# SOUL TRACKER

## By Bill Myers

*The Face of God*
*Blood of Heaven*
*Threshold*
*Fire of Heaven*
*Eli*
*The Bloodstone Chronicles* (children's fantasy)
*McGee and Me* (children's book/video series)
*The Incredible Worlds of Wally McDoogle*
    (children's comedy series)
*Blood Hounds Inc.* (children's mystery series)
*Secret Agent Dingeldorf* (children's comedy series)
*Faith Encounter* (teen devotional)

Novellas
*Then Comes Marriage* (with Angela Hunt)
*When the Last Leaf Falls*
*The Wager*

# BILL MYERS

## SOUL TRACKER

**ZONDERVAN**™

GRAND RAPIDS, MICHIGAN 49530 USA

## ZONDERVAN™

*Soul Tracker*
Copyright © 2004 by Bill Myers

Requests for information should be addressed to:
Zondervan, *Grand Rapids, Michigan 49530*

**Library of Congress Cataloging-in-Publication Data**

Myers, Bill, 1953–
   Soul tracker / by Bill Myers.
      p. cm. — (The soul tracker series ; bk. 1)
   ISBN 0-310-22756-9
   1. Loss (Psychology)—Fiction. 2. Children—Death—Fiction. 3. Single fathers—
   Fiction. 4. Teenage girls—Fiction. 5. Future life—Fiction. I. Title.
   PS3563.Y36S67 2004
   813'.54—dc22                                                    2004007352

Published in association with the literary agency of Alive Communications, Inc., 7680 Goddard Street, Suite 200, Colorado Springs, CO 80920.

*Interior design by Michelle Espinoza*

*Printed in the United States of America*

04 05 06 07 08 09 10 /❖ DC/ 10 9 8 7 6 5 4 3 2 1

*For Nicole:*
  *Who will always own a piece of my heart.*

*"Whoever lives in love lives in God, and God in him."*

*John 4:16*

# part one

# one

It had started again. The voice. Five hours earlier in Wal-Mart. He'd been doing his usual stalking up and down the aisles, this time for laundry detergent. Why was it every month they moved at least one item to a new location? Over the years, since Jacqueline left, he felt he'd become quite the veteran shopper—reading labels, clipping coupons, even watching as the cashier rang up each purchase on the register. But this moving of products, especially to the least likely places, always frustrated him. He was reaching the peak of just such a frustration when he heard the child crying one row over.

"Daddy! Daddy, where are you?"

The fear in her voice brought him to a stop. It was the same panic, the same desperation that had haunted him for weeks.

"Daddy, come get me!"

The tone was so similar to another's that David forgot the laundry detergent. He hesitated, then pushed his cart to the end of the aisle. He slowed as he rounded the corner and peered up the next row. A little blonde, about kindergarten age, sat alone in a cart. She was bundled in a bright red coat, pink tights, and shiny black shoes. Tears streamed down her face as she cried.

"Daddy, please don't leave me!"

He scowled, glancing around. There was no one near. What parent would leave a child like this? Had the father no sense of responsibility? He pushed his cart up the aisle toward her. "Sweetie, are you all right?"

She turned, eyeing him, then took a brave, trembling breath.

He continued to approach. "It'll be okay, darling. I'm sure your—"

Suddenly her face brightened as she looked past him. "Daddy!"

He turned to see a concerned young man in a green fleece jacket and worn jeans stride up the aisle toward them. In his hands he held a new push broom, grasped tightly enough to assure David he would not hesitate to use it if necessary. David forced a reassuring grin. The young man sized him up and said nothing as he brushed by and joined his daughter.

"Oh, Daddy." The little girl sobbed as she stretched out her arms.

"I was just around the corner." Laughing, he scooped her out of the cart. "Did you think I forgot you?" She nodded and he hugged her. Then, pushing aside her damp hair, he kissed her cheek. "You know I wouldn't do that." Again, she nodded, but continued to whimper—an obvious attempt to make him pay penance.

David thought of stopping and turning his cart around, but that would be clumsy and awkward, only adding fuel to the parent's suspicion. So he continued up the aisle. As he passed, he felt he should say something to the young father, something instructive, something to remind him what a precious responsibility he held in his arms. He said nothing.

But the voice remained. A whisper in the back of his mind. It remained through the wooden conversation between Grams, Luke, and himself over dinner. It remained through the forced laughter as Grams recounted some scene from one of her daytime soaps. It even remained as David rode his son about the poor progress report they'd received in the mail from school.

And now, several hours later, as David Kauffman stood alone in the dark, silent living room, the whisper grew louder, becoming a more familiar voice. The one that always filled his head and swelled his heart to breaking.

*"Daddy, I'll be good! I promise . . . please . . . please!"*

He approached the overstuffed chair from behind, reaching out to its back to steady himself. He had not bothered to turn on a light. Across the room on the mantel, he heard the clock ticking. Outside, a faint stirring of wind chimes. He caught the shadowy movement of the cat—her cat—scurrying past and up the stairs to safety. David hated this room. Tried his best to avoid it. The memories were too painful—as bad as the upstairs bathroom, its lock still broken from when he'd busted through it to find her opening her veins . . .

The first time.

*"Daddy . . ."*

David closed his eyes against the memories, but he could still hear feet scuffing carpet, attendants' muffled grunts as they grabbed her flailing arms, pinning them to her side. And, of course, her pleas.

*"I'll do better, I promise! Please, don't make me go!"*

Images flashed in his head. Flying hair, twisting body, kicking feet, the appearance of a pearl-white syringe . . . Emily's eyes widening in panic.

*"Daddy, no!"*

*"To help you relax,"* the attendant had said.

*"Don't let them take me . . ."* She no longer sounded sixteen. She was four, five. So helpless. *"Daddy . . ."*

He leaned against the chair, his throat tightening.

*"Daddy . . ."*

That was the deepest cut. The word. *Daddy.* Protector. Defender. *Daddy.* The one who always made things right. That was the word that had gripped him in Wal-Mart. The word that sucked breath out of him every time he heard it, that drew tears to his eyes before he could stop them. Even in front of Luke.

He tried his best not to cry when he was with his son. The boy had been through so much already. What he needed now was stability, and David was the only one who could provide it. If his twelve-year-old saw tears it would spell weakness, and weakness meant things were still out of control. No. Now, more than ever, Luke needed to know things were returning to normal, that there was someone he could depend on.

But David was by himself now. Alone. Luke was upstairs sleeping (or more likely working on the Internet) while Grams snored quietly just down the hall.

Emily's voice returned, softer, thicker. The drug taking effect. *"Daddy . . ."*

*"Just a few weeks, honey,"* he had promised. *"You'll get better and then you can come home."*

He remembered her eyes. Those startling, violet blue eyes. Eyes so vivid that people assumed she wore colored contacts. Eyes glassing over from the drug. Eyes once so full of anger and confusion and accusation and—this is what always did him in—eyes that, at that moment, had been so full of trust.

He had held her look. Then slowly, with the intimacy of a father to his daughter, he gave a little nod, his silent assurance.

And she believed him.

She still sobbed, tears still ran down her cheeks, but she no longer fought. In that single act, that quiet nod, her daddy told her everything would be all right. And she trusted him. She *trusted* him!

David leaned forward onto the back of the chair, tears falling. He remembered the front door opening—bright sunlight pouring in, flaunting its cheeriness.

*"I'll be right behind you,"* he had promised. *"Grams and I will be in the car right behind you."*

She could no longer wipe her nose. She could only nod and mumble. *"Okay."*

The last word she ever spoke in the house. *Okay, I believe you. Okay, I'm depending on you. Okay . . . I trust you.*

David dropped his head against the chair. He was trembling again, trying to breathe. The house was asleep and he was alone. "Where are you, baby girl?" He whispered hoarsely. "Just tell me. Let me know so I can help."

The screen door groaned. He looked up and quickly wiped his face. This was no memory. The boy was here. He'd called half an hour ago, asking if he could come over. David straightened himself, listening. There was a tentative knock. He took a breath and ordered his legs to move. Somehow they obeyed. He reached out to the cold door. He took another breath, wiped his face, and pulled it open.

The boy wore a gray sweatshirt with the word *Panthers* and red paw prints across his chest. He was tall and lanky, around six feet, with curly brown, unkempt hair. Long, dark lashes highlighted even darker eyes. His chin was strong and his nose slightly large, almost classical. David blinked. In many ways he was looking at a younger version of himself, back when he was in high school.

He forced a smile. "Rory?"

"Cory," the boy corrected. His voice was clogged. He coughed slightly and plumes of uneven breath came from his mouth.

"Well"—David opened the door wider, as if to an old friend—"Come in."

The kid swallowed. "No thanks, I gotta"—he shifted—"I gotta be going."

David's heart both sank and eased. Though he wanted this confrontation more than anything, he also feared it. This was the famous Cory. Cory, the sensitive. Cory, the "You'll really like him, Dad, he's just like you." Cory, the boy Emily couldn't stop talking about the last few times he'd visited her at the hospital.

And now this same Cory had come to meet the parent. A bit ironic. Maybe even macabre. But better late than never.

With long, delicate fingers the boy produced a cloth-covered notebook. "This is what I was telling you about." He cleared his throat again. "I know she'd want you to have it."

David took it into his hands, but he barely looked down. Instead, he was drinking in every detail of the boy, every nuance—those dark eyes, the frail shoulders under the too-big sweatshirt, his nervous, painful energy. He'd just been released from the hospital the day before yesterday. And, if possible, this meeting seemed even harder on him than David.

"She left it in my room the night she, uh . . ." He lowered his head, examining the porch.

David nodded, watching. He looked at the notebook. It was six inches long, four wide, and nearly an inch thick. The cover was pale pink with a white iris on the front. It felt like silk. He stared at it a long moment.

The boy shifted.

Coming to, more on autopilot than anything else, David repeated, "You sure you don't want to come in?"

"No"—the boy cleared his throat again—"no, thanks." He motioned over his shoulder to a van that was idling. "I've got people waiting."

"Oh . . . right." Hiding his neediness, David forced a shrug. "Well, maybe we can have coffee together or something sometime . . . if you want."

Cory glanced up to him. "I'd like that." His eyes faltered then dropped back down. Speaking softer now, and still to his shoes, he added, "She was pretty amazing. I mean, I never met anyone like her. Never." He took a breath, then looked up.

David saw the sheen in the boy's eyes, felt his own starting to burn. "Yeah."

Cory glanced away, studying the porch light above them. "So . . . uh . . ."

David came to his rescue. "I'll give you a call next week, how does that sound?"

Cory gave the slightest nod.

David watched, waiting.

As if he'd completed an impossible mission, the boy took a deep breath and blew it out. He nodded more broadly and turned to start down the walk. David watched, absorbing everything.

Halfway to the street, Cory paused and turned. "I just, uh . . ." He cleared his throat. "It just doesn't, you know, seem right."

David swallowed, then nodded.

"I mean, she was getting so strong . . . so healthy. She was really happy, Mr. Kauffman. The happiest I'd seen her."

David wanted to respond, but he no longer trusted his voice.

Cory shook his head. "It just doesn't . . . things just don't seem right." With that he turned and headed toward the van.

David remained at the door. Moisture blurred his vision as he watched Cory arrive at the vehicle, open the door, and climb into the passenger's side. A moment passed before the van slowly pulled away. The boy never looked up.

It wasn't until the vehicle disappeared around the corner that David glanced down to the journal in his hands. He was trembling again. The meeting had taken a lot out of him. And it was still taking. Because he knew exactly what he held.

Emily's journal. Her final thoughts and hopes and dreams . . . and nightmares.

He turned and reentered the house, easing the door shut behind him. But he could go no farther. He leaned against the closed door and lifted the notebook to his face with both hands. He inhaled deeply, hoping for some fragrance, some lingering trace of his daughter. There was nothing. Only the faint odor of smoke and antiseptic. He brought the cover to his lips and kissed it. This was all he had left. All that remained.

"Where are you, baby girl? Where are you?"

Y ou never get married?" Nubee cried.

"It is possible."

"But, must be somebody . . ." He hesitated looking for the right word.

"Somebody what?" Gita asked.

"Somebody blind enough to think you look beautif—*ow!*"

Gita gave her little brother a playful smack upside the head. Well, most of it was playful. It made no difference that he was thirty-two, so physically disabled that he could not look after himself, and that she was pushing his wheelchair on the walk past other residents. There were some things she just wouldn't cut him slack on.

"Help me!" he cried to Rosa, a passing staff member. "Help me! Help me!"

"You picking on your sister again, Nubee?"

"She beating me! Cruelty to animals, cruelty to animals!"

Rosa smiled. "How's it going, Dr. Patekar?"

"Very well," Gita answered. "And you?"

"Still breathing."

Gita smiled. "That is a good sign."

"At least around this place." The plump Hispanic chuckled as she started up the ramp toward the building.

Gita and her brother continued along the walkway. She lifted her face and closed her eyes to feel the warmth of the winter sun flickering through the bare mulberry branches. In her faster-than-the-speed-of-light world, these few hours a week spent with her little brother always brought a certain peace. Many saw her visits as compassion for her only living relative, but the truth was she needed them more than he did.

Gita had flown Nubee over from their home in Nepal as soon as she'd settled in. That was part of her agreement with the Orbolitz Group. She would work for them and commit her sizable experience to their new Life After Life program, a series of studies designed to scientifically track the soul after death. All they had to do was offer reasonable pay and pull a string or two to bring her little brother to the States so she could look after him. To her surprise, not only did they agree, but they made certain Nubee was admitted to one of the finest nursing homes in Southern California, and picked up the tab for his room and board. It was a gracious offer, but typical of Norman E. Orbolitz. Granted, he was an eccentric recluse, a billionaire who owned one of the world's largest communication empires. It was also true that he was a master at playing hardball with any and all competitors. But he was known equally well for his generosity and philanthropic outreaches. That fact as much as any other convinced Gita to move halfway around the world and join his organization.

As a thanatologist, someone who studies death and dying, Gita had made a name for herself by exposing one of Great Britain's most famous psychics as a fraud. It wasn't intentional, just the outcome of her unwavering, dogged research. But it had created a stir that caught the attention of the Orbolitz people. In a matter of months they'd convinced her to leave her position at Tribhuvan University in Nepal and join their Life After Life program in the States.

Unfortunately, her focus quickly became something more along the lines of *Hoax* After Life. Apparently the Orbolitz Group—more precisely Gita's department head, Dr. Richard Griffin—wasn't as interested in her research as he was in her ability to expose false psychics, particularly those who exploited the grief-stricken with promises of contacting their deceased loved ones. It wasn't exactly the program she'd signed up for, but she had always seen the importance of truth, the need to separate fact from fiction. And, like it or not, she was getting quite good at it. No surprise there. Dr. Gita Patekar enjoyed success at everything she put her mind to.

Well, almost everything ...

"So, nobody in all world think you pretty?" Nubee was doing his best to get another rise out of her.

"I am afraid you are correct." She sighed, playing along. Unfortunately, the opposite was true, and she knew it. For better or worse, she'd been attractive all of her life. And not just to the Asian community. Her petite frame, high cheekbones, coal black eyes, and well-endowed figure made her fresh meat in any male shark tank—even at the church singles' group. Then there was the problem of her intellect. It was supposed to be one of her better features, but she found herself having to use it mostly as a weapon of self-defense.

Last night's fiasco with Geoffrey Boltten was the perfect example. Was there some unspoken law that said after the third date men were entitled to have sex with a woman? Was that the new definition of lifelong commitment? Because, just like clockwork, after a romantic dinner and enjoying Mozart's "Magic Flute" at the Civic Arts Plaza, Dr. Boltten, respected surgeon and churchgoer, felt he was entitled to make his move.

Gita had barely let him inside her townhouse, supposedly to use the bathroom, when he grabbed her shoulders. Always the understanding type, she stepped back and tried to defuse the awkward situation with an obvious scientific explanation.

"It is okay, I understand. It is simply your phenylethylamine. Do not worry. Some was bound to have been released during our time together this evening."

"Oh, Gita," he gasped, pulling her to him. "I can't stop thinking of you." It was an old line, an even older move.

She shrugged him off and tried pivoting away. "With the rise of your PEA levels, you knew this would happen. You also know that further touching will increase both of our dehydroepiansdrosterone levels, which will lead to a rise in oxytocin." She was being as kind and forthright as possible.

"Oh, baby . . ." He grabbed the back of her head, pulling it toward his, forcing his mouth over hers.

Coming up for air, she tried one last time. "And now we must contend with testosterone and vasopressin. Doctor, you know you are merely reacting to chemicals being released within your—"

"No more talking." He yanked her toward him. "No more talking." That was when Gita realized the time for talking had indeed come to an end. All it took was one quick knee raise followed by a sharp blow to his larynx and the good doctor was on the floor, writhing, unsure what part of his anatomy to be holding in pain.

She looked down at him and sighed wearily. No doubt here was yet another man who would never call her again.

Nubee continued his teasing, pulling her from the memory. "Not to worry. We find somebody. Somebody blind . . . maybe deaf too."

She smiled weakly, because it wasn't just the culture's sexual promiscuity that she struggled against. There was something else. Something deep inside of her. And the books she'd read, the counselor she'd been seeing, they all pointed to the same cause. They insisted it stemmed from the nightmare childhood that she and her brother had lived while on the streets of Katmandu.

"These things can take a long, long time to heal," her counselor had said. "Someone who has endured your level of abuse may take years, even decades, to fully recover."

Gita hated that thought. She fought against it with every fiber of who she was. But deep inside she knew it was true. Deep inside she knew that loving another, that sharing her heart and soul with a man would be difficult. No, *difficult* wasn't the word. For her, there was another. And it was one that frequently brought tears to her eyes when she slept alone at night. It crippled and hobbled her heart as much now as when she was that eleven-year-old girl sleeping with men for food, for rupees, for anything to keep her and her brother alive. Because, as much as she wanted to give herself to another, as much as she begged God to free and heal her, Dr. Gita Patekar feared that when it came to love, she would now and forever be . . . *unable*.

"You make me listen to Bible now?"

She barely heard her brother.

"Gitee?"

They had arrived at their favorite bench, the one between two eucalyptus trees. Coming to, she answered, "Yes, it is time to make you listen to Bible again. What part do you wish to hear today?"

"More Revelation."

"Again?" She reached down and locked the wheels of his chair. She pulled the wool blanket up around his chest. "Are we not always reading Revelation?"

"I like the angels. I like the monsters."

"Of course," she sighed, "then we shall read Revelation." She sat on the wooden bench across from him and produced a small New Testament from her pocket. And there, in the warmth and cold of the winter light, she opened the book and began to read.

I'm hearing something now," the boy said. "Kind of a low hum, like a machine."

"Yes," Dr. Richard Griffin agreed, "that's fairly normal. Just try to relax." He caught a reflection of himself in the stainless steel tray on the bedside table. Who could believe he was fifty? Early forties would be his best guess, as long as he held in his stomach and paid close attention to how he combed and sprayed his hair.

He glanced at the digital readout over the subject's bed. It cast a blue-green glow upon the white tiles of the cubicle. They were coming up to the seven-minute mark. Seven minutes since he'd injected the kid with three milligrams of dimethyltryptamine, a hallucinogenic better known as DMT.

"Do you see any movement?" He peered at the boy. "Any type of . . . beings?"

"No."

"Be patient, they'll show up," Griffin assured him. "And when they do, stay calm, don't panic."

Seventeen-year-old Jason Campbell nodded. He licked his lips in nervous anticipation and no doubt a little fear.

Dr. Griffin had picked him up as a volunteer from their "off-campus" site near Hollywood Boulevard. Kids, mostly runaways and street ilk, came to the place in droves looking to sell themselves as volunteers for various medical experiments. Experiments that weren't always legal, but that were absolutely necessary if the human longevity division of the Orbolitz Group was to stay on the cutting edge of its research. For the most part, the procedures were harmless and everyone benefited—the kids got their money for drugs, important data was secured without jumping through bureaucratic hoops, local authorities were provided enough financial incentive to look the other way—and on those rare occasions when Griffin needed to cross divisions and secure a subject for his Life After Life program, they were there for the taking. It was win/win for everyone involved.

"There, I see something."

"The creatures?" Dr. Griffin asked. "Do you see the creatures?"

Jason's acne-ravaged face twitched under the silk eyeshades.

"Jason?"

"Yeah . . ."

"Do you see them?"

"Yes . . ."

"How many?"

"Just one."

Earlier, the boy had assured Dr. Griffin that he was a frequent user of psychedelics—LSD, ketamine, MDMA, he said he'd tried them all. Griffin had his doubts, but it really didn't matter. Although DMT was classified as a hallucinogenic, its devotees more commonly referred to it as the *spirit molecule.* It was a rare chemical that they insisted opened them up to a strange, mystical world, often populated by gargoyles and troll-like creatures. Creatures identical to several of the near-death experiences Griffin had recorded. If that was the case, if the same creatures that appeared in near death experiences also appeared while using the drug, then it was important he add at least one of the drug experiences to his database.

"There's another," the boy said.

"That's two?" Dr. Griffin asked.

"No, three . . . four, five." Jason's voice grew shaky. "They're everywhere!"

Griffin tried to soothe him. "Just relax. That's not unusual. Let them approach. It'll be okay." He threw a look over to Wendell Nordstrom, a wiry technician with red hair and a stringy goatee. Nordstrom stood on the other side of a portable console, watching the boy's readouts—heart rate, blood pressure, EEG . . . and one very peculiar video monitor off to his left.

Jason's face twitched again. He scowled, then lifted his eyebrows, raising a black wire and fabric skullcap. The cap contained paper-thin electrodes strategically placed throughout it. These picked up the electrical firings from a handful of neural synapses within his brain. Firings that were amplified, sorted, and eventually fed into PNEUMA, the project's giant, fifteen-teraflops supercomputer.

Initially the skullcap was a cumbersome helmet that recorded tens of thousands of impulses. But gradually, thanks to the research of scientists such as Francis Crick of double helix fame, a small set of neurons leading from the back of the cortex to the front were isolated. To some, these few neurons were the elusive location of human consciousness—a small group of cells connected in such a way that they made us different from animals by making us self-conscious.

To others, it wasn't the cells or even their connections that mattered. Instead, it was what resided *within* those cells. Something the more religious might call . . . the soul.

In either case, this drug, this DMT, seemed to stimulate those same neurons, particularly in the frontal lobe where so many near-death experiences are registered. And if those very same neurons were being fired by the drug, then their experiences had to be entered into the system.

"I can't . . ." Jason scowled. "They're trying to talk, but I can't, I can't hear what they're saying."

"Relax. Let them have their way."

Jason gave the slightest nod. A thin veneer of sweat appeared across his forehead and above his upper lip.

Griffin looked at the clock. They were almost at the eight-minute mark.

Wendell's voice came from behind the console. "We're getting images."

Dr. Griffin nodded. This was the pivotal point of the experiment. For nearly four years they'd been studying the brain functions of the dying. They recorded those last few moments as the subject approached death, followed by the six to twelve minutes as the brain slowly shut down from the outside in. Theirs was an extensive, nationwide program involving over eighty hospitals and nearly two hundred hospice organizations. Each case was handled with care and sensitivity, as the terminally ill and their relatives were seldom in the mood to participate in experiments. Yet in the name of science—and with the added incentive of $2,500 per subject (thanks to the very deep pockets of Norman E. Orbolitz)—nearly thirteen hundred patients had agreed to wear the small, unobtrusive skullcap to record the last electrical firings of their brains as they died.

"Jason, can you hear them yet? Can you tell me what they're saying?"

The kid rolled his head. "I can't . . ." His face twitched again. "I can't make it out. But they're everywhere."

Dr. Griffin glanced at the empty syringe in the stainless steel tray. They'd given the kid three milligrams. The experts claimed that was more than enough to "interact" with the creatures. But if this was all the further they could go, after investing all their time and energy, then the experiment was essentially a failure. Griffin did not have time for failures.

He glanced at the vial beside the syringe. It contained another six milligrams. "Are they coming any closer?"

Jason shook his head.

"You must be holding them back. Relax, there's nothing to fear. Give in to the drug. Let them have their way."

Jason scowled again. It was obvious he was trying but still failing.

Griffin looked back at the vial on the table. He knew the answer to their problem, but hesitated. Not for ethical reasons. As far as he was concerned, ethics were man-made restraints created by timid moralists. This was science. More important, this was *his* science. Besides, Jason was homeless—street flotsam and jetsam that would never be missed. No, it wasn't ethics or even the fear of being caught that gave Griffin pause. It was simply the bother of having to go back to the Boulevard and begin the screening process all over again.

But the kid gave him little choice.

Dr. Griffin reached for the vial and syringe. He drew out another three milligrams, hesitated, then continued until the entire six milligrams was in the syringe.

"Dr. Griffin?"

Griffin didn't know if his assistant was calling out a word of caution or if he'd seen something of interest on the monitor. It didn't matter. The decision was made. He inserted the needle into the boy's right arm and emptied the syringe.

"Okay, Jason, I've increased the dosage. Now I want you to—"

"Inside . . . ," the youth whispered. "They want . . . inside."

"Inside? Inside what?"

Jason gave no answer. His face twitched again, then again. He began to roll his head. Harder. Faster. He flinched, then began to squirm.

Griffin reached for the leather restraint on the bed rail and buckled down the boy's right arm. "Jason . . . Jason, can you hear me?" He crossed to the other side and repeated the process.

Then to each of the ankles. "Jason? You said they wanted inside. Inside of what?"

Faint crescents of sweat appeared under the arms of the kid's hospital gown. The sheen on his face had beaded into drops.

"Jason?"

His head continued to roll. Faint whimperings escaped from his throat.

"Jason? Jason, can you hear me?"

He opened his mouth, panting in uneven gasps. The whimperings grew louder.

Wendell called from the console, "Dr. Griffin, you need to see this."

Suddenly the boy's body contracted. His arms and legs yanked at the restraints. His head flew back, then rolled faster and faster. His whimperings grew to choking cries.

"Dr. Griffin!"

The doctor hurried to join Wendell behind the console. Readouts showed the boy's pulse at 148, his blood pressure skyrocketing. But it was the TV monitor to the left that grabbed Griffin's attention. The images were crude, like an eighties' video game—the result of raw data being translated by a portable, in-lab computer. They would become much more refined when fed into PNEUMA and prepared for the virtual reality lab. But for now there was no missing Jason's form, or at least how he perceived his form. He was floating in a dazzling star field. Closing in on him from all sides were the gargoyle-like creatures—some with amphibian faces, others more reptilian—all with sharp, protruding teeth and long claws. Several had already leaped on top of the boy's chest. More followed.

No wonder he was writhing.

"Jason?" Griffin called. "Jason, can you hear me?"

But Jason did not answer. His chest heaved then went into a series of convulsions.

"Pulse 185!" There was no missing the fear in Wendell's voice.

The boy screamed—then swallowed it into gagging coughs and gasps.

"*Jason!*"

"Two hundred!"

Griffin spun back to the monitor and stared. Two of the creatures had pried open the boy's jaw with their claws. Even more astonishing were the creatures on his chest. One after another raced toward his head and leaped into the air. As they hovered over his face they dissolved into a black, vaporous cloud that rushed into the boy's mouth and shot down his throat. Creature after creature followed. Black cloud after black cloud. Leaping and entering with such frightening speed that they soon became a thick, continuous stream of blackness.

Jason tried to scream but could only choke and gag.

"Jason!"

An alarm sounded.

"He's in V-fib!"

"Get the medical team here!"

Wendell nodded and hit the intercom as Griffin raced to the bed. "Jason! Jason, close your mouth!"

But the boy's mouth was locked open as he continued gasping, choking.

Griffin ripped aside the kid's hospital gown, yanking off a handful of the sensors taped to his chest, ready to begin CPR if needed.

The alarm continued.

The boy gagged as Wendell called for the medical team again.

But even as his assistant's voice echoed through the complex, Dr. Griffin changed his mind. Slowly and quite deliberately, he stepped back from the bed. It was better to do nothing. He knew that. And if the kid was lucky, the medical team would arrive too late to help. Granted, there would be some inconvenience in disposing of the body, but it was best for the boy. Griffin had seen these creatures before in the virtual reality chambers. He had seen what they did to a select handful of dying. The mental agony those patients endured, the impossible anguish they suffered . . . it was a horror worse than any pain of physical death.

It was a horror that the kid should not have to take back with him into the land of the living.

—

*Things are finally falling into place. Bryan actually came up to my locker and started talking, which seriously is such a great emotional high. I feel like I could just run around twirling and jumping in the bright shining sun. I want to embrace life and give back so much. I know he's working up the courage to ask me to the dance. Kind of a spastic thought, but this gives me a great outfit to plan. I was thinking about like an off-white or purple dress. I have always liked purple; it has such an amazing regal feel to it. Seriously, I think that the hot guy in my math class might get jealous of Bryan, and what if Mr. Hot asks me to dance! How incredibly stellar would that be!!! I just want to bask in this moment of pure happiness and imagine two great guys fighting over my company. "Oh, I am sorry, were you talking about dancing with me?" Here is where the band breaks out into a slow, romantic tune and we gaze lovingly into each other's feverish eyes. His enchanting mocha browns settle deep into my dazzling violet blues. He softly joins in, singing to me, and my entire heart just melts. Ha-ha. I am so psyched!! I want to glide and sway here forever.*

David lifted his glasses onto his forehead and rubbed his eyes. He'd been at Starbucks since the place opened three hours ago, sitting at the window counter, reading her journal. Of course he'd read it earlier, had been up all night devouring its two-hundred-plus pages. But like a man too starved to taste food, he'd gobbled down sentence after sentence, entire paragraphs without fully comprehending. And he wanted to comprehend, he wanted to savor every moment of his daughter's last few months. So, here he was, a mile from the house at his favorite writing hangout near the corner of Topanga and Ventura Boulevard, nursing his third cappuccino, trying to stay focused.

He might have had more success if it wasn't for the street preacher. The black, barrel-chested old-timer sporting the latest fashion from the Salvation Army stood just outside the window, as he often did, giving no one within earshot a break.

"You, brother!" His voice reverberated against the glass as he dogged a passing shopper. "Yes, I'm talking to you! Have you found the Lord? Have your sins been washed in the blood of the Lamb? Repent! Repent, or burn in the fires of hell that have no end!"

David watched with quiet distaste. The two of them had been coming to this shop for months, each plying their trades—the preacher outside searching for lost sinners on the sidewalk, David inside, struggling with his next novel on his laptop. Normally, the old-timer's rantings didn't bother him much—just another layer of coffee shop and street noise. But today, with no sleep and spent emotions, the self-righteous railings grew more and more irritating.

David sighed, pulled down his glasses, and turned the page to the next entry.

> *I feel nothing. I just want to lie here in my warm, safe bed. Living has so entirely drained my blood of substance to the point that my parched veins are screaming for any form of liquid to fill them. My blood has been sucked out venomously by that stupid leach that I so often refer to as Kaylee. What a hypocritical jerk if I ever saw one. Honestly, I consider Kaylee my best friend in the entire world. Why would she not consider me the same . . . is Amanda such a great friend considering she*

*ditched you, Kaylee? I seriously stuck through everything with you! Just because I didn't know you as long as Amanda doesn't mean we can't be better friends than you and her. It's stupid, I know. All I do is wallow in this mental slush, swimming in the sewage hour after hour, holding my breath, unable to come up for air.*

Talk about emotional whiplash—one page exhilaration, the next, devastation. But apparently roller-coaster emotions came with the territory of female adolescence.

He remembered one of their very first counseling sessions, the ones they started not long after his wife left. Emily was burrowed into the corner of the sofa, feet drawn up, playing with her hair. "It's just that he's like always shouting all the time."

He recalled his jaw going slack. "What? Honey, I never shout."

"Yeah, right." She smirked. "Like yesterday when I didn't empty the cat box?"

David turned to the woman counselor, lifting his palms. "It had been nearly two weeks. I merely made it clear that—"

"By shouting," Emily interrupted.

"I don't shout."

"Yes, you do."

"No, I don't."

"You're doing it now."

"Disagreeing with someone is not the same as—"

"Told you."

"Told me what?"

"You're shouting."

"I am not."

"Yes, you are."

"Emily!"

She turned to the counselor and shrugged. "See?"

David smiled at the memory. At the tender age of fourteen his daughter was already playing him like a fiddle. He recalled another session where he'd asked the counselor, "Does *every*thing in the house have to be ruled by emotion? Surely, truth and logic must count for something."

Once again the therapist broke out laughing. Apparently, he had lots to learn.

But the laughter didn't last long. The frenetic, topsy-turvy world of emotions eventually led to bouts of depression, which only seemed to grow darker and deeper until finally—

"Repent! 'I am the way, the truth and the life. No man comes to the Father but by me!' Turn to Him! Turn to the Lord before it's too late! Turn or burn!"

David squinted at the journal, trying to stay focused. But the lunchtime crowd was filtering in, opening the door more and more frequently, allowing the preacher's rantings to intrude more and more loudly.

"Time is short. You don't know what tomorrow will bring! Turn to Him and flee the torments of hell, where the worm does not die nor the fire is quenched!"

David shifted on his stool, trying to concentrate on the words before him. Emily loved to write. Sometimes the rambling stream-of-consciousness that he saw before him now, sometimes short stories, sometimes poetry. She cherished words. No surprise there. As the child of an author, she was always surrounded by stacks of books and magazines. Her favorite reading haunt? The tub . . . which occasionally made for some careful maneuverings in the bathroom.

"I just want to find the toilet in the middle of the night without breaking a toe," he complained once over breakfast.

She nodded with the obvious solution. "Maybe you should drink less liquids before bedtime."

Again David smiled. It was true, when it came to books and writing he gave her plenty of leeway. Particularly with her mother gone. For Emily, reading was a way of affirming her emotions, of discovering what other women thought and felt. And her writing, no matter how emotional or over-the-top, was her way of exploring her own thoughts and feelings.

So often she'd enter his garage office unannounced and plop down on the worn sofa behind his desk to write. And write and write and write.

He treasured those times together—back when she was open and sunny, back before the shadows of the disease had begun hiding her from him. For years she read to him from that sofa, those incredible eyes looking up, so eager for praise. And he gave it, abundantly. He never criticized, sensing that any negative comment would crush her already oversensitive heart. Instead, he would find authors she loved and encourage her to copy their work in longhand. That was how writers in the old days learned. It forced them to slow down and study each phrase, sip each word, and, most important, begin to understand the workings of the craft.

She practiced this advice religiously. Snips and fragments of great literature filled her journals. She was particularly fond of the poets. Emily Dickinson, her namesake, was her favorite. He flipped through the pages of the journal until he spotted one of the famous writer's poems:

*Some, too fragile for winter winds,*
*The thoughtful grave encloses, —*
*Tenderly tucking them in from frost*
*Before their feet are cold.*

*Never the treasures in her nest*
*The cautious grave exposes,*
*Building where schoolboy dare not look*
*And sportsman is not bold.*

*This covert have all the children*
*Early aged, and often cold, —*
*Sparrows unnoticed by the Father;*
*Lambs for whom time had not a fold.*

He tried swallowing away the tightness in his throat. Tears were coming again. How could someone so young, so full of life, become so lonely and full of death? He was near the beginning of the diary, before her hospitalization. During those black, nightmare times when she would not get out of bed, when her grades plummeted, when the two of them continually fought, shouting oaths and threats that he'd give anything to take back now. Those awful times when he had to physically force her to take the medication. Those beggings, those pleadings, those—

"Excuse me, brother?"

David looked up with a start. Through the moisture in his eyes he saw the preacher.

"This seat taken?"

David glanced at the stool beside him, then around the shop for an alternate choice. There was none. The place was packed. Exhausted, emotional, and with an overdose of caffeine, he replied, "Go ahead." He cleared his throat. "Just spare me the hellfire."

Unfazed, the man gave a crooked-tooth grin. "Some folks would say it's a pretty important topic."

David fought to hold back his anger. What right did this person have to talk to him about hell? He had no idea what he'd been living through these past nine weeks. The sorrow, the hopelessness, the absolute . . . finality. But instead of making a scene, he exercised all of his self-control and quietly seethed. "And what makes you an expert?"

The preacher pulled out the stool and eased himself onto the seat with a quiet groan. "I guess 'cause I've been there."

"We all have. Some of us more than others."

"Maybe." The man brought a latte up to his thick lips and slurped the foam. "But I'm talkin' the real deal."

David glanced away, angry that he allowed himself to be pulled into the conversation. But the old-timer wasn't finished. Not quite.

"You know what I'm talkin' 'bout. The real hell." His eyes peered over the cup at David. "That place you're so afraid your daughter is."

# two

W ho are you!"
Those sitting at their tables looked over at the commotion. Others standing in line turned with mild interest. Surprised that he was on his feet, David glared down at the old man, trembling.

The preacher simply stared at his coffee. "I ain't nobody special. You see me here all the time."

David remained standing, breathing hard, unsure how to respond.

"Please." The big man motioned to David's stool. "Please."

Hesitating, feeling the eyes on him, he eased himself back down.

Preacher Man said nothing.

"How did . . ." David struggled to keep his voice even. "How did you know?"

"Terrible thing when a young person takes their life."

David quit breathing.

The preacher looked out the window, sadly shaking his head. "World's an ugly place for 'em. Gettin' uglier by the minute."

Measuring each word, David repeated, "How did you know?"

The man nodded to the counter. "The boys told me. You're that famous author, right?"

Closing his eyes a moment, getting his bearings, David muttered, "Used to be. That was a long time ago."

"Four or five years if I remember." Taking another sip of foam, he added, "You was all the rage. Some family adventure thing, wasn't it?"

David drew in another breath. More calmly, he repeated, "You said something about hell. That I was afraid my daughter was in hell."

"Aren't you?"

He set his jaw, revealing no information.

"That's most people's fears, when a loved one takes their life. Will the good Lord show mercy, will He understand the pain they were trying to stop?"

Against his better judgment David half asked, half scorned, "And what's your take?"

Once again the big man glanced out the window. The answer came more softly. "His love paid a lot for us up on that cross, brother. I imagine He'll do everything in His power to insure a return on His investment."

David looked down to the journal.

Softer still, the old-timer continued. "You'd give anything to talk to her, wouldn't you?"

The words came before David could stop them. "If I just knew . . . if there was some way I could reach her." His voice grew husky. "If she could just let me know she's all right."

The preacher took another sip. "Dangerous stuff—tryin' to connect with the other side."

"She's a child . . . all alone. What if she's out there . . . lost?" He searched the table, unable to swallow the ache in his throat. "If there was some way I could help her. Some way I could . . ." He took another breath, then looked up at the preacher. "You said, you mentioned that you were, that you'd been—"

"To hell?"

David nodded.

"Comin' up on three years now."

"What, like a dream or vision or something?"

"No, brother, it was no dream."

David continued, more quietly, "Tell me."

Preacher Man shot him a look. But David held his gaze, making it clear he was sincere. The man frowned hard at his coffee. "No . . . it was no dream."

Another pause.

David ventured, "You had a near-death experience?"

"Wasn't nothin' *near* about it. I was dead. Deader than a stump." The fanatic edge to the old man was disappearing.

David persisted. "If there's something you can tell me . . ."

Preacher Man took a long, slow breath, then blew it out. It was clear this was not something he'd intended.

"Please. Anything . . . anything at all."

Finally, almost imperceptively, he started to nod. And then he began . . .

"People make a big deal 'bout dying. Like it's all painful or something. Shoot, ain't no more painful than a hiccup, or skipping a heartbeat. Anybody can do it. Fact is, we'll all get our chance . . ." Quietly, he added, ". . . a few of us more than once."

Equally as soft, David said, "Tell me."

He shrugged. "You know the routine—floatin' over your body in some hospital room, sucked through a tunnel toward the Light . . ." Again he dropped off.

David gently pursued. "What else?"

Another moment of hesitation before the old-timer fully gave in to his memories. "Folks are right when they talk 'bout the Light. It really is incredible. More love than you ever felt in a lifetime, a hundred lifetimes."

David watched and listened.

"I never made out no face or nothin'—just them eyes, them incredible, blazing eyes."

"Blazing? With what?"

"Fire . . . and love. For me. All of it burning for me. I was in the presence of the Lord God Almighty and He was burning with love for *me.*"

"Because you were one of his workers, a preacher."

"A what?" He threw a glance to David, then shook his head. "I was no preacher. Though I s'pose we both made our living off the eternal. No, brother, I was a mortician—well, a mortician's assistant, 'fore I got the call."

"But you were religious."

The man chuckled. "Wrong again. That was my Dorothy's department. Only time I ever used the Lord's name was when I reached the end of a bottle or I was cussin' someone out on the freeway. But I recognized them eyes . . . immediately. And I knew they loved me. I knew *He* loved me. And that's what made the leaving all the harder."

"You mean coming back, returning to Earth?"

"No."

"I'm sorry, I don't—"

"The closer I got to that Light, the more I felt His love till I was bathed in it, covered from head to toe. That's when I realized . . ." He swallowed. "That's when I realized I didn't want it."

"Want what?"

"Him. I mean I did, then. But it was too late."

David waited as the preacher struggled to find the words.

"It's like . . . like I'd spent my whole life tellin' Him no, I didn't want Him around, I didn't want His company. And now, now He was simply respectin' my wishes. It broke His heart, I could see it in His eyes . . . and it broke mine." The man's voice thickened. "All that power. All that love. But He had to respect my choice. *I* had to respect my choice."

"But," David gently persisted, "you could have made a different choice. You could have changed your mind."

"I can't explain it. It's like . . ." He cleared his throat. "It's like . . . clay. When I was here, living, I was soft and pliable, I could say yes or no anytime I wanted. I could be anything I wanted. But once I made my decision, once I truly decided and made my choice, then the clay was set. My death was the furnace, the kiln that fired and hardened it . . . that made me become what I'd chosen to become."

"And there was no changing?"

He slowly shook his head. "I'd become what I'd chosen to become. I had decided what I would worship—or not worship—for eternity."

"What happened next?"

Preacher Man scowled. "Suddenly I was falling. Ripped from the Light. From Him. I was back in the tunnel and I was falling. Fast. And the faster I fell, the darker it grew." He took another breath, exhaling with the faintest shudder. "But it wasn't darkness like you and me are used to. No sir, this was a darker darkness. I mean, even at midnight, even in a pitch-black room with the covers over your head, there's still some light, still some of His presence." Another, more ragged breath. "But not there. Not where I was."

"Just darkness?"

The man barely heard. He was lost, drifting someplace far away. When he resumed, he whispered, "And the screaming . . . I heard it all around me. Terrible. People crying, shrieking in rage."

"At the Light? For sending them there?"

Preacher Man's scowl deepened. "No . . . that's just it. *We* did it." The veins in his temple swelled. "*We* wanted it. *We* chose it. He only did what *we* had decided."

David watched as the old-timer closed his eyes and lowered his head. The story had taken much out of him. David glanced away, then to his own coffee, giving the man his space while trying to absorb all that he'd heard. But there was more. And he had to ask. "So how did . . . you know, how did you get back?"

There was no answer. David glanced back to the face. The man's eyes remained closed. He looked down at the black, leathery hands gripping the cup. A moment passed and he tried again. "If there were no second chances, how did you get back?"

The preacher took a long, slow breath and let it out. Finally, he answered, "That was the strangest thing of all. 'Cause in the midst of all that cryin' and carryin' on, I heard another voice. My Dorothy's voice." He cocked his head as if straining to hear while at the same time quoting: "'Dear Lord. Don't let him die. Not without knowing You. Not yet, Lord, not yet ...'"

"Your wife was praying?"

Preacher Man opened his eyes. They shined with moisture. "To beat the band. The old girl just wouldn't let up." He glanced at David with a smile. "And believe you me, I know what it's like to be on the other end when she makes up her mind. And the more she prayed, the brighter it got. Not like when I was with Him, but enough to see I was moving again. And before I knew it, I was in the hospital, racing toward my body, slipping into it as easily as if they were an old pair of trousers."

"And she was right there, praying over you."

"Yes, exactly." He took another breath. A cleansing breath. "She was praying to the only One who could save me." His strength was returning and with it, his fervor. "That's when I gave my life to Him." He wiped his eyes. "That's when I received Jesus Christ as my Lord and Savior. Glory be to God!" Turning to David, he continued, "And, brother, you can do it too. Anyone can. All they got to do is ask. That's why I stand out there all day long. You gotta repent, you gotta turn from your ways and accept Him while you still have the chance."

David felt his jaw tightening.

"Repent! Now, while the clay is still soft. Say yes to Him now, 'fore your heart gets too hard and you—"

"And I what?" David interrupted, "Go to hell? Is that where I'm going if I don't accept your Jesus? Is that where my daughter is because she didn't say yes to Him? Is that where this great loving Light would send her? Some innocent girl who didn't even—"

"No, no, that's the whole point. *We* choose to go to hell, *we*—"

"So how do I know?" David's voice grew louder than he intended. He struggled to bring it down but it quivered under the restraint. "How do I know what she chose? How can I help her?"

"I don't think you can, brother."

"Your Dorothy, she helped you, didn't she?"

The man started to answer but stopped.

"Didn't she!"

"I don't think you can."

"Don't tell me I can't! I'm her father! I'm supposed to protect her! I'm supposed to be there for her! She's sixteen years old." His voice cracked. "Sixteen!"

He hesitated, noticing how quiet the coffee shop had grown. He glanced around, once again realizing he was the cause. He took a breath to steady himself. "Look, I'm, uh, I'm sorry. I—"

"No, I understand. Believe me."

"What do you mean, you understand? Have you lost a kid?"

"Well, no, but—"

"Then don't tell me you understand."

"We've all—"

"No!" He was nearly shouting again. He brought it back down, practically hissing. "Until you can say the word *dead* and your child's name in the same sentence, you understand nothing!"

The old man looked down, quietly taking the blow.

David had had enough. He closed the diary and rose from his stool. Struck with sudden light-headedness, he reached out to the counter and steadied himself. As he did he saw the preacher writing something on a napkin, then shoving it at him.

"What's that?"

"When they found out 'bout me dying and all, some folks in the area interviewed me. It's a program that looks into the type of stuff you're talkin about. If anyone can help you, maybe they can."

The dizziness cleared and David looked down at the napkin. On it, in uneven scrawl, were the words:

*Life After Life.*



**D**r. Griffin watched as Norman E. Orbolitz stepped out of one of Life After Life's three virtual reality chambers. He was a tall, emaciated man in his seventies with translucent skin almost as white as his closely cropped hair. He wore a blue, tight-fitting bodysuit that in some ways looked like the uniform of a speed skater. He removed his 3-D goggles to reveal a pair of dark sunglasses that he was required to wear from his most recent operation. He placed the goggles in a clear case recessed in the outside wall of the chamber and turned to greet a half-dozen children who raced up and clambered around him. As always, there was plenty of horseplay and laughter. Mr. Orbolitz required it. And for good reason. More than one study indicated that this type of socializing strengthened the immune system and actually increased life spans. And since living forever (or as close to it as possible) was a passion of Mr. Orbolitz, these children and their parents were paid healthy salaries to increase those odds.

Of course, no one knew for certain when he was in the VR chamber. Because of the great vulnerability whenever he was inside it, that information was held in the strictest confidence. Still, the kids had a pretty good idea whenever they were hustled down to the VR lab "just for fun."

"Hey there, Dick." He spotted Griffin standing on the elevated platform behind the control console. "Haven't been waiting too long, have you?"

"No, sir." Griffin stepped down to join him.

Mr. Orbolitz picked up a husky six-year-old and playfully slung him across his bony shoulders. He was surprisingly solid for a man so underweight. Of course the lack of weight was intentional, all part of his fourteen-hundred-calories-a-day diet. Studies of rats with similarly restricted diets indicated they lived thirty to forty percent longer. This translated to an extra thirty years for humans. And thirty extra years wasn't a bad start for a man who used everything within his sizable influence to achieve such things. Everything and then some. It was the "then some" that Griffin suspected had summoned him into the great man's presence this afternoon.

Lowering the boy to the floor and shooshing him away with the others, Mr. Orbolitz asked, "How long this time, Wendell?"

Griffin's assistant answered from up at the console, "Almost fifty-eight minutes, sir."

Orbolitz flashed him a grin and Griffin saw every tendon and cable in his neck. The man was pleased. The virtual reality that PNEUMA created from the data of all those dying brains had become very authentic. So authentic that, unless you built up resistance, exposure to only a few minutes of the information would fool your own system into thinking it was dying and cause it to actually start shutting down. Theory had it that it would take younger, more elastic brains longer, but for first-timer adults, six minutes was the maximum. Orbolitz, who had built up resistance from many sessions, could last nearly an hour.

"Did you see anything new, sir?" Griffin asked, as they turned from the VR chambers and headed into the hallway. Though it was indoors, the hallway's floor was covered in a carpet of grass sod, along with ferns, flowers, bushes, even an occasional tree. Everything was real, including a handful of birds, some smaller wildlife, and a few of the more pleasant insects—butterflies, ladybugs, and a dragonfly or two. But since there were no windows in the vast complex, as sunlight contained ultraviolet rays which break down human cells and shorten life span, the vegetation had to be constantly replaced.

"I seen that river again," Mr. Orbolitz said. "And the garden. Say, did I ever tell you that the ancient word for *paradise* means 'walled garden'?"

"No, sir."

"Well, I tell you, ol' buddy, it is one fascinatin' place."

Griffin smiled. The good-old-boy persona was one of his boss's many eccentricities. Some thought it was a way to purposefully irritate the rich and influential, to rub their noses in his success. Others knew it was more calculated—to lull his competition into underestimating his abilities so he could strike and take them by surprise. Whatever the reason, as his empire grew and expanded, so did this persona.

"But them faces . . ." Mr. Orbolitz shook his head. "Way too many faces in the garden. Your boys may want to put some sort of filter on that. All them past reunions with all them dead friends and relatives can tucker a fellow out."

Griffin nodded. It was one thing to piece together an afterlife from thirteen hundred people's experiences, quite another to see each and every one of their past acquaintances come to greet them.

"I hear you had a little excitement over at the lab this morning."

Griffin nodded. "A little."

"Another one of them hell encounters?"

"Hard to tell. PNEUMA is still processing. I'm isolating it to chamber two's system until we make sure it isn't some crazy person's hallucination."

"Good idea."

A pretty assistant, California beach blonde, midtwenties, approached. She carried a tray holding an eight-ounce glass of carrot juice with the appropriate electrolytes to balance his metabolism from the VR workout. Orbolitz gave her a wink and she returned a dazzling, picture-perfect smile as he took the glass.

"How the other projects comin'?" He gulped down the drink and replaced the glass with a nod to the girl. She continued the smile and drifted away. "What's happening with them longevity studies?"

Griffin hesitated, unsure where to begin. How much detail did his boss want to hear, and in what area? Oxidation, free radicals, caramelization? Or did he wish for an update on the hormone replacement therapy or their genetic research? Uncertain, Griffin decided to focus on the latter, while being careful, as he always was, to insulate the man from any legally gray areas.

"We seem to be having quite a bit of success with telomerase right now."

"Telomerase . . . the enzyme us old fogies stop producing?"

"Yes, sir."

"Remind me what it does again?" He chuckled, pointing to his head. "Old age, you know."

Griffin laughed, uncertain whether the man was playing stupid or had actually forgotten. It was another aspect of the good-old-boy charm that kept his employees on their toes. "It protects the shortening of our chromosomes," Griffin answered. "Which occurs every time our cells reproduce."

"Which they do . . ."

"Most of the cells in our body die off and are replaced every few years."

Mr. Orbolitz nodded.

"Without telomerase the chromosomes in those cells become shorter and shorter until the cell ceases to function."

"Fifty or so reproductions, if I remember right, then we're history."

"That's the Hayflick limit, yes, sir. But by injecting genetically altered telomerase into some cells we're actually increasing those cells' reproduction rate up to twenty more generations."

Mr. Orbolitz shook his head in quiet wonder. "The Tree of Life."

"Pardon me?"

"From the Bible. When Adam and Eve sinned in the Garden, they weren't allowed to eat from the Tree of Life. And when they couldn't eat its fruit, they up and died."

"Ah." Griffin chuckled good-naturedly. "A piece of fruit no doubt containing a cousin to the telomerase enzyme. I get it."

Mr. Orbolitz grinned. "Imagine if such a fruit really existed—or just a piece of it so we could copy its DNA?"

"It would certainly put me out of work."

Mr. Orbolitz laughed, slapping him on the back. "Maybe I oughta start up another division and get some archaeologists working on it, what do you think?"

Griffin chuckled. "Who knows, maybe you should."

Still laughing, Mr. Orbolitz added, "Who knows, maybe I have."

The merriment continued, though Griffin wondered if the old guy was crazy enough to actually try it. He'd pursued just about everything else they could think of. Not that Griffin blamed him. In fact it was one of the many things he admired in Orbolitz. If you've got all the money in the world and only one life, why not do everything you can to prolong that life? Forget the charitable organizations. Forget wasting wealth on the poor or other parasites who could never return it. Spend it on what really mattered. Survival of the fittest. Darwinian pragmatism at its finest.

Over the years, Griffin had read a half dozen biographies on the man. Nothing spawns public interest (and unauthorized biographies) like a reclusive megapower. There were various theories on his birth that he neither confirmed nor denied. The most popular had him the illegitimate offspring of a Catholic priest and a young nun. When the Mother Superior refused to buy immaculate conception and when the girl refused to put him up for adoption, baby Norman and Mommy were cloistered away in some rural, ultrarestrictive convent with little to feed his heart and mind but a growing hatred for the Church and its God. Pop legend said that as a child his loathing was so intense he used to pray to God to allow him to become the Antichrist. As far as anyone could tell, that prayer had never been answered. But it didn't stop the man from trying to go toe-to-toe with God on the eternal life issue . . . while building a multibillion-dollar communication empire on the side.

The two approached an indoor waterfall and pool, complete with carp, water lilies, more ferns, and a tiny pygmy bunny that froze at their appearance. The pool narrowed to a small stream that meandered down the hallway.

"Dick," the old man said, "I got a gift I want to give someone—a special favor for a buddy of mine."

Griffin almost smiled. Despite the public's perception of Mr. Orbolitz as a charitable man (a perception fueled by Orbolitz's own media machine), in Griffin's eleven years of employment, he had never seen Orbolitz give away something for nothing. Everything had a price. If he could spin it to look like philanthropy, so much the better. But when it came to Mr. Orbolitz, nothing was free; everything had a string.

"Seems Congressman Hagen is having some congenital heart problems. They say it's pretty serious."

"Really?" Griffin said. "I didn't know."

"You ain't supposed to." The pigmy bunny decided to make a run for it. Dashing in front of them, it raced for the nearest clump of ferns several yards downstream. Mr. Orbolitz continued. "'Course they got him on all the ORO lists, waiting for a new ticker, but you and I both know that'll take months, maybe years."

"Even for a congressman?"

"First come, first serve. We're all equal in the eyes of the government."

"So I hear."

With a chuckle, he added, "Though some of us are a tad more equal than others."

The bunny arrived at the ferns and did its best to hide.

"Anyhow, I'm expecting that your research projects, with all them volunteers . . . well, I wouldn't be surprised if you discovered some private donor willing to help the congressman."

Now, at last, Griffin understood the reason for their meeting. "They've certainly come forward in the past, haven't they, sir?"

Mr. Orbolitz flashed him a grin, enjoying their little joke. After all, it was Griffin who had personally secured Orbolitz his most recent upgrade, not to mention the pair of healthy kidneys and pancreas he'd received some three-and-a-half years ago. He'd also lined up a future liver and heart donor, should the need ever arise. Organs do wear out. Especially for a diabetic. And should you ever need one and have the means to replace it, you'd be a fool not to plan ahead. And Norman E. Orbolitz was no fool.

"How close of a match do we want?"

Mr. Orbolitz came to a stop above the bunny. It remained perfectly still in the ferns, obviously hoping it was unseen. "Nothing as extravagant as mine," he said. "There's no need for him to entirely miss the joys of drug therapy."

More chuckles. Both knew the physical and emotional discomfort that antirejection drugs bring. A discomfort that Griffin had made certain his boss would never have to endure.

"Still," Mr. Orbolitz continued, "try to make the match as close as possible, given our tight time frame."

"How tight?"

The old man stooped down to the bunny. "I'd like him back on his feet in a couple three months."

"So we're talking an immediate transplant."

"The sooner the better."

Griffin nodded, then frowned slightly.

Sensing his unease, Mr. Orbolitz looked up. "Something on your mind, son?"

"It's just . . . well, isn't Congressman Hagen a strong advocate of gay rights?"

Mr. Orbolitz turned back to the bunny. "So I hear."

"And given your feelings toward homosexuals . . ."

"I'm not sure what you're talkin' about, Dick."

"In the past, you've always expressed to me—that is to say, you've always felt they were . . ."

"Deviant throwbacks?" Mr. Orbolitz asked. "Useless mutations that serve no purpose on the evolutionary ladder 'cept to deplete resources from folks who actually propagate the species?"

Griffin chuckled. "Well, yes, something like that."

Mr. Orbolitz slowly lowered his left hand in front of the bunny. "Actually, if you were to have deeper conversations with the good congressman, you'd find his sympathies and mine aren't all that different."

"Seriously?"

"Oh, yeah." He stealthily lowered his other hand behind the creature, unseen.

"But his policies," Griffin persisted, "his public positions—"

"Rather necessary, I should say, given his district includes some of the largest gay populations in the country." Having distracted the animal with his left hand, he quickly slipped his right hand in and caught it. Pleased with his success, he rose, holding the squirming creature.

Griffin continued, trying to understand. "So the fact that you share similar views on homosexuals is enough to merit the risk of—"

"Nah, not at all." Then with a sly twinkle he added, "I may be a bigot, son, but I ain't a stupid one." He held the bunny before his face, looking it in the eyes, then returned it to the safety of cupped hands against his chest. "There's another matter far more important to both of us."

He resumed walking, holding the shivering creature, stroking it and calming it. "Come next legislative session, the good congressman will propose a bill to legalize embryo stem cell research. And he'll use his sizable influence to pass it."

Griffin's heart quickened. Was such a thing possible? Imagine the doors that a bill like that could open for research.

To finally have their hands untied and legally study the most vital of all human cells. Still, other politicians had tried and failed to legalize it in the past.

"What about the religious right?" Griffin asked. "That's a political hot potato for anyone to handle."

"You bet it is." The stream drifted to the right, pushing them so close to the wall that Mr. Orbolitz's shoulder nearly brushed it. "But, given the fact that he'll soon be owing me his life, so to speak, well, I'm sure he'll be able to put his whole heart into the program." He chortled over his joke. "His whole *new* heart."

Griffin smiled. This was the Mr. Orbolitz he knew—the one who never gave something for nothing. As always, what started off as a carrot would turn into a stick.

"I understand, sir."

"Good. Now I want you to contact your division heads and—*ah!*"

Griffin gave a start as the man angrily yanked the bunny from his chest and slammed it hard against the wall.

"Stupid creature!"

"What happened?"

"It bit me!" He cursed as he brought the animal before them. It was injured from the blow, writhing and twitching in his hands. With another oath, he took the head in one hand, the body in the other and gave a quick, sharp twist. There was a sickening crunch of breaking vertebrae. The rabbit stopped moving. In disgust he threw it against the opposite wall. It hit with a dull thud and slid into the grass.

Griffin reached for Mr. Orbolitz's hand. "Are you okay, sir?"

"Yeah, I think so." They carefully studied each of his fingers. "No broken skin, at least. Stupid animal." He produced a locket from around his neck and pressed its large, round button. "Better safe than sorry, though."

Griffin nodded. "Absolutely." Within seconds he knew that the medical team would materialize. They would examine the bite and decide if any cautionary steps would be needed. If they did their job well, Mr. Orbolitz would praise them and give a reward. He was always quick to praise and reward. Just as long as you pleased him.

Griffin looked over to the dead bunny lying in the grass. It was important that you always please him.

I f David Kauffman didn't believe in ghosts before, Alcatraz was enough to change his mind. At least that's what he thought as he stood fighting off the chill in the corridor outside Cell 14-D. Of all the unsettling places on this thirty-three-acre island of rock, the solitary confinement cell at the end of the row was the spookiest, considered by many to have the greatest "negative energy." Over the years a dozen guards, psychics, and reporters claimed to have felt a sinister evil lurking inside. Several experienced a "breathing cold spot" near the left back corner. And more than one had seen glowing red eyes emerge from the darkness, accompanied by a malicious smile with a silver front tooth.

David glanced up to the wire-meshed windows towering above him—their dirty, opaque glow quickly fading in the setting sun. Everything about this place gave him the creeps. Including its history. Proportionately, Alcatraz had more mental breakdowns and attempted suicides than any prison in the country. In one year alone fourteen men had gone insane here. Hardly the place for somebody who wrote warm-hearted action/adventure novels. Unless that somebody wanted to talk to an expert about the possibility of contacting his dead daughter.

Three months ago he would have written off anybody with such ideas as a nutcase. But a lot can happen in three months. Besides, with so many psychics on TV, the radio, and in the papers, maybe there was some truth to it. Of course he figured most of the claims were false, but with all of that smoke, maybe, just maybe, there was the tiniest trace of fire.

In any case, that's why he was here. To talk to an expert. To see if there was some, if there was *any* possibility of breaking through and communicating with his child.

It had not been difficult to track down the Life After Life people. They were part of the Orbolitz Group, one of the largest media empires in the world and well-known for its charitable outreaches. Its sprawling headquarters were located just outside Los Angeles in the Santa Monica Mountains, practically in David's own backyard. Tracking them down was one thing, spending time with the right person was another. Those in the department agreed it should be Dr. Gita Patekar. If anyone could help him separate truth from fiction, she could. But the woman was perpetually busy. Nonstop. Still, he continued calling and e-mailing, insisting he would meet her anywhere, anytime that she had a moment. As a result, though they lived twenty-five minutes apart, he was now four hundred miles up the coast, watching her ply her trade, waiting for the event to end. When it was over she had promised she could spend up to an hour with him before jetting off to her next appointment.

"I'm feeling something," the psychic was saying. "Yes, yes, there's someone here. Definitely an entity . . . yes."

The nervous banter and joking of the reporters quickly came to an end as silence filled the corridor. Now there was only the intermittent ringing of a bell buoy and the distant moan of a foghorn.

David pulled his coat tighter and looked back to the cell.

Just outside the open door sat Morrie Metcalf, acclaimed psychic and host of the nationally syndicated TV show *Beyond the Grave*. His head was tilted back, allowing his silver-gray curls to rest on his black Dior Homme sports coat.

"Yes, I'm feeling . . . a him, it's definitely a him."

Beside Metcalf, around a clear, Plexiglas table, sat three other people. The first was J. L. Burton, the religion editor from the *Los Angeles Times*. The second was Janice Strommer. She claimed to be the great-niece of a murderer who was killed a few hundred yards from this spot in an escape attempt that took five lives. And finally, dressed in a white blouse and navy blue skirt, sat the petite and thoroughly professional Dr. Gita Patekar. She appeared Asian, perhaps Indian. And, though they'd only met for a moment, David found her accent as intriguing as her soft-spoken directness.

Several months earlier, in a *Times* interview, Dr. Patekar had mentioned that Morrie Metcalf was one of several fake psychics who were bilking grieving families of millions with false promises of contacting their dearly departed. Metcalf had taken issue with the article and had challenged her to test his abilities right here, in one of the hottest psychic places of the West Coast. Patekar had readily agreed to the challenge, and now here they were, surrounded by a handful of print reporters, TV lights, and two documentary crews—one from Metcalf's own show, and the other from the supposedly unbiased Psychic Network. It was a definitive showdown that everyone wanted to document.

"Yes . . ." Metcalf frowned. He rolled his head and whispered, "Yes . . . yes . . ." He grimaced then gave the slightest jerk, before his face relaxed into a smile. With eyes shut, he quietly whispered, "He's here."

No one spoke. Dead silence—except for the clicking of still cameras and their whirring autowinds.

"Yes," Metcalf whispered. Eyes still closed, he turned to the group. "He wants to know if anyone has a cigarette."

"Uh . . . sure." One of the reporters reached into his pocket and produced a pack of Camels. "Right here." Walking over to Metcalf, he tapped out a cigarette. The psychic opened his mouth and took it, then waited as the reporter fumbled for his lighter.

Once it was lit, Metcalf inhaled deeply, savoring the pleasure. He smiled, then spoke. "He says it's been a long time." He took another drag. And then another, blowing the smoke out over the table, where it hung in the still air.

More clicking and whirring of cameras.

The *Times* reporter cleared his throat. "Ask him, ask him who he is."

Metcalf smiled, then chuckled. "First, he wants to know who the hot dishes are."

Dr. Patekar and Janice exchanged glances. The young woman spoke first. "My name is Janice Strommer. Ask him if he knew my uncle, Joseph Cretzer?"

Metcalf took another drag and exhaled, thickening the haze over the table. "He says he knows Joey. Sometimes they hang out together. The prisoners from here have like a special fraternity."

"What about a name?" the reporter persisted. "What is his name?"

Another drag, then the answer. "Burgett."

Several eyes shifted to Dr. Patekar's young male assistant, who sat to the side quickly scanning a laptop screen until he found the name. "Edward Burgett?" he asked.

"Aaron Burgett," Metcalf corrected. Then he chuckled. "He says, nice try."

Others in the group softly laughed. The assistant glanced to Dr. Patekar, who appeared unfazed. She leaned toward Metcalf. "May I ask Mr. Burgett a question?"

Another smile. "He says anything . . . from a gorgeous toots like you."

Ignoring him, Patekar asked, "Is there some way to verify that he really is Aaron Burgett? Is there something he could tell us that only he would know?"

Metcalf nodded, paused a moment as if listening, then answered. "He says he tried to escape in 1958. September of '58." He took another puff and blew it out as he listened, then relayed more. "His body was missing for twelve days, and on the thirteenth day they found—"

"Yes," Dr. Patekar interrupted, "that is very impressive, but it is also well documented. Is there something else, some information that only he would know, that we could verify and—"

Suddenly Metcalf dropped his head forward and groaned. "No . . ." He rolled it to the left, then to the right. "No . . . don't hurt them, don't—They only want to know . . . No, don't hurt . . ."

Tension filled the corridor.

"Don't hurt who?" the reporter asked.

"There's somebody else here," Metcalf gasped. "Somebody who—" He jerked back his head, his face shiny with perspiration. "Who are you?" he cried, eyes still shut. "What do you want? No! No . . ."

The group exchanged uneasy glances.

Metcalf continued pleading, shaking his head violently. "No . . . she didn't mean for you to—She doesn't want you to—"

Then David saw it. He blinked, thinking his eyes were playing tricks.

"No . . ."

As Metcalf continued protesting, a faint orb of light appeared over the table. Indiscernible at first, but quickly taking shape.

Excitement swept through the crowd. Cameras clicked and whirred nonstop, as the video crews repositioned themselves and zoomed in.

The image grew clearer. Though transparent, it appeared to be a head. In the thick haze of smoke hanging over the table, a human head had materialized. The back of it was toward the reporters while its face looked directly at Metcalf.

"Who—who are you?" Metcalf cried. "What do you want?" The thing remained hovering, unmoving, yet apparently communicating. The psychic's face grew ashen. "No! Don't hurt these people! No!"

Obviously afraid, Janice and the *Times* reporter leaned as far from the table as possible. Dr. Patekar, although surprised, seemed more intrigued than frightened.

Slowly, the head started to rotate. The crowd fidgeted. The thing continued turning until it faced the *Times* reporter, who stared wide-eyed in fear, unable to move. But it did not stop. It continued rotating until it looked directly at Janice—who wasted little time rising to her feet, kicking over her chair, and stumbling to get away. And still it turned, until it finally came to a stop, directly facing David and the reporters . . . with its white, transparent face and glowing red eyes.

The crowd braced themselves. One or two stepped back. David tried to swallow, but his mouth had gone dry.

The lips of the face curled, parting into a malicious sneer. The front left tooth gleamed of silver.

*"Aaaaah!"*

David spun around to one of the video engineers wearing a headset not far from him. He was swatting at some invisible force. "Stay away!" he shouted. "Stay back! Stay—No! *Nooo!"* His entire body convulsed, raising him onto his toes as if lifted. He gave a chilling scream, then dropped back to his heels. But when he did, his entire countenance had changed. Slowly, he lifted his head. Now, like the floating face, he was also glaring.

"Bobby?" one of his colleagues called out. "You okay, bud?"

But he did not seem to hear. Instead, his arm shot out and he yelled, *"You!"* His finger pointed directly at the psychic. "What do you know of Burgett?"

Metcalf's eyes widened.

"What do you know of any of us?" Ripping off his headset, the engineer approached Metcalf, his face glowering, his voice guttural. "You are a fraud!"

Metcalf rose unsteadily to his feet. "What . . . what's going on here?" Turning to the video crew he asked, "Who is this man?"

"Bobby," someone from the Psychic Network called out. "Bobby Green."

*"Fraud!"* the engineer roared. *"Liar!"*

Fighting back his fear, Metcalf turned to Dr. Patekar. "You put him up to this?"

Dr. Patekar did not answer but slowly rose, keeping a careful eye on the engineer as he approached. "Mr. Green? Mr. Green, what are you doing? Mr. Green, stop right there."

The engineer slowed to within five feet of them.

"Mr. Green?" she repeated. "Bobby?"

Still looking at Metcalf, the engineer sneered, "Bobby can't come to the phone right now, but leave a message and he'll get back to you. Beep."

Metcalf took a half step closer, his voice unsteady. "Who are you?"

"You know who we are," the engineer growled. "*You* brought us up."

"I . . . I don't understand."

The engineer turned from Metcalf to the head floating above the table. "Do you hear that? He doesn't understand." He burst into a taunting laugh.

And then, to everyone's astonishment, the head opened its mouth and joined in the laughter, its voice an exact duplicate of the engineer's.

Metcalf spun to the head, staring in disbelief.

"What's the matter?" the engineer seethed.

Metcalf jerked back to him.

Then the head spoke, sounding identical to Green. "I think we've startled him."

Both the head and engineer laughed again.

"Who . . . who are you?" Metcalf demanded. He was trembling now.

"You don't know us," the engineer taunted, "but we know you . . . Don't we, Mr. Metcalf? Or should I say . . . *Tubulardude.*"

Metcalf's jaw dropped. Barely audible, he gasped, "What?"

"Isn't that your password when logging onto the kiddy porn site?"

The head broke into more laughter. The engineer joined in.

Panicking, Metcalf cried out as much to the cameras as to the ghosts, "I don't—I don't know what you're talking about!"

More laughter.

"Who are you?"

"Nothing is hidden from our world," the engineer snarled.

"But this . . . this is not possible!"

"We know everything," the head agreed.

"No!"

"Like those thank-you gifts you never mention to the IRS."

"What are you—"

"You don't think they're interested in that twenty-eight-foot cabin cruiser?"

"This isn't possible, it can't be happening!"

The head laughed, exactly as before.

"You're not real. I . . ." He pointed at the head. "You can't be real, we programmed you ourselves!"

"Programmed?" the engineer asked.

"Yes, yes!" In desperation Metcalf stepped forward and waved his hand through the head. "You're an image! A holographic image that we programmed three days ago!"

"Would a holographic image know about your sweet young thing in Orlando?" the engineer sneered.

Metcalf spun around to him.

The floating head joined in the laughter.

"My what—"

"What is she, fifteen?"

"Stop it. You're not real, you're a fake!"

"Too young to have a baby. At least that's what you keep telling her."

"Stop it! This isn't real! This isn't—"

"Too bad she's not listening."

"Please, stop!"

"Maybe you should tell your wife—"

"In the name of God—"

"—maybe she can convince her!"

"Stop it! Whatever you want. Just stop!" Turning to his young producer, he ordered, "Mel, stop tape. Guys, this isn't real, this can't be—"

Then, before everyone's eyes, the floating head started to morph. It began sprouting ears, then an animal's snout. Soon, it looked very much like a famous, all-American icon. And, should there be any doubt of its identity, it began to sing, *"M-I-C . . ."*

Metcalf watched in terror and confusion.

The engineer joined in. *". . . K-E-Y . . ."*

Then the rest of the Psychic Network crew finished the song. *"M-O-U-S-E!"*

When they ended, they broke into applause. Suddenly, the engineer relaxed. Returning to his old self, he grinned while being slapped on the back and congratulated by his fellow crew members.

Realizing the ruse, Metcalf shouted, "You think this is funny? Do you?"

No one paid attention as more congratulations were shared and the cameras continued running.

"You won't think it's funny when my lawyers slap a suit on you. All of you! Defamation of character, destruction of livelihood! You play one foot of that tape and I swear to God . . ."

Ignoring him, Dr. Patekar produced a remote control from her coat pocket. She clicked it at a case very close to the Plexiglas table, and the entire projected image of the head vanished.

Metcalf's face grew beet red as he sputtered. "But that's— that's *our* holograph! That was our, our—"

"Your what, Mr. Metcalf?" she quietly asked. "Your fraud? Your lie?"

"But how did you reprogram it? How did you get it to—"

Dr. Patekar's assistant spoke up as he closed his laptop. "Let's just say one of your technicians has recently become a devoted Orbolitz Group employee . . . with a very enviable raise in pay."

The engineer grinned at her. "So what did you think of my performance, Dr. Patekar?"

For the first time during the encounter, the petite lady broke into a smile. "I think you may have missed your calling, Bobby."

"How so?'

"Perhaps you should have pursued a career in front of the camera instead of behind."

More laughter as someone messed his hair and others taunted with good-natured quotes: "You don't know us, but we know you!" "Sweet young thing from Orlando . . ."

Finally understanding the ruse, David smiled at the camaraderie then glanced over to Dr. Patekar, who had turned to gather her papers. He was deeply impressed. Not only by her quiet beauty and gentle modesty, but by her intelligence. If she could detect and expose such a complex fraud, then surely she would know if there was someone who could help him make legitimate contact. He continued to watch, silently. And, as he watched, for the first time since his daughter's death, he began to hope.

A night wind had kicked up, putting a slight chop to their return ride from Alcatraz. But Gita barely noticed. She sat at the thickly varnished table in the cruiser's galley sipping hot Darjeeling tea and unwinding from the evening's event. All had gone well—except for the total destruction of a man's career and his personal life. She took little pleasure in that part of her work. But she had accomplished her task. Truth had again prevailed and that was the bottom line. For her, truth was always the bottom line.

Across the table sat David Kauffman, a ruggedly handsome, unkempt writer in his midforties. The years had treated him well, and it was clear he worked out just enough to make sure they kept doing so. But the faint stirring she felt inside of her had little to do with his looks. There was a tenderness about the man, a vulnerability that she found both touching and unnerving.

"This is, uh . . ." He fumbled with a photo and carefully pulled it from his shirt pocket. "This was her junior picture—taken at the beginning of the school year." He passed it to her. She noticed his hands trembling slightly. It may have been the cold, but she doubted it.

The girl was pretty. Long, raven-black hair, strong chin, dark brows. Though her features were more refined, there was no mistaking the resemblance to her father. Except for the eyes. They were startling in color—deep blue-violet. Beautiful. Despite her grin, they seemed to have a searching quality, almost an urgency.

"She's a good kid. I know that's what parents are supposed to say, but she really was."

Gita glanced up. He remained staring at the picture in her hands, not taking his eyes from it.

"I mean, we had our differences, what family doesn't. And we were struggling with her through some clinical depression, but she's a good person. You would have liked her. Everybody likes her."

Gita nodded, moved by how the man spoke in both past and present tenses. What love he had. What love he has. Yes, he suffered greatly, there was no missing that. But to be able to love so deeply, with such passion . . . Not that she didn't love. Of course she loved, that was her duty as a God-fearing Christian. But with this man, it was somehow different.

"I, uh . . ." He cleared his throat. "I ran off a copy of her diary." He produced a thick, spiral-bound notebook. "Maybe you could look at it—you know, see if there are any clues or anything."

She knew where they were going—had been down the road with dozens of others. And the last thing in the world she wanted to do was inflict more pain. "Mr. Kauffman, please . . ."

"I know you're a busy woman, but maybe if you saw something in her writing, in her thoughts . . ."

Gita started to protest, but he continued talking, as if afraid she'd cut him off. "I've tried calling the hospital a half-dozen times. But I can't get hold of the doctor. Maybe *you* can see something here, some sort of clue."

His dark brown eyes looked up, earnestly holding hers. So much love. So much compassion. Almost against her will, Gita started to nod. Relief filled his face and she smiled sadly. Reading the journal would be the easy part. What she suspected was coming next would be hard.

He cleared his throat. "What you did back there to Metcalf—I mean, I know he was fake and everything, but—"

She waited, sadly knowing the question.

"—but what about the real ones?"

"Real ones?" she asked.

"You know, real psychics. There must be a few who actually make contact. I mean, aren't there some legitimate ones out there somewhere?"

"Yes," she conceded, "there are a few."

"I knew it!" There was no missing his excitement. "Then could you—I mean, do you have names? People I can contact?"

"Mr. Kauffman—"

"I'm not asking you to recommend me or anything, but if I could simply—"

"Mr. Kauffman."

He stopped, anxious and hoping.

She wanted to soften the blow, but didn't know how. Truth was truth. "Mr. Kauffma—"

"David," he interrupted.

She frowned slightly. "David. In all of my experience, there has not been a single, legitimate contact ever made with the dead."

He blinked. "But . . . you just said, you just said there were real psychics."

She nodded. "There are psychics who make contact with another world, that is correct. The evidence is irrefutable. But there are many clever entities from that world. Beings who have observed the deceased when they were alive. Beings quite capable of impersonating them after they have died."

"You mean . . ." He tried to form the words.

She helped him. "They are not the dead. They are only beings, evil entities who take pleasure in counterfeiting the dead."

David scowled, his mind searching. "But, surely . . . I mean, you've not interviewed every psychic in the world."

"That is true. But I can tell you this much . . . David."

He looked at her, waiting.

She took a breath. Here it came. "As much as you wish to contact your daughter, you will not be able to. For that I am very sorry."

She watched as the truth hit him, then saw him struggling to recover, refusing to give up. "But . . ." He searched her face. "There must be . . ."

She held his gaze and slowly shook her head. "I am truly sorry."

"But—"

"And if you decide to seek her out, through mediums or psychics, you may indeed contact something. On that you have my word. However, I can also promise you that it will not be your daughter."

He said nothing, trying to understand.

She continued. "And . . . in doing so, you will put your own safety at risk."

"I don't care about that."

"Yes," she answered more softly, "that I can see." She watched as he looked away, trying to digest the fact. "Tell me, Mr. Kauffman—David—are you a religious man?"

He looked at her, then shook his head. "Not really."

"But you believe in the supernatural."

"I don't . . . I'm not sure . . . That's why I'm here."

She nodded. "When you return home, will you do me a favor? Will you find a Bible?"

"Sure."

"Look in the Old Testament. In fact you may want to write this down."

He checked his jacket and found a pen. But there was no paper. She reached for a napkin on the table and handed it to him. "Please write down Deuteronomy 18:10–12." She waited as he wrote. Then continued, "Exodus 22:18. Leviticus 19:31 and 20:27."

He nodded, repeating each as he scribbled.

When he had finished, she resumed, "Each of those verses forbid any contact with the dead. In fact, those last two give strict orders that a practicing medium should be put to death."

He frowned. "Why?" Then realized the answer. "Because of the danger you mentioned?"

"Yes, to protect people. The spirit world, it is a very dangerous place."

"But ..." He was struggling again. "There must be something. Some way ..."

"I am truly sorry. I wish there was. But the fact is ... there is no way you will be able to contact your daughter—not this side of heaven."

"Or hell," he quietly murmured.

"Pardon me?"

He shook his head, then took a discreet wipe at his eyes.

She looked on, feeling his heaviness in her own chest, wishing there was some way to ease the pain that her truth had once again inflicted.

# three

Dad and I had another crazed screamfest this morning. About the medicine. Big surprise, it's always about the medicine. He keeps yelling at me to take it and I keep going, "I feel better without it!" But the doctor keeps saying it's good for me and that it'll stop me from going over the edge again (I guess once is enough when it comes to seeing your kid carve up her arms in your bathtub) so I can see why he thinks it's important I take it. But still . . .

I snuck out and visited our tree again. I visit it a lot. The one down at Picador Beach that me and Dad carved our initials in back when I was in eighth grade. We were both having the world's worst day, so he text-messages me, saying he's going to call the school office in a couple minutes and say there's some major emergency but there really isn't so don't freak. Mrs. Lee then pulls me out of third period and I go "What's wrong?" and she goes, "Not sure." Then I see Poppy all sad eyed at the office desk, signing me out. We make our escape, CD blasting, hit KFC (long live popcorn chicken!), and wind up at Picador, where basically we just disappear off the face of society for the rest of the day. Seriously, how cool is that!

Then knowing inquiring minds will want to know, we put our devious writer heads together and came up with this awesome excuse about Mr. Tibbs, my cat, which is like a member of the family. Seriously, he's higher up the evolutionary chain than Luke, my subhuman brother, will ever be. Anyway, Tibbs supposedly

*swallowed these goldfish of mine that Mom supposedly*
*gave me before she ran off (I've never owned a goldfish*
*in my life) and Dad and Grams raced to the vet to see if*
*she could pump his stomach. But something goes*
*majorly wrong and he winds up in kitty ICU. Dad*
*thought the stomach-pumping part was over the top, but*
*he let me put it in. And you know what? They bought*
*it! Hook, line, and goldfish! What a team we are! Even*
*when I can barely handle him, I think back and care for*
*him more than any guy I've ever felt for . . . I love him so*
*much. I know I flap my wings too hard sometimes and*
*he gets hurt (hey, I'm just learning to use 'em), but he*
*puts up with it and is usually so cool. So I suppose I'll*
*take the stupid medicine, even though it makes me*
*majorly crazy. Then I'll call up the station and dedicate*
*that goofy "YMCA" song to him. The one we're always*
*dedicating to each other. The one where he threw his*
*back out at my cousin's wedding reception. He'll know*
*it's my way of saying sorry. And why not. I owe him that*
*much. I owe my daddy everything.*

Gita looked up from the journal, feeling a tightness in her
throat. Such love. What a lucky girl this daughter was. How
she could have killed herself was beyond understanding—
though the bouts of depression she had written of earlier
sounded like some very dark times.

Gita glanced out the window of the Gulfstream 5, but she
barely saw the moonlit Rockies passing below. It had been
ninety minutes since she'd said good-bye to David Kauffman.
He was on his flight back to LA while she was here, winging
high over Utah. She knew she should be prepping for tomorrow's meeting, but the emotions, the joys and heartaches in
this little diary had so captivated her. Such life bubbled up
from its pages. What a remarkable relationship this girl had
with her father.

And what a remarkable man her father seemed to be.

Of course she had serious reservations about his honesty.
How could he lie so his daughter could skip school? What was

he thinking? What type of example was that to set for a young, impressionable girl? And yet . . . here there was something beyond lying—something beyond breaking the rules. And though Gita couldn't put her finger on it, it made her uneasy. Friends occasionally teased her of being legalistic. Well, maybe they were right, maybe she was too focused on rules. But without rules everything would turn to chaos. Without rules and carefully prescribed order, people could never protect themselves.

But there was a depth and connection between these two that she would give anything to have. The thought had barely formed in her mind before she scowled at herself. She shook her head in silent contempt. Here was a man struggling to keep his head above emotional waters and all she thought about was her own needs. How selfish. And—she took a deep breath, slowly letting it out—how typical.

No. She could never experience this type of love. Didn't deserve it even if she could, not with her disgusting past. It was a double-edged sword, that's what the counselors said—the abuse of her past made her starved for affection . . . while the guilt of that past made it impossible for her to ever receive it.

Gita Patekar reached for her cup of tea and looked back out the window. She took a long, slow sip, allowing the warmth to ease her throat's tightness.

Then, against her better judgment, she picked up the diary and continued to read.

T his is my room! Get out of here!" Twelve-year-old Luke Kauffman charged at his father, but David managed to hold him off with one hand while rifling through his desk drawer with the other.

"I smelled smoke!" David slammed the top drawer and opened the next. "Cigarette smoke."

"Grams!" Luke spun to David's mother, a portly woman with blue-gray hair who stood at the door. "Make him stop! This is my room! He has no right to—"

"It'll be okay," she said, trying to calm him. "It'll only be a minute."

David shut the last drawer and turned to the mammoth pile of clothes on the floor. "Don't you ever pick up after—"

"Dad—"

"This place is a sty!"

"David," his mother cautioned.

"My kids don't live like this!" He was vaguely aware that he spoke of them as plural, but it didn't matter. He'd made so many mistakes with Emily, been such a rotten father, let her get away with so much, he wasn't about to go that route with Luke. "Just tell me where you hid them! Where are the cigarettes?"

"Why?" His son stood glaring in defiance. Dark hair spilled onto his forehead. Already the soft round face of a boy was taking the sharper, more angular features of a man.

"Because they're dangerous!" David stooped down and began digging through the clothes. "Because they'll kill you!"

"What do you care?" the boy shouted.

David turned to him. "What?"

"What do you care? Maybe I *should* take up smoking. Yeah. Then maybe I can hurry up and die of lung cancer."

The phrase stunned David. "What's that supposed to mean?"

"It means she's still getting more attention than me. Even now! Even when she's dead!"

Slowly, David rose from the clothes, staring at his son in disbelief. He turned to his mother, who looked away, not letting their eyes meet. The ground under his feet started to shift.

"It's been nine weeks, Dad! *Nine* weeks!"

David's eyes dropped back to the pile before him. What was he doing? He loved this boy. More than his own life. He looked over to the desk. This wasn't like him. What was he doing?

"You don't think I miss her too?" Luke choked out the words.

David was lost. Getting more lost by the second. He looked about the room. Spotted the door.

"Don't you think I'm always wondering what I did wrong—how I could have saved her?"

If he had an answer, he couldn't give it. He started toward the door.

"Don't you?"

He arrived and stepped into the hall.

"David?" his mother called.

But he barely heard her. What did he think he was he doing? Accusing his son? Destroying another child? Wasn't one enough? His feet shuffled across the carpet. To his left were a dozen pictures on the wall. Instinctively, he lowered his eyes. He never looked at them. Couldn't. He'd tried once and it had nearly destroyed him. Those penetrating, violet eyes. Full of such curiosity, such hope for the future. But now there was no hope. Or future. Everything had ended. That's why he couldn't look. The ache of no future outweighed any joy he might have of the past.

But there were other pictures—pictures of his boy. That goofy one Luke hated and David loved of his son with both front teeth missing, wearing the baseball cap. And another. Father and son holding their catch of the day—nine-year-old Luke grinning proudly with four rainbow trout, David with an empty hook and broken arm.

*"That looks pretty dangerous,"* his son had shouted as David scaled up the rock face alongside the waterfall.

*"Not for me,"* David had shouted back. *"You stay there and catch the young stupid fish. I'm going up here and hit that pool where the big smart grandpappies hide out."*

He remembered Luke watching him in awe and wonder. Any suspicions he had that his dad wasn't a real man's man were quickly being dispelled. More might have been dispelled if David had not slipped from the rocks, fallen, and had to have Luke drive him to the nearest ER.

Now, on the verge of adolescence, his son stood yelling at him from the bedroom door. "Nine weeks, Dad!" Emotion cracked and ruined the boy's voice. "Nine weeks and you won't even go into her room!"

David couldn't answer. He couldn't turn. What was wrong with him?

"Dad . . ."

Nine weeks and he was no better. Worse, since the numbness had worn off. Now there was only this raw, gaping wound with pain that never stopped. A giant hole of what "could have been." Every *Seventeen* magazine that greeted him at the mailbox was a mockery. Every college advertisement addressed to her was a taunt. Nine weeks and no relief . . . except for those brief moments each morning when he woke, before reality crushed his chest. Most mornings it was an accomplishment to simply get out of bed, let alone put on clothes and go through the motions of the day. Because that's all they were . . . motions. Meaningless repetition. He floated through them—like a visitor from another world—watching, talking, listening to people he once knew who were no longer part of his reality.

"Dad . . ."

And his son. Powerful currents had ripped them from each other. They reached out but kept slipping further and further away. He loved the boy. Knew his son loved him. But it had gone wrong. Topsy-turvy. A whirlpool spinning and tumbling them farther and farther apart.

He passed her closed door. It was always closed. But that didn't stop Mr. Tibbs, her cat, from sitting there each night, waiting for her return. Not that he blamed him. His heart still skipped when the phone rang late in the evening, or he heard keys rattling in the door. Grams and Luke had tried adopting Tibbs, but he would have none of it. He was faithful to the end. Only, the end had come and gone and he didn't know it. Nobody knew it.

Except David.

And Luke.

And Emily, wherever she was.

That's him on the left? Hector Marquez?"

"The tall skinny one, yeah."

Dr. Richard Griffin leaned past a thick muscular brute with a bald head and a dozen rivets in his ear, to stare out the limo window. There, on the corner of Hollywood and Highland, stood a clump of teens smoking, drinking from a paper bag, shouting to passing cars. A couple were gang bangers with shaved heads, white T-shirts, and baggy pants looking for action. Others were homeless runaways—girls in skimpy shorts, boys slouching with faces hidden under hooded sweatshirts. They were looking for another type of action—something to pay for eats or another fix.

"And he's AIDS free?" Griffin asked.

"Last time we tested."

Griffin glanced at the laptop computer in front of him. On the screen was a detailed tissue-type chart of Hector Marquez. "All right. Tell him to come here."

His associate rolled down the window. The street smelled of diesel and smoke and urine. "Luis," he shouted. "Hey, Luis!"

The shortest Latino looked up.

"Luis, come here."

Glancing to his friends, the kid butted out a cigarette and sauntered over to the car, baggy pants falling enough to reveal his boxer underwear.

"Bro," he called.

"'Sup man?"

He arrived and they gave a handshake as complex as any secret society's.

"The man here wants to talk to your cousin, Hector."

The kid stooped lower to look at Griffin, then shook his head. "Don't think so, Bro."

"Why?"

"Hector ain't switch hittin' no more. 'Specially not with old white raisins." He flashed Griffin a grin that showed a dying front tooth.

"We ain't talkin' party, Bro. He got some other action comin' down."

"Yeah?" The kid sized up Griffin again, then shook his head. "Don't think so, man."

As if understanding an unspoken language, Griffin's associate magically produced a twenty-dollar bill.

The kid grinned and snatched it. "I'll see what I can do." He turned and sauntered back to the group.

The associate turned to Griffin and explained, "Handling fee."

Griffin nodded. "He's not turning tricks anymore. This is a good sign."

The man nodded. "You'll still want tests. Make sure he's clean."

"We'll do that during cross match."

"Everything else works?"

Griffin motioned to the computer screen. "His tissue types are very close. In all three groups."

"Cool."

They turned as Luis approached with Hector.

"Happening, Bro?"

Hector shrugged.

"The man here wants to talk to you."

Hector glanced up the street, then waited.

Taking his cue, Griffin extended his hand. "My name is Griffin, Dr. Richard Griffin."

Hector simply stared at the hand.

With a smile Griffin pulled it back. "Do you remember the blood test they ran on you over at the drop-in center a couple months back?"

"I ain't sick."

"No, no you're not. In fact, what we've discovered is that you may have some very remarkable blood running through those veins of yours. So remarkable that we'd like to run a few more tests, to see if our data is indeed correct."

Hector's eyes held his, carefully evaluating.

"Of course there'd be some remuneration, payment for your time."

"How much?"

"How does one hundred dollars sound?"

The associate's wince indicated that Griffin had offered too much. Before he could respond, Luis stepped in.

"One-fifty."

"One hundred and fifty dollars?" Griffin asked in surprise. "No, I don't—"

"Take it or leave it. He's a busy man."

Griffin hesitated, glancing to his associate for clues. There were none. "Well, all right, then. One hundred and fifty dollars."

"Plus a safety deposit."

"A what?" Griffin asked.

Luis explained, "You pay me safety deposit money and I'll make sure he gets there safely."

Now Griffin understood. Extortion. Protection money. But would he really harm his own cousin? It didn't matter. "All right." Griffin produced a twenty and handed it over to Luis, who waited patiently for him to produce a second. Griffin complied.

The kid flashed his dead-tooth grin. "Where and when?"

"Tomorrow, one o'clock, at 2540 Las Posas."

"The Freak Shop?" Luis exclaimed.

"The what?"

"Where you run them experiments."

"Actually, we share those facilities with several other medical groups and—"

"Right." Luis nodded at the obvious lie. "But no experiments on this one. We don't run no experiments on my man with the remarkable blood."

"No, no, of course not."

Another grin. "At least not for no hundred fifty bucks."

"That is correct. No experiments."

Luis spoke something in Spanish to Hector. The kid nodded, turned, and slunk back toward the curb. Before joining him, Luis leaned farther onto the window. "I got some fancy blood too, you know. Special discount rate."

"Don't think so, Bro," the associate said, reaching for the electric window.

"Also got friends who specialize in raisins, if you're interested." The window rolled up, forcing Luis to pull back. "Okay, maybe some other time then."

～

*He fumbles at your spirit*
  *As players at the keys*
*Before they drop full music on;*
  *He stuns you by degrees,*

*Prepares your brittle substance*
  *For the ethereal blow,*
*By fainter hammers, further heard,*
  *Then nearer, then so slow*

*Your breath has time to straighten,*
  *Your brain to bubble cool, —*
*Deals one imperial thunderbolt*
  *That scalps your naked soul.*

Gita sat in her hotel room, staring at yet another poem by Emily Dickinson. She didn't understand it all, but was struck at how David's daughter, this other Emily, had valued it so much that she had written it down. And not just this poem—dozens of similar ones filled her journal. Some by Dickinson, some by other poets. Each seemed rich with meaning. In fact, more than once, Gita found herself skimming over the daughter's written thoughts to focus upon the poems that so intrigued the girl. That so intrigued Gita.

As she read the journal, she had noticed a gradual shift in the daughter's tone—particularly in the last portion, during her final weeks at the hospital. Here, she'd met a Christian kid, some heartthrob by the name of Cory. And here, her hunger for spiritual things seemed to awaken. The poem that she'd entered on the following page by a J. Quarles and H. F. Lyte of the seventeenth and eighteenth centuries was a perfect example:

*Long did I toil and knew no earthly rest,*
*Far did I rove and found no certain home;*
*At last I sought them in his sheltering breast,*
*Who opes his arms and bids the weary come:*
*With him I found a home, a rest divine,*
*And I since then am his, and he is mine.*

*The good I have is from his store supplied,*
*The ill is only what he deems the best:*
*He for all my friend I'm rich with naught beside,*
*And poor without him, though of all possessed;*
*Changes may come, I take or I resign,*
*Content while I am his, while he is mine.*

*Whate'er may change, in him no change is seen,*
*A glorious Sun that wanes not nor declines,*
*Above the storms and clouds he walks serene,*
*And on his people's inward darkness shines;*
*All may depart, I fret not, nor repine,*
*While I my Saviour's am, while he is mine.*

*While here, alas! I know but half his love,*
*But half discern him and but half adore;*
*But when I meet him in the realms above*
*I hope to love him better, praise him more,*
*And feel, and tell, amid the choir divine,*
*How fully I am his and he is mine.*

Interspersed among the poems were pages of conversations with Cory—particularly the ones they had during their secret rendezvous in the laundry room where they talked and she asked questions until dawn. Questions about God. About Cory's faith. And, nestled between one of those conversations, Gita found a poem the girl had written on her own. It was no masterpiece, but again it showed the depth of something happening inside:

*I see Love's scarred hands*
*outstretched from Calvary.*
*"Come, come, come."*

*"But my filth and failures —*
*can't you see*
*my shame, shame, shame?"*

*"I see not your dirt,*
*I count not your losses.*
*Come, come, come."*

*"But I am worthless,*
*with nothing to bring but*
*Shame, shame, shame."*

*"You've not even that,*
*For I've taken it all, even*
*your blame, blame, blame."*

Yes, she was going through deep changes, making the transition into a life of faith—which made her suicide in the hospital all the more tragic. But there was something else. A small bit of info that Gita had run across earlier and still couldn't shake. She looked up from the diary and stared out the hotel window into the evening. Something wasn't right. Something about the hospital tests. She was no psychiatrist and she was clueless about the medications the girl mentioned, but she did find it strange that the staff had run a series of tissue-type tests on her. Those were the words she had used. Not blood type, which might be understandable should an emergency arise, but the battery of tests they'd run was to determine her tissue type. Why would a mental health hospital need tissue type?

She glanced at her cell phone charging on the nightstand. There was one possibility. She knew the Orbolitz Group sometimes asked for such information from hospitals who benefited from their grant programs—and from individuals who agreed to participate in their medical studies. They'd even asked for permission from her brother, Nubee. The idea was to encourage as many as possible to consider becoming organ donors—typical of the Orbolitz Group's humanitarian focus.

She reached for the phone. It was almost two in the morning Salt Lake City time, one on the Coast. But she knew her boss, Richard Griffin, was as much a workaholic as she. He'd still be up working on something. She'd give him a quick call to see if either the hospital or the girl was in their system.

N ormally Griffin paid for much higher-class call girls. He could certainly afford them. And normally they'd drive themselves to his Santa Monica penthouse. But this evening he'd been down on the Boulevard and saw such an abundance of youth that he thought a little diversion might be good for the soul. So, after dropping off his associate, he picked up a couple street brats for a little drive-time party before heading home. They'd just entered the limo when his cell phone rang. He read the name on the LED, motioned for the girls to be patient, and answered, "Good evening, Gita."

"Dr. Griffin, did I wake you?"

"You know better than that." He glanced at his reflection in the window, adjusting his hair. "Just got your report on Morrie Metcalf. Nice work. Sounds like some major slicing and dicing."

"I hope I did not completely destroy him."

"Nonsense. He got what he deserved." Griffin pulled one of the girls, a redheaded Goth, to his side. "He was a fake and you exposed him."

"Yes, I suppose."

Griffin chuckled. One thing he enjoyed about Gita Patekar was her straight-arrow approach. You always knew where you stood with her . . . which meant you could always manipulate her. Except, of course, when it came to compromising her morality. Pity. He'd certainly put in enough effort . . . and he wasn't about to stop. She was too tantalizing of a morsel. Other than that imperfection, she was the model employee—as faithful and dependable as any household dog.

"What's up?" he asked, turning his face from the smell of the redhead's greasy hair.

"I was wondering. Do we have any philanthropic programs running at Valley Care Health Facility? It's in Agoura Hills, California?"

"Where?"

"Agoura Hills?"

"Why do you ask?"

"I met a man this evening. A Mr. David Kauffman."

"Go on."

"He has a teenage daughter, or had, by the name of Emily Kauffman. She was institutionalized at Valley Care Health until her successful attempt at suicide nine weeks ago. As you can imagine, he is quite traumatized by it."

The redhead nuzzled into Griffin until he shrugged her off. Gita definitely had his attention. He chose his words carefully, trying to sound casual. "What does that have to do with us, Gita?"

"I was simply curious if we had any programs running there. Or perhaps we are sponsoring some of its patients."

"Doesn't ring any bells." There was a pause at the other end. He quickly added, "I'd have to check the files to be certain, though."

"Would that be a problem?"

"For you, of course not."

"It appears they ran a tissue type on her, which seems rather odd in an institution such as that."

Griffin closed his eyes, striving to keep his voice even. "Yes, it does. I can't get to a computer right now. But first chance I get, I'll be happy to look into it. What's her name again?"

"Kauffman. Emily Kauffman. I am sure it is nothing. But he is a very nice man, and as you can imagine, he is tormented by many questions."

Griffin forced a laugh as he opened the laptop before him and quickly searched the screen for a folder. "Nice, is he?"

"He is very sensitive, yes."

The redhead tried again and he pushed her away. She pretended to pout, sliding to her friend who was putting down her second or third mini-bottle of rum from the bar. "Well, you be careful of those nice men, Gita. You know where that can lead."

"Dr. Griffin, please." He could hear the embarrassment in her voice. "I am simply trying to be helpful."

"Right." He found the folder labeled *Surveillance* and clicked it open. "Well, you be careful, just the same."

"Thank you for your concern, Doctor."

He smiled. Was that sarcasm he heard? Was she finally getting acclimated to American culture?

"You know I'm always looking out for you, Gita." He pulled her name from the file and brought it up on the screen.

"I am certain you are."

Yes, that was definitely sarcasm. He forced another chuckle. "I'll have an answer for you within twenty-four hours."

"Thank you, Doctor."

"Is there anything else I can do for you?" He tabbed over to her phone numbers and saw three entries—cell, home, and work. Beside each was a box with the word *monitor.* He rapidly checked all three. Now Security would record and review all of her calls.

"No, that is all, Dr. Griffin. Thank you."

"Are you certain?" He continued to tease, though there was no smile on his face. "Because if there's any other service I can provide, you know I'm always here."

"Thank you, Doctor, that was all I needed. Good night."

"Good night, Gita." He hung up, then paused a moment to think. If the father, David Kauffman, was asking questions, if he had somehow connected his daughter's death to the Orbolitz Group, then he'd have to be diverted. And the sooner the better. Griffin hit the menu tab on his cell phone, then clicked to phone book. He scrolled until he found the number. There was no name beside it. Griffin had never known the name. He had never wanted to. Just the extension: 3316. That's the number that would evaluate the problem. That's the number that would suggest how best to contain and, if necessary, remove it.

# four

"You really think that's true?" David adjusted the phone and rose to his feet. "That she became a person of faith?"

"Please look at the entry dated . . ." He heard the drone of Gita's car as she leafed through her copy of the journal. ". . . October 13."

He reached down to his desk and flipped toward the back of Emily's diary. It was just before noon. Dr. Patekar had already flown halfway across the country, arrived at the airport, and was driving home. David, on the other hand, had managed to record his answering machine message (six times), wash every windowpane of the French doors to his office (inside and out), and connect all fifty-four paper clips he'd found in his desk drawer. It was one of his more profitable days. Of course no writing came. Not anymore. He hadn't been able to write since the accident. Actually long before that.

Originally he'd thought his paralysis came from the success of his last book and the fears of trying to match that success with his next. But as the months dragged into years, he suspected he'd run up against a much greater problem—the problem of catching truth on paper. He saw the beauty of life all around him. He saw it in breathtaking vistas, he saw it in tiny details. But, no matter how hard he tried, he could not find the words to capture that life. Everything he wrote felt

cliché... artificial... clunky. His phrases glanced off truth
like a butter knife trying to sculpt marble. And, though
Emily's death was his latest excuse, he knew his ineptness
had been lurking underneath long before that.

He found the page Gita had mentioned and asked, "Is it
the Edwin Hatch poem she copied?"

"Yes. Please take a moment to read it."

"You're sure you've got the time?"

"In this traffic," she sighed, "I may have all day."

David smiled. He liked this woman—her intriguing
accent, her gentle directness. More than that, there was a
quality about her, a type of centeredness, that he found very
engaging. He sat on the edge of his desk and read from the
journal:

> Breathe on me, breath of God
>   Fill me with life anew,
> That I may love what thou dost love,
>   And do what thou wouldst do.

He stopped. "I've read this before, a couple times."

"Yes. But in the context of her conversations with Cory?"

"The boyfriend."

"Yes."

"Well, no, not— "

"Please, read it again, David. I think you may see something."

"All right." He returned to the poem and continued, forcing himself to slow down and read it with fresh eyes.

> Breathe on me, breath of God,
>   Until my heart is pure:
> Until with thee I have one will
>   To do and to endure.
>
> Breathe on me, breath of God,
>   Till I am wholly thine,
> Until this earthly part of me
>   Glows with thy fire divine.

*Breathe on me, breath of God,*
    *So shall I never die,*
*But live with thee the perfect life*
    *Of thine eternity.*

He paused a moment. "It is lovely. Maybe you're right, maybe she was becoming, you know, more spiritual."

"I believe it is more than that."

"How so?"

"Turn, if you will, to the end of the diary, to her second-to-last entry."

As David flipped through the pages he heard call waiting beep, but decided to ignore it.

"November twentieth?" he asked.

"Yes."

As before, he forced himself to read slowly, savoring the words:

*Well, the big IT finally happened. With Cory, I've gone and done the deed. No bells no whistles no earth moving. Just the exquisite, rapturous joy of completely giving myself over to someone who has been beckoning me, pursuing me, doing everything in the world to prove he loves me. I got to tell you, it's not the way anybody describes it. Not Cory, not anybody. I mean, you can read about it all you want, but until you actually take the step, the words are just words. Such rapturious joy. There really is no other word for it but Divine. All around me. So pure and perfect. I will never experience something this great with another human being.*

David swallowed. "I thought . . . When I read that I thought that she and Cory were, that they'd—"

"Made love?"

"Yes."

"I do not think so. As I read of their conversations, and her thoughts, and these poems, I believe she was being romanced by somebody. But I do not believe it was Cory. And, I believe here at the end, she has given herself over to that somebody."

"You mean . . . God?"

"More precisely, Jesus Christ."

David stared at the final entry. "And that's important, because . . ."

"Because we now know with certainty where she is."

He rose stiffly from the desk and wandered toward the French doors. "You mean heaven."

"Yes."

"You sound like a preacher I know."

"I am no preacher, David. But I am a scientist. And truth is very important to me."

"A scientist who believes in the Bible?"

"And the claims of Christ."

"I didn't know there were such people."

"Of course. There is more than sufficient empirical evidence to prove—"

"Whoa, whoa," he forced a chuckle. "'Empirical evidence'?"

"Yes."

"How . . . where?"

"I do not think this is the time to—"

"No, please." He turned from the French doors and ambled back across the office, going no place in particular. "I mean, if you have a few minutes, I'd love to hear your thoughts."

There was silence.

"Hello? You there?"

"Yes."

"I'm serious. If you don't mind, I'd like to hear what evidence you're talking about."

"All right . . . Empirical evidence can be found in any one of several disciplines. History, archaeology, mathematic—"

Call waiting beeped again, and again he ignored it. "You can prove the claims of Jesus Christ mathematically?"

"According to the laws of probability, there is little doubt that He is the Messiah."

David frowned. He really did like this woman. And he enjoyed talking to her. But this . . . "Dr. Patekar, I don't mean to be argumentative, but . . ."

She completed his thought, "You are asking how?"

"Well, yes—if you don't mind."

"If you don't mind me sounding like your preacher friend."

He smiled. "Please."

"As we can best determine, there are up to three hundred Old Testament prophecies of the Messiah that were fulfilled by Jesus Christ."

David arched an eyebrow. "What type of prophecies?"

"His actions, the location of His birth, the precise time of His appearance—not to mention specific details of His cru- cifixion—a form of execution not even invented when the prophecies were written."

David started back toward his desk. "Couldn't some of that be coincidence?"

"Perhaps, but the odds of one man fulfilling only eight of the major prophecies is roughly one in ten to the seventeenth power."

"That's steep."

"The equivalent of covering the state of Texas in two feet of silver dollars, painting one red, and giving a blind person one chance to pull it out."

David sat back on the edge of his desk, quietly absorbing the information. "So, in your mind, that makes Jesus Christ the Messiah."

"Among other evidence, yes. And, if that is the case, I must accept His claims."

"Which are?"

"Several. But the one that should give you the greatest comfort is His promise that those who put their trust in Him will not die but live forever in heaven."

"And you believe that."

"I believe truth. And if I believe the claims of His messiahship, then I must also believe His other statements."

David nodded silently and looked back to the journal. *With Cory, I've gone and done the deed.*

Was it possible? Had she—

Once again, call waiting beeped.

"I'm sorry, Dr. Patekar, I've got someone on the other line trying to get through."

"I believe we are finished."

"Listen, I really appreciate your taking the time."

"In spite of the sermon?"

He chuckled. "In spite of the sermon. Maybe, if I have further questions, would it be all right . . ."

"I would very much enjoy talking to you again, David."

And he believed her. In her gentle directness, he believed she enjoyed the conversation as much as he did. "Thank you."

Call waiting continued to beep.

"You are most welcome."

"Good-bye."

"Good-bye, David Kauffman."

He found himself smiling as he switched lines. "Hello?"

"Mr. Kauffman?"

"Yes."

"This is Lincoln Middle School. I'm afraid we have an incident with your son, Luke."

He was immediately on his feet. "What's wrong, is he okay?"

"I'm afraid he's a bit . . . inebriated."

"He's what?"

"Drunk, Mr. Kauffman. We found a bottle of vodka in his locker and he is quite intoxicated. He's in the nurse's office and—"

"I'll be right there." David hung up without saying good-bye. He raced to his office door, head spinning. Was it happening again? With Luke? What was he doing wrong? Would it ever end?

N ow what's the problem?" Griffin sighed. "Didn't we have a deal?"

"Yeah," Luis said, stepping into a dust-filled shaft of sunlight in the deserted hall. "But the rates, they gone up."

"Have they?" Griffin was in no mood to be back in Hollywood. Especially in the middle of the day. But he'd been told there was an "issue," and that the kid would only speak to him.

"Way I figure, goin' price for this special blood of Hector's is two, maybe three hundred now."

"Three hundred dollars?"

Luis shrugged. "Way I figure."

Griffin wearily shook his head. It was just the three of them—Luis, the bald associate with the rivets in his ear, and himself. They stood in the dank, plaster-peeling hallway of an abandoned building. Well, nearly abandoned. Behind him was the closed door to their off-campus site—the special suite of rooms where volunteers to their longevity program were tested, examined, and, of course, paid.

"We had a deal, Luis."

"I don't see no contract."

"We had a gentlemen's agreement."

"'Gentlemen?'" The kid snorted in disgust. "You don't think I know what comes down in your little freak shop here?"

"A gentlemen's agreement," Griffin repeated.

"Well, this is what I think of you as a gentleman." Luis slowly raised his right hand, making an obscene gesture directly in Griffin's face.

"Luis." Griffin shook his head. "That is so tasteless. If you're trying to communicate as one businessman to another, you need to speak in terms that I can hear."

"Really?" The boy broke into his dead-tooth smile. "Then let me improve your hearing." He duplicated the gesture with his other hand.

"Such vulgarity."

Luis shrugged. "Freedom of speech, man."

Griffin nodded then simply glanced to his associate who, with lightning speed, grabbed the kid's finger.

"Ahhh!" Luis cried. He struggled to get free. "Let go! Freedom of speech, man! I can say whatever I want!"

"Yes, you can," Griffin agreed. "But I'm afraid your audio-visual aids are experiencing some technical difficulty."

"What? What are you—"

There was a sickening crack—like someone eating crab legs at Red Lobster—followed by the boy's scream. "*Augh!* My finger, man! He broke my finger! He broke my finger!"

"Only one?" Griffin asked.

The kid looked to Griffin in terror. The associate grabbed the other finger.

"No!" Luis squirmed and fought, dropping to the floor, trying to kick away, yelling, cursing—until his assailant expertly used the finger as leverage to flip the boy onto his back. Once down, he rested a heavy boot on his chest to help hold the kid in place. Suddenly, Luis was wide-eyed and helpless, his finger nearly twisting out of its socket. "We can work this out! We can—" He winced while struggling to breathe. "All right. Whatever you want, man! Whatever you want!"

Griffin looked down, impressed at the boy's flexibility—his finger was nearly touching his elbow. "So you'll bring Hector in?" he asked.

"I don't know where—"

The associate applied more pressure.

Luis screamed, cursing in Spanish. Griffin didn't understand all the words, but appreciated the sincerity. Finally the kid gasped in English. "Yes ... yes! I'll bring him! I'll bring him!"

"I'm sorry," Griffin cupped his hand to his ears. "Remember, my hearing isn't so good."

"Yes! Yes!"

"Are you certain? Because I would hate to make another trip down here to—"

"I'll bring him in, man. I swear, I'll bring him."

Griffin gave the slightest nod to his partner, who released Luis's finger and removed his foot. The boy scampered to his feet, grabbing his finger, cussing a torrent of Spanish.

"Same time tomorrow?" Griffin asked.

Luis glanced over his shoulder to the metal door behind him. Still holding his hand, he backed toward it—struggling to regain his machismo while anxious to retreat. "Got it, man. Same time tomorrow. No problem. Same time."

Griffin nodded as the kid arrived at the door. "And Luis?" He looked to him.

"Tomorrow, your rates are lower."

Luis frowned.

"Tomorrow, they're free."

The kid started to protest until he shot a look at the associate, prepared for more action. "Okay, man. Free, I hear you." He pushed the door open. Bright sunlight glared in. "I hear you." He continued backing out. "Tomorrow for free. I hear you." And then he was gone.

The door fell shut, returning the hallway to its dimness. Outside, the thumping bass of low riders and a distant car alarm could be heard. As his eyes adjusted to the darkness, Griffin turned to his associate. "You think he'll show?"

"Don't matter."

"You planted the tracker?"

"Inside, lower cuff. If he don't bring Hector to us, he'll bring us to Hector."

T he flames flickered softly in the fireplace that set in the corner of the small library adjacent to his bedroom. Sitting with Emily's open journal, David took another sip of coffee. He'd built the addition in hopes of saving his marriage. This was where he thought Jacqueline and he would spend their late evening hours after the kids went to bed—this was where they could read, listen to the radio, and grow old together. But, of course, that never happened. By the time he'd completed building it, Jacqueline had found enough excuses to leave.

Now he sat alone in this quiet place of thought and solitude. Frequently Emily and Luke would join him, either with homework to be explained or fights to be resolved, but it was still *his* room—the fire, the books, his overstuffed chair . . . and Jacqueline's. He wasn't sure why he never removed her chair. Maybe it was nostalgia. More likely, it was his ever-persistent and silent hope that she would return.

He still didn't understand how their marriage had fallen apart. Much of it, he figured, was his fault. He could have been more thoughtful, less absorbed in his work, more attentive to her needs. But, strangely enough, most of their friends seemed to think otherwise. They suspected it had more to do with her romantic dreams of being an author's wife—the respect, the notoriety, the money. She'd even been willing to endure those first few macaroni-and-cheese years to reach those dreams.

But, once they were reached, something inside her was still unsettled, still searching. She began looking for it in their new friends, in the parties, the glitz and glamour. He'd never been comfortable with any of those trappings, but if that was what she needed, he tried to oblige. Still, it seemed he could never quite keep up with her in the fast lane—especially when the booze, drugs, and all-night binges began.

Next, they tried kids. Maybe that was the missing piece. For David, becoming a father revolutionized his life. He had no idea a person could love so deeply, that he could be so committed to the care of another. But for Jacqueline they became more weight to tie her down. In fact, when they had discovered their unplanned pregnancy with Luke, it was all David could do to talk her out of an abortion.

Fortunately, Luke stayed. Jacqueline, on the other hand, did not. Her departure came gradually—David fixing the kids breakfast, then driving them to school, then to soccer practice, then showing up solo at school events—Jacqueline coming home later and later from parties until she began not coming home at all. Of course they had fights; he wasn't blind to what she was doing or with the various persons she was doing it with. But for the children's sake, he endured it—the extra work, the humiliation, the rising debts. After all, half of a mother for the children was better than no mother.

Then one night she'd quit coming home altogether. She'd run off to Europe with an actor.

Luke took it the hardest—at least in the beginning. Nearly every night he'd found some excuse to pad on down the hall and join his father in bed. Occasionally Emily would join them too, but not often. After all, she was becoming a young lady, the woman of the house. Luke, on the other hand, was still a child, the one who needed his mommy the most ... or so they thought.

Emily's first bout with clinical depression began within a year of Jacqueline's departure. Noticing her sullen withdrawal and growing moodiness, David decided to bring in his mother. She was a thoughtful, understanding woman, and she and Emily always got along famously. He hoped the added female presence would help. It did, but only for a while. Soon, the darkness returned ... and grew. Although the doctors agreed that Jacqueline's abandonment triggered it, they also felt Emily's illness had been waiting in her chemistry, ticking away like a time bomb, looking for the opportunity to explode.

Of course, he hated himself for waiting so long before seeking medical advice. He'd just hoped it was something she'd snap out of. But she didn't snap out of it. Instead, she kept falling deeper and deeper into the abyss—grades spiraling, barely eating, friends disappearing—until it finally ended in her failed suicide attempt.

The first hospitalization at Valley Care had been a success. With the right therapy and drugs, Emily fought hard to get back on her feet. And she succeeded. Though a little unsteady from the blow, and struggling with the "nutcase" stigma at school, she was definitely on the road to recovery. That's why the relapse had caught them so off guard. A relapse that included manic episodes leading to three A.M. calls to the doctor, changes in medication, fights to make her take that medication ... each step plunging them further and further into darkness.

*"Daddy, I'll be good! I promise ... please ..."*

He pressed his fingers to his eyes.

*"Daddy, don't make me go! Daddy, I'll be good!"*

Then came her second trip to the hospital ... and her last. This time even the doctors couldn't help. And yet, during those final weeks, she really did seem to be improving. Dr. Patekar was right, she really did seem to have a peace. He looked back at Emily's journal. Why hadn't he seen it before, her growing interest? Jacquelyn had been a churchgoer once, before their marriage. But he'd never felt a need for it. Nevertheless, he now read with excitement the changes that had taken place in his daughter. And the more he read, the clearer those changes became. Despite the demons she had been unable to defeat that final night, his daughter had, indeed, been experiencing some sort of spirituality. Some sort of ... fulfillment.

He wiped his eyes and looked down to another poem she had written in longhand. It was by the eighteenth-century poet John Byron:

*My spirit longeth for thee*
    *Within my troubled breast;*
*Although I be unworthy*
    *Of so divine a Guest.*

*Of so divine a Guest,*
    *Unworthy though I be;*
*Yet has my heart no rest,*
    *Unless it comes from thee.*

*Unless it comes from thee,*
   *In vain I look around:*
*In all that I can see,*
   *No rest is to be found.*

*No rest is to be found,*
   *But in thy blessed love;*
*O, let my wish be crowned,*
   *And send it from above.*

What a relief if it was true. If she really had found this rest. If he knew for certain that she really was someplace safe, with someone whose "blessed love" rivaled his own. Wishful thinking? Perhaps. Though Gita Patekar certainly didn't think so.

Once again his thoughts drifted to the woman. What a remarkable person she was—her kindness, her quiet strength, that gentle persistance for truth. How refreshing in this age of uncertainty and floating standards to know that someone actually held convictions that they could back up. He smiled, thinking again of her accent, how she held him with those earnest, liquid dark eyes. Eyes so deep a person could get lost inside—

*What are you doing?* he scolded himself. *Your daughter's dead and you're daydreaming about a woman?* Angry at his betrayal, he pushed Gita from his thoughts and focused back on the journal. But only for a moment . . .

"Dad, you seen Tibbs?"

He looked up at Luke standing in the doorway. He was thinner and taller than David remembered. Lately he always seemed thinner and taller. Mostly legs and arms, with a voice cracking and creaking—when he chose to use that voice. Because, like it or not, his son was entering that age of brooding, male monosyllables. David smiled sadly. It was true, Luke was leaving his childhood behind. He would miss that. And yet, in many ways, his son had already left. They still tried to talk, but there were always those other things in the way—their grief, the fear of hurting each other by bringing up Emily, David's sudden unsureness of being a parent.

And now the drinking. Was it starting all over again? Was he making the same mistakes he'd made with Emily? Did he love them too much? Did he love them wrong? The school had suspended Luke for three days, and David stepped in with a month's grounding. He'd also insisted on a five-page paper on the dangers of alcohol (writing was the price you paid for having an author as a parent). But was that enough? Should he be doing something else? What?

"Dad?"

David blinked, trying to remember the question. Something about the cat. "He's not by Emily's door?"

Luke answered in his usual frustration. "Right, like I wouldn't have checked."

David wondered which was worse, the monosyllables or the attitude. "Sorry. You didn't let him outside?"

"Daa-ad."

"I don't know, maybe he's—" David stopped cold. On the radio, in the background, he heard the opening bars to a song by the Village People. "YMCA."

"Dad?"

He hadn't heard it since her death. Since before the relapse.

"Dad, what's—"

"Shhh!"

The DJ was introducing it with a dedication: "... from a young lady by the name of Emily to a very dear and special person in her life ... her dad."

David's heart stopped.

Luke stared, stunned.

The voice continued, "She says she loves and misses you ... and she wants you to hurry and come visit her." With a warm chuckle, the voice concluded, "So pay attention there, Dad. This one's for you."

The music came up but David remained frozen, not breathing.

Luke finally asked, "Is that . . . *our* Emily?"

David didn't answer.

Luke stepped farther into the room. "Dad, was he talking about *our* Emily?"

David still couldn't speak. Something in his pocket chirped. He frowned, disoriented. What on earth?

"It's your phone. Dad. It's your cell phone."

He nodded and numbly reached into his pocket. Only the immediate family had this number—his mother and the children. But Grams was in bed and his children—well, his only remaining child—stood in the room before him. He fumbled with the phone, turning it over to read the display. It glowed two words: *New Message.*

Luke moved closer as David opened the phone. The print read:

    1.View

    2.Ignore

"I don't . . ." He turned to Luke. "I don't understand."

"It's a text message, Dad. Press number one. Press *View,* see what it says!"

David pressed the key. Suddenly, a new screen appeared with different type:

    I miss u

    Come c me

    Emily

David's hands began to shake.

Luke leaned over his shoulder to read. "It's from Em!"

"What? How?"

"'I miss you. Come see me.' She wants to see you, Dad! She wants you to see her!"

David stared, still in a stupor.

"Call back!" Luke cried. "What's the call-back number?"

David stared at the screen. He didn't understand. There was the date and time, both current, but—

"Here!" Luke yanked it from his hands. "Hit the call-back number." His son pressed a single digit and watched the little screen.

"What's it . . ." David tried to swallow. "What's it say? Who's it from?"

Luke stared. Finally, he half-croaked, half-whispered, "It's . . . her number." He slowly looked up to his father, his face gone pale. "It's the number to Emily's cell phone."

The two stared at each other. The silence was absolute—save for the crackling fire and the song's continuing chorus.


D avid, I can appreciate your hope, but—"

"No, you don't understand. It's a code, like a secret message. Whenever we wanted to say hi or apologize or something, we'd get the station to play the song."

"Yes, I read that in the journal."

"Then—"

"But there must be another explanation. Did you call the station, did you—"

"They said it came in on a fax. No return number."

"Perhaps it was one of her friends. Perhaps she told them and they were playing a trick on—"

"And the text message? Coming right on top of it?"

"Did you check that number?"

"That's just it. It was her old cell number. I disconnected it last week. They couldn't have possibly given it out. Not yet."

"And you tried calling?"

"Got a recording that it was out of service."

Gita sat behind the teak desk in her bedroom, frowning. She'd been working on the Salt Lake City report when his call came in. She was pleased to hear his voice again, but this . . .

"Also, her cat, Mr. Tibbs, is missing. I know that's not a big thing, but there's something else. I didn't mention it before, but when this boy she mentions, this, uh—"

"Cory?"

"Yes, when Cory got out of the hospital and dropped off the diary, he said something about her death not seeming right. 'Things don't seem right,' that's what he said."

"Meaning?"

"I don't know. Meaning maybe she's still alive, maybe she's—"

"David—"

She heard him taking a breath, calming himself. "Look, I'm sorry I called so late, but—I didn't know who else to talk to. Is there a possibility . . . is there a possibility that you're wrong? That maybe things somehow got screwed up on the other side? I mean, nature always has abnormalities, right? Isn't it possible that she is actually trying to contact me?"

Gita's heart quietly ached for the man. Such hope. Such passion. "I am sorry, David," she spoke as gently as possible. "If your daughter has passed away, she cannot contact you."

"But—"

"Regardless of the circumstances, it is not possible. My best guess is that it is a counterfeit, human or otherwise, and that—"

"A counterfeit, you mentioned counterfeits before."

"Yes, malevolent forces that enjoy evil and—"

"Like the Devil? Are you saying this could be like the Devil?"

"There are numerous cases of fallen angels who try to seduce others into believing—"

"But how can you be certain?"

"David."

"No, I'm just asking. I'm—look . . ." He took another breath. "I'm a little on edge here. Is it possible—I know you're busy, but is there any way for us to get together again?"

"I wish there was, but my schedule is very—"

"If we could just talk, go over the facts, see if I'm missing something, if you're missing something."

"I am afraid I will be at my office, catching up on paperwork for the next several days . . . and evenings."

"Could we meet before work?"

"Before work, I jog."

"Great! Where? I'll join you."

"David, please."

"Dr. Patekar . . . Gita, that's my daughter out there. Do you understand? My little girl is trying to contact me. She's begging me. I can't turn my back on her. Do you understand? My child . . ." She heard his voice thickening. ". . . She needs me."

Gita stared at the cup of tea growing cold before her. She took a deep breath, and against her better judgment, answered, "All right. There is a park on Las Virgenes, just past Mulholland Drive."

"The old Paramount Ranch."

"Yes. Shall we meet there at six A.M.?"

"Six is great!"

"That is not too early for you?"

She heard him laugh. "How can it be too early if I'm not going to sleep?"

"All right then. Six A.M."

"And bring her journal."

"Yes."

"And Dr. Patekar . . . Gita?"

"Yes?"

"Thank you. I can't tell you how much this means. From the bottom of my heart, thank you."

"You are most welcome, David. But please, do not get your hopes up. You are too good a man to be hurt again."

"Pardon me?"

Gita caught herself, surprised by what she'd said. "I simply mean, I do not wish for your hopes to be hurt."

"I understand. Thank you."

"You are most welcome. Good night, David."

"Good night."

She slowly hung up the receiver, puzzled—not only by the circumstances, but by her behavior. Despite her workload, she was actually grateful that he had called, pleased for the opportunity to meet again. She knew better than that. This was not good. She noticed her heart pounding. She glanced at the tea, hoping it was the caffeine. Returning to her work, she tried to focus. But her mind kept returning to the conversation. This was not good at all.

A thick fog had rolled in, making it impossible for Dr. Griffin to see beyond the glass walls of his Santa Monica penthouse. On clear nights the view of the beach and the pier with its lighted Ferris wheel was to die for. But tonight, nothing was visible. He was cut off from the rest of the world and he loved it. He loved the absolute privacy as he floated in his silent, fog-shrouded cocoon.

He read the computer screen in front of him as the last of the text from the phone call appeared:

> Patekar: I simply mean, I do not wish for your hopes to be hurt.
>
> Kauffman: I understand. Thank you.
>
> Patekar: You are most welcome. Good night, David.
>
> Kauffman: Good night.

Griffin reached over and picked up the phone. He punched in Gita's home number. It rang only once before she picked up.

"Hello?"

"Gita, Richard here."

"Dr. Griffin, what may I do for you?"

"Just calling to see how you are."

"At 11:52 in the evening?"

"Sure. I knew you'd be up. And I figured you were probably thinking about me."

"Thank for your concern, Dr. Griffin. I am fine. Is there anything else?"

Griffin got to the point. "We have some big government fish coming to discuss Life After Life and examine the virtual reality chambers early tomorrow morning. I know this is inconvenient, but I'll need you there, say around 6:15."

"6:15?"

"I know it's early. But I figured for you, that's not a problem. It isn't, is it?"

"Well, no, but, that is . . . I did have an appointment."

"At 6:15 in the morning?"

"It was somewhat urgent. What time will the group be arriving?"

"That's just it. Could be any time, six, eight, ten. We just need to be there when they show up."

"I see."

He paused, waiting for her to take the bait. She didn't respond. He gave a little push. "That won't be a problem, will it?"

"No, sir. I . . . Dr. Griffin?"

"Yes."

"Would it be possible to bring my appointment up to the complex tomorrow morning?"

"Somebody I know?"

"I have mentioned him before. David Kauffman. His daughter committed suicide several weeks ago."

"Gita, you know how Mr. Orbolitz feels about strangers coming on site. Particularly to the VR lab."

"Yes, but—"

"Have we run a background check on him?"

"I would be very surprised if he was a security risk."

Griffin smiled, unable to pass up the opportunity. "Sounds like you know him pretty well."

"I do not believe he is a risk, but we could still run a check on him this evening, could we not?"

He paused for effect. "All right, Gita. If he's good enough for you, then he's good enough for me. Call security and order a prelim on him tonight. If he passes, his name will be at the front gate tomorrow morning."

"Thank you, Dr. Griffin."

"I'd do anything for you, Gita. You know that. Anything at all."

"I appreciate—"

"And I trust you feel the same about me."

"Good night, Dr. Griffin."

"Good night, Gita."

They disconnected and Griffin immediately dialed another number. He had two more calls to make before wrapping up the evening. First was to the VR lab, giving orders for them to program PNEUMA with all of the information they had on sixteen-year-old Emily Kauffman. Everything they could find on her. The more personal the better. They'd done a fine job luring Kauffman to the lab. Soon, all of his fears would be put to rest. More importantly, he would no longer be asking questions.

The second call would be to 3316. He needed to let 3316 know about the daughter's boyfriend, this—Griffin scrolled up the text—Cory. Apparently Cory had found a diary that no one knew about. Even more troubling was the comment he'd made to the father that "things don't seem right."

Griffin shook his head and sighed wearily as he dialed the number. Why did things always become so complicated?

# five

"So, in these three rooms, it's actually possible to catch a glimpse of heaven?" David asked.

"Or hell," Dr. Griffin added. "With the help of test subjects around the country we have successfully recorded over thirteen hundred experiences of the first six to twelve minutes of death. That information is allowing us to successfully build a virtual reality program that can be experienced inside any of these three chambers."

"Virtual reality," David repeated. "Like those rides in Disneyland where the seats shake as you watch a movie?"

"Actually"—Dr. Griffin flashed a knowing smile to Gita—"we're a bit more sophisticated than that. Our computer alone, a fifteen teraflop that we call PNEUMA, is one of the largest in the country, costing us roughly thirty million dollars." With a grin he added, "Which of course includes a three-year service and maintenance agreement."

David added, "Never buy a computer without one."

Griffin smiled, "To be frank, Mr. Orbolitz feels even that is a small investment if it will ease people's fear of death . . . and lessen the pain of those who have lost loved ones."

Gita's eyes shot to David, who was already looking down, obviously struggling to hide his emotions.

Dr. Griffin moved to one of the three chamber doors as they continued their tour of the VR lab. Initially Gita was pleased that her boss had taken such a liking to David. Pleased and puzzled. David had barely arrived in the complex's lobby before the doctor appeared, introduced himself, and after some minor chitchat, magnanimously offered to show him around. The two of them hit it off immediately, making Gita feel a bit like the odd person out. Now she stood up on the control platform a few yards away with Wendell Nordstrom, Dr. Griffin's prized techie. Wendell Nordstrom, who, just last summer, tried to strike up a romance with her. Wendell Nordstrom who, unlike the others, waited until their fifth date before trying to bed her. (Techies can be a bit shy.) But regardless of whether it was the third date or the fifth, his moves were identical, which brought identical disaster.

"Twelve minutes isn't long," David was saying, "but what an incredible opportunity to see even that much into—"

"Actually," Griffin interrupted, "by your and my measurement of time, twelve minutes isn't much. But if we're talking a reality where time is infinite . . . minutes may seem like hours, even days." Turning to Gita, he asked, "What does your Bible say, Dr. Patekar? To the Lord a day is like a thousand years?"

Gita cleared her throat and quoted, "'With the Lord a day is like a thousand years, and a thousand years are like a day.'"

Griffin chuckled. "It's nice to have a resident Bible scholar. Of course, Gita will never know the experience, as this little contraption terrifies her, doesn't it, Doctor?"

"I believe one death per lifetime is more than sufficient."

"Right," Griffin teased. "Unless, of course, you believe in reincarnation—something else our good doctor is opposed to."

"An unhealthy superstition," Gita retorted, "for the weak-minded." The surprise in David's eyes said she'd overspoken. She hated it when she did that. Normally, that sort of thing only happened when she was nervous. But what did she have to be nervous about? There was just Dr. Griffin, Wendell, and—she looked down at the console, finding a monitor to frown at.

Dr. Griffin chuckled. "When it comes to other people's faiths, Dr. Patekar is, how shall we say, a bit intolerant. Fortunately, it has not affected her scientific objectivity. Has it, Doctor?"

Gita looked up. "Truth is truth. One may believe whatever one wishes, but it does not change the absolutes." She glanced down, wincing. She was doing it again.

"Yes." Dr. Griffin smiled. "Truth and absolutes; they are very important to our good doctor."

She involuntarily glanced to David, who was now sharing Dr. Griffin's smile. Suddenly her face felt very warm.

Griffin continued, "She is correct, though, when it comes to the absolutes of the program. There are some dangers that we've had to take precautions against."

"Precautions?"

"Here, let me show you."

They headed to the door of one of the pie-shaped chambers. Gita stepped down from the console to join them, moving self-consciously in her baggy khaki pants. These along with an oversized beige sweater were the least flattering of all her wardrobe. She'd purposely worn them—as much for David's protection as for her own. She could sense his interest on the phone, feel her own excitement at the sound of his voice. And that must not be. He was too good of a man for that.

The outside wall and doors of the chambers were painted in jungle images—vines, leaves, a monkey or two—with colors that looked more like a preschool play area than cutting-edge technology. This was part of Mr. Orbolitz's edict to maintain an atmosphere of fun and playfulness. Beside each door was a small, glass-enclosed shelf, holding what looked like a cross between expensive sunglasses and the silver wrap-around band worn by the blind fellow in *Star Trek*.

Griffin reached to one of the shelves. The glass door opened automatically, and he scooped up the pair of goggles. "These are for visual input." He passed them to David. "When they're activated, they become miniature movie screens, but in 3-D."

David examined them. "Very impressive."

"Actually, too impressive. We discovered that our technology is so advanced that we can actually fool the brain into believing it is shutting down . . . so it does."

"You mean you can fool the brain into believing it's dying?"

"Something like that. Fortunately, it's possible to build up resistance to the stimuli, but that takes time. Which is why we've included a little readout in the left corner of the goggles. It shows each user how much time he or she has remaining. When they approach the end of their time, a series of alarms begins to sound, warning the participant to stop the exercise."

"Otherwise"—David motioned to the console platform—"you have to shut it down from up there?"

"Actually," Gita said, trying to rejoin the conversation, "we discovered that abruptly ending the program creates a trauma to the neural system that is just as dangerous as staying too long."

Dr. Griffin continued, "Which is why the chamber doors lock from the inside and why it's nearly impossible to pull the plug up at the console."

"So you're on the honor system," David said.

"With rather disastrous results if you break it."

"May I look inside?"

"Certainly." Dr. Griffin stepped aside. "There's really nothing to see, but you're welcome to take a look."

David poked his head into the doorway of chamber one. A warm, orange light came on. Gita had seen the insides of the chambers a hundred times. Nothing but a room the size of a walk-in closet with every square inch covered in black sound-absorbent material. And an ingenious treadmill that rolled any one of 360 degrees.

David stepped back out, marveling. "So you actually see things we see when we die?"

"Not just things," Griffin replied, "but people as well."

"People?"

"Deceased friends and relatives who frequently come out to greet the newly departed."

"You mean you can see other people who've passed away?"

Gita fired a look to David. She knew exactly what he was thinking.

Griffin nodded. "That's one of the kinks we're trying to work out. Apparently, the first thing many deceased see when they arrive is family, loved ones, and acquaintances. And with thirteen hundred past subjects, our VR participants have thousands of people they have to wade through before they can continue the program."

David shook his head, his voice sounding further away. "Imagine, seeing people who have died."

"More than see," Griffin corrected. "See, hear . . . and feel."

David turned to him, trying to understand. "Hear, as in you have speakers in the rooms?"

Dr. Griffin nodded.

"And these goggles are for the seeing. But how do you feel?"

"Ah, that's the best part." Griffin walked a few steps to the opposite wall and spoke: "Dr. Richard Griffin. Suit." There was a slight hum as a door slid aside to reveal a blue, Spandex-like, virtual reality suit—complete with matching gloves and boots.

David approached as Griffin unsnapped the gloves from the hanger. "Each of these gloves, and the suit itself, is filled with tiny bladders of air." He handed a glove to David. "When you reach out to an image projected in the goggles and try to touch it, the computer reads your movements, and at the moment of supposed contact the bladders expand. They push against your skin with exact pressure to give the feeling that you're actually touching it—or even picking it up."

Gita added, "You may feel the object's temperature as well."

"Or if it's vibrating, or if there's wind, or any combination of tactile sensations."

Holding the glove in his hand, David pieced together the information. "So, between the 3-D visuals, the sound, and these suits, it's like you're completely there."

"That's the idea." Then, as an afterthought, Griffin asked, "Would you like to try it on?"

"The gloves?"

"The whole suit."

David looked at him, surprised.

"Sure." Griffin grinned. "We can find a size close to yours and borrow it. The sensations won't be entirely accurate, but close enough to give you the feel. In fact"—he motioned toward the chambers—"you're more than welcome to spend a little time inside, if you'd like."

"Dr. Griffin?" The concern surfaced before Gita could stop it. Both men turned, and she tried a more tactful approach. "Did you not say—were we not having guests this morning? Should we not be preparing for them?"

"Oh, didn't I tell you?" Griffin asked. "They called just as you were signing in. Looks like they've cancelled." Before she could respond, he turned back to David. "So what do you think, Dave? Want to give it a whirl?"

David was practically speechless. "Are you serious? I mean . . . are you sure it's okay . . ."

"Absolutely. All I have to do is get approval from the head of the department and—oh, wait a minute, *I'm* the head." Griffin laughed at his little joke.

"Dr. Griffin?" Gita repeated evenly. "Are you certain it is safe?" She looked at David. "Have you experienced a virtual reality environment before?"

Griffin laughed again. "He'll be fine, Gita—as long as we stay within the six-minute limit." He turned to David. "That's the parameter we give first-timers since, as I said, the brain needs to become sensitized to the experience. Now if you were a child, we could push you further, since their minds are more elastic, but for you, six minutes is the max." Another thought came to mind. "But listen, if you're at all concerned, I'd be happy to accompany you in another chamber. I'd be at your side, traveling with you the entire time."

David, still overwhelmed, stuttered, "That would be . . . that would be great . . ."

Dr. Griffin grinned and reached out to rest a hand on David's shoulder. "Then let's find you a suit and we'll go together." Turning to Gita he added, "Unless *you'd* prefer to accompany him."

Gita shook her head.

He called up to the console. "What do you think, Wendell?"

"Shouldn't be a problem, Dr. Griffin. I'll need some time to get things up and running, but it shouldn't be a problem."

"Excellent." Turning back to David, Griffin asked, "It's okay with you, then?"

Still dumbfounded, David looked from Griffin to Gita then back to Griffin. "Yes . . . yes, that would be, that would be . . . incredible!"

Thirty minutes later, David sat with Gita in the large, mostly vacant cafeteria. Tiny quartz bulbs hung from silver girders which rose to form a futuristic cathedral of skylights and steel. Earlier they'd found a virtual reality suit for David and now they were sipping their respective coffee and tea, waiting as Wendell prepared PNEUMA and VR chambers one and three. Of course David was excited—thrilled, to be exact. But he still had important issues to cover, and once he and Gita were settled in, he pursued them.

"So you think the song on the radio, the phone call, you think they were all coincidence?"

Gita shook her head, her dark hair shimmering in the morning sun. "The more I think on it, the more I am certain someone is playing a hoax on you."

"How can you be so certain?"

"The dead do not return, David."

He hesitated, not wanting to offend, but not completely buying it either. "According to *your* beliefs."

"According to truth."

He took a silent breath and let it out. So they were back to that. "Gita, may I ask you a question?"

She looked up from her tea with those liquid black eyes.

"I've always found the notion of reincarnation kind of, well, intriguing. But back there . . . you sounded so adamant."

The briefest pain flickered across her face and she lowered her cup. "I must apologize. I did not wish to be rude. But when you know something to be false, is it not dishonest to pretend that you don't?"

David felt himself smiling. He so enjoyed her childlike honesty. But this was no child before him. This was somebody so honest, so intelligent, that he never tired of talking with her. More than that, he found himself energized just to be around her.

Misinterpreting his smile, she glanced down, obviously embarrassed. "I'm sorry if my candidness has offended—"

"No, no," David interrupted, "I like your candidness. Really. I think it's great." His words were supposed to put her at ease, but somehow they made her more embarrassed. He tried again. "Actually, it's your finest, well, one of your many . . ." He was only making things worse. "What I mean is, I enjoy it." He shrugged. "I enjoy you."

She scooped up the tea bag with her spoon and carefully wrapped the string around it. Still not looking at him, she returned to the original subject. "I have simply found reincarnation to be a dangerous and most brutal belief."

"Brutal?"

"Yes."

"Well, I'll grant you, to some it might seem a little silly—but dangerous and brutal? Isn't that a bit of an exaggeration?"

She looked up at him, surprised. "I never exaggerate, David."

He smiled. "I know, I know. Because that would be dishonest."

Seeing his humor, she relaxed slightly.

He continued to tease. "And you believe in truth."

"Yes." She nodded. "I am afraid so."

"The whole truth and nothing but the truth—"

"Yes, yes." She smiled.

"—so help you God—"

"—yes—"

"—*especially* the God part."

She broke into a gentle laugh. It was the first time he'd heard it, and it made him feel warm and good inside. He savored the moment, taking a drink of his coffee. She responded by sipping her tea.

When they had finished, he continued, "So tell me . . . how do you see it as dangerous?"

Gita glanced up, those incredible eyes searching his for any trace of insincerity. There was none. She cleared her throat, then frowned slightly. He continued to wait until she began.

"Theologically speaking, reincarnation makes Christ's sacrifice on the cross irrelevant."

"How so?"

"If one can work off one's evils by living over and over again until they reach perfection, then they do not need Christ to suffer and pay for those evils on the cross."

"And that's dangerous, because . . ."

"According to Christ, no one is good enough to face God on their own. That is why He said He must die to take our punishment."

David nodded, understanding. Then, somewhat gently, he countered, "So it's dangerous to the Christian faith."

"More than that. If Christ was speaking truth, than it is dangerous to anyone who tries to stand before God on their own."

"And if He wasn't?" David asked. "Speaking truth, I mean?"

"Then, as many have said, He is either delusional or a bold-faced liar."

Again David nodded. She had obviously thought this through. He continued, "You used the word *brutal*. How do you consider it to be brutal?"

Gita shifted in her chair. He waited. She rechecked the tea bag then glanced at her watch. "It is nearly time. We should return to the—"

More softly, he repeated, "How is it brutal, Gita?"

She looked up at him. He could see her searching again, making sure he could be trusted. She swallowed and glanced back down at the tea.

Finally, quietly, she explained. "I grew up in Nepal. With my brother. Hinduism was our state religion. Nearly everyone embraced it. Everyone believed in reincarnation." She hesitated.

"Everyone but you."

"No, we believed it as well."

He gently persisted. "What happened?"

She lifted the cup to her lips. He noticed slight tremors rippling across its surface. She returned it to the saucer and continued. "When I was ten and my brother was five, our parents were killed in an automobile accident near Katmandu."

"I'm sorry."

She nodded, dropping her eyes to the tea. "Because we were orphaned, our neighbors and family turned their backs on us, refusing to take us in."

David scowled. "Why?"

"They believed we were being punished for the evil of our past lives. They believed that is why our parents were killed, because of bad karma from our past."

"I don't understand. You were just children. Why wouldn't they help you?"

"They believed they were helping us. They believed that the more quickly we suffered and died, the more quickly we would pay for our sins and reincarnate into a higher life."

David felt anger starting to grow. "That's terrible."

She barely heard, losing herself to the memories. "Our local village expelled us. We were forbidden to reenter it . . . or any other village that knew of our plight."

"How did you eat? How did you survive?"

"We drank the water from irrigation ditches, from puddles of mud. We ate what we could find or steal—vegetables from gardens, cats, dead rats. Sometimes my little brother . . . sometimes I would catch him eating dirt, just to fill his belly, just to stop the ache . . ." Her voice trailed away.

David sat, watching her struggle, wanting to help but not knowing how.

She swallowed and continued. "Later, we were picked up by a man who . . ." She took a breath and forced herself to continue. ". . . who sold us to other men . . . for their pleasures. Sometimes for a night. Sometimes for days." Her voice grew thick. "Me, mostly." She looked back down at her tea, blinking. David was about to reach out and stop her—there was no need to continue. But she pressed on.

"I had just turned eleven. Soon, I became his prized possession. His biggest moneymaker. And Nubee . . ." She took another breath. "One night my brother tried coming to my rescue. He was beaten so badly that he suffered severe brain trauma. For a long time we thought he would not survive. But he did . . . though he was never the same after that." She raised her hand to her forehead, rubbing it with her fingers. David watched a single tear slip from the corner of her eye.

"How did . . ." He cleared his voice. "How did you get away?"

"There was another man." She sniffed, quietly regaining her composure. "I cannot tell you his real name because what he did was very illegal."

"Another monster?"

She shook her head. "This was no monster. At that time it was illegal to speak to anyone outside your immediate family about Jesus Christ. You would face at least one year's imprisonment for doing so. But this man, this Christian, he saw our great need—he saw dozens of orphans like ourselves living along the roads. And he began to adopt us. One at a time. Covered in lice. Disease ridden. But he would adopt us. He would take us in. Clean us. Feed us. Enroll us in school."

Her chest rose and fell before she continued. "And because we had become official members of his family, he could legally tell us about Jesus Christ. And we listened. We listened because we knew what he said was truth. We had already lived in hell, and now his truth allowed us to experience heaven."

David nodded, greatly moved. "How many of you were there?"

"When I left for college there were sixty of us."

"Sixty!"

"But there are thousands of others who will never be helped. Children and adults—sick, crippled, in need, who will always suffer—because no one wishes to interfere with karma."

She took another breath and wilted ever so slightly. She was done. The story had taken much out of her. Unsure what to do or how to help, David reached across the table and clumsily took her hand. She tensed slightly, but did not withdraw it. How self-centered had he been? How stupid and thick? Did he think he was the only one who suffered? Who continued to suffer? And sitting there, David Kauffman understood something else. He understood why truth was so important to this incredible lady. For her it was more than just an exercise in self-righteousness or morality. For her, truth was invaluable because she knew, she had experienced firsthand the ugliness of falsehood.

H ang on, Dave, it's quite a ride."
  Griffin was right, it was a ride. Suddenly the two of them were shooting through a long tunnel. And at the far end? What else but the proverbial blinding light.

David turned to Griffin, who appeared to be beside him, but of course he wasn't. He was actually in another chamber, wearing a similar VR suit and experiencing the same, identical program. The powerful computer merely projected the image of his body onto David's goggles as if he were floating right there beside him. The 3-D rendering was nearly perfect—except for Griffin's blowing hair. It appeared much thicker than David remembered. It was either a glitch in the system or a bit of vanity Griffin had insisted be programmed in. David suspected the latter.

"This tunnel ... the light, it's exactly what I've read about," David shouted over the sound of rushing wind coming through the speakers.

Griffin's image nodded. "Yes," he called back. "People have reported a tunnel and light for centuries."

David turned and squinted toward the light. It was blazing white. Around its edge was a deep vivid red, turning to orange, then yellow, green, and finally ending at the outside parameter in rich blue and violet. "It's gorgeous!" he shouted. "Like a rainbow!"

Dr. Griffin agreed. "From our interviews, most NDEs, near-death experiences, describe an accompanying sense of euphoria. Of course you and I won't be feeling any of that, as we're only dealing with sight, sound, and touch."

"It's euphoric enough!" David exclaimed. "I can't believe the realism. You're sure I'm still inside the chamber? What would happen if I took off these goggles; would I still see the light?"

"Not at all. And the sudden shock to your system would be so traumatic that, like others, you'd probably fall to your knees and start vomiting."

"Wonderful."

"Or go into seizures."

David looked at Griffin. "Think I'll keep wearing them."

"Good idea." Griffin grinned. As before, his image was entirely convincing. Earlier, he'd pointed out the cameras inside each chamber that recorded both their body movement and facial detail. These images were run through PNEUMA and transmitted back to the goggles within milliseconds.

Over the roar of the wind, David began hearing a sound. "Is that . . . music?"

"Yes, sir. The closer we approach the light, the louder it will become."

"Incredible." He strained to listen. "I've never heard anything like it."

"Audio analysis indicates it's not coming from instruments. The best we can tell, it's produced by living organisms—but not human."

David nodded. Eventually his attention was drawn to the sides and ceiling of the tunnel. By practicing what Wendell had shown him, he began floating closer to the top. "We designed the suits to respond the way scuba divers navigate," the technician had explained. "The more air you take into your lungs, the higher you will rise. The more you exhale, the lower you will sink."

"What are you doing?" Griffin called.

"I'm going to check out the roof of this thing."

"That's not a good idea."

"Why not?" David looked at Griffin, who now appeared several feet below him.

Instead of answering, Griffin called, "Wendell?"

Wendell's voice reverberated from all sides. "Yes, Doctor."

"Slow us to three-quarter time."

"Three-quarter time it is."

Suddenly their speed decreased.

"Are we stopping?" David asked.

Griffin shook his head. "Wendell's just retarding the program a moment—like dropping us into slow motion. Now, take another look at that ceiling above you."

David tilted his head and gasped. Instead of a smooth, dark roof blurring past him, he was now traveling slow enough to see that the ceiling, a black, quartzlike substance, was swarming with faces! And bodies! But not human. Some appeared to be froglike, others more like reptiles, others grotesque gargoyles. But they all had one thing in common— they writhed and screamed, lashing out at one another with daggerlike claws and protruding fangs. Most were brown or green. Some were covered in scales with warts and spines. All glistened to one extent or another in dark, shiny blood from their multiple cuts and wounds—some of those wounds oozing, others flowing freely.

Their appearance was so terrifying that David sucked in his breath—which caused him to rise even faster. Spotting his approach, the creatures shrieked and snarled, lunging for him with their webbed hands, slashing at him with their claws.

"Exhale!" Griffin shouted.

"What?"

"Drop down! Exhale! Exhale!"

The nearest creature, a large, amphibian-like gargoyle, leaped at him. Although it could not leave the ceiling, one of its long talons barely missed David's face.

David cried out in surprise.

"Breathe out!" Griffin shouted. "Exhale!"

But panic forced David to breathe in deeper, causing him to rise faster. The creature lunged again. This time its claws caught his left shoulder and sunk in deep, just above the clavicle. The pain was intense. But not as intense as David's fear ... for the thing began dragging him toward the ceiling, toward itself and the others.

"Exhale!" Griffin shouted. "Exhale!"

The host of smaller creatures scrambled closer, jockeying for position, gnashing their fangs in eager anticipation.

Blind with terror, David began punching and kicking, doing all he could to get away. Griffin appeared at his side, trying to pull out the claw, while dodging others that sliced precariously close. David landed a powerful blow to the creature's snout and felt the breaking of gristle and cartilage. The thing howled. Griffin took advantage of the distraction, prying loose the claw, pulling it out of David.

"Exhale!" he shouted into David's face. "Exhale!"

David blew the air from his lungs and they fell. The creature lunged at them again, its talons barely missing David's head as the two men dropped out of reach. Defeated, angry that its catch had slipped away, the thing bared its fangs, and tilted back its head with a howling screech.

B ack at the control console, watching the images on the monitor, Gita shouted, "Bring them back! You must order them back!"

Wendell nodded and pressed the intercom button. "Dr. Griffin? Mr. Kauffman? Dr. Patekar suggests we end the program."

There was no answer.

Wendell tried again. "Dr. Griffin?"

At last the doctor answered. He was breathing heavily but didn't sound panicked. "I think we'll be okay now."

Gita reached past Wendell to the intercom and pressed it. "Dr. Griffin, this has been too traumatic for his first session." She glanced at the medical readouts to the right. "His pulse and BP are both elevated. I strongly advise you consider ending it."

"We'll be okay," came the response. "Bring us to full speed, Wendell."

Wendell nodded and reached for the controls.

"Dr. Griffin," Gita repeated, "I strongly advise that you reconsider."

As she spoke, a red light appeared above the intercom button.

"What is that?" she asked Wendell.

The technician glanced over to the light and answered. "He cut you off."

"Pardon me?"

"He's turned off the intercom."


Y ou okay, Dave?"

"I think so," David said. He poked his fingers through the ripped VR suit and examined the wound in his shoulder where the talon had sunk in.

"Don't worry," Griffin chuckled. "Remember, it's all an illusion. Worst you'll have when we get out is a slight bruise from the air bladder slamming against you. Now, heads up. We're approaching the opening."

David looked up to see they were shooting through the tunnel at a faster speed, once again approaching the light.

"About that light . . ." David turned his head from the glare and looked to Griffin. "Is that . . . could it be . . ."

"God?" Griffin grinned. "Actually, we haven't been able to figure out what it is. It seems to come from a central structure. And it registers more brightly than any sun or natural phenomena we know of. Our best guess is that the senses of the test subjects somehow overload when they see it. Whatever it is appears to be beyond their comprehension, so they translate it into an impossibly bright light."

David nodded and noticed a quiet throbbing had begun in his ears. "What's that noise?"

"Noise?"

"A low pulsing sound."

"How much time do you have left?"

David glanced to the left-hand corner of his goggles. A blue-green digital timer read:

    00:01:55

"One minute, fifty-five seconds," he answered.

"That's your first alarm. We wasted too much time at that wormhole."

"Wormhole?"

"The little friend you ran into, along with a few other million, seem to be guarding a labyrinth of wormhole-like tunnels that lead someplace entirely different and very less pleasant."

"Where?"

"Another time. Right now we need to pick up the pace. We'll be exiting the tunnel and entering the garden. Once there, you'll need to exhale and lower to the ground. You'll feel the extra pressure on your feet when you land."

As if on cue, the two emerged from the tunnel and entered a beautiful park lit entirely by the light. The ground was carpeted in thick lawn and there was a myriad of jade-green trees shimmering, almost to the point of glowing. Just as interesting were the people gathering below. They were of every race and age, and they appeared to be coming specifically to greet them.

David exhaled and descended until his feet touched the lush turf. Griffin landed beside him. The people did not rush in or crowd, but simply strolled toward them as if they had all the time in the world. Some waved, several called out names. Everyone smiled with such genuine friendliness that David couldn't resist smiling back.

"Who are they?" he asked Griffin. "It's like we're old friends, but I don't recognize a single one."

"You won't. Remember, you're viewing a compilation of other people's experiences. These are the deceased loved ones who've come to greet them. Friends and relatives who have previously passed away and who are—"

But David no longer heard. Because there, at the front of the group, was someone he did recognize. She was wearing her favorite white pants, pink linen top, and jean jacket.

"Emily!"

A petite teen with long dark hair broke from the crowd and ran toward him. He did the same, his eyes suddenly burning with emotion, his voice breaking. "Emily!"

As they met he scooped her into his arms, holding her for all he was worth. "Emily ... Emily ..." He pressed her face to his chest, kissing the top of her head over and over again. "Emily ..." Hot tears spilled onto his cheeks. Through the blur he saw other people approaching, smiling warmly.

The two continued embracing until he finally pulled back to look at her face. It radiated joy. And those eyes, those beautiful, violet eyes brimming with tears of their own. They hugged again and he murmured into her hair, "I was so afraid ... I didn't ... I didn't know if you were ... I ..." but that was all he could say. Now there were only tears.

Another alarm filled his ears. A shrill, *beep-beep-beep-beep*.

Griffin must have heard it too, for he called, "Dave."

But David barely noticed.

He tried again, louder. "Dave, look at your time. Dave, we have to go back."

But he didn't care about time. He finally had his girl. After all these weeks, she was finally safe in his arms.

"Dave ..."

He glanced down to the digital display just as it tripped to:

*00:00:54*

"Dave, we have to go."

The images in David's goggles had begun to pulse, overexposing to white with each *beep*. "Not yet," he whispered hoarsely, clenching his eyes against the tears. "Not yet."

"Dave, we've got to go now."

"It's okay, Daddy." Emily spoke into his chest, barely discernible over the alarm. "I'm okay." Her voice seemed lower than he remembered. "Daddy ..."

He pulled back and she looked up at him through those incredible, trusting eyes.

"You have to go back," she whispered. "It's not time for you."

He started to speak, but could not.

She reached out and adjusted his collar. "Not yet."

"I'm—" Emotion clutched his throat. He tried again. "I'm not going to leave."

The beeping increased in volume. Instead of overexposing to white, the images began to pulse red.

"Dave!" He felt Griffin take his arm. "Dave, we have to leave!"

He shrugged him off.

"Daddy?" He looked back into her eyes. They were concerned. "You've got to go."

"But—"

"Now, Dave!"

"I'm all right," she said, gently unclasping his arms and stepping back. "I'm okay. I'm okay and I'll be here waiting for you. But not yet. Not now."

Griffin grabbed his shoulder. "We have to go *now!*"

He reached for her. "Em—" But she took another step back.

"*Now!*"

She smiled bravely at him, tears again springing to her eyes.

His throat constricted. "Em—"

"Breathe!" Griffin shouted.

Greater concern filled her face.

"Breathe in deep! Now, Dave! *Now!*"

She nodded for him to listen, urging him to obey. And that's what did it. Her concern. Her insistence. Were it not for that, he would have stayed forever. But, for her, for Em's peace of mind, he would obey. He raised his right hand and pressed his five fingers together, forming a type of mouth with their tips. When she was little this was how they kissed

good-bye through car windows and later from a distance—his
fingertips kissing her fingertips. Somehow the ritual had followed them through junior high and, from time to time, high
school.

But, instead of responding, Emily simply looked at him
and smiled. The response left him puzzled and a little sad.

"Dave!"

It was time to go. He forced himself to return the smile,
then took a deep, uneven breath and began to rise. She tilted
back her head, watching him float higher and higher. She gave
a quick wipe of her tears and her smile broadened. He was
doing the right thing, he could see it. She began to wave, then
called to him, though he saw the words more than heard
them. "I'm safe here, Daddy. And I'll wait for you. I promise
I'll wait!"

Suddenly, as though he'd entered a powerful current,
David was sucked back into the tunnel. He picked up speed.
Over his shoulder he saw the crowd and garden quickly disappear, the light shrinking. Soon there was only the persistent beeping and the red, flashing image of the tunnel.

"It's going to be close!" Griffin yelled. "Close your eyes!"

"What?"

"Close your eyes, it'll make the transition easier!"

David didn't understand, but obeyed. He felt only the sensation of roaring speed, heard only the *beep-beep-beep beep*
of the alarm . . . until both faded. Until everything faded.

Until there was nothing at all.


I t was just past noon when Griffin received word on his
office computer of Congressman Hagen's successful cross-
matching. The procedure involved mixing Hector's white
blood cells with a small portion of the congressman's blood.
If Hector's cells died it would indicate that the congressman's
blood contained antibodies to some of the antigens in Hector's blood. Translation: Even though Hector's blood type and

HLA were near perfect, if the congressman's blood killed Hector's cells, it would also reject and kill Hector's heart.

Luckily for the congressman, it didn't.

Not so lucky for Hector. It was time to pull him from the street and force him to exercise his patriotic duty. Griffin reached to the recessed keyboard in his desk and began typing the orders when Gita Patekar suddenly appeared in his doorway.

"May I speak to you, Doctor?"

He continued typing. "Is it important?"

"I am having difficulty understanding your purposes this morning."

Without looking up, he asked, "What do you mean?"

"I mean it was not possible for David Kauffman to see his daughter."

"Perhaps one of the subjects we recorded had known her. Perhaps she was a friend or a relative."

"No."

He glanced up at her. "No?"

She held her ground—a little nervous, but held it nonetheless. "I have checked. There is no record that any of the 1300 subjects were relatives of the Kauffmans or, as far as I can tell, acquaintances. You and I both know that the only way his daughter's image could have appeared in the VR chamber was if someone had purposely programmed it."

Griffin finished typing the message and hit *Send*, forever sealing Hector's fate. Now, he leaned back in his chair to give Gita his full attention. "You have been busy, haven't you?" He caught a glance of his hair in the tinted window and adjusted it.

"Why?" she asked evenly.

"How is he feeling?"

"A little nauseous, some AWS sickness."

Griffin nodded. "To be expected. Did you tell him? When you walked him to his car, did you say anything?"

"I expressed my doubts that it was his daughter. I mentioned the unlikely probability of—"

"Did you tell him that we programmed her into the system?"

"I . . . even if I was sure, the poor man was so excited that he would not have listened to me."

Griffin smiled, rocking slightly in his chair. "Good . . . good."

"Dr. Griffin—"

"So, we have somebody happy, who can finally be at peace because he thinks his daughter is safe. He's happy, Mr. Orbolitz is happy, everybody's—"

"Mr. Orbolitz knows about this?"

Ignoring her, he continued, "Everybody's happy, Gita." As he spoke the word, *Security* began flashing on the lower toolbar of his monitor. He reached to the keyboard, entering his access code. "And you should be happy too."

"Are we the ones who called him with the text message, pretending to be his daughter?"

Griffin hesitated, then resumed opening the security file. "Dr. Patckar, there are some things you should not trouble yourself—"

"Are we the ones who dedicated the song to him on the radio?"

"There are some things you should not concern yourself with."

"We are, aren't we?" Her voice grew the slightest bit unsteady. "Why?"

He paused a moment to look up at her. "Tell me, Gita. How is your brother these days? How is Nubee?"

She scowled. "He . . . is fine."

"I'm glad, that's quite a relief."

"What . . . what does my brother have to do with this?"

"Nothing. Nothing at all." He frowned as he saw David Kauffman's name appear on the screen. Quickly he typed in the access code and continued, "Of course that could all change.

Everything could change should you feel a need to compromise our security."

"Compromise security? I am sorry, I do not understand."

"I'm merely suggesting that with all the medical care your brother is being given at the Orbolitz Group's expense, it would be a shame to have a slipup . . . for some staff member to accidentally distribute the wrong medication, or treatment, or the thousand and one things that can go wrong in such a facility."

"What do you mean?"

"What I mean, Doctor, is that your silence will do much to insure your brother's safety. And we all want that, don't we? He's too sweet and vulnerable to wish anything else."

He could see her stiffen. She'd gotten his point. Good. "Now, if you will excuse me"—he turned his focus to the screen as the text to the latest phone transmission appeared—"I have work to do."

He wasn't sure how long she stood before she left. He didn't care. Besides, there was a more pressing matter to attend to. He stared at the completed transcript from security. The one from David Kauffman's home phone line:

> Incoming Call: Tuesday 12:04 P.M. PST
>
> Answering Machine: This is the Kauffmans. Please leave a message and we'll get back to you as soon as we can.
>
> Caller: Mr. Kauffman, this is Cory. Cory Boller. Emily's friend from, uh, the hospital? Remember how I said things didn't seem right, how it was so weird for her to, you know . . . especially then? I don't think she did. Mr. Kauffman, I think . . . check to see what medicine she was taking. I think it was the medicine. Not her. It was the medicine. Don't call me back here.

*You might want to erase this message after*
*you hear it. We'll talk later.*

*End of Transmission: 12:05 P.M. PST*

*Duration 00:00:32*

Griffin stared at the screen. Would this problem ever go away?

With a heavy sigh, he reached for the phone and again dialed 3316. This would have to be the final call. With the congressman's upcoming operation, they could not afford to take any more risks. The leak would have to be contained once and for all.

# part two

# six

David Kauffman stood in front of his daughter's closed bedroom door, quietly marveling.

*"I'm safe, Daddy. And I'll wait for you. I promise I'll wait."*

After all these weeks, to see her so happy, so healthy, so ... safe. That was the important thing, to see her safe. Of course he'd heard Gita's comments in the parking lot, knew what she was trying to say, but she was wrong. In this she was wrong. It was not coincidence. It was not mistaken identity. How could he mistake his own daughter? And what about that song dedication from her earlier? And her text message, pleading with him to visit her. *"I miss u. Come c me. Emily."*

No, he wasn't sure how she did it, but somehow Emily had gotten through. Their love had helped her get through. And she was safe.

As he drove from the Orbolitz Group's parking lot he didn't think it was possible to experience such lightness. It was as if somebody had lifted a giant boulder from his chest, an entire mountain. He was actually able to breathe more deeply—which he did, again and again. And, for the first time in weeks, he didn't mind arriving at a silent house with Grams outside gardening and Luke holed up in his room with the computer. He even had the strength to stand alone in the living room a minute, before making an even bolder decision to head up the stairs and down the hall to her room.

And here he stood. But only a moment. With another deep, cleansing breath he reached to the knob, turned it, and opened her door. The closed blinds kept it dark and it smelled stale from being shut up for so long. But it was still her room. The place she'd spent so much of her childhood—

*"Daddy, just one more story, please, I'm not sleepy . . ."*

*"Daddy, can we put curlers in your hair again . . . please . . ."*

And the place where she'd grown up—

*"What do you mean, 'It's just a dress'?"*

He remembered leaning against the door with a smirk. *"I mean it's fine, if you're trying to be a chick or something, but — ow!"* He also remembered the punch to his gut and the door slamming in his face.

He stood there. But he would not enter. Not yet. The place was still too sacred. He could smile, though. He could smile at the fashion magazine cutouts plastered on her wall, the dozen bottles of perfumes and lotions on her dresser, the stuffed orangutan hanging from one of her many shelves overflowing with books.

Yes, he missed her, he always would. But now he knew they would not be separated forever. It was as if she was away at camp. A beautiful camp where he'd eventually join her. A camp that, with Gita's and Dr. Griffin's permission, he hoped to visit from time to time.

How long he stood in the doorway, letting the healing flow, he didn't know. But eventually he turned and headed back down the hall, lightly taking the stairs, feeling a joy and peace that he'd forgotten was possible . . . until he entered the kitchen.

Until he saw the flashing red light on the telephone answering machine.

Until he approached it, pressed *play*, and listened:

*"Mr. Kauffman, this is Cory. Cory Boller. Emily's friend from, uh, the hospital? Remember how I said things didn't seem right, how it was so weird for her to, you know . . . especially then? I don't think she did. Mr. Kauffman, I think . . .*

*Check to see what medicine she was taking. I think it was the medicine. Not her. It was the medicine. Don't call me back here. You might want to erase this message after you hear it. We'll talk later."*

Sitting in Nubee's room, Gita read another poem by Emily Dickinson, handwritten by David's Emily:

*He touched me, so I live to know*
*That such a day, permitted so,*
  *I groped upon his breast.*
*It was a boundless place to me,*
*And silenced, as the awful sea*
  *Puts minor streams to rest.*

*And now, I'm different from before,*
*As if I breathed superior air,*
  *Or brushed a royal gown;*
*My feet, too, that had wandered so,*
*My gypsy face transfigured now*
  *To tenderer renown.*

Gita stared at the page, shaking her head. This time she understood the words. Perfectly. The very thing that she read was happening ... to her. She was the one being touched, she was the one being changed, she was the one being transfigured. And it filled her with guilt and shame. And confusion. The ground that had once been so firm and rational under her feet ... was shifting. Ever since she'd met him it had started to shift, and there seemed little she could do to stop it.

Even in the compound's cafeteria. Hadn't she purposely exposed herself? Hadn't she poured out everything about her that was vile and sick and disgusting? But instead of turning and running, instead of seeing the wrecked goods and backing away like any reasonable person—he had reached out and held her hand. *He had held her hand!* She couldn't have made it any plainer. What was wrong with him? Couldn't he see? Couldn't he hear who she was? What she was?

Gita took a deep breath, surprised at how ragged and uneven it came out. No, she could not let it continue. He was too good of a man for this. And if he couldn't see it, at least she could.

But what of this other matter? The greater matter involving Nubee? She looked across to her little brother dozing in bed. As if things weren't confusing enough, there was this new concern, the one that had tightened her stomach into an impossible knot.

*"What I mean, Doctor, is that your silence will do much to insure your brother's safety."*

Silence of what? Silence that they had purposely programmed Emily's likeness into the VR program? That they'd planted the song dedication on the radio and the phone text message to drive David to them and consequently to her image? But why? To make some stranger they didn't know feel good about a lie? That was not Emily he had seen. Her likeness had been programmed into PNEUMA. But why go to all that effort? What were they hiding? Something illegal? If so, then she'd have to notify the authorities. After all, laws were laws. Truth was truth.

But what of Nubee?

*". . . some staff member could accidentally distribute the wrong medication . . ."*

"You make me listen more Bible?"

She gave a start and looked up to see Nubee stretching, giving her that lopsided grin that always melted her heart. A slight trickle of saliva escaped from the corner of his mouth.

*"He's too sweet and vulnerable for anything to happen . . ."*

He was her little brother. What course did she have but to protect him?

"Gitee?"

But what of truth? Not only with the authorities, but with David? How could she let this man that she so deeply—that she so greatly respected—how could she let him keep believing a lie?

"You make me listen more Bible?"

She rubbed her temples.

"Gitee?"

To protect him, to love and protect them all, she was expected to remain silent? To live a lie? How could lying be love?

Her eyes dropped back to the journal, recalling the section where David had helped Emily ditch school. And his daughter's response? Gita had read it a half dozen times: *I love him so much sometimes my chest actually hurts.*

To love so greatly, to be loved so deeply. But with lies? She took another ragged breath.

"You make me listen to Revelation?"

She looked to her little brother—the trusting face, the lopsided grin.

"Gitee?"

"Again?" She forced a smile, beginning the same litany they went through every time he wanted her to read. Wearily, she pulled the Bible from her satchel and pretended to complain, "We are always reading Revelation."

He giggled, eager to give the expected answer. "I like the angels. I like the monsters."

"All right," she sighed, continuing the ritual, "then we shall read Revelation."

But even as she turned the pages, even as Nubee gave a shudder of delight, her thoughts spun and roiled.

Returning to Valley Care Health Facility was the hardest thing David had ever done. Ninety minutes earlier, he'd been enjoying his first peace in months. And now, with one phone message, it had not only been torn away, but was accompanied by unspeakable, crushing fear. Now, he sat in the hospital's lobby with its Monet prints, its pastel green carpet, and its whitewashed oak tables. His face was covered in sweat and he was feeling very, very cold.

For months this had been his private chamber of horrors—the place he'd battled a parent's worst fears . . . while fighting to look relaxed and upbeat when they led him down the hall to her room. It was always important that she see him relaxed and upbeat during his weekly visits to hell.

But those memories were only the tip of the iceberg.

*"Check to see what medicine she was taking. I think it was the medicine. Not her. It was the medicine."*

Wiping his face, he winced at the pain in his shoulder. Dr. Griffin had been right; it was tender and there was definitely a bruise forming. But there was no broken skin. Although he had seen the razor-sharp talons sink into his shoulder, there was no broken skin.

*"Don't call me back. You might want to erase this message after you hear it."*

What was the boy saying? And why such fear and paranoia in his voice? Of course David had immediately returned the call, but there was no answer. And of course he'd tried calling the doctor here at the facility—twice from home, once from his cell in the car, but with the usual results.

*"Not her. It was the medicine."*

He'd been in the lobby over an hour—his gut churning, his head swimming. Was it possible? And if the boy was correct, what of David's relentless demands that she take the medicine? Wouldn't that mean that he'd actually been part of her—

He pushed the thought out of his mind and looked back over to the receptionist.

"You don't have an appointment?" the shiny-faced girl had asked when he first arrived.

"No, it's, uh, it's kind of an emergency."

"You're a patient?"

"Uh, well, no. It's about my daughter, Emily Kauffman."

"Is she a patient?"

David could only stare. Two months and already forgotten?

"Your daughter is a patient?" the girl repeated.

"No, I mean she was. Emily Kauffman. Look, I've been calling the doctor for weeks. Three times this afternoon, and he's never returned a call, not one."

"Well, Dr. Schroyer is very busy—"

"I know he's busy!" David snapped. "We're all busy." Then regaining control he said, "I just need to ask him a couple questions, that's all. About Emily's medication. That's all."

"Well, have a seat and we'll see what we can do."

That was 3:50. Now it was nearly five o'clock.

*"Not her. It was the medicine."*

Sitting in the chair, David closed his eyes, forcing himself to hear another voice, to see another face.

*"I'm safe, Daddy."*

How she glowed with joy, those beautiful sparkling eyes, her hair shimmering. Everything was perfect, exactly as he remembered. Well, except for her voice.

*"I promise, I'll wait."*

And, of course, their finger kiss, their secret way of saying good-bye. How strange she would ignore that. It was how they'd said good-bye through windows, across distances, in crowds, anyplace a real kiss would embarrass her. But that wasn't his concern now.

*"It was the medicine."*

What did the boy mean? Had he known that was the cause of so many of their fights?

*"I hate it! I hate you! You can't make me—"*

*"Don't push it, Em!"*

*"It gives me nightmares. I see stuff. I won't—"*

*"The doctor said—"*

*"You can't make me!"*

*"Take it, Em!"*

*"You can't make—"*

David wiped his face again, this time noticing his trembling hand. He glanced at the clock on the wall. Straight up five. He rose to his feet and crossed back to the receptionist's window. "Miss?" She had her back to him, checking a file. "Miss, would you mind trying—"

"Mr. Kauffman"—she turned to him—"the doctor knows you're here. As soon as he has a moment he will speak with you."

David nodded and looked at the locked door leading to the hall and offices. Beyond them was another door and another hallway—the one leading to the patients' rooms, the final place where she—

He wiped his face again and headed back to the chair. As he sat he heard a muffled conversation approach the door from the other side. He strained to listen. Women's voices. No Dr. Schroyer.

The door opened and the lock gave a distinctive click. Two women appeared. One an obvious doctor in a casual but professional gray skirt and jacket, but with tennis shoes—the other a bit frumpier in a white UCLA sweatshirt and too-snug navy blue pants. They stood in the doorway, chitchatting, taunting him with the ease that the chosen could pass through.

As he watched, an idea came to mind. He reached for the nearest magazine on the table, some fitness thing, and found a mail-in subscription card toward the front. Quietly, he tore it out, then folded it once, twice.

They continued talking. Another thirty seconds passed before they said good night and parted. Frumpy Lady bid the receptionist, "Good evening," and exited, as the doctor reentered the hallway with the door shutting behind ... but not before David stealthfully rose and inserted the folded card between the lock and its catch. He moved back to his seat just as the receptionist looked up. Smiling, he returned to his magazine. She returned to her work.

Now what? There was no way he could open the door without attracting attention; it was always within the girl's view ... except when she moved to the files behind her. He quickly threw together a plan. With a heavy sigh he rose. She stole a glance up. He pretended not to notice while making the pretense of stretching. As he did, he crossed to the other side of the room and sat down . . . just out of her sight. Then he pulled out his cell phone and hit redial.

One ring and the receptionist picked up. "Valley Care Health."

He cupped his hand over the mouthpiece. "Yes, this is Charles Cooper. I need to check on my outstanding balance."

"Certainly, Mr.—did you say, Cooper?" He heard her chair roll back to the files.

"Yes," he answered, "Cooper, with a C."

He rose silently, took a peek to make sure she was back at the files, then made his move. He opened the door, slipped through, and quietly shut it behind him. He paused, holding his breath to listen. She was still looking for the file. He released his breath, then took another, trying to clear his mind, but barely succeeding . . .

*"It gives me nightmares. I see stuff. I won't—"*

*"The doctor said—"*

*"You can't make me!"*

*"Take it, Em!"*

*"You can't—"*

He closed his phone and headed down the hall to find Dr. Schroyer.

I n-A-Gadda-Da-Vida," the long version, blasted through the portable CD boom box as the thoracic surgeon sliced a perfectly straight line down Hector's chest, exposing his glistening breastbone.

Griffin watched with fascination as the surgeon called for the sternal saw.

Initially they had chloroformed Hector, transporting him to the motor home which served as a mobile operating room. The anesthesiologist, part of the same team they had used for

Mr. Orbolitz's new kidneys, had then injected the kid with succinylcholine—a curare type of drug that paralyzes the muscles but leaves the patient conscious. However, because he felt the boy shouldn't have to be awake during the removal of his own heart, he followed up with an IV of Pentothal to put him out. After all, they weren't monsters. Finally he had intubated him and began pumping a mixture of oxygen and nitrous oxide into his lungs.

In a normal operation, they would have attached a pulse sensor to his fingertip, EKG tabs to his temples, and a blood-pressure cuff. But this was not a normal operation. None of those were needed. Only the black, neoprene body bag off to the side.

The electric saw fired up.

Griffin leaned past the scrub nurse and watched as the blade whined through the bone, kicking up a tiny cloud of dust whose smell reminded him of sitting in the dentist chair having his teeth drilled. Not pleasant, but not nauseating. At least to Griffin.

A moment later the cutting was finished.

The surgeon, an Asian who called himself Gus (only Security knew their real names), took the scalpel and carefully cut through the pericardial membrane. And, despite their experience, a reverent hush fell over the team as they looked down at the young, beautiful, beating heart.

"Okeydokey, let's keep going." Gus nodded to the boom box. "We're running out of time."

The group quickly moved into action as the song's drum solo began. A rhythmic throbbing of the bass—*boom, boom, boom, boom*—with flourishes and accents on various tom-toms.

Griffin frowned. He knew speed was important, but it seemed like the team was moving faster than usual.

On a small cart a nurse prepped two pails of chilled saline solution as the doctor expertly sliced and cut his way closer to the beating heart.

A bass guitar joined the drums and Gus called out, "Six hundred cc's of potassium."

The syringe was passed to him. He pressed the needle into the stem of the aorta and injected it. A moment later the boy's heart quivered to a stop.

Hector was dead.

The nurse reached for the first pail of saline solution as the lead guitar joined in the drums and bass with its own solo, a wailing feedback that sounded like elephants trumpeting. She dumped the pail into the chest cavity while Gus returned to serious cutting.

The wailing continued.

Eventually the second pail was poured in.

It wasn't until the song returned to the vocal with a "Two, three, four!" that Gus finally pulled the heart out of the boy. It reminded Griffin of raw liver before his mother cooked it. A stainless steel bowl with more iced saline was passed to the doctor, and he carefully eased the organ into it.

The song was coming down the homestretch.

Gus rinsed the heart in the saline, squeezing out excess blood, as another nurse produced a large plastic baggie that was full of more cold saline. Carefully the doctor lifted the organ and slipped it into the bag. More solution was added to top it off, before the bag was sealed and placed into a second bag which was twisted shut and closed with a bread-wrapper fastener.

And finally, as the Hammond organ repeated the brief riff that had opened the song some seventeen minutes and two seconds earlier, the heart was placed into an ordinary picnic cooler filled with ice. From here it would be handed to a man who would motorbike it back into town and Mercy General where Congressman Hagen eagerly waited.

A cheer rose from the team as the lid to the cooler was closed. Congratulations were given and high fives shared, as the music pounded out the ending phrase. It was close, but they had beaten their own record. The good doctor and his team had killed a man and taken his heart within the expanse of a single song.

D avid tapped on Dr. Schroyer's office door. There was no answer and it was no surprise. Through the small, wire-meshed window, he saw that the lights were off. Cupping his hands against the glare of the glass, he also saw there was no briefcase, no coat, or any evidence that the man was there. Nevertheless, he knocked again.

With identical results.

He glanced down the hall. It stretched fifty feet farther before coming to another locked door—steel and dark blue. On the other side were the living quarters for the residents, or "guests" as they were called. David had walked down that hall, entered through that door more times than he could count . . . and he dreaded it more than he could explain. Some parents attend soccer games on Saturday; he visited the loony bin. On the other side of the door had been the smell of disinfectant and bug spray, a TV blaring from the dayroom, a dozen curious eyes belonging to children dressed in robes and pajamas, and a daughter who could be in any one of several moods—sometimes depressed, sometimes volatile—until those last few weeks, those last few weeks when . . .

*"She was really happy, Mr. Kauffman. The happiest I'd seen her."*

He took another breath and forced himself to relax. He glanced the other direction toward the lobby and saw two more deserted offices with their lights off. He reached for the doorknob. It turned in his hand. He gave a push and a moment later found himself standing inside a room with dark green walls, diplomas, and an Ansel Adams photo of Yosemite. Behind the desk, light filtered in through white shutters and struck a group of three oak filing cabinets.

*"She was really happy. The happiest I've seen her. Things just don't seem right."*

He stared at the files, blinking. How many times had he left messages for this man? And he'd not returned a single one. Not since her death.

*"It was the medicine. Not her . . ."*

Over the past few weeks, with his mother's gentle encouragement, the two of them had slowly started disposing of the more painful memories—a little at a time, in fits and flurries. The medicine was the first to go.

*"You can't make me take it!"*

*"You'll take it or you're going back to the hospital!"*

*"I hate it! I hate you! You can't make me—"*

*"Don't push it, Em. You know what the doctor—"*

*"It gives me nightmares. I see stuff. I won't—"*

*"The doctor said—"*

*"You can't make me!"*

*"Take it, Em!"*

*"You can't—"*

*"Take it!"*

David closed his eyes against the memories. Against the shouting, the tears, the physical struggles. And against the boy's message.

*"Not her. It was the medicine. Not her . . ."*

Was it possible? Had they prescribed the wrong medication? Worst of all, had his constant insistence that she take it, had that been what . . . what . . . He reached out to the desk to steady himself. Could he have actually been responsible for—

"No," he whispered fiercely. He would not think it. He would not lose control. Not here. He looked back at the filing cabinets, their form a blur through his tears.

*"It was the medicine. Not her . . ."*

His heart pounded as he moved around the desk to the files. He pulled at the top drawer. It was locked. He tried the one beside it. Locked. Turning to the desk he opened its first drawer. He quickly rummaged through it finding nothing but papers, an address book, and business cards. He shut it and reached for the next drawer. Envelopes, stationery goods, index cards. Growing more impatient, he opened the next, rifling through Visine bottles, tissues, a box of staples, paper clips, minicassette player, cassettes, and—there, in the front corner. A set of two, black-headed keys on a ring. He pulled them out and turned to the filing cabinets.

He inserted the key into the first drawer and unlocked it just as the phone rang. He froze. Nothing happened, only the red glow on the phone indicating that voice mail had picked up.

He turned back to the cabinet, carefully opening the top drawer, and began flipping through the files: Albert, Aquine, Cobert, Dorsey . . .

He shut the drawer and tried the second: Farmington, Headwell, Kaster, Kauffman—there! . . . Emily Kauffman.

His heart hammered harder as he pulled out the file, set it on the desk, and opened it. The first page had a photograph clipped to it—her junior class photo, the one with her hair all up. Below it were typed statistics: date of birth, race, home address, siblings. He turned the page, once again noticing how his hand trembled. On the second page were scrawled paragraphs, some long, some short, each one dated. The same was true with the next page and the next. They were too sloppy to read, at least in his current state. He'd have to study them later. He closed the cover and slid the file into the back waistband of his pants, covering it with his coat.

Suddenly he was very anxious to leave. He started for the door, then stopped and returned to shut the cabinets. He replaced the key and straightened the chair before heading back to the door. Once there, he glanced out the small window to make sure the coast was clear, then he stepped outside.

Good. Now, how to leave? Not the lobby. The receptionist could still be there. Surely, there had to be another exit—the one the doctor had ducked out of. He turned and saw the dark blue steel door in the distance. It was the last direction he wanted to go. He certainly had no intention of passing through that door, couldn't if he had to. No, there had to be another exit or stairway before it. At least that's what he hoped.

He ordered himself forward. He'd only taken a few steps before he noticed his face growing wet again. And cold. Not just his face. He was wet and cold all over. And breathing hard. He looked at the dark blue door. Knew it was the reason. He hadn't been here since . . . since . . .

He tried to swallow but his mouth had become leather. His eyes filled with moisture as the door floated ahead. Beyond it was where his daughter had lived and fought and struggled for so many months . . . and where she had finally lost.

He stumbled slightly and frowned at the yellow beige linoleum. But it wasn't the floor. It was his legs. They were losing feeling. He looked back up at the dark blue door. It lay two dozen feet ahead. Beyond it were her friends . . .

Carrie, always pulling her turtleneck up to her mouth and hiding behind her hair.

Mary, who cut herself to cleanse herself, to relieve the pressure constantly building inside her.

The door floated closer.

And Valerie, sweet, giggling Valerie. A stick figure who went through teen magazines collecting body parts, creating a collage of the perfect human form. Valerie, whose protruding cheekbones always startled him. Valerie, whose parents brought her fashion magazines which she devoured not for fashion, but to study where she was failing.

He was nearly there.

These were the sick children. The ones Emily had told him about. These were the ones she would hear crying at night. The damaged ones, the broken ones—other people's children, not his—they were the ones at risk. They were the ones whose conditions were so serious, who were in danger of . . . Not Emily. Not his girl. The others, not her. Not his own flesh and blood, not his—

*"Daddy, don't make me go. I'll get better, I swear!"*

Not his only . . .

*"You can't make me take them!"*

*"Take them or you'll—"*

"No!"

"May I help you?"

*"Daddy, please ..."*

"Sir, may I help you?"

David wiped his faced and turned. A staff member was approaching. He smiled stupidly, then leaned against the wall for support.

"How did you get in here?"

He wiped his face again, still frozen in the stupid grin. "I, uh ... Dr. Schroyer. I came to see Dr. Schroyer."

The orderly was a big woman in her fifties. "Dr. Schroyer left half an hour ago."

"Oh, really." David sounded anything but convincing. "I didn't, uh—"

"I'm going to have to ask you to leave."

"But, Dr. Schroyer."

"I told you, Dr. Schroyer is not in."

"Right, but—"

"If you don't leave, I'll have to call the police."

"Right." He nodded then pushed himself away from the wall, a little wobbly, but okay. "Leave," he repeated, then looked about. "How? Where is the—"

"How did you get in?"

"I don't, uh ..."

"You don't know how you got in?"

"Uh ..."

"Follow me, please."

David nodded. Then wiping his face again, he started forward and followed the woman, away from the locked door, away from the nightmare memories as her shoes rhythmically squeaked against the yellow beige linoleum.

Gita made it though chapter six of Revelation, the opening of the seven seals, before Nubee had fallen asleep again. She paused, sitting in the steel-framed chair with the sticky black vinyl. How could she allow Griffin to force her to compromise truth? Yet how could she risk Nubee's welfare? And what of David? She closed the Bible and rose, looking tenderly down upon her sleeping brother.

"Please, Lord," she whispered, "there must be another way. Everything is so twisted, so mixed up. Please, show me how to fix it."

She waited a moment. But of course there was no answer, no great flood of inspiration. She didn't expect any. She knew God loved her; the Bible said so. For whatever reason, He had obligated himself to that fact. It was all part of the covenant, the binding legal agreement. But to actually feel something, to experience some sort of cosmic embrace ... well, some things just weren't meant to be. And that was okay. What she'd already received from Him was more than she ever deserved.

She reached down and pulled up Nubee's covers. She stood another moment before moving away and heading out the door.

"Dr. Patekar."

She turned to see Rosa Rodriguez, a plump, good-natured staff member approaching from the end of the hallway. The two had become friends from their first meeting—Rosa, a doctor from Nicaragua who had only achieved nurse status in the States, and Gita, a fellow Third-World immigrant who understood the difficulty of earning recognition in the West.

"You're in late today," Rosa said.

"Yes." Gita nodded. As she waited for the woman to arrive, a thought formed. "Rosa ... have there been new prescriptions for my brother, any changes in medication or procedure?"

"Not that I know of."

"Would it be possible ... when you have the chance, would it be possible for you to check his records?"

"Sure. I'm heading there now. We could do it now if you like."

"Yes. Thank you. I would appreciate that."

A light drizzle had started to fall. David shoved his hands into his coat pockets as he waited outside on the brick porch. Although it was not in a gated community, the home was still in one of the more expensive areas of Westlake Village. He reached out and rang the doorbell a second time.

Bolts clicked and one of the large double doors opened to reveal a white-haired gentleman in a green velour robe. He had just stepped out of the hot tub or shower.

David immediately recognized him. "Dr. Schroyer."

"Yes, what may I—" He came to a stop. "What are you doing here? How did you find my address?"

"You're in the book. There aren't many Dr. Schroyers in—"

"What do you want?" The old man's eyes darted past David to the street beyond.

"I've been trying to contact you for weeks, but—"

"Her case is closed."

David was startled by the abruptness. "Pardon me?"

"She's gone, Mr. Kauffman. And there's nothing you or I can do about it. That's reality."

David felt a flash of anger but strove to keep his voice even. "I can appreciate that, Doctor, but—"

"You need to get on with your life. She's gone and the sooner you accept that, the healthier you'll be."

David's jaw tightened. He hadn't come for a lecture, nor to hear his daughter's death treated like some minor misfortune that he had to suck up and get over with. Until then he'd been unsure if he was going to produce or even mention the file he held under his arm. Now he had no choice. He raised the folder, opened it, and flipped through the pages. "I just have a couple questions about her medication."

"Where did you get that?"

"From your office." David looked up. The man had noticeably paled. He pressed on. "I can read most of your writing, but the medication, it looks like it's in some sort of code. I was hoping you—"

"Y–you broke into my office and stole—you stole my file?"

David had to admit, it felt good seeing the man sputter. "Uh, actually, it's my daughter's file."

"That is private property."

"I suppose. But my point is—"

"Give that to me." Schroyer moved for it.

David turned, easily blocking him.

"If you don't give that to me, I shall call the police."

David frowned, surprised at the doctor's intensity. "Sure. I'll give it to you. In a second. But if you could just explain to me what—"

"I demand that you give it to me now."

David's frown deepened. "Why is it so important to you? Didn't you just tell me the case was closed?"

"That is confidential information."

"I can appreciate that, but—" David stopped. The old man was distracted by something up the street. He turned to see a white panel van approaching, perhaps a bit slower than normal. On its side was the logo of a grinning repairman with "Agoura Heating and Cooling" scrawled in bright blue letters.

David turned back to the man. "Dr. Schroyer?"

The doctor's eyes darted back to David. "If you do not hand over that file this instant, my attorneys will be contacting you."

"All I'm asking is that you—"

The van drew closer. Schroyer's agitation increased.

"This conversation is over, Mr. Kauffman. If that file is not on my desk tomorrow morning, there will be serious repercussions."

"But, if you'd just—"

The man stepped back and quickly shut the door—just as the van passed and continued down the street.

# seven

H ere are our residents . . ." Rosa's stubby brown fingers
flew across the keyboard as thirty-two names appeared
on the computer screen in alphabetical order. She scrolled
down to Nubee's name and double clicked. "And here is your
brother."

Gita stood beside her at the nurse's station as they scanned
Nubee's medical records . . . drug prescriptions, physical therapy, doctor's notes, mental and emotional evaluations.

"Everything looks normal to me," Rosa said.

Gita nodded, feeling a wave of relief—though knowing
there was no guarantee for the future. Unless . . .

*"Your silence will do much to insure your brother's safety."*

She scowled hard at Griffin's words then noticed something at the bottom of the screen. "What is this?"

"His blood and tissue type. To be a recipient of an
Orbolitz grant, we're required to ask if residents will submit
themselves to testing for both blood type and tissue type."

Gita nodded, well aware of the fact.

Rosa continued, "It is a harmless test. The idea is to
encourage us all to think in terms of becoming organ donors.
Pretty commendable, don't you agree?"

"Yes," Gita said, half reciting, "the Orbolitz Group always
prides itself on its humanitarian outreaches."

Rosa nodded while casually clicking the heading and
bringing up the file. A chart with hundreds of boxes and letters

appeared. She pointed to the first row. "Here is your brother's blood type. Good old-fashioned *O.* "

"The most common," Gita agreed.

"Almost half of the population has it." She motioned to the rest of the chart. "And here is his tissue-type info. You understand how it works?"

Gita stared at the boxes and letters. "Not entirely, no."

"With organ transplants, besides matching blood type, it's also important to get a close tissue-type match."

Gita nodded.

"There are basically three tissue-type divisions or human leukocyte antigens . . . HLA-A, HLA-B, and HLA-DR. We receive one set from each of our parents."

Gita concluded, "And just as it is important for organ donors to have the same blood type, they must have the same HLA types as well."

"To a point, yes. But a perfect HLA match is nearly impossible."

"Why is that?"

"Each of the three HLA groups have different antigens within them—59 different ones in the HLA-A group, 118 in the HLA B group, and 124 in the HLA-DR group."

Gita saw where she was going. "And the probability of all of these antigens perfectly lining up is extremely unlikely."

"Which is why recipients have to take all those anti-rejection drugs with their various side effects."

"Side effects?"

"Facial swelling, weight gain, severe depression, restlessness, nightmares."

"But the closer the match . . ."

"The less the medication and the fewer the side effects . . . at least in theory."

Gita looked back at the screen. "And all of this tissue-type information is gathered . . ."

"So if we ever have a fatality, and the resident has agreed, we can send the information to the proper authorities for organ placement."

Gita nodded. "That is a very thorough system."

"Sure is."

"What is this?" Gita pointed to bold type in red coloring that read: **MATCH CHECK**.

"Oh, that. After entering the information we're required to run the results past a template."

She double clicked the bold type. Immediately, Nubee's chart with its hundreds of antigen boxes was superimposed over another. The boxes that lined up as matches glowed amber. Those that did not glowed blue.

Gita frowned. "I do not understand."

"Me neither. But we're asked to compare every result to this one."

Gita squinted at the screen. "This is somebody's tissue type?"

"Most likely."

She turned to Rosa. "Whose?"

Rosa shrugged. "Who knows? But should a perfect match ever result, we are to immediately report it."

"Report it? To whom?"

"Let's see here." Rosa moved the mouse to the bold type at the bottom that read **Report**, and double clicked. Immediately the program changed to an e-mail program with a name and address appearing in the *Send To* box.

Gita leaned forward and read a complex address ending clearly with the name:

DrGriffin@OrbolitzGroup.com

Her frown deepened. What did tissue matches and organ transplants have to do with Dr. Griffin? Bits and pieces of the puzzle flashed by.

"... *he's happy, Mr. Orbolitz is happy, everybody's —* "
"*Is Mr. Orbolitz a part of this?*"

But, try as she might, she could not fit them together ...
"'*Things don't seem right,' that's what Cory said.*"
"*... there are some things you should not be concerned —* "

"Dr. Patekar?" Rosa asked.

Gita blinked, then came to. "Yes, I—Rosa, would you do me one more favor?"

"What is that?"

"May we print a copy of this chart?"

"The template?"

"Yes . . . just this page."

"Sure. No problem."

H ello, may I speak to Cory, please?"

"Who's this?" The voice was female, wafer-thin.

"My name is David Kauffman. He and my daughter, they were, well, they'd become good . . ." He paused, hearing someone sniffing. "Hello?"

There was a clunking and rustling of the phone. A different voice came on. Male. "Hello?"

"Hi, my name is David Kauffman. I was wondering if I could speak to Cory . . ." He glanced down at Emily's diary. ". . . Cory Boller?"

"Cory's . . . There's been an accident."

"An accident? Is he all right?"

There was no answer.

"Hello?"

"Yes, uh—"

"You said there was an accident. Is Cory—"

"Cory is dead. He was hit by a car."

David stopped breathing. "I'm sorry, what—"

"Can you call back later?"

"Yes, uh—certainly. I—"

*Click.*

"Hello? Hello?"

No answer. David lowered the phone and stared at it, his thoughts reeling. The boy had called just a few hours ago. Left a message on this very phone.

*"You might want to erase this after you hear it."*
It wasn't possible.
*"Not her . . . the medicine, not . . ."*
He raised his hand to his head, trying to focus.
*" . . . She was the happiest I'd ever seen her."*
Slowly he pressed the disconnect button.

He may have stood there seconds, minutes, he wasn't sure. But a thought eventually surfaced. He reached to his billfold, pulled out Gita's card, and dialed her office number.

After two rings her voice mail kicked in. He didn't leave a message but looked back to the card, read her cell number, and dialed it.

She immediately answered. "Hello?"

"Gita? David."

"David—"

"Cory's been killed." He took a breath, trying to slow down. "The boy from Emily's journal has been killed and I have her medical records."

"Dav—"

"He thinks she might not have killed herself. He thinks, he thought it was her medicine."

"David."

"I went over to her doctor's house—Dr. Schroyer. I couldn't make out what he wrote on the chart so I went over to ask—"

"David, do not talk to me."

"What?"

"Not on my cell."

"Why, what—"

"I do not think . . ." She hesitated. "I do not think we should be talking over my cell."

His mind raced. "Why not?"

"I just—do you remember last year, that place you and Emily went the day you helped her leave school early?"

David frowned.

"It is in her journal, do you remember?"

"You mean—"

She interrupted before he could answer. "The place where the two of you carved your initials in a tree?"

"Well, yes, but—"

"We will meet there."

"What? Now?"

"Hey, Dad." It was Luke, entering the kitchen. "What did you find out?"

"In forty minutes," Gita replied.

"Gita, I don't—"

"In forty minutes, please." Then, for the second time in as many minutes, someone hung up on him. He stood blinking.

"Dad, what did you find out about the song?" He was numbly aware of Luke rummaging through the fridge. "Those guys find anything out about that song and the text message?"

*"Cory's dead."* Thoughts still raging, David managed to mumble, "What's that?"

"I said did you find out anything about—"

*"I do not think we should be talking over the cell."*

He rubbed his head.

"Dad?"

"Huh?"

With a sigh of exasperation, the boy slammed the refrigerator door. "Never mind."

David turned, still on autopilot. "I'm sorry, what's that?"

Luke slunk into the living room. "I said never mind."

Trying to change gears, David called, "No, Luke, what did you say?"

His boy tromped up the stairs. "Forget it."

"Luke?" There was no answer. "Luke!"

He'd done it again, lost another moment with his son. *"Cory's dead."* He'd make it up to him, he was his dad, he loved him. But now . . . he looked to the back sliding glass door. *"Forty minutes."* He hesitated, then took a breath for resolve and started forward. He arrived at the door, slid it open and stepped out into the cold, wet drizzle.

David?" Gita was breathing hard as she approached the summit of the cliff. It had been a steep climb up a switchback trail of dirt and crumbling rock. "David?" She could see nothing beyond the sage and chaparral that surrounded her, but she knew he was there. His Jeep Cherokee had been the only vehicle in the wet parking lot below. A dozen more steps and she reached the top, the path leveling out as the Pacific Ocean came into view. The water sat flat and gray in the cold mist—the same mist that formed tiny, pearl-like droplets on her black wool coat. The black wool coat still holding a copy of Emily's diary.

Although her concerns over Nubee had not been answered, she knew the solution lay, in part, with this man. The man Griffin had gone to such lengths to deceive. The one who loved beyond reason, beyond true and false, beyond death. The person who, despite all of her efforts, she could not stop thinking of.

She spotted him near the edge of the cliff—tall, lean, dark hair. He rested his arm on the trunk of a large elm, head lowered, lost in thought. For the briefest moment she wanted to run to him, but of course checked herself with a scowl and curt reminder that when the time was right she'd cut it off. For her. For him.

The crashing surf drowned out the sound of her approach. When he finally looked up he appeared startled, then guilty. He straightened himself and quickly wiped his face. "I, uh, didn't hear you coming."

She nodded, then glanced to the tree. Although brown and worn from weathering, the initials were still clearly visible.

She felt her throat tighten and turned to him. But he would not look at her.

"It was a silly thing. I'd helped her skip class and she wanted to, uh ..." He swallowed. Gita watched him struggle, feeling her own ache. "'... make a memory,' she called it."

"Yes," Gita gently replied. "I read it in the journal."

"Oh, right. Sorry." He looked out over the ocean.

She stood in the silence, wanting to help, not knowing how.

"I thought once I knew where she was ... I thought that would make things easier, but something ... something's not right."

She dreaded what she would say, knew it would tear him apart. But he had to know. She took a breath. "David ... David, I think you are being deceived. I think we are deceiving you."

He turned to her, not understanding.

She took another breath. "The song you heard on the radio? The text message that appeared on your phone? The virtual reality chamber where you thought you saw your daughter—I believe it is all our doing."

"What?"

She nodded.

His eyes searched hers. It was her turn to look away.

"*Why?*" His voice was thick with confusion.

She shook her head. "I cannot say for certain. But I believe we are doing something very wrong."

"You keep saying 'we.'"

"The Orbolitz Group."

"It has something to do with Emily's death? With Cory's?"

"I do not know."

"He left a message on my machine, just a few hours ago. Said he thought she'd been given the wrong medicine, that her suicide really wasn't ..."

Gita closed her eyes as he continued.

"Remember, he said it didn't seem right? Remember, he said she was the happiest he'd seen her?"

She looked back at him. He was still searching, still desperate. She cleared her throat. "You said something about a file."

"Yes." He fumbled in his coat and produced a file folder. "I asked the doctor about it. He didn't write out the drug but used some sort of code. I asked him what it was, the medicine, I mean, but he wouldn't tell me."

"Why not?"

"I don't know. He pretended to be angry, but I think he was frightened. He seemed really frightened."

"May I see it?"

He opened the file for her to look. She stepped closer as he flipped through the pages of handwritten notes. "He mentions all the other medicines by name except this one, see?" He pointed to a dosage, ten milligrams, followed by the initials ZY. He flipped to another page. "Here it is again." There were the same initials but with an increased dosage of twenty milligrams. "And here, and here, and all the way through— every once in a while increasing the dosage. Do you have any idea what that means?"

Gita shook her head. "Have you any of the medication remaining?"

"No. It was the first thing we got rid of. Too many memories."

She nodded. "Maybe we should check with the pharmacy?"

"That's just it, he always had free samples. Said it was really expensive and he could give us free samples."

She frowned. Somebody was being very thorough. She motioned to the file. "In there, did you see anything—" She reached into her coat pocket and pulled out the paper Rosa had printed up. She unfolded it to reveal the tissue-match chart with the hundreds of boxes. "Did you see anything similar to this?"

"Sure." He flipped through the notes to a separate typed chart near the back. "Right here."

She caught her breath. It was the same chart. She brought her paper alongside to compare the antigen boxes. Her heart began pounding, as row after row, box after box, revealed a perfect match.

"Gita, are you all right?"

She said nothing, continuing to compare, to recheck, not believing what she saw.

"Gita, what is it? *Gita!*"

She looked up, startled.

"What's wrong, what is that?" His cell phone chirped, but he ignored it.

"This is a tissue-match chart." She was breathing harder. "It is used in determining organ donors and their recipients."

"Okay." He obviously did not understand the significance.

She gave a little shiver and pointed to the chart in David's folder. "That is the tissue match of your daughter." Referring to the sheet in her hands she continued, "And this is the tissue match of someone in the Orbolitz Group. Someone very important."

"And . . ."

"It is most difficult to have them line up closely. The odds are very unlikely, but—"

His phone began again, momentarily distracting her.

"Go ahead," he said.

She took another breath. "The best I can tell is that your daughter's chart and this chart are identical—they are a perfect match."

"What are you saying?"

"Did you ever sign papers for Emily to be an organ donor?"

David frowned and shook his head.

"Are you certain? At the hospital, did you perhaps sign—"

"No, I'd remember something like that. Why, what are you saying?"

"I am saying someone in my company has an identical tissue match to your daughter . . . and if they ever needed an organ, your daughter would be a prime candidate."

David's mouth opened. He could only stare.

Gita's heart pounded harder.

When he finally spoke, his voice sounded strange, detached. "You think someone . . . killed her?"

"I didn't say—"

"For her organs?"

The phone began chirping again.

"David, we cannot be certain—"

"You think because she had a perfect match with someone in your organization, that they killed her so they could have . . ." This time he couldn't finish the sentence.

She watched the range of emotions flicker across his face—horror, rage, disbelief—until it drained into an eerie hardness.

The phone continued ringing and he pulled it from his pocket. Opening it, he demanded, "What?" Then a little softer and surprised, he continued, "Dr. Schroyer?"

Gita strained to listen.

"Yes, I understand, but why can't you just tell me—hello? Hello, Dr. Schroyer?"

There was no response. David lowered the phone.

"What did he say?" Gita asked. "What did he want?"

"He wants . . . he wants me to come over so he can explain."

"When?"

"Now."

Thirty minutes later the two of them stepped from their respective cars outside the doctor's house. Gita had suggested she drive, but David had declined. And, as he wound back and forth through the steep curves of the Santa Monica Mountains, he felt the numbness settling in. The same numbness that had seized him during those first weeks of his daughter's death. He was floating again. Functioning on impulse power.

They arrived at the front door. He knocked and discovered it was slightly ajar. "Hello?" He knocked harder, deliberately giving a push. "Dr. Schroyer?" Still no answer. He looked at Gita then pushed the door wider and stepped inside. "Hello? Dr. Schroyer. It's David Kauffman."

They stood together in the dim entry hall—green marble tile, large antique mirror, cherry bureau, matching coatrack, crystal chandelier.

"At last you have arrived."

He gave a start and turned to see a tall blonde man in his midthirties standing in the shadows. He had a slight accent—possibly French. "I was afraid you were not coming."

David squinted into the darkness. "We're here to see Dr. Schroyer. My name is David Kauffman and this is—"

"Yes, yes. He has been waiting for you." As the man spoke he motioned to the wooden sliding doors behind him.

David was immediately suspicious. There was something about his tone, his demeanor. And, as his eyes grew more accustomed to the dimness, he found other reasons to distrust the man. Like the surgical gloves he wore on both hands. And the gun he held in his right.

"Come." Again he motioned toward the doors. "Please join us."

Instinctively, David stepped in front of Gita to protect her.

The man grinned humorlessly. "Please, we have little time for that."

"Who are you?" David demanded.

"I am nobody special. Simply a messenger."

"A messenger?" Gita asked.

He moved toward them, pulling a business envelope from his leather jacket and holding it out to David. "The doctor, he wishes for you to read this."

"What is it?"

"Take it. Please."

David hesitated.

The man nodded to the gun. "I am not in the habit of asking so many times."

David reached out and took the envelope. He turned it over, saw his name scrawled in the same sloppy handwriting that was in Emily's file.

"Open it."

He turned it back over, pulled out a letter, unfolded it, and read the typewritten words:

> *Mr. Kauffman,*
>
> *I need so desperately to beg your forgiveness. You guessed correctly, I was indeed giving your daughter too great a dosage of some very special, psychotropic drugs. I do not expect you to understand what torture my work has been to me these many years, or my loneliness. Nor will I use it as an excuse for my behavior. But you, above all people, must understand how lovely your daughter was. What a delight. And so very, very beautiful.*

David gripped the letter tighter and continued reading.

> *Initially, she refused my advances. However, with a little experimentation, I soon found the right combination of medication that reduced and eventually removed her resistance. However, I had not anticipated her accompanying guilt, which became far too great for her young psyche to bear.*
>
> *I hold myself entirely responsible for her death and loathe all that I have done. I will call the police first thing in the morning and turn myself in. I am, however, leaving this message in your mailbox, as a personal apology, offering you my sincerest and most humble regrets. If you should ever find it in your heart to speak to me personally, one on one, please do so any time, day or night. My home address is 1233 Roman Drive,*

*Westlake Village. Until then I remain most humbled and broken.*

*Sincerely,*
*Dr. Peter L. Schroyer*

David looked up, shaking with rage, the words roiling from his gut. "Where is he?"

The man motioned toward the sliding doors. "As I have said, he is waiting."

"Is this true?" David demanded.

The man chuckled. "Of course not. Schroyer is a raging homosexual—although he is of the old school, with most of his raging done in the closet."

David scowled, his mind spinning. "I don't ... understand."

"I am sure the doctor will explain it far better than I." He motioned them forward with the gun. This time David did not hesitate.

The man slid open the doors and there, on the hardwood floor near the desk, lay Dr. Schroyer's body. A dark pool of liquid surrounded it.

David froze. He heard Gita gasp.

"Please." The man motioned them inside.

Neither moved.

"You are making me ask again."

David felt Gita take his arm as the man repeated his order. "Come."

They entered the room—a richly decorated den with maple furniture, built-in bookshelves, French doors over-looking the backyard, and an antique desk, its chair tipped over not far from the body.

As the man slid the doors shut he called, "Dr. Schroyer, your guests are here." Then turning, he feigned surprise over seeing the body. "Dear me, he seems a bit indisposed."

The words caught in David's throat. "What's ... going on ... what happened?"

"Perhaps you should tell me."

"He called ... half an hour ago, he called me ... he said—"

The man's grin cut him off. In his left hand he'd raised a mini digital recorder.

David frowned.

He pressed *play*. Immediately Schroyer's voice began: *"Mr. Kauffman. Please come to my house. We must talk in person, do you understand?"* There was a brief pause followed by: *"I will explain when you get here. Come at once."*

"That was you?" David asked. "On the phone?"

The man shook his head. "No. It was our beloved doctor, prerecorded—though I was here, able to provide him with some much-needed incentive."

"But, this ..." David held up the letter trembling in his hand. "I don't ... What's this?"

"That, Mr. Kauffman, is your motive."

"Motive?"

Gita stepped forward. "Who are you?"

"Just a fellow employee, Dr. Patekar."

"You know my name."

"Of course. We had some messy in-house business to clean up, but I think it is finally taken care of." Then, turning to David, he added, "Except, of course, for your arrest."

"My arrest?" David asked.

The man tilted his head, listening. In the distance there was a faint siren. He broke into another grin. "Right on cue." Still holding the recorder he pressed *play* and this time they heard:

*"Hello, I need to report a break-in at 1233 Roman Drive."* Again, it was the doctor's voice. It sounded forced, but believable. *"A Mr. David Kauffman, father of one of my patients, and a woman friend who—what are you doing?"* Suddenly the voice sounded much more believable. *"No! No, I'll do what you say. No. Please, don't shoot. In God's name, please. You want money, I'll give you money, but please, please don't—"*

A loud explosion filled the tape. The doctor half yelled, half gasped. Two more shots followed in rapid succession and then there was silence.

The gunman clicked off the recorder.

The sirens had grown louder.

"Let us see . . ." He motioned toward the letter in David's hand. "We have the motive—the original still on his computer, of course." He nodded to the phone. "We have our call to 911." He pretended to think. "I believe that just leaves . . ." In one fluid motion he tossed the gun at David, who instinctively caught it. "The method."

The sirens were much closer.

"So, as far as I can see, my work is complete." He turned and started for the open French doors.

"Just a minute," David croaked, his voice coming from that distant, faraway place. "You're forgetting who has the gun."

The man slowly turned. There was that grin again. "I know very well who has the gun, Mr. Kauffman. So well that I know he will not fire it."

David raised the weapon. It trembled violently in his hands.

"David," Gita warned.

The man remained standing, grinning. There was no way David could fire the gun and everyone including David knew it. Finally, slowly, he lowered it until, in a burst of adrenaline, he quickly raised the weapon and pulled the trigger.

It gave a feeble *click*.

The man arched an eyebrow. "Perhaps he is not such a coward after all." His grin broadened. "While I, of course, am neither a fool."

David pulled the trigger with another *click*. And pulled it again . . . and again.

"Well, this has been most enjoyable, but if you'll excuse me, I must be off." He strolled through the doors, then stopped just outside. "You may wish to consider leaving, as well. Though, of course, you will have no place to hide." He smiled tightly. "As you will discover, we have been most thorough." Turning, he headed across the yard to the neighbor's cinder-block wall which he effortlessly scaled, disappearing over the other side.

Gita broke toward Schroyer's body, dropping to her knees, searching for any sign of life. "Dr. Schroyer!" No response. She turned him over. His chest was soaked in blood.

David felt himself drifting further away, growing even colder.

Sirens came up the street.

Gita turned to him, obviously trying to think it through. "We will stay and explain what has happened. Yes, we must tell the authorities the truth and we must, we must—"

"Truth?" The word erupted before David could stop it—along with a scornful laugh.

The sirens were nearly there.

"We will explain," Gita argued. "They will believe us. They must believe us!"

In refute, David held up the letter in one hand, the gun in the other. Both shook beyond his control.

Gita stared at them. She opened her mouth . . . but had no response.

He looked back to the gun in his hand, suddenly feeling its awful weight, its terrible history. He let go, allowing it to slip away and clatter to the floor.

The sirens pulled in front of the house.

Gita sprang to her feet. "You are right, we must go." She took his arm and started forward. He tried to move, but could not find his legs. "We will think of a solution on the way." She pulled harder. Finally, he stumbled forward, moving one foot in front of the other.

He stepped around the body, stared at the gaping wound.

Suddenly, they were outside—Gita still tugging. "This way. We must go this way!"

Now they were running across yards.

"Hurry, David . . . hurry!"

G ita threw a glance to David, marveling at his strength.
Each time they knocked him down he got back up. Not
as quickly, and not as strong, but he always got back up. The
two of them had traveled less than three blocks across yards
and down streets before he reached into his coat, pulled out
his cell phone, and hit speed dial.

"David, who are you—"

He covered up his ear to listen, then spoke: "Mom, Luke—
if you're there, pick up. Guys? Guys?" His voice was thin, still
shaky, but he pressed on. "Listen, I, uh, I can't explain it now,
but I want you to call the police. I want you to call the police
and tell them there's been a, that someone is threatening your
lives. Have them come to the house immediately. Tell them
it's an emergency, do you understand? I'll, uh, I'll explain
when I get there. I love you guys. Bye."

Amazing. After all he'd been through, his first thought
was still for his family. She reached into her own pocket to
follow suit. She would call the hospital. She would tell Rosa
to alert the staff and block any visitors from seeing her
brother. But she'd barely pulled out her phone before the
police car slid around the wet corner in an obvious hurry to
join the others at the scene of the crime.

They were sitting ducks. Completely exposed. David
grabbed her hand to pull her behind a sparkling new Hummer—
one of those huge, all-terrain vehicles so necessary for freeway
driving. But she refused. If they'd already been spotted she knew
the action would only incriminate them.

Instead, she stepped off the curb and headed into the road.

"Gita!"

She gripped his hand, pulling him along until they were in
the center of the street.

"Excuse me!" She waved her arms at the approaching
vehicle. "Excuse me!"

The driver hit the brakes and the car skidded to a stop just
feet from them. She crossed to the driver, who was already
rolling down his window in exasperation. "Lady, are you—"

"Excuse me!"

"I almost hit—"

"Excuse me! Have you seen a cute little French poodle?"

Incredulous, the officer demanded, "What?"

"A cute little white poodle? Have you seen one?"

"Ma'am, we're on an important—"

"Answers to the name of Foo-Foo?"

"Ma'am, step away from the car."

"But—"

"Ma'am, we have matters more urgent than a missing pet."

"I can appreciate that, but—"

"Step away from the car."

"But—"

"Ma'am."

Reluctantly, Gita obeyed.

Without a word, the officer shook his head as they pulled away—but not before Gita caught the name on his badge, *R. Diego*, and made a mental note to call his station when things were over to apologize for the lie. Though technically it wasn't a lie—she'd simply asked if he'd seen a dog, never said it existed. Still, it was as close to the nontruth as she cared to get.

Turning to watch the car accelerate down the street, she was unnerved at how easily her performance had come, how quickly her street-survival skills had resurfaced. She threw an embarrassed glance to David. He said nothing, which was fine with her. After all, this was the old Gita. The one she had never intended upon seeing again.

# eight

G ita tried talking David out of hiring a cab to his house. She tried explaining that it would be the first place the police would look. But, as with everything else involving those he loved, the man would not listen to reason. Nor would he stop looking for ways to help . . . even those he could no longer help.

They'd called for the taxi from his cell phone and had barely ridden fifteen minutes, before he pulled himself together enough to ask, "So if that wasn't Emily in heaven . . . if it was some fake virtual reality program, then . . ." The words came hard, but he forced himself to continue, "then she's still lost. We still don't know where she is."

Gita hesitated, then responded the best she knew. "As I have mentioned, if Emily was serious about committing her life to Jesus Christ, then there is little doubt that she is now with Him in heaven."

She could see frustration filling his face. He looked out the window, attempting to hide it.

"I am not trying to preach, David, but that truth should provide some comfort."

He continued staring outside, perhaps nodding slowly, she couldn't tell. Then, out of the blue, he turned back to her. "Even if she committed suicide?"

The candidness surprised her, though she suspected the subject had been on his mind for some time. "Pardon me?"

He cleared his throat, his voice hoarse and raspy from the day's emotions. "What if we're wrong, what if she *did* . . . kill herself? I mean, doesn't your Bible say something about murder . . . about where murderers go?"

The vulnerability in his eyes made her chest tighten. She answered gently and honestly. "I am sorry, I do not have an answer for that. But according to Jesus, He will forgive any sin—if we put our trust in Him."

"Trust?" David scorned. "Like what Cory had? Like Emily? Trust in a God who would turn around and let them be killed?"

Gita started to respond, but had no answer. No facts and figures this time. She glanced down, then out her own window. The cab, which had taken the Topanga exit and turned east onto Ventura Boulevard, now headed south into the residential area.

A half minute passed before he spoke again—thick and gravelly. "I'm . . . sorry. There are just some times . . . I know you mean well . . . and you probably have all the truth and evidence in the world. But sometimes truth . . . sometimes it just isn't enough."

The words cut deep. If he only knew how accurate they were. Quietly, she answered, "I am sorry too, David. I do not know . . ." She swallowed. "I do not know what else I can offer you." It was true, she could provide all the truth she had, quote all the Bible she knew, but it would not be enough. Not even close. And that fact caused her chest to tighten even more, her eyes to burn with moisture.

"Turn left here!" he suddenly called to the driver.

The taxi turned onto an upscale, residential street. Just the type she imagined he would live on—except for the three patrol cars with their flashing lights parked in front of the fifth house. And the group of neighbors who had gathered on its front lawn.

"Quite a crowd," David observed.

Gita agreed. "More than you'd expect from an emergency call."

He looked to her, then back out the window, nodding. "Good news travels fast." He called to the driver, "Stop the car up there."

"No, don't!" Gita ordered. "Keep going."

David turned to her. "What?"

She motioned to the house and lowered her voice so the driver couldn't hear. "Your family is safe; no one is going to approach them with the officers here."

"Right, but—"

"The police are waiting for you, David. You are the only reason they are here."

"But—"

"If they arrest you, they'll leave. Your family will have no one to protect them." She held his eyes making sure he understood.

"What will it be, folks?" The driver was glancing in the mirror.

"Keep driving," Gita answered. "We are not stopping."

They eased past the house as the red and blue flashing lights of the patrol cars filled the cab. David slumped down, looking away and toward Gita.

"What do you see?" he whispered.

She looked past him. "There are many people and many officers."

"What about Luke? My mom?"

She spotted a child standing with an older, heavyset woman. They spoke to a policeman who was busy taking notes. Unable to resist, David turned his head and rose to steal a look.

"David, be careful."

He didn't listen.

"Is that them?" she asked, though she didn't have to. She clearly saw the resemblance, particularly in the boy—lean, strong chin, dark hair. As she glanced at David, she could see his helplessness and frustration at being unable to join them.

"Where to now?" the driver called.

David continued to stare out the window, not answering, probably not hearing.

It had started to rain and the driver turned on his wipers. "Folks?"

Gita spoke up. "Can you take us to Sherman Oaks?"

"Sherman Oaks?" the cabbie repeated as they approached the end of the block.

"Yes, it is not that far away."

"It's your money," he said, taking the corner and heading back to Ventura Boulevard.

David turned to her. "What's in Sherman Oaks?"

"My townhouse."

"Gita"—he lowered his voice to another whisper—"I can't have you taking—"

"I know what you are thinking. It is inappropriate for you to spend the night. But I believe in this instance—"

"Actually . . ." He cleared his throat. "That's not what I was thinking."

She looked to him in surprise. "You weren't?" For some reason she felt her face growing warm.

He shook his head. "If the police have found my place, won't yours be next?"

Gita nodded, surprised and embarrassed that she had not thought of it herself. The wipers continued their quiet *swish-swish* as the taxi turned onto Ventura and she ran other options through her head. Friends? No, she did not have that many, and what few she had she would not want to entangle with the law or endanger their lives. Hotel? That would mean credit cards, which could be traced unless they paid cash. And the only way they could get enough cash would be—She looked out her window at the passing stores. "Excuse me?"

The driver glanced into the mirror.

"If you see an ATM, would you stop at it, please? There must be an ATM in the vicinity."

"There's a bank up ahead. They probably got one."

"Yes," Gita agreed, "let us stop there."

He nodded.

She sat back in her seat and stole another look at David. He was drifting away again. Losing himself to some far-off place.


The rain fell harder as they stepped back from the ATM. But David felt neither wet nor cold. He was not surprised that both his and Gita's ATM cards had been rejected. There was little that surprised him now. If they could kill his kid and get away with it, if they could set him up for a murder he didn't commit, what couldn't they do? What had the gunman said, *"You will discover, we have been most thorough."* Well, he got that right. Here they were, less than a mile from his own house, a block from his favorite Starbucks, trapped with no place to go. Once again he thought of heading home to his family, and once again he knew Gita was right—if he stayed away, his loved ones would be safe. As soon as he arrived and was arrested, they'd be left unguarded and vulnerable. She was also right about—

"Hey, brother."

—not endangering friends or—

"Brother, is that you?"

David looked up through the rain. Gita was at the cab haggling with the driver over money. But there, pulling up behind them in a rattling, 1970s, smoking Ford Galaxy was—

"What you doin' standin out in the rain like that?"

—Preacher Man.

"You okay, brother? Hey, you all right?"


Gita was grateful for the ride and to be out of the rain. She would have been more grateful if the back of her throat wasn't burning from the exhaust. "Are you certain this is safe?" she asked from the front passenger seat.

The black man threw her a grin. "I'm still breathing, ain't I?"

She coughed, wondering if the old junker had a tailpipe, and if it did, why its fumes were channeled directly into the car. She'd not seen a vehicle this old on the road for some time—and she was beginning to understand why.

"If you get to feelin' sick, just stick your head outside for some fresh air. Always works for me."

Gita looked out at the cold, drizzly darkness wondering if it was better to die from lung cancer or pneumonia. The car gave another lurch—one of several since they'd first accepted the ride. Seeing her worried expression the old man laughed. "Don't worry, it'll get us there . . . long as we stay off the freeways and don't go over forty, we'll get there."

"Where is *there?*" David asked from the backseat.

"Kids call 'em 'squats.' Lots of 'em in Hollywood."

"Hollywood?" Gita asked with concern.

"Yes, ma'am. That's where I do my night preachin'. Great location, plenty of street action, and I got lots of friends there who'll give you a hand."

The thought brought a chill to Gita. She knew all about Hollywood . . . and the Boulevard—the street kids, the filth, the immorality. In many ways it was the West's version of where she'd grown up, the memories and past she had worked so hard to forget.

The old man continued, "I know the accommodations ain't so great, but you'll be safe. Lotsa people with lotsa history—nobody asks too many questions." Glancing to David in the mirror, he added, "And given your sudden popularity, no questions is exactly what you need."

"You're sure it was us on the news?" David asked.

"They showed your picture, brother. And mentioned your name—two separate channels."

"But not mine," Gita said.

"Just a 'female accomplice.'"

"So we *could* go to my place."

"Except"—David coughed—"the Orboltiz Group knows."

"And somebody thought enough to block your card," the preacher reminded her.

Gita sighed.

"No, sir, far as I can tell, you two are in the same boat." Turning to Gita the preacher added, "'Cept you missed out on your fifteen minutes of fame."

"How could the news pick it up so fast?" David asked.

Gita ventured a guess. "The Orbolitz Group is a communications empire. I would not be surprised if they had financial interests in one or more of the local stations."

"Or know folks who do," the preacher added. "Yes, sir, sounds like you've run yourself smack-dab into one of them big-time Goliaths. Mercy."

"And you are sure"—Gita coughed again—"you wish to be involved with this?"

"I like the odds." The big man flashed another grin.

Gita eyed him.

"'Sides, the good Lord, He always fought for the down-and-out. 'I did not come to bring peace, but a sword.' Them's Jesus' very words."

"You may be taking that out of context," Gita pointed out. "Was He not speaking more in spiritual terms?"

"I don't know what terms He was speaking, darlin', but it's a right fine quote to have handy."

Gita scowled, obviously wanting to clear up the fact, but not knowing how.

The man coughed, rolled down his window, and spat. "Glory." Then, turning to David, he asked, "So . . . you think these bad guys, they may have taken your daughter's life just so they could get her organs?"

Gita feared the question was too harsh for David and stepped in to field it. "The tissue match was exact. The odds of such an event happening are extraordinarily high."

The old man nodded, then looked back up at David in the mirror. "So all we got to do is prove it."

"But . . ." David coughed. "How?"

The preacher shrugged. "Guess we check the hospitals, see who's had an organ transplant."

Gita shook her head. "From what we have seen, they would have covered those tracks."

The preacher nodded. A moment of silence. Then, from the back, David spoke, his words sounding cooler and more detached. "We could examine the victim's body . . . see what's missing."

The preacher's eyes shot to the mirror. "Your daughter?"

Gita turned to David, his face barely visible in the shadows. "Yes . . ." was all he said.

She stared another moment, then turned back, troubled. Silence again filled the car.

This time the old man broke it. "That would mean exhuming the body."

"No," Gita immediately replied. "There must be another way. Besides, for such a thing, we would need a court order."

The preacher nodded. "Which might be a bit difficult, given your current popularity."

Another moment.

"Didn't you tell me . . . aren't you a mortician?" David asked. "Couldn't you get one?"

The preacher glanced in the mirror. "*Ex*-mortician, son."

"But you could still help, right?"

Once again Gita heard resolve growing in his voice. She turned back to him, cautioning, "David—"

But he had already sat up, leaning toward them in his seat. "Couldn't you help us, couldn't you find out what happened?"

The preacher took a deep breath, then released it. "I could find out what happened, yes."

"When?" David asked. "How long would it take?"

"David—"

He barely heard. "It's got to be soon. The sooner the better."

The old man scowled. "Well . . ."

"If they catch us, who knows what will happen, we may never find out."

"Let me see . . ." He paused, thinking.

"Well?"

Finally looking at the mirror, he asked, "I don't suppose tonight is too late?"

"Tonight?" David croaked.

"How is that possible?" Gita demanded. "How can you do such a thing legally on such short notice?"

"Legally?" the man asked. "Who said anything about legally?"

"You would break the law?" Gita was surprised. "As a preacher of the Gospel, you would break the law?"

"The way I figure it, a man's child is a man's child."

"Yes, but there are proper channels that must be followed."

"The same channels that are tracking you two down for murder?"

"That is an entirely different matter."

"Maybe it is, maybe it isn't."

"It is a sin to break the law."

"Maybe." Then, quoting again, he said, "'But if you sin, sin boldly, and trust in Christ's grace more boldly still.'"

"That is not in the Bible."

"Nope. Martin Luther, but it's another one of them nice quotes to have around."

"What of the law?" Gita insisted.

The big man turned to her. "What of love?"

One hour later, Gita sat huddled on a lumpy, paper-thin mattress. The heavy smell of pine cleaner filled the air, though she knew it was better than the other smells lurking beneath. Her cot was shoved against a dirty window that glared with flashing, sequential lights advertising the Pussy Cat Theater across the street.

What was God doing? This was the last place she wanted to be. Surrounded by such filth and squalor . . . and memories. What was He doing?

"First timer?"

She gave a start and turned to see a fleshy-faced girl, cigarette dangling from her mouth, suddenly plop down on the cot beside her. Despite the thick maroon lipstick and raccoon eyeliner, she was obviously a child—fourteen at best. Her blonde hair hung in greasy strands and even the pine cleaner couldn't hide the smell of her body and the booze on her breath.

"Yes," Gita said, trying to smile. "I guess you could say that."

"Old man beat ya?"

"Pardon me?"

"You're too old to be a runaway, too dressed to be hooking." She took a drag from her cigarette and blew it out. "That leaves druggie or the old man's punching bag."

Discretely trying to pull back, Gita caught a throat full of smoke and began coughing.

The girl grinned. "Nasty habit, ain't it?"

Gita kept coughing as the girl took another drag and blew it up and over their heads.

Finally catching her breath, Gita threw a look past the dozen or so empty cots to the open door and hallway beyond. There, at a cheap metal desk, Adrianna, a volunteer staff member from some church, kept guard. She was a heavy black woman, just slightly younger than the preacher. And from the way the two had bickered and chided each other, it looked they had some history between them. Whatever the relationship, they were close enough for the preacher to fast-talk Adrianna into allowing Gita and David to spend the night, no questions asked. That had been twenty minutes ago, just long enough for Gita to settle in and for David and the preacher to head off to the cemetery—something she'd strongly protested against and had no intention of participating in.

Now, here she sat, too close to some unbathed child who nervously jiggled a foot on the floor, making Gita feel more than a little uncomfortable. But it wasn't just the girl that unsettled her. It was the memories. Memories of a similar child with a similar attitude in a similar world—but a child that was now dead and buried—far, far away, in another lifetime.

Gita stole a look back into the hall. Hadn't Adrianna known the girl was drunk? And what about the smoking? Surely, they wouldn't allow children to smoke here in the shelter.

The blonde took another drag. Outside the window, car stereos throbbed, horns honked, and in the distance there was the *thump-thump-thumping* of a police helicopter. She flipped her greasy hair to the side and leaned closer. "Lots of lowlife here, Chiquita. They'll be rollin' in from tricks any time now."

"Tricks?" Gita repeated, trying not to breathe.

The girl looked at her, then giggled. "You are fresh meat, aren't you?"

Gita searched for an excuse to pull away.

More foot jiggling. "If you got money, you better hide it. Drugs, you better do 'em now. 'Cause I guarantee you, they won't last the night."

"I—" Gita coughed, waving away the smoke, feeling a little nauseous. "I have very little money."

"Right, or you wouldn't be here. And drugs?" Her watery eyes searched Gita's. "Chiquita got drugs?"

Memories rushed in—of the old days when she'd have a kid like this on the floor, face down, tearing out her hair. Unnerved at the thought, Gita swallowed then blinked. "Why do you call me Chiquita? I am not Hispanic, I am from Nepal. And I have no drugs."

"No?" The girl continued to stare.

"Well, perhaps some Tylenol, but nothing of any—"

"Tylenol?" The blonde broke out laughing, which turned to a hacking cough. "Tylenol?"

Gita said nothing.

The girl laughed harder, coughing up a small wad of spittle. It landed on Gita's arm, and she flinched. Regaining her composure, she calmly brushed it off.

But the girl had seen Gita's reaction and laughed harder. "What's a matter?" She drew closer, purposely invading Gita's space. "Chiquita afraid? Chiquita afraid of catching something?"

Gita felt her insides tighten, grow steely. But she held herself in check. The child's rancid breath made her eyes water, but she would hold herself in check.

The girl shoved the cigarette back into her mouth, took another long drag, and held it. Then, just when Gita was positive she would blow it into her face, she turned her head and exhaled, breaking into more hacking. Once she'd finished, she held out her hand and introduced herself. "The name is Starr, with two r's."

Gita looked at her a moment then took it. "Gita."

Flashing a grin of yellow teeth, the girl rose unsteadily to her feet and half walked, half stumbled the few steps to her cot. Turning, she smiled and said, "Pleased to meet you," before breaking into another fit of coughing and dropping onto the cot.

Gita closed her eyes. She took a purging breath. And then another. *What are You doing?* she prayed. *What are You doing to me?*

It was three in the morning by the time they started digging in the cemetery—Preacher Man and a couple boys he'd picked up from the shelter. They'd parked his car outside the fence, easily broken the gate's lock, and silently traipsed through the wet darkness with their shovels. The boys were runaways, fifteen/sixteen, wearing the standard uniform of hooded sweatshirts and baggy pants. They claimed to be new converts and insisted that the good Lord had told them to help. David suspected it had more to do with the twenty bucks Preacher Man had promised than with any moving of the Holy Ghost. Either way, they now had second thoughts as they complained while digging in the mud and rain.

"Man, how deep does this go?"

"This dirt's like rock."

"When do we get a break?"

Preacher Man showed little mercy as he stood at the edge of the grave with a flashlight. "What we need is a lot less whining, and a lot more digging."

"Yeah, but—"

"'Whatever you do, do it as unto the Lord.' That's the Bible, boys. You wouldn't be complaining if you was doin' this for the Lord, would you?"

"No, sir, but—"

"Then keep digging, my children, keep digging."

David stood thirty feet away under a dripping pine. Initially, he'd insisted upon helping, but after the first shovelful, Preacher Man had seen how pale his face had become.

"I think you better sit down, friend. Go back outside and wait in the car. We'll tell you what—"

"No, I'm okay," he had insisted. "I'm okay." He'd been so adamant that he nearly pulled it off . . . until he doubled over and puked his guts out.

"Just stand over there, brother, outta the way. Me and the boys, we'll take care of it."

David had protested, until the second set of retchings. Now he stood with his hands in his pockets, shivering and fighting back macabre imaginings as they dug up the body of his firstborn.

"Don't you be worrying," Preacher Man called over to him. "Nine weeks ain't nothin'. If your mortician did his job, it won't be bad at all. I know of some bodies that have lasted for—"

"All right!" David cut him off. "I'll take your word for it."

They continued digging as David fought the images of Emily's helpless body exposed to the dirt and rain. But he hung on. He would make it through this, he had to. For her.

Nearly forty minutes passed. They were up to their waists in the hole when the first scraping was heard.

"Hit something?" Preacher Man asked.

"Must be a rock?" the youngest one croaked.

"No rocks here," Preacher Man said. "That's the lid to the vault."

"Vault?" the older asked.

"Yes, sir, concrete vault, required by law. Grab that sledgehammer there and start breaking through it."

"Man, you didn't say nothin' 'bout—"

"That's not a complaint I hear, is it, son?"

"But—"

"'Cause I could sure use this here money for other works of the—"

"It ain't no complaint."

"Good. Then grab that sledgehammer and get to work."

The older kid traded his shovel for the sledgehammer and started swinging.

Each slam felt like a blow to David's chest. He looked the other direction until, suddenly, he retched again, this time dry heaves. When he'd finished he heard concrete breaking, then scraping, then more slamming and breaking, until finally—

"There we go." The beam of the flashlight swung over to David. "A bronze casket, brother?"

David looked up, face covered in sweat. "Yeah. No. I don't remember."

The beam swung back to the hole.

"Okay, boys, get that all cleaned off nice and pretty for me."

There was more scraping and shoveling. David felt his head growing light. He bent down, leaning over his knees.

Finally he heard, "Nice work, fellas. Now climb on out and let me get in."

He glanced up as the boys crawled from the hole. They were drenched and exhausted. They took only a few steps before dropping to the ground and rolling onto their backs, gasping for breath.

Preacher Man eased himself down into the opening accompanied by his own set of gasps and groans.

Mustering all of his strength, David called, "Need some help?"

"Not from you."

David nodded, grateful for the reply.

Preacher Man bent out of sight. Although exhausted, the boys couldn't resist rising and moving back to the edge of the hole for a look. He handed the flashlight up to them and they kept it directed into the grave. Now all David saw was moving shadows between their legs. He strained to hear, listening for any movement, fighting his writer's imagination that wanted to fill in the blanks.

There was no talking, only silence as Preacher Man went about his business. From time to time David saw the man's bobbing head, but that was all.

"Brother?"

"Yes . . ." David had no voice. He tried again. "What?"

"There's been no incision—not in her chest or her back."

"What . . ." It had grown difficult to breathe. "What does that mean?"

"It means no one removed her heart or her kidneys or any other organs, as far as I can tell."

Relief washed through David . . . until he glanced over and caught a glimpse of long, dark hair. Her hair. Suddenly, everything started going white. He fought to stay on his feet, until his knees betrayed him and buckled. He was out before he hit the ground.

When he opened his eyes, they blinked against wet grass and mud. He lifted his face, guessing he'd only been unconscious a moment or two—no one had noticed, Preacher Man was still talking.

" . . . lookin' fine. Nothing unusual. Nothing—hold it."

David caught his breath. He struggled to his knees. "What's . . . wrong?"

"Her eye caps."

"Her what?"

"We put 'em under the lids to keep them from opening. They're like Ping-Pong ball halves, only rough."

"What's wrong with them?"

"Hang on."

"What?" David demanded. He tried rising to his feet but was too unsteady. "What's wrong?"

"Nothing wrong with the eye caps, but underneath—"

"What?" Anger welled up inside. "What's underneath?" He watched frantically as the boys moved in for a better look. "What's going on? What's underneath?"

"Cotton balls."

"What?"

"Nothing but cotton balls."

"What does that mean?"

There was no answer.

He tried rising but slipped, falling back into the mud. "What does that mean?"

"It means . . . someone has stolen your daughter's eyes."

~

*Love bade me welcome; yet my soul drew back,*
  *Guilty of dust and sin.*
*But quick-eyed Love, observing me grow slack*
  *From my first entrance in,*
*Drew nearer to me, sweetly questioning*
  *If I lacked anything.*

*"A guest," I answered, "worthy to be here."*
  *Love said, "You shall be he."*
*"I, the unkind, ungrateful? Ah, my dear,*
  *I cannot look on thee."*
*Love took my hand, and smiling did reply,*
  *"Who made the eyes but I?"*

*"Truth, Lord, but I have marred them; let my shame*
  *Go where it doth deserve."*
*"And know you not," says Love, "who bore the blame?"*
  *"My dear, then I will serve."*
*"You must sit down," says Love, "and taste my meat."*
  *So I did sit and eat.*

Gita looked up from the poem Emily had entered by George Herbert, a seventeenth-century poet. By now it was clear exactly what—or more precisely *Who*—"Love" was in her entries. For Emily, the words "God" and "Love" were interchangeable. One and the same.

Gita glanced at her watch and sighed wearily. She'd been reading the journal by the light of the Pussy Cat Theater—partially to stay awake until David returned, partially to avoid any contact with the dozen or so kids, both girls and boys, who staggered in from a long night of working the streets. By all appearances, her tactic had worked. Not a one of them had spoken to her—though she suspected her success had as much to do with their exhaustion as with her plan.

Two cots over, Starr thrashed in a fitful sleep, whimpering as she twisted her sheets into a wadded knot. Gita could make out none of the words but one: "Momma." She heard it twice, three times, the universal plea for help in so many languages. "Momma"—the cry of another girl, so long ago on the streets of Nepal—locked in the tiny "discipline room."

"*Momma ...*" whimpered in the dark, the girl rocking herself, huddled in a ball on the dirt floor against the cold—all alone except for the rats scurrying over bare ankles and arms, curious noses poking and sniffing, whiskers brushing her cheek.

*"Here you will stay until you show them respect!"*

"Momma . . . ," she sobbed, longing for those caring arms that could no longer hold her—arms replaced by thick brutish ones, with hair-covered chests, and hungry, suffocating mouths, reeking with alcohol, making her gag as she fought to breathe—and the pain, the searing pain.

*"You are their property. You will do as they say!"*

"Momma . . ."

*"For your sake. For your survival. For your brother's."*

Gita closed her eyes, forcing the memories away. She wiped her face and looked off to the hallway where Adrianna sat at her desk. Why the woman allowed boys and girls to sleep in the same room was beyond her. Just like the smoking and the permitting of drunks and druggies to enter. Where did she draw the line? Wasn't this supposed to be a church ministry? Still, by the look of things, these kids were not interested in sex. All they wanted was sleep.

She looked back at the journal, wondering what Emily would do in Adrianna's place. Or, for that matter, what she would do. Follow the rules, call the cops, close the place down? Or ignore their overt sins and gross immorality, pretending God didn't care about truth and holiness?

Another child, a boy, cried out in his sleep, so loud that he woke his lover in the next cot over. She swore at him to shut up, then reached over and shook him from whatever hell he was visiting—before she turned and drifted back into her own. Gita watched, a convoluted knot of revulsion and pity and guilt. The ache in her stomach grew worse.

Her cell phone chimed with the distinct ring that she'd programmed for it. She reached into her wool coat, folded neatly at the foot of her bed, but the phone wasn't there. It rang again. It was not coming from her coat but from Starr's cot. Gita rose and crossed to the girl. Apparently she had lifted it during their earlier meeting. It rang a third time . . . from under her pillow. Carefully, trying to touch as little of the greasy hair as possible, Gita tilted Starr's head to the side and slipped her hand under the pillow to retrieve it.

She opened the lid and whispered, "Hello?"

"Gita ..." It was David; he was breathing hard as if running.

"David? What did you find out?"

"They didn't take her organs."

She felt a wave of relief. "Thank goodness."

"They took her eyes!"

"What?"

"Her eyes. They took my baby's eyes!"

Gita's mind raced. "What are you talking about? Where are you now?"

He was still gasping. It wasn't from running. "They took her eyes! The most beautiful part. They killed my baby and took her ..." Static filled the line.

"David—David, are you there?" More gasping. "David?"

"All right, they ... play hardball, we'll ... hardball!"

"David, you're breaking up."

"I'm calling ... at the *Times*. He used to be a reviewer, now ... I don't know why I didn't think ... He knows important ..."

"David?"

" ... bust some heads. Fire with fire ..."

"David, can you hear me?"

"Fire with fire!"

"David?"

But the line had gone dead.

Extension 3316 stared at the message on his screen with contempt:

    Kauffman: " . . . bust some heads. Fire with
    fire . . ."

    Patekar: "David, can you hear me?"

    Kauffman: "Fire with fire!"

    Patekar: "David?"

He had struck as much as Griffin had allowed him to strike. But it was obvious it wasn't enough. It was equally obvious that Griffin was holding him back . . . because of the woman. He hadn't even allowed her name or photo to be released. Maybe it was to protect the company, maybe there was more, he didn't know.

But that would all have to end.

The transplant with Hagen had gone off without a hitch. The paperwork at Mercy General had been expertly handled, not a question asked. Everything had gone as planned. Everything except this business with Patekar and the girl's father.

It was time to stop the hemorrhaging. But not with soft-hearted threats toward Patekar's brother, or entrusting Kauffman to the police. Even the death of the girl's boyfriend had not been enough. No, it was time to override Griffin's weakness and do what should have been done in the beginning.

# nine

D avid and the preacher had not returned by dawn, and Gita had no idea where they were. Although reluctant to use her cell phone, she had tried David's number several times. Apparently the battery was dead. At least that's what she hoped. At least that's what she prayed. But no matter what she hoped or prayed, she couldn't stop the fear rising up inside of her. It was bad enough to be thinking about the man all of the time, but now to be worrying about him . . .

At eight o'clock, Adrianna had asked her to give a hand in making sack lunches for the kids. Gita was more than grateful for the diversion . . . and to be in the company of someone who bathed. The woman was no-nonsense. Her ebony hands were thick and scarred and she wore no wedding band. As a volunteer from her church, she staffed the shelter four nights a week. Together, the two of them worked in the cramped, musty hallway that served as reception area, counseling center, and apparently kitchen. The lunches were nothing fancy—peanut butter and jelly, apple, and a juice box.

"I wouldn't be worrying about them, sweetheart," Adrianna said as she slapped a thick layer of peanut butter on another piece of bread. "They probably just stopped off for a bite to eat." She grinned. "Billy Ray loves those Denny's breakfast specials. Either that, or he found some potential convert to harass, in which case he may not be back for hours."

Gita snapped open another lunch bag and dropped in an apple. "If it was only that simple."

"Why? What else is he up to?"

Gita started to answer but Adrianna threw up her hands. "No, no—best you not tell me."

Gita looked at her as the woman chuckled, then shook her head. "That boy's always getting into mischief, believe me."

The words gave Gita little comfort.

"But I'll tell you one thing, he's got twice the heart of anybody I ever saw. Says he met the Lord once and now he can't stop loving folks the way God loves them."

The phrase slowed Gita to a stop. Before she could ask any further questions, the door to the dormitory room opened. A tall, thin young man with shortly cropped hair, carefully dressed in black jeans, sweater, and trimmed goatee, appeared.

Adrianna greeted him. "Well, look who's up in the middle of the night. Good morning, Lawrence."

"Good morning, Adrianna." His speech and manners were effeminate enough for Gita to feel her disgust rising.

"So what's the occasion?" Adrianna asked.

"If you must know, I have a job interview this morning."

"Very cool, with who?"

"Microsoft."

Adrianna whistled. "Guess they're getting tired of you hacking into their systems."

"I suppose."

"So they're buying out the competition."

He grabbed one of the sack lunches from the table and nodded to a beat-up steel cabinet behind her. "May I have a bleach kit, please?"

"You sure you'll be needing it? For today?"

"I *like* to be prepared."

She gave him a look and he glanced away with an exaggerated sigh of impatience. Finally, she pulled a key from her pocket and turned to the cabinet. She unlocked it and pulled out a sealed sandwich baggie. Inside was a strip of paper and what looked like instructions printed on a small orange card. She handed the pack to him.

The boy responded sarcastically, "Thank you," and headed toward the exit. He pushed the heavy metal door open and it screeched against the outside concrete.

"Go with God," she called.

He said something that was drowned out by the morning traffic as the door scraped shut behind him.

"And God go with you," she finished quietly.

Gita waited a respectful moment as the woman shut and locked the cabinet. "What are those bleach kits?" she finally asked.

"Not much. Just paper treated with rubbing alcohol, water, and bleach."

"I do not understand."

Starting another sandwich, Adrianna explained, "For cleaning needles so they can use them again."

Gita nearly gasped in surprise. "You help them clean drug needles?"

"Yeah. We used to pass out free ones, but folks in the church objected. I tell you, some of them can be so legalistic."

"Legalistic?" Gita repeated. "How can objections to helping them use drugs be considered legalistic?"

"No one's helping them use drugs."

"You are making it easier for them."

"We're making it safer. Big difference."

Gita frowned. "I fail to see how—"

"You tell me what's more loving, child. Turning our backs on them and letting them get infected with all sorts of diseases, maybe dying of AIDS—or meeting them where they're at with the love of God."

"The love of God also involves truth."

"It sure does. Unfortunately, more people use truth to hide behind and throw rocks from, than to reach out in love and change lives."

Gita felt her defensiveness rise as the woman continued, "Real love is a dangerous thing. It involves getting your hands dirty once in a while. Getting your religion a little shook up. Not like Billy Ray—sometimes that fool goes way overboard. But I'll tell you this—religion, rules, and regulations, they're a hundred times easier to follow than God's love. Nice and neat, no mess. No risks . . . and no need to listen to His heart."

"But these are children," Gita argued. "You, you—"

"We what?"

"You allow them to smoke, to come in here drunk, you help them clean needles. How can you say God would endorse such activities?"

"He wouldn't—not with you or me. They're sin. Most of what they do and live and breathe is sin—vile, ugly, hated-by-God sin. And if you or I ever took it up, He'd come down on us harder than a ton of bricks. But these *children*, as you call them, these poor, lost souls—He would meet them wherever they're at without judging them, even if it meant risking His reputation. What does the Bible say—Christ didn't come to condemn the lost, but to save them?"

"Yes, but—"

"As far as I know, the only ones He ever condemned were the religious folks who claimed to be so righteous."

Gita shifted, not missing the implication. "So, you would say that love is greater than truth?"

"I'd say they're equal." She quoted, "'The law was given through Moses; but grace *and* truth came through Jesus Christ.' He's both grace *and* truth."

"You know your Bible," Gita admitted.

Adrianna shrugged. "Kinda necessary for a doctorate in theology."

Gita choked. "You have a—"

"Does that surprise you?"

"Well, yes, I mean no, I mean—"

"Just 'cause I'm old and black and fat don't mean I'm stupid."

"I didn't mean to imply that you were. I just, well, what I mean was—"

Adrianna grinned and patted her arm. "I know what you mean, girl, and don't be worrying about it. It's my dirty little secret. We try not to let it get around."

Gita slowly nodded.

The woman gave another chuckle, sealed the sandwich in a baggie and dropped it into a bag with an apple and juice box. "My point is this—real Christianity is both grace *and* truth. It's like that sign up there." She motioned to the placard above the door that read, "Jesus Saves." "That sign is truth, but it just sits there. It can't come down off the wall and love people like you and I can. It can't even save them. It's pure truth, but it's pure useless—like most Christians I know. They got truth all neatly wrapped and preserved, but they're afraid of getting it dirty—they're afraid to come down off the wall and soil their hands."

"So truth is only good if it is soiled?"

The woman grinned and started another sandwich. "I'm just saying that real love is messy. So messy that it could get you killed—especially by the truth keepers. Just ask Jesus."

Gita scowled.

"But I'll tell you this." She looked up, holding Gita's eyes. "And listen carefully. You listening?"

Gita waited.

"Jesus will never judge anybody with His truth that He didn't first die for with His love. And unless you and I have that type of love, our truth is vain and empty and useless. Like Paul says, without love we're an obnoxious clanging cymbal."

Gita started to answer, but couldn't. Her frown deepened. According to this woman it all came down to the very thing she felt so detached and clumsy and incapable of.

She hesitated then asked, "What about love without truth?"

"What do you mean?"

"I work for an organization that sincerely believes in helping others. But, by the look of things, they are not always so interested in the truth."

"You mean the Orbolitz Group?"

Gita's mouth dropped. "How did you—"

"Billy Ray said something 'fore he left."

Gita nodded. "They are a good company. A most human-itarian organization, but—"

"Maybe they are, maybe they're not."

"What do you mean?"

"I mean I'm just as suspicious of people who have truth without love . . . as those who have love without truth."

Gita scowled, searching the woman's face for more. "Is there something you know that you are not telling me?"

Adrianna worked a moment on the sandwich, obviously weighing what she should say. When she finally spoke, she did not look up. "Once we're done here, there's somebody I'd like you to meet."

"All right . . ." Again Gita waited.

But Adrianna said nothing more as the two worked together in the lengthening silence.

The message was on the computer when Luke woke up. After hitting his snooze alarm the mandatory three or four times he finally rolled onto his back and opened his eyes. The light from the window was dull and overcast. He stared up at the ceiling hearing the *pat-pat-pat* of water dripping from the overhead tree onto the roof. His school suspension for drinking was over today. He could finally go back. Yeah, right. With the police stuff last night and his dad's picture all over the news, no way was he leaving the house. Not until he found out what was going on.

Was he worried? Of course. Dad always came home at night. Well, at least the part of him that was left always came home. And the other part? That part had left weeks ago, and by the looks of things it would never return. Because it wasn't just Em who had died that Saturday morning. So had much of his father.

In the old days they were always doing stuff together, joking, fooling around. Sure, they kept a special eye on Emily with her depression and all, but that didn't stop the teasings and ribbings, the weekend mountain biking, the one-on-one basketball matches down on the driveway which, by the way, he had been getting closer and closer to winning . . .

*"Nine to nine,"* Dad had panted, bouncing the ball, stalling to catch his breath. *"One more point and you're history."*

*"No way. It's got to be two over!"*

*"Says who?"*

*"Those are the rules, Dad."*

*"Maybe your playground rules, sonny boy."* Dad shot him a sly grin. *"But not for us pros."*

*"David—"*

*"'Cause when you're playing with the big boys—"*

*"David!"* Grams stood at the back door holding the phone. *"It's the hospital."*

He stopped bouncing the ball. *"Is everything all right?"*

She held the phone out to him, her face white and pale.

He flipped the ball to Luke. *"Hang on to this. I'll be right back."*

But, of course he never came back. Not all of him.

Luke threw off the covers, crawled out of bed, and shuffled toward the hall bathroom. He didn't know which was worse—to have the man pay attention to him, which meant being suffocated and quizzed over every detail of his life so he didn't wind up dead like his sister—or to be ignored, even when they were in the same room pretending to have a conversation.

Either way they had never played basketball again.

Luke passed the computer on his desk and tapped the space bar, kicking out the screen saver of spaceships blasting alien invaders, to check for instant messages.

As always, there were tons. But only one caught his attention. It was from *Litchick–16* . . . his sister's old address. He came to a stop, then reached down and punched up the keys bringing it on screen:

> Y r'nt u and Daddy helping me!!!!!
>
> Em

I cannot believe I have worked for the Orbolitz Group this long and have never heard of such a place."

"Big company," the kid replied.

"Yes, but—"

"Don't imagine they want this gettin' 'round."

"I understand. Particularly if what you have said is accurate, but—"

Luis Ríos interrupted by calling out in Spanish to a friend across Hollywood Boulevard. The friend shouted back, motioning to Gita, causing Luis to flash his dead-tooth grin. She had no idea what was being said, but somehow suspected Luis had claimed to be more than just her guide for the morning.

It was barely after nine and the street was already alive. Brightly clothed tourists gawked down at the Walk of Fame stars, bleary-eyed shop owners pushed aside metal gates protecting their windows and doors. Not far away a statue artist painted in silver, absolutely frozen with boom box blasting and hat on the ground for donations, was hard at work. A weary hooker passed—coming home late, miniskirt askew, barefoot with stiletto heels in hand, and makeup so thick that in the harsh morning sun she looked like a clown.

Gita glanced away from her, forcing the image out of her mind. She turned back to Luis. "We may be a large company, but if what you are saying is accurate, then we should be part of the same or related division."

"Division?" Luis asked, checking his reflection in one of the windows.

"Yes, Life After Life. My boss, Dr. Griffin, heads up both research and—"

"Griffin?" Luis slowed. "Dr. Richard Griffin?"

"Yes, do you know him?"

Luis cursed. "He has my cousin. Over seventy-two hours now. Nobody knows where he is."

"Dr. Griffin?" Gita asked in surprise. "Richard Griffin?"

"Yeah, yeah." Luis continued forward. "I met him at the place we're goin'." He held up his hand, displaying a finger in a dirty white splint. "His goon did this to me."

"Dr. *Richard* Griffin?" she repeated.

But he seemed not to hear, his anger boiling. "Love to meet him again." He swore and spat on the sidewalk. "Without his buddy."

Gita stared at the boy. "He would not be at this place now, would he? Dr. Griffin?"

The kid shrugged. "Somebody's there. Somebody's always there."

Gita nodded. Less than an hour ago, Adrianna had called Luis on his cell phone (everyone in LA appeared to own one) and asked him to stop by the shelter. She wanted him to show Gita something they called the "Freak Shop." At first he'd been reluctant, but when Adrianna had promised him two dozen bleach kits, which could bring a dollar apiece on the streets, he had agreed to squeeze Gita's tour into his busy schedule.

They rounded the corner and approached an electronics shop—TVs playing behind a barred window, mariachi music blasting from an open door. Beside it was a dark entranceway. Inside, a skin-and-bones couple were shooting up. The girl couldn't have been over thirteen. The knot tightened in Gita's stomach, nearly making her ill.

Catching her expression, Luis gave a scornful laugh. "Welcome to the big city." Before she could respond, he continued, "You folks from the suburbs, you need your morning coffee—down here, we need somethin' a little stronger."

Gita said nothing. For twelve hours the images had been mocking her—the immorality, the filth, the smells of bodies and exhaust and urine. It was as if God was purposely torturing her, rubbing her nose into her past, refusing to let her forget what she was.

She forced herself back to the subject. "What I find most difficult to believe is that they would allow people to experiment on their bodies."

Luis shrugged. "Why not? They sell 'em for everything else 'round here, why not for taking a few extra pills or a hit or two." He slowed. "Okay, here we go."

They stopped at what looked like a vacant building. Gita glanced up and saw the number 2450 painted on the dirty window above the door. Luis pulled the handle and motioned for Gita to enter first. She hesitated, then ducked under his arm and stepped into the darkness.

It took a moment for her eyes to adjust. Morning light filtered through the upper window revealing peeling plaster and brown tile. The place looked as deserted on the inside as it did on the out. At the end of the hall was a wooden door painted in shiny black lacquer. Luis took the lead as they approached. When they arrived he knocked loudly.

As they waited, he turned to Gita and repeated, "So Dr. Griffin is your boss, huh?"

She nodded.

"What do you know." He shook his head, muttering in Spanish. "What do you know."

He knocked louder.

A moment later, the door opened to a brightly lit room. A muscular man in white slacks and a blue polo shirt stood before them. Seeing Gita and Luis, thinking they were both Hispanic, he asked, "Si?"

"Dr. Griffin in?" Luis asked.

"Who?"

"Richard Griffin."

The man frowned. Gita couldn't tell if he failed to recognize the name or was merely acting. She tried another direction. "My name is Gita Patekar."

He waited for more.

"I am, uh ..." She fumbled in her bag and produced a company I.D. badge. "Dr. Gita Patekar from Life After Life."

"You a doctor?"

"Yes, from Life After Life."

He leaned down and peered at the badge, then at her.

She gave a nervous smile.

"You want to see Dr. Horton?"

"Yeah," Luis answered, "Dr. Horton, that's the guy we came to see."

The man scowled at Luis, then examined the I.D. again. Finally, he opened the door wider and Gita entered. The room was warm, close to eighty. When she turned back, the man had blocked Luis's entrance.

"Only the doctor," he said.

"Yeah, but I'm with her, kinda like an escort."

"Only the doctor enters the clinic. Come back this afternoon if you wish to sign up for a program."

"I ain't interested in no program." Again Luis tried to enter and again he was blocked. "I'm with her, man."

"You don't enter."

The kid swore, but it was obvious he could not get by. "All right," he conceded, "but I'm waiting right here for her." Calling past him, he shouted to Gita, "You hear that? If they try anything funny, you just holler, I'll be right here, waiting."

"I doubt she'll be needing any assistance from you."

"Yeah, well, we'll just see, won't we?"

With what may have been a smirk, the big man started to close the door.

"And see if they got a Hector in there," Luis shouted. "Hector Marquez! That's my cousin. If they got him strapped down somewhere, you be sure to—"

That was all Gita heard as the door shut.

S till on his feet before the computer, Luke typed:

> who is this . . . u still there?

There was no answer. "Come on, come on," he muttered, staring at the screen. He was about to type some more when the response finally appeared:

> wheres daddy!?

With heart pounding but still very suspicious, he typed:

> is this really u?

The response came quicker, ignoring his question.

> y hasnt he come 4 me?!!

Luke took a breath to calm himself, then typed:

> where r u?

Another pause, then:

> its cold and creepy. luke, seriously i'm
> scared. wheres dad!

Thrilled, but knowing he should still be skeptical, he tried one last time:

> how do i know its REALLY u?

The answer appeared:

> didnt u get my text message?

He started to type:

> yeah . . .

She continued:

> the YMCA song?

Luke hesitated.
As if sensing his reluctance, another sentence appeared:

*hows mr tibbs?*

His heart pounded harder. He noticed his hands shaking as he typed:

*who?*

The reply was fast:

*MY CAT MORON*

That was all it took. This was his sister, he was sure of it. Quickly he typed:

*he misses u—we all do*

The words rapidly appeared:

*luke, u and daddy gotta help me!!!*

He wondered if he should tell her about the police, about the TV news. Then, deciding she had enough worries, he wrote:

*how! wat can we do?*

The answer returned:

*these people have some machine*

He frowned and typed:

*machine?*

She replied:

*im not sure how it works, but its how im talking to u*

Anxiously, he typed:

*ok, so how do I get to u? where?*

The answer quickly formed:

*brb sum1's here*

Luke typed:

*NO WAIT!!*

He stared at the screen, holding his breath. There was no response. He tried again:

*Em U there? EM?!*

But there was no answer. She was gone.

A mber, I'd like you to meet Gita Patekar. She's a very famous colleague of mine who studies about death and the afterlife."

The gaunt teen barely nodded her shaved head as she sat on the examining table. Though she was hidden in a thick winter coat, her sunken eyes and cheeks gave clear signs that she was undernourished.

"And Amber here, she is one of our star subjects. Been with us how long, sweetheart?"

The girl shrugged.

The doctor, Benjamin Horton, a pudgy man in his late fifties, answered for her. "Almost eighteen months now."

She gave half a nod and mumbled, "Can I go now?"

"Certainly. Everything is fine here. See Mr. Jackson on your way out to get your medicine."

The girl scooted off the table, wrapped the coat tightly around herself, and shuffled to the other side of the room where the big man who had admitted Gita sat behind his desk.

Calling after her, the doctor added, "And no more than one every twelve hours. You know the rules. That's why your heart was racing. One tablet every twelve hours. No more."

Without turning she gave a half-raised hand as she moved off.

Horton nodded as he dabbed the sweat around his comb-over. Gita had met him ten minutes earlier and, after learning they both worked for Griffin, he was only too happy to show her around the clinic. It wasn't much—a large room with a reception area, desk, filing cabinets, and a couple worn sofas near the door. Black lab benches with cupboards stretched the length of both walls. And two curtained-off cubicles served as examination rooms at the far end where they now stood.

"Will she be okay?" Gita asked. "What is wrong with her?"

"Speed freak," Horton said as he began filling out her chart.

"I do not understand."

"Speed freaks don't eat. What better subjects to test for low caloric intake than kids who don't eat." He glanced up to see the puzzled look on Gita's face and explained, "We know that animals on low-calorie diets live longer. Cutting the intake of rats, say thirty percent, increases a life span of up to forty percent. In human terms that would mean a total of 120 years."

"But . . ." Gita scowled. "She is obviously suffering from malnutrition."

"The beginning stages, yes. Which explains her inability to stay warm. The body generally drops a degree or two when it switches from growth to survival mode."

"But," Gita sputtered, "I do not understand. She is just a child, she is starving. Surely you—"

"Ah." He nodded. "I see your concern. Actually, according to her I.D., she is nearly twenty. And as far as the malnutrition, she would be starving anyway, wouldn't she? Her use of methamphetamine already destroys her appetite, so we're merely taking advantage of the situation and recording the results."

Gita stared over to the reception desk as the big man handed the girl a small package. "You mentioned medicine. What is she taking?"

"As I said, she is a speed freak."

"You're supplying her with drugs?"

"She'd get them anyway. This is merely a safer way to obtain them. Instead of sleeping around or doing who knows what to earn money to buy a drug that may be dangerous, we provide a safer, more modified version of it. It really is a win-win situation. We provide her a safer form of what she would be taking anyway, and she provides us with valuable information."

Gita turned back to him in astonishment as he resumed writing in the chart. "That is what you do here? Provide drugs so you can record children hurting themselves?"

He continued to write. "You're misinterpreting my words, Doctor. Believe me, we've studied all the arguments and this is an amicable solution."

"Amicable sol—"

"And no," he interrupted her. "That's not all we do. However, a low-calorie diet is one very important element in our longevity studies."

"One?" Gita asked. "You are conducting others?"

Finishing the chart, he paused to look at her, obviously weighing how much to say. He closed the cover and continued, "There are two other avenues of research that we feel may lead to greater longevity. One is our hormone therapy program."

"Hormone therapy?"

"Yes. As you may or may not know, great strides have been made with insects, roundworms, and of course rats. By manipulating insulin-like hormones which signal the endocrine system to release other hormones, some fruit flies have lived up to eighty-five percent longer. Imagine what the right combination of insulin, human growth hormone, and thyroid hormone may someday accomplish for humans."

Gita's incredulity only increased. "You subject these children to hormone treatments?"

"As I've said, none of our subjects are children. All are over eighteen and they have been carefully screened. Each has given their signed permission to participate in a program where they receive moderate doses that are kept under strict and very careful supervision."

Gita could only stare.

Horton chuckled. "Don't look so shocked, Doctor. The rich and famous are doing the very same thing for hundreds of thousands of dollars a year. We're providing the exact service to a select group of young adults for free."

"And it is safe?"

"Absolutely."

She showed her doubt and it was his turn to be incredulous. "Please, Doctor, it's not as if we're living in the 1900s."

"Pardon me?"

"Nobody's grafting sex glands to the body."

"They did that?"

"Certainly. And celebrities like Noel Coward, Somerset Maugham, even Pope Pius XI participated in other various treatments such as sheep fetus injections."

Gita closed her eyes.

He chuckled again, "We've come a long ways since then, Doctor, and as I've said, our subjects are carefully monitored. They visit once a week for treatment, walk out five minutes later with a handful of cash—and maybe, just maybe, a few extra years added to their life."

The idea still made Gita shudder. "What about the other?"

"The other what?"

"You said there were three areas of research?"

"Did I?"

"Yes. Restricted calories, hormone therapy, and . . ."

"I misspoke. For us, there are only those two."

She caught something in his eyes and he glanced away. Seeming to sense her suspicion, he turned back to add, "There is a third area of experimentation, though we are not a part of it. However, in my humble estimation, it will prove more promising than the other two combined."

"What area is that?"

"Gene therapy."

"The manipulation of DNA?"

"Precisely."

She waited for more. She'd heard both his enthusiasm and hesitancy, but like every scientist committed to a study, she suspected his enthusiasm would win out. She was right. He took the bait—cautiously at first, but with growing excitement. "There seems to be a small handful of genes that either speed up the aging process or slow it down."

She nodded and waited.

"One of science's favorites these days is something called the klotho gene."

"The klotho gene?"

"Yes, named after the Greek goddess who controls our life span. And rightfully so, because it does seem to retard the aging process. In fact, when strains of mice are created without this gene, they age much, much faster and quickly suffer diseases common to old age—atherosclerosis, osteoporosis, emphysema. Not unlike humans who suffer from Werner's syndrome or even progeria."

"Progeria? I have heard of that."

"Yes. The disease where humans age so rapidly that they die by the time they reach their late teens or early twenties."

Again, Gita remained silent.

"It, too, is triggered by a single gene or, in this case, a mutated gene. One you'll be pleased to know has recently been discovered and isolated."

"Here?"

"No, no. Overseas."

"So . . . you do not experiment with such things."

"Don't be ridiculous." He sighed heavily. "No, as promising as it is, I am afraid progress in the States is much, much slower. Worms, fruit flies, someday primates—unfortunately it will be years before the authorities will allow for human testing."

Gita felt a certain relief, and a little foolish over her suspicions.

Horton smiled and turned to direct them toward the reception area. "So, as you see, Doctor, we are not creating monster children in some secret laboratory. Or, what do they call it on the street—a 'Freak Shop'?"

Gita nodded, her embarrassment growing. "It is easy for rumors to spread."

"Yes, especially among people with such hopelessness and pain." He took a weary breath and exhaled. "Still, even with the rumors, we must turn dozens of volunteers away a week."

"Life is very hard for them."

"Yes, it is. Yes, it is." They arrived at the orderly's desk. Apparently the tour was over. "In any case, if you continue to work with these people, please do what you can to convince them that we are on their side. We are on everybody's side. After all, their contributions may someday be the determining factor in—"

"Dr. Horton!"

He turned to see a small Oriental nurse entering from a door at the far end of the room.

"Janelle," she cried, "she is having a seizure!"

"She's what?"

Motioning for him to come, she repeated, "A seizure!"

The doctor nodded to the male receptionist, who immediately rose to his feet and strode across the room. Turning to Gita, Horton quickly explained, "One of our inpatients." He turned, moving to join the other two, and called over his shoulder, "It was a pleasure meeting you, Doctor. Please, you'll have to excuse me. I trust you can find your way out."

"Yes." Gita nodded as he arrived at the far door and followed the others through. That's when the word hit her. *Inpatients?* He'd said nothing to her about inpatients. She watched as the door shut behind him. For a moment she stood alone in the silence. But only a moment. Immediately, she headed across the room to join them.

She arrived at the door and pushed it open. A white screen panel blocked her view. She noticed the lights were much

dimmer, incandescent instead of fluorescent, making everything feel warmer and homey. She rounded the screen and
saw three hospital beds separated by curtains—each surrounded by state-of-the-art monitoring equipment and each
with a patient. It was the center patient that held the attention of the nurse, Horton, and his assistant. The girl appeared
to be suffering a Grand Mal.

But it wasn't the seizure that sucked away Gita's breath. It
was the patients. All three of them. They lay in their beds
shriveled, their muscles atrophied, and looking very, very old.
There was little to no hair on their bodies, and their paper-thin
skin was stretched over tiny, brittle bones. One was curled
into a fetal position. The other had an oxygen tube in his nose,
IV tubes taped to his pencil arms. But these patients were not
old. They were children. She could see it in their faces, their
hollow, frightened eyes. They were teenagers. Teenagers
trapped inside old bodies. Young people suffering from—

*Progeria* . . . the word resurfaced in her mind.

She turned to Horton who was shouting, "Janelle, Janelle,
can you hear me?"

Suddenly it became clear. The caution Horton took when
speaking about gene therapy—his enthusiasm, particularly
over the klotho gene, his failure to mention these patients,
the rumors on the street . . . and the lengths her employer
went to accomplish his objectives.

No, this doctor wasn't speaking of some gene in a test tube.

"Janelle? Janelle?"

He was already experimenting and replicating it.

"Janelle!"

It was already being tested. And not on rats. But children!
Children of the street. Children no one would miss. Children
who—

"What's she doing here?"

She saw the receptionist motioning at her.

Horton turned and looked up. "Dr. Patekar."

She took a step back, her eyes darting from one crippled
child to the next.

He left the bed and started toward her. "You are making a mistake. It's not as it appears."

She stumbled backward into an unused IV stand. It clanged, scooting across the floor.

"Dr. Patekar ..."

She turned.

"Doctor—" He stretched a hand toward her but she darted away, back around the screen.

"Dr. Patekar!"

She threw open the door, squinting against the brighter light, and started running—running from the man, from the children, from everything that was unraveling around her.

"Dr. Patekar, if you would let me explain!"

With heart pounding she raced across the room and passed the reception desk. Footsteps echoed behind her.

"Doctor—"

She arrived at the door, fumbled with the handle.

The footsteps were nearly there.

The latch clicked and she flung open the door. In the dim hallway she saw Luis, head jerking up. "What the—"

"Dr. Patekar!" Horton's voice was behind her.

Running into the corridor, she shouted at Luis, "Let's go!"

"What?"

She grabbed his arm. "We must go!"

"Go? I ain't afraid of no—"

She pulled, causing him to stumble down the hallway with her. "Please!"

"Dr. Patekar!" Horton and the orderly had entered the hall.

"I will explain later!" she shouted at Luis. They arrived at the door and she threw it open. They hit the sidewalk and started running.

"Doctor ..."

She continued, pulling the protesting Luis—until they rounded the corner and hurried down the Boulevard, the doctor's voice fading into the sounds of the city.

# ten

David had been sitting at the hallway table, nursing a second cup of Adrianna's thick coffee, when the door scraped open and he looked up to see Gita arriving.

"David!" She raced around the table and he barely had time to rise before she was in his arms, practically knocking him over. "Are you all right? What happened? I was so worried!"

It had been a long time since he held a woman, and despite his bone weariness she felt good and natural. "I'm okay," he had assured her, "I'm all right." But it lasted only a moment before they were both struck with embarrassment and separated somewhat clumsily.

"I am sorry." She looked anywhere but to him. "I was just . . . That is to say, I was merely—"

"No, no." He cleared his throat. "That's all right. I appreciate the, uh, concern." Feeling a bit light-headed, he reached out to the table to steady himself. She spotted the movement and motioned him to his chair.

"Please, sit, sit."

He nodded, only too happy to comply. It had been a long night. Actually, a couple of them. And, after the ordeal at the cemetery, he, Preacher Man, and the boys had traveled the last few miles to the shelter on foot. The "smogmobile" had finally given up the ghost around Echo Park, and for some reason, LA motorists didn't feel inclined to pick up four male hitchhikers in the dark, predawn hours.

When they finally arrived, Preacher Man had told the boys that after a brief rest they'd return to the car for a little laying on of hands . . . and a crescent wrench or two. The kids had groaned as they dragged themselves into the dormitory room for some sleep, but not before he left them with another dubious quote, "'Whatever you repair for the least of these, you repair for me.' Just look upon it as Jesus' car, boys; you're just fixin' the good Lord's car."

That had been forty minutes ago. Another fifteen minutes passed before the six of them had gathered around the hallway table . . . David, a stringy-haired resident by the name of Starr, Preacher Man, Adrianna, Gita, and some loudmouthed Hispanic kid who answered to the name of Luis. Although everybody sympathized and shared David's outrage, it was Luis who seemed the most agitated. He had barely sat down before he was back on his feet, the news of Emily fueling his fury. "So this Griffin jerk—he's like the point dude, right?"

Gita carefully chose her words. "He is the one they contacted regarding Emily's tissue type, yes."

"I knew it!" The kid swore and began to pace. "I knew he was scum the minute I set eyes on him!"

The group exchanged glances. Adrianna asked the obvious. "And you think that's what happened to your cousin? That they took him for his organs?"

He spun back to her. "It's the same man, what do you think!" Angrily he quoted, "'He's got a rare blood type, come to our clinic, we want to run some tests.'" He resumed pacing. "I figured they was just going to give him some pills, that's all, like the others. I should have seen it." He swore again. "I should have seen it!"

Gita tried to calm him. "Perhaps he was merely screening him for future—"

"He wasn't screenin' nobody! He's nowhere to be found, lady! My family, friends, nobody's seen him! And he ain't in that Freak Shop, you said so yourself!"

"That is correct, but—"

"He's gone! They killed him!" He motioned to David. "Just like they killed your kid."

"But why?" Adrianna persisted. "I mean, people are donating organs every day."

Preacher Man shrugged. "Maybe they couldn't wait."

"Or maybe..." David's voice was low and thick. "... they didn't have to."

Adrianna began to nod. "Particularly, if they have the power." The group looked to her. "If they happen to be one of the largest communications empires in the world."

Silence stole over the table, broken only by Gita's flat observation: "The Orbolitz Group."

More silence.

"But why her eyes?" Adrianna asked. "Needing a cornea isn't a life-threatening situation. Surely it's not worth murdering somebody over."

No one had an answer.

Preacher Man finally nodded over to David. "Whatever the reason, our brother here got too close to the truth, and last night they turned the tables on him 'fore he could blow the whistle."

"But ...," Gita ventured, "all of these lives? Emily's, Cory's, Dr. Schroyer's—all of this killing, for a pair of eyes?"

"And Hector," Luis spat out. "Don't you forget my cousin."

No one seemed to disagree.

Finally, Adrianna asked, "So where does that leave us?"

Another moment of silence before Luis turned to David. He spoke with quiet intensity. "They kill your kid, my cousin, then turn the tables on us ... I say we turn the tables back on them."

"Luis," Adrianna sighed, "we're talking one of the largest communication conglomerates in the world. You just can't come out and attack a powerful corporation."

"She's right," Preacher Man agreed. "It's not like some gang war."

Luis turned on him and challenged, "Says who?"

Preacher Man looked at him, somewhat surprised. Surprised and with no answer.

Gita turned to David. "Did you put a call in to your friend at the newspaper?"

He nodded, coughing to unclog his throat. "But if it is Orbolitz . . . if they have so much power . . ."

Preacher Man concluded, ". . . they'll persuade him to keep quiet."

"So we got no other option," Luis insisted. "We either sit around moaning like a bunch of old ladies, or we get up and start swinging."

"Swinging, Luis?" Adrianna scoffed. "At what? At who? We don't know where the organs went, we don't know who got them, or why, or when, or—"

"But we know who took them!" He turned to Gita. She held his gaze, unblinking. He broke into his dead-toothed smile and reached into his jacket to pull out his cell phone. "So all we gotta do is find out what he knows."

"How do you propose we do that?" Preacher Man asked.

Still looking to Gita, Luis said, "You got his number, right?"

"Dr. Griffin's? Yes, certainly, but—"

"What are you thinking?" Adrianna asked.

"Just give me his number."

Gita looked around the table. It was clear she hoped for somebody to speak up with a voice of reason. No one did. Reluctantly, she reached into her coat pocket for the phone. It wasn't there. She tried the other pocket, then frowned. "I seem to have misplaced it. It is not—" She came to a stop as Starr pulled it from her own jeans pocket.

She handed it to Gita with a shrug. "Sorry."

David looked on as Gita opened the phone and scrolled down her directory until she found the number. "Here it is." She read the number to Luis, who immediately dialed it on his own phone.

"Luis," Adrianna repeated, "what are you—"

"Watch and be amazed," he said, punching in the numbers. "Watch and be amazed."


**M**r. Orbolitz?" Griffin headed toward him as he stepped out of the VR chamber. The sinewy man had already removed his 3-D goggles and, as was his custom, would change out of the VR suit in his office. The children were there to greet him, but he waved them away. He had more important matters on his mind. Unfortunately, Griffin knew who those matters pertained to. "Mr. Orbolitz?"

The man did not glance up as he started down the grassy hallway toward the offices. His tone was cooler than usual. "Hello, Dick."

Arriving at his side, Griffin asked, "You sent for me?"

"I'm not real happy right now, son."

Griffin's gut tightened.

"You know why?"

"Well, sir," he hedged, "I'm not entirely—"

*"Do you know why?"*

Griffin remained silent, knowing he'd soon find out.

"I hear a relative of one of our donors is making some waves."

"Yes, sir."

"Discovered your trail of incompetence and is tryin' to go to the media."

Griffin had no doubt of the source of Orbolitz's information. 3316. He was the only one who knew the details. He was the only one who had questioned Griffin's actions. Now he'd apparently finished his questioning and had pulled an end run.

"Actually," Griffin explained, "I believe we've managed to sufficiently discredit him."

"'Sufficiently discredit'?" Orbolitz gave him a dubious look. "And his girlfriend? One of our own, I hear?"

Griffin swallowed. Apparently *all* of the laundry had been aired. "Dr. Gita Patekar is one of our employees, yes. An unfortunate distraction."

"Seems to me there's been too many 'unfortunate distractions.' And, rumor has it, she's a bit of a distraction for you."

Griffin started to protest, then closed his mouth, accepting the rebuke.

"I suggest you do more than 'sufficiently discredit' them, son. I suggest you clean up this whole mess and do whatever it takes to end it. I don't imagine I have to remind you of the stakes."

"No, sir."

They continued down the hallway, past the waterfall and along the meandering stream.

"The father and this Patekar gal have gone into hiding?"

"Yes, sir. I thought their fleeing an arrest would be the best way to silence any doubt that—"

*"The best way?"* Mr. Orbolitz slowed to a stop. *"The best way?"* He shook his head. "You know the *best* way . . . and I suggest you get to it." He resumed walking.

Griffin followed. "Sir, there have been so many casualties already."

"And there will be more if this business ain't cleared up. It's time to cut out the infection and cauterize it, Dick. *All* of it."

Griffin nodded. "Security has established a link to the son, in the event we should need to get to the father."

"Then I suggest you use it."

Griffin agreed, wondering if that meant disposing of the boy as well.

"Oh, and Dick." Once again they came to a stop.

"Sir?"

"You and me, we've had ourselves some history together."

"Yes, sir."

"But as we both know, I ain't one to get stuck in the past—I always like lookin' to the future."

Griffin tried reading what was going on behind the man's sunglasses. He didn't have to try hard.

"Don't disappoint me, Richard. You know how I hate disappointment."

"Yes, sir."

Mr. Orbolitz broke into a smile and clasped him on the shoulder. "Good ... good. Now, if you'll excuse me." He turned and continued down the hall. "Have a good afternoon, son."

"Thank you, sir. And you."

Griffin watched as the wiry man followed the stream toward the offices. He was about to turn and head back toward the VR lab, when his eyes caught the newly painted portion of wall across from him. The portion that had recently been splattered with the blood of a pigmy bunny—a reminder of Mr. Orbolitz's response to disappointment.

His cell phone rang, pulling him from his thoughts. He flipped it open and answered. "Hello?"

"Dr. Griffin."

He detected an accent. "Who's this?"

"I know about Hector."

"What? Hector who?"

"The kid from the Boulevard you offed."

His heart quickened. "What are you talking about? Who are you?"

"It's your amigo, Dr Griffin. The friend with the broken finger."

Now he recognized the voice. Keeping calm, he responded, "So tell me, 'friend,' how did you get this number?"

"The same way I found out about the girl whose eyes you stole."

Griffin caught his breath. When he could trust his voice he calmly answered, "Girl? What girl? What do you mean 'eyes'?"

"Check out her grave, man. We dug it up last night. For some reason the chick is missing both eyeballs. Pretty weird, wouldn't you say?"

Griffin swallowed.

"'Course, we know the reason, don't we, amigo?"

"And why would that be of interest to an inconsequential cockroach such as yourself?"

"Oh, it don't interest me, man. I don't even care about her dead boyfriend or the shrink you killed."

Griffin felt his body stiffen.

"See, I don't give a rat what you did with any of them. But Hector, he was my cousin, man. Family. And what you done to him and his organs, man, well, I take that real personal."

Griffin played for time, gathering his wits. "There seems to be no end to your imagination, nothing you don't think you know."

"That's the beauty of cockroaches, we're everywhere—in your floors, your walls, you name it and we're—"

"Why exactly are you wasting my time with these fabrications?"

"It's just good manners."

"What?"

"A courtesy call. On the streets we always warn our marks 'fore we destroy them."

Griffin forced a laugh. "Destroy *me?*"

"Not just you, man. Everyone involved with Hector's death. You, your company, all the way to the jerk who got his organs—all of you, man."

Griffin shook his head at the bravado. "Let me get this straight, you're saying a little, know-nothing cockroach like you is going to take on somebody like me?"

"Not just you, man. You're only the warmup. I'm takin' on everybody. You're all comin' down. Every last one of you."

Griffin chuckled. "Right, you and your delusional world are going to take on an entire corporation *and* bust a major-league politician. You're going to 'bring us all down.'"

"If that's what it takes."

"Listen, my friend, besides being acutely misinformed, you're acutely insane."

"Like I said, I'm just being polite."

"Well, find somebody else to practice your manners on."

"Suit yourself, man."

"I always do."

"And have a nice day . . . whatever's left of it."

The kid disconnected, leaving Griffin standing, his mind racing.

Got him." Luis snapped shut his cell phone.

"What do you mean?" Adrianna asked.

"Some hotshot politician's got Hector's organs."

"He told you that?"

Luis shrugged. "I'm the master. Don't go messin' with the master."

"He told you?"

"I pushed him, threw a couple fakes to the left, then *wham*, got him with the right." Grinning in satisfaction, he concluded, "Never saw it coming."

"He give you a name?" Adrianna persisted.

Luis scoffed, "Don't be stupid."

"Wouldn't hurt to have a name."

Before he could respond, the heavy metal door scraped open. Gita looked up to see the young gay she had met earlier.

"Hey, Lawrence," Starr called, her face lighting up.

He sighed wearily. "Hello."

Adrianna turned to him. "How'd the interview go?"

"If they have any thought life they'll hire me." Looking around the table he asked, "You having some sort of meeting?"

"We're having a strategy session," Starr chirped. "Want to join us?"

Ignoring her, he turned to Adrianna. "What's going on?"

"Looks like Luis here has uncovered a genuine murder plot."

Lawrence looked at him. "You found out what happened to your cousin?"

"Took his organs, man. Killed him and took his organs."

"Only we don't know who got them," Starr explained. "We think it's some politician, but—"

"Hagen," David quietly interrupted.

Gita turned to him.

He continued, voice low and raw. "I saw the headlines in the newspaper racks on the way here."

"Congressman William Hagen?" Adrianna asked.

David nodded.

"I've heard that name," the preacher said.

Adrianna gave him a look. "He's been our congressman for the last fifteen years."

He nodded with confidence. "Told you."

Rolling her eyes, she turned to Lawrence. "Pull it up on the Internet; let's see what it says."

Lawrence nodded, peeled off his vest, and headed to the desktop computer in the corner. "Congressman Hagen? He's on our side, isn't he?"

Adrianna replied, "If you mean is he a proponent of gay rights yes, for years."

The preacher closed his eyes, shaking his head.

Lawrence took a seat and quickly worked the computer, bringing up the latest edition of the *L.A. Times*.

As he did, Gita spoke up, "The time frame would make sense."

Luis looked at her. "How's that?"

"There is only a small window available from the harvest of an organ until its transplant. So if they removed—"

"Here we go," Lawrence interrupted. "'Congressman receives new heart.'" The group sat quietly as he scanned, reading the excerpts. "Yesterday afternoon . . . Mercy General

. . . no complications, excellent prognosis . . . wife and children rejoicing."

"Glad somebody's happy," Luis seethed.

"Well, at least we know who the 'who' is," the preacher said. "Not that it'll do us any good, but—"

"Says you," Luis interrupted. The old man turned to the kid, who continued, "Who says we can't use this information?"

"What you going to do, Luis?" Adrianna scorned. "Give Griffin another call, get him to confess this time?"

"Not him."

"Not him?" the preacher repeated. "Then who?"

"If this Hagen dude is so cool, maybe he'll help us."

"That's extremely unlikely," Lawrence scoffed. "Just because he is a supporter of gay rights doesn't mean that he would risk—"

"He'll deny everything," Adrianna agreed.

"That's right." Lawrence nodded. "Provided he knew anything in the first place."

"So"—Luis shrugged—"we'll help him know what he should know."

"How?" Lawrence sighed.

"We'll tell him the truth and give him the choice. He can either work for us . . . or against us."

"Oooh, that'll scare him." Starr pretended to shudder.

Luis shot her a look.

"We have no proof, son," the preacher said. "It's our word against theirs."

"Actually . . ." Gita cleared her throat. "We do have some proof. It may be circumstantial, but we—"

"Circumstantial is all I need," Luis interrupted. "The rest is a piece of cake."

"What?" Adrianna mocked. "You gonna con a congressman now?"

"Why not? Ain't that what politicians do to us?"

"How?"

Luis looked at her, lifting his palms. "You still don't know who you're dealing with, do you?"

She arched an eyebrow.

"Look around the room, woman. We got plenty of resources here." Flashing his dead-tooth grin, he added, "With a little time to figure it out, and in the hands of an expert like myself—we got all the resources we need."

~

luke? luke u there?

Griffin stared at the screen impatiently waiting for an answer. It had only been a few hours since he'd contacted him. Surely the kid wouldn't just wander off—not if he thought he'd been talking to his dead sister. Of course Mr. Orbolitz was right. It was time to clean up the mess. Time to follow through with the contingency and use the son as bait.

He rose from his desk and headed to the cherry minibar to pour a Scotch. He'd barely closed the decanter when he heard the familiar *ding*—the sound that a message had arrived. He quickly returned to the monitor and read:

Em, is it u? where u been?

He sat and, forcing himself to take his time, finally typed:

thats just it, i dunno

He hesitated, thinking of writing more, but decided to let the kid run with it. A moment later the question appeared:

r u alive?

He smiled and typed:

i dunno . . .

Another moment and another sentence appeared:

u said somethin bout a machine

His smile broadened. This was going to be easier than he thought. He typed:

> daddy saw me in it. didnt he tell u?

The response was immediate:

> NO WAY! when? where?

Griffin chose to ignore the questions. Instead, he made certain the hook was set.

> i'm trapped inside. i can't get out!

A question repeated:

> where?

He remained silent, patiently waiting. More words appeared:

> EM! tell me where U R—I CAN HELP!

Another pause. Waiting. Waiting. He took a sip of his drink.

> EM!!

Another sip. Finally, he typed:

> grab some paper

The reply was instant:

> ok go

Griffin typed:

> decker canyon, santa monica mountains cor-
> ner of mulholland/decker

The answer appeared:

> got it-im out

He typed:

> how will u get here?

There was no response. He tried again, deciding to add a touch of sisterly concern:

> luke, be careful

But there was no answer. His smile reappeared. The kid was already gone. The bait was set.

G ita listened to Luis and marveled. The kid was such a con artist that he nearly had *her* convinced it was possible. According to him, all they had to do was confront the congressman with the facts and trust that he'd respond. He could play dumb, he could claim ignorance, it didn't matter to them. But once he knew that someone else knew and could blow the whistle, then he'd have to play it safe and protect his backside by calling for an investigation.

"It's still our word against his," Adrianna insisted. "Even if we contact him, he's not going to admit having heard from us."

Eager for drama, Starr suggested, "We could plant a wire on him and record our conversation."

Lawrence impatiently replied, "It would be much easier to simply speak to him and openly videotape it."

David rubbed his temples, his voice quiet and husky. "Are you saying we just saunter on up to the congressman's room with a video camera and confront him?"

"Why not?" Starr quickly changed positions and came to Lawrence's defense. "I seen something like that on *NYPD Blue.*"

The preacher pointed out, "Security might have a little problem with that, darlin'."

"No." Adrianna shook her head. "In this case security would have no problem."

They looked at her as she turned to Lawrence. "What hospital is he in again?"

Glancing at the screen Lawrence read, "Mercy General." She nodded, almost smiling.

"What's going through your head, girl?" the preacher asked.

"One of our own alumni had been servicing their head of administration."

The group exchanged glances.

Adrianna continued, "Jodi Brunnel—had been his mistress for years."

"Had?" Lawrence asked.

Adrianna nodded. "Got dumped recently for a newer model."

"Is he married?" the preacher asked.

"With children."

"Then we're in." Luis shrugged. "She turns the heat up on him—"

Starr jumped in. "—by threatening to tell the missus—"

Lawrence continued, "—and he pulls some strings."

"And we're in," Luis repeated.

Gita scowled. "But—wouldn't that be ... blackmail?"

Luis grinned. "We call it 'leverage.'"

Before she could respond the preacher asked, "What about the video camera?"

"What about it?" Luis said.

"It's one thing to talk to the congressman. Quite another to do it in front of someone holdin' a camera."

"Who says that it has to be a someone?" Lawrence asked. The group turned to him and he explained, "They would certainly have video security, particularly in VIP rooms like his. We simply patch an audio into it, run it through their system and into our own."

"Is that possible?" the preacher asked.

Lawrence nodded. "With an engineer or two, it would take less than an hour."

"Seems to me we might be a little short on video equipment," Adrianna pointed out.

The preacher agreed. "Not to mention engineers."

There was a moment's pause until David turned to Gita, his exhaustion more evident. "What about your guys?"

"Pardon me?"

"The engineers who helped you at Alcatraz?"

"It was only one and he now works for the Orbolitz Group. I hardly think he would—"

"No, no. The ones who worked for Morrie Metcalf, his TV show."

"I imagine they are now all unemployed."

"Exactly." She watched as he once again summoned up some hidden, unknown strength. "Thanks to the Orbolitz Group, they're out of work. If you ask me, they just might relish the opportunity for a little revenge."

"Cool," Starr giggled.

"A little eye for an eye," Luis agreed.

Again, Gita expressed her concern. "I wonder how appropriate it is to capitalize on somebody's hunger for revenge, when what we really—"

"It may not be *appropriate*," Lawrence argued with a touch of sarcasm, "but it is brilliant. If we could have a real video crew hook things up, that would be terrific."

Others nodded. Starr agreed, "Sweet."

Gita frowned, turning first to David, then Adrianna and the preacher. But they were all nodding with the rest.

"Now . . . ," Luis thought out loud, "we just need the messenger."

Lawrence agreed. "Someone to relay the information."

"They need to appear trustworthy," Adrianna said, glancing about the group.

The preacher fidgeted. "Don't look at me."

"I wasn't," she replied.

Luis continued, "They need to look respectable. Like establishment. All honest and clean like."

"I suppose . . ." David coughed. "I could . . ."

Preacher Man shook his head. "You're in no shape, brother. 'Sides, your picture is all over the news."

"What about the lady?" Luis asked.

All eyes turned to Gita.

Startled, she looked at them. "Surely you are not thinking of me?"

Glances were traded.

She swallowed. "But I too was on the news."

"Not really," the preacher corrected. "Not your picture."

More glances were exchanged.

Gita shifted uneasily.

Adrianna leaned forward and quietly explained, "All you have to do is present that man with the facts, just the truth, we'll do the rest."

She looked from one face to another until her eyes landed on David's. He was so tired, so exhausted. But there was no missing the gentleness in his voice. "Truth *is* your specialty."

"Yes, but I am not qualified to—"

"What are you saying?" Luis asked. "You telling us you ain't qualified to tell the truth?"

"Well, no, but—"

"That's all anyone is asking you to do," Lawrence said.

Hoping for an ally, she looked back to Adrianna. But the woman held her gaze and calmly repeated, "All you have to do is tell the truth. We'll take care of the rest."

With rising desperation, she glanced around the table one last time until she was again looking at David. Sensitive, understanding David. His answer was kind, but equally clear:

"Just the truth, Gita. All we're asking is that you tell the truth."

An hour later, Dr. Gita Patekar lay on her cot trying to get some rest. Rest? Who was she kidding? In less than two hours she would be weaseling her way through a hospital administrator who was being blackmailed by some prostitute to tell a U.S. congressman that he was an accomplice to the murder of a victim whose heart was beating inside his chest . . . all this while teaming up with some of the city's most immoral and unsavory characters!

No way was she resting.

Minutes earlier, she'd put another call in to Rosa. The nurse had offered to work a double shift to continue keeping an eye on her brother. She had also passed word to the rest of the staff to be on the alert, which started all sorts of rumors only adding to their vigilance.

After that, Gita had tracked down the video engineer of Morrie Metcalf's show—actually, his ex-engineer. As expected, the Alcatraz segment was aired not only on the Psychic Network, but *Entertainment Tonight* (two evenings in a row), as well as becoming sound bites for the morning news shows. This had been enough to cause the sudden pullout of all sponsors, which led to the immediate cancellation of the show, which of course led to the immediate layoff of the video department. Initially, the engineer, Sean Morris, was leery of her offer. But when Gita had mentioned there was a good chance of implicating the Orbolitz Group, the ones responsible for his sudden unemployment, he thought it might be worth chucking his poker night, "borrowing" the company's van, and working out a little clandestine operation.

But it was more than the upcoming events that filled Gita's mind and drove away all peace. It was also her association with these people, these . . . dregs of society. Her unease around them had not decreased. If anything, it had grown worse as more and more memories were dredged up. This was the very thing, the very people she had struggled so hard to forget, to be free from. And now the Lord had brought her full circle, returning her to her childhood, with all its filth, its immorality, its disgusting sins. And, if that wasn't bad enough, there was her own confusion and embarrassment for being so judgmental. David certainly didn't have trouble associating with these kids—and, she guessed, neither would have Emily, not with her great compassion . . . and love.

Swallowing back the knot of conflicting emotions, she reached under her cot for Emily's journal. She flipped to the first poem she had read so long ago, at the beginning of this long and all-too-revealing journey. A poem by the other Emily:

*He fumbles at your spirit*
  *As players at the keys*
*Before they drop full music on;*
  *He stuns you by degrees,*

*Prepares your brittle substance*
  *For the ethereal blow,*
*By fainter hammers, further heard,*
  *Then nearer, then so slow*

*Your breath has time to straighten,*
  *Your brain to bubble cool, —*
*Deals one imperial thunderbolt*
  *That scalps your naked soul.*

Was this what was happening? Was God stripping her naked? Was He tenderly but relentlessly scalping her soul? But for what purpose? For the love she had longed and prayed for? The love she had seen in David? In Emily?

But what of truth? Holiness? Purity?

*"Real love is a dangerous thing, child. It involves getting your hands dirty once in a while."*

She understood Adrianna's words. Of course. But Scripture plainly teaches that truth is truth. We're never to compromise the Word of—

*"'The law was given through Moses; but grace and truth came through Jesus Christ.'"*

Yes, but—

*"'. . . grace and truth.'"*

She closed her eyes. Then, opening them, she flipped a few pages further into the journal and reread:

*He touched me, so I live to know*
*That such a day, permitted so,*
  *I groped upon his breast.*
*It was a boundless place to me,*
*And silenced, as the awful sea*
  *Puts minor streams to rest.*

*And now, I'm different from before,*
*As if I breathed superior air,*
*    Or brushed a royal gown;*
*My feet, too, that had wandered so,*
*My gypsy face transfigured now*
*    To tenderer renown.*

She was being touched. She was different than before. But this? This is not what she had planned. This did not fit in with her faith. Not by any stretch of the—

*"I'm just sayin' that real love is messy. So messy it can get you killed. Just ask Jesus."*

Again she closed her eyes and took a breath.

"I thought you were going to get some rest."

With a start she looked up and saw David smiling at her. He eased himself down on her cot.

"And what about you?" she asked.

"It's been a long day," he admitted.

"Or three or four."

He tried smiling, but she could see the depth of his fatigue.

"Are you going to be okay?" she asked. "How do you feel?"

He took a deep breath. "Angry. Outraged. But most of all . . . most of all, I still need to know if she's okay, if she needs my help."

Moved with feeling, Gita reached out and touched his arm.

He looked down and nodded. "I know—you believe she's with God. But . . ."

She said nothing, watching him struggle.

Finally he looked up. "But I really do think what we're doing—what we're planning is the right thing—exposing the truth, I mean. The truth is going to clear up a lot of stuff and maybe"—he took another breath—"maybe save some other lives in the future."

She nodded in silence.

Musing, he repeated, "*Truth.* Seems to be a word that keeps coming up. Don't know where my sudden interest in that began—must be the company I'm keeping."

It was her turn to glance down. "You have been through a great deal, David Kauffman."

"And so have you, Gita Patekar." She looked back up, back to those caring, exhausted eyes. "I can't even imagine how difficult this is for you."

She glanced away.

"For you to associate with these people—to have to work side by side with them." Her eyes shot back to his. Though spoken with kindness, the words hurt more than he could imagine. Misunderstanding the pain on her face, he tried to explain, "You know what I mean—prostitutes, gang members, druggies."

Tears sprang to her eyes. She tried to blink them away, but they kept coming.

"What's wrong?" he asked in sudden concern. "What did I say?"

She shook her head, could not speak.

"I'm sorry . . . I didn't mean—"

"No," she answered hoarsely, taking a quick swipe at her eyes. "You are right. I pray to God it is not true, but you are right. It is hard for me. It is very hard and it should not be."

David frowned. "What do you mean? I'm sure they bring back awful memories. To put you in a position where you have to work with them, live with them, sleep with them . . ."

He still didn't understand. She looked up to him. "And what about you?"

He stared at her. "What about me?"

A strand of hair had fallen into his eyes. She resisted the urge to push it aside. "How do you do it—without feeling . . . so unclean, so dirty?"

"I guess"—he took another breath—"I guess I know there's not that much difference between us. I'm not selling my body or doing drugs, but I've certainly got my own baggage." Growing more quiet, he added, "And when you get down to it, I suppose in my own way, I'm just as lost."

She looked back down, her voice thick with emotion. "You are a very good man." She swallowed, unsure if she could continue. "But me? I am so busy hiding behind truth that I do not know the first thing about people, about caring and—"

"Whoa, whoa," he interrupted. "What are you talking about? I'd give anything to have what you have."

She looked up at him.

"Your faith, that assurance of absolutes—those are hard commodities to come by. Especially today. I mean it, I'd give anything for them."

"You would?" she half-whispered.

"Of course. And maybe, after this is all over, maybe we can talk some more about it."

She almost laughed. "You would want me to continue rattling on about such things?"

"I would love to hear you rattle on. About anything."

The phrase sucked the breath from her. She wanted to respond but didn't know how. And he didn't wait for her to try. Instead, he leaned over and gently kissed her on the forehead. "Please, get some rest."

She nodded.

Wearily, he rose to his feet. Without thinking, much less understanding, Gita reached out and took his hand. He looked down at it, then to her face. Tenderly, he raised her hand to his lips and kissed it. She looked on, her heart nearly bursting. Then he turned and silently headed toward his own cot across the room.

# part Three

# eleven

Gita pushed open the door to the shelter's only restroom and was greeted by the smell of vomit and disinfectant. Just inside, Adrianna worked on her hands and knees cleaning the floor with a worn sponge.

"Watch your step," she warned.

"Somebody was sick?" Gita asked.

"Too much partying. And by the looks of things, the booze has got his ulcer bleeding again. Poor child. Poor, stupid child."

Gita simply stared.

"You all set?" Adrianna asked.

Coming to, Gita stepped around her and headed toward the single stall. "Almost." Then, turning back, she asked, "Do you not ever tire of this?"

"Of what?"

"This . . . this continual cleaning up of their messes, their mistakes?"

"Every day."

"But you're still here."

"I'm still here, 'cause God's still here."

Gita softly replied as much to herself as to the woman, "I wonder . . ."

Adrianna stopped mopping and looked up.

Gita felt her face redden. "I apologize but . . . I know what we spoke of this morning, but do you not sometimes wonder if they are simply bringing this all upon themselves, that you are somehow . . ."

Adrianna returned to her work. "That I'm interfering with God's justice? That I'm preventing them from reaping what they're sowing?"

"Well, yes, does that not ever concern you?"

The woman paused a moment, then answered, "I've been here almost twelve years. Seen a lot. And you're right, the sad fact is many of these kids will never make it. Some are gonna die from overdose, or some sort of violence, or disease. Others, they may keep their bodies alive, but their souls will have died. God only knows how many will actually ever receive Jesus Christ."

Gita remained silent, listening.

"And sometimes . . ." Adrianna stopped to wipe her forehead with her arm. "Sometimes I gotta say, the saved ones give me almost as much worry as those who aren't."

"Why is that?"

"Because they're the ones who often forgive the least."

Gita shifted her weight, feeling uncomfortable. "How— how is that possible?"

"I'm not sure." Adrianna looked up at her. "I suspect they just don't know how forgiven they are."

Gita blinked but held her ground.

Adrianna returned to her work. "Oh, they say God loves them and everything, but deep inside they think He's still holding a grudge. Deep inside they think He's forgiven them, but only because He has to."

Gita turned toward the stall, but her feet would not move.

"It's like they can't fully love others . . . 'cause they don't know how fully loved they are."

Without turning, Gita spoke. "And how do they"—she cleared her throat—"how will they ever know this love?"

The woman quit scrubbing again. Gita could feel the eyes in her back. "I guess they just have to stop trying so hard. They just have to stop and let Him love them."

Gita swallowed, remaining silent.

"'Cause that's what He *wants* to do, isn't it? He doesn't *have* to ... He *wants* to."

Gita felt her eyes burning.

"Amazing, isn't it ... The Creator of the whole universe loves us more than His own life. Makes no difference who we are, what we've done—He loves us. Isn't that what He proved on the cross? That He loves us more than His own life? And once we get ahold of that, I mean, once we really understand and accept that, then the love, it just starts gushing out, doesn't it—it just starts gushing, and there's nothing we can do to stop it."

Gita nodded and sniffed quietly. She headed to the stall. Once inside, she closed the door, leaned against the side, and wrapped her arms around herself. Only then did the tears that were welling in her eyes finally spill onto her cheeks ...

Forty-five minutes later, Dr. Gita Patekar stood inside the office of Gerald Larson, head administrator of Mercy General.

"You'll have three minutes," he said.

"I understand."

"Three minutes, not a second more. We've already had a repair crew in there working on the security camera; he doesn't need any more interruptions."

Gita nodded as the bald, middle-aged man, complete with spreading paunch, continued, "There will be an LAPD officer outside the door and a security agent in the room. You will be accompanied by my own head of security the entire time."

"You are being very thorough."

"Why shouldn't I be? You people are not exactly a trustworthy lot, are you?" Once again his eyes swept over her body. She tried not to fidget, though it had been a long time since she'd felt such unabashed leering. There was little doubt what story Adrianna's call-girl friend had invented to explain her acquaintance with Gita.

She stole a glance out the window of the third-story office. Just up the street sat the remote video van. Somewhere in this building Sean Morris, the engineer from Alcatraz, and Luis, posing as his assistant, were at work—thanks to a "requisitions order" Lawrence had earlier hacked into the hospital's computer. By the time Sean and Luis arrived, security was already waiting for their system's "repair and upgrade."

Larson moved around his desk, the edge to his voice softening. "So where are you from originally?"

"From?"

"Yes. The accent, the demeanor? I'm guessing India."

"Originally I am from Nepal."

"Nepal." He moved closer. "So tell me, what do they do differently in Nepal that they don't do here?"

"I am not certain I understand."

"Oh, I believe you do." He arrived and set a pair of pudgy hands on her hips. She managed not to flinch and wondered whether he'd had garlic or onions for lunch. "So, what do you think? What could a person like myself learn if I went . . . international?"

Resisting the urge to hurt him, she smiled tightly. "I have come here to meet the congressman."

He paused, apparently seeing the steel in her eyes. Then with feigned indifference he removed his hands and turned back to his desk. "And so you shall. I told his people that you are a business friend of mine and that you have an extremely influential voice in the community—which, of course, is the only reason he would see you. He knows nothing of your occupation. See to it that remains." Glancing back to her, he added, "That can be our little secret—which I trust we will explore at some future time."

David stared impatiently at the computer screen. He felt frustrated and guilty over allowing Gita to confront the congressman on her own. He had tried to convince the group that it was best for him to tag along, to at least stay in the video van, but they wouldn't listen.

"Not enough room," the engineer had insisted. "Between me, Luis, and the equipment, things will already be too cramped."

There was also the matter of David's name and photograph all over the news. It was too risky for him to be seen in public. And finally, there was his exhaustion. He could still push himself, he was certain of it—but no one seemed to believe him. So, here he sat in the shelter's hallway—a type of central command with Lawrence and Preacher Man watching everything that came into the computer through the streaming video.

The screen was split. The left half showed Luis and Morris, the engineer, in the van. The right half showed the congressman, a distinguished-looking man with flowing white hair, lying in his private room joking with one of his aides. The sound still wasn't working, but Morris, who was busy under the mixing board, promised it would be up and running in minutes.

"Hey, Lawrence." Luis leaned into the van's minicam. He wore the matching overalls that he and Morris had donned while working in the building. "Check it out, man. Not only do we get local"—he pointed to their monitor showing Congressman Hagen in bed—"but we get cable too." He motioned to another monitor that displayed what was playing on Congressman Hagen's TV. With a grin, he pressed a selector switch and suddenly changed channels on the congressman's set. Fortunately, neither the congressman nor his aide noticed.

Lawrence spoke into the mic beside the monitor. "Don't screw around, Luis."

But the kid, who was obviously enjoying himself, continued pressing the selector. "So what channel should he watch?"

"Luis . . ."

"Nickelodeon?" He paused, looking at a cartoon for a moment. "Nah." He resumed his channel surfing. "Hey, what's that local gay channel you girls watch?"

"Tell him to stop fooling around," Preacher Man ordered.

But Luis continued punching the selector until he stopped on a talk show featuring some provocatively dressed gays. With an effected lisp he said, "Oh yess, I think thiss is jusst what the doctor ordered."

"Luis—"

As David watched and waited, he was again tempted with the thought of calling home. "Lawrence, how much time do we have?"

Lawrence spoke into the mic. "What's our time frame, gentlemen?"

"Three, maybe four minutes," Morris replied from under the board.

David nodded and reached for his cell phone. All day he'd been dying to check on his family. But everyone kept warning him about the possibility of his call being traced. In fact they insisted he keep it turned off for that very reason. But now, with just a few minutes to go, what did it matter? He'd keep it short. Thirty seconds. And even if they did trace it, by the time the police arrived it would all be over. Thirty seconds. Just to hear his son's and mother's voice. Just to assure them he was all right.

He quietly rose and walked to the far end of the hallway. Hitting speed dial, he glanced at his watch and waited.

His mother picked up on the second ring. "Hello?"

He covered his mouth and whispered into the phone, "Mom ..."

"David! David, are you okay?"

"I'm fine."

"You were on the news. The police were here. Are you—"

"I'm all right, I'm okay."

"What's going on?"

"I can't explain right now, but—"

"We've been worried sick. There's a warrant out for your arrest. They say you're a suspect for murder!"

"Yes. It's a huge mix-up. But I promise I'll clear it up. Very shortly. How's Luke? How is he doing?"

"Didn't go to school today. Too much hubbub. David, the people from the TV trampled all over our yard. My flower beds are—"

"I'm sorry, Mom. We can get you more flowers. Where is he now?"

"Luke? Where else but upstairs with the computer."

"Can you get him for me?"

"Hang on." She covered the receiver and shouted, "Luke!" Then, back to David, "Can't you tell me anything?"

"Not yet. I don't understand it all myself. But soon, very—"

"But the murder of this doctor—"

Striving to keep his voice even, he repeated, "I'm not responsible for that, Mom." He glanced at his watch; they'd just passed thirty seconds. "I promise as soon as we get this straightened out I'll explain everything. Can you hurry Luke up?"

More rustling as she covered the mouthpiece. "Luke, honey, come downstairs. Luke!" Returning to David she said, "Hang on, I'll take you up to him."

He looked at his watch. Forty-five seconds. "Mom, I'll have to call back."

She was shouting again, "Luke . . ."

"Mom?"

He hesitated, then reluctantly closed the phone. He walked back and joined the other two as they watched the monitor. The congressman and his aide had finally noticed the TV and were exchanging remarks.

"Got it," the engineer said. "We've got sound."

"Bring it up," Lawrence spoke into the mic. "Let's hear what they're saying."

The hospital room's volume increased and they heard the aide speaking. He was a tall, good-looking man with a radio announcer's voice. "These queers," he said, shaking his head. "I don't know, you give them an inch and they take a mile."

David blinked, wondering if he'd misunderstood.

The congressman nodded. "One wonders which is worse, pushy Jews or pushy queers."

"What?" Luis asked. "What did he say?"

Lawrence shushed him.

"I hear you," the aide chuckled as they turned back to the TV.

"Lawrence," Luis spoke to his camera, "I thought you said this jerk was a supporter of you girls."

"Be quiet, Luis," Lawrence snapped. He leaned closer to the screen. So did David and Preacher Man.

Suddenly, both Hagen and his aide groaned and shook their heads in disgust. "I told you," the congressman said.

"Like termites infesting a house," the aide agreed. "They're everywhere."

Hagen nodded. "And if we're not careful, someday they'll destroy the entire infrastructure. By the way, you did screen my nurses, right? The orderlies?"

"Yes, sir. Not a pervert in the bunch."

"Good. I don't want any of them sneaking up on me when I'm asleep, if you know what I mean." They both chuckled. "I tell you, sometimes just to have them touch me makes my skin crawl."

"I understand."

"And campaigning—shaking all those limp-wristed, pasty-white hands—I mean, who knows where they've been. And not being able to wash, sometimes for hours." He gave a shudder. "It can literally make you sick to your stomach."

"I don't know how you do it, sir."

The congressman sighed wearily. "Jews, wetbacks, everybody has a coalition these days."

Luis swore softly. "I gotta be hearin' things."

No one responded. They simply stared at the screen.

"I tell you," the congressman concluded, "if there was one mistake we made in history, it was stopping Hitler too soon."

"What do you mean?"

"Don't get me wrong, the man definitely had his share of problems. But after he was done removing the Jews, next on his list would have been the homosexuals."

Luis swore again. "All right. That does it."

David glanced to the other side of the split screen to see Luis rise to his feet.

"Where you going?" the engineer demanded.

"It's time we give this scum sucker a wake-up call."

"Luis," Lawrence warned.

"Not now, girl."

"You'll ruin everything, you'll ruin our plans."

"Yeah, well, plans have just been changed."

"Luis—"

"This one's for you, Larry . . . and for my cousin."

The screen flared white, as Luis opened the van's door.

"Luis!" Lawrence shouted.

David's cell phone rang. Checking the number and flipping it open, he answered, "Mom!"

"David, he's not here."

"What?"

"He's not here," his mother repeated. "His computer's on but he's not here."

Having heard the phone, Preacher Man turned to David. "Brother, what are you—"

David held up his hand for silence. "Could he have gone out—to the store or something?"

"He would have told me, especially today. There's something else, too. A message on the computer. He'd been talking to someone."

"Who?"

"Brother, you shouldn't be—"

Again David motioned for Preacher Man to be quiet. "What does the message say?"

"It's somebody pretending to be Emily. They say she's trapped in some sort of machine and needs to be rescued."

*"What?"*

"They say she saw you there. David, who—what is this?"

He struggled to stay calm. "What else does it say?"

"Luke says he's going to rescue her."

"Rescue her?"

"That's what he wrote: 'Hang on, I'm coming to get you.'"

The bottom dropped out of David's stomach. "Is there anything else?"

"That's it, except for an address. Something in the Santa Monica Mountains—Mulholland and Decker Canyon."

Growing numb, David forced out the words, "Is that all?"

She hesitated. "No."

"What?"

No response.

*"Mom?"*

Finally she spoke. "I'm looking out his window, down to the driveway."

"And? What is it? Mom?"

"My car, it's missing."

# twelve

Congressman William Hagen heard a knock. He glanced from the TV and saw the tall security agent open the hospital door. There was a brief discussion before the agent finally stepped aside to admit one of the surveillance technicians who had been there earlier—the Hispanic kid with the broken finger.

Hagen sighed and turned back to the TV as Steven Maxwell, his senior aide, addressed the boy. "You back again?"

"Sorry, man." The kid headed toward the TV. "Forgot somethin'. It'll only take a sec."

"Well, make it quick, the congressman needs his rest."

"Sure, man, no problem. Hey, I see you're watching Fag TV."

The comment amused Hagen, though he was careful to hide it.

"I beg your pardon?" Maxwell asked.

"You know, the homo station. I tell you, those guys are everywhere, aren't they?"

Maxwell replied, "If you mean the homosexual community, don't you believe it's about time they receive the respect and recognition they deserve?"

The kid shrugged, setting his toolbox on the chair below the TV. "Do you?" he asked.

"Of course."

He turned to the congressman. "You too?"

Hagen glanced at him then nodded.

He returned to his toolbox. "Well, that's good, man, that's good." Then, looking back to the congressman he added, "Especially for you."

"What do you mean?" Maxwell asked.

"Well, considering, you know, whose heart he's got and everything—considering where it came from."

Hagen frowned and cleared his throat. "I beg your pardon?"

"Your heart, your heart, man. Considering it came from my cousin—Hector, I mean."

"Excuse me?"

"Yeah. Used to be a switch hitter on the Boulevard." Rummaging in his toolbox he continued, "Big-time homosexual hooker. Best on the street, I hear. Top dollar. Till Dr. Griffin had him killed so they could put his ticker inside you."

Hagen threw an alarmed look to his aide.

The kid glanced up and pondered. "Wonder what that's like, you know, havin' a homo heart inside you. Personally, it would creep me out, you know what I mean. I'd be afraid it would make me start, you know, lookin' at guys different. You haven't noticed a difference or anything, have you?"

With growing anger, the congressman started to answer, but the kid cut him off, lowering his voice and speaking directly to Maxwell. "I don't know, if I were you I'd be careful, man. I mean, who knows what that things doin' to his mind. Unless, of course, well, you know, unless you're also a—"

"Who are you?" the aide demanded.

"Me?" The kid flashed him a smile with one dead tooth. "Just your everyday TV repairman."

Maxwell repeated louder, "Who are you?"

"I'm a cockroach, man. Just ask Dr. Griffin."

"How do you . . ." Hagen tried unsuccessfully to hide his agitation. "How do you know Dr. Griffin?"

"From the Orbolitz Group, man. Yeah, we go way back— all the way to his Freak Shop on Las Posas." Without missing a beat, he continued, "Listen, I've got another cousin, owns a gay porno shop over on Sunset. I mean, if you're looking for different action now. He's got some very, very specialized—"

"Get him out of here!" Hagen called to the security agent.

The agent started forward.

"Get him out!"

"I'm going, man, I'm going." The kid closed his box. "No need to be inhospitable. But listen, next time you see Dr. Griffin—"

"*Out!*"

The agent grabbed him by the arm and led him toward the exit just as the door opened revealing Gerald Larson, the chief administrator, along with some Asian girl.

"Excuse us," the agent said, strong-arming the boy through the door—but not before the kid greeted the girl. "Hey, Gita, I just told the congressman 'bout Hector's heart."

"You what?"

"Fill him in on the details if you want, but he seemed pretty excited about it. Told him how Griffin killed my cousin so he could—"

"Out!" Hagen cried. "Get him out!"

"Congressman," the administrator started, "I apologize if there's—"

"Out! All of you! Out!"

The agent spread his arms, forcing all three back through the door, as the kid called over his shoulder, "Don't forget 'bout my uncle—he can set you up with anything you—"

The door closed. It was only then Hagen noticed how heavily he was breathing. He couldn't seem to catch his breath. Maxwell moved to his side. "Sir, are you all right?"

Struggling to keep his voice calm, he ordered, "Call Griffin."

"Sir, I don't think that's such a—"

He pointed at the phone and ordered, "Call Dr. Griffin and call him now!"

"Try it again," Preacher Man called from under the hood. David turned the ignition. Nothing. Just like the last half dozen times.

"Hang on."

David rolled his head, trying to work out the tightness that had gripped his skull. Precious minutes were slipping away. Luke was already heading to the Orbolitz complex, no doubt to the VR lab. And then what? To try to save Emily? *Hang on, I'm coming to get you*—weren't those the last lines he'd written? Gita had insisted that it wasn't Emily, that someone had programmed her into the computer. Maybe they had, maybe they hadn't. He didn't know anymore. He was so spent and exhausted, there wasn't much he did know . . . except that they had killed her. They had killed his daughter and he had let them. More than that—by forcing her to take the medicine, he had helped them. And now they were going after his son!

David shuddered, remembering his own experience in the VR chamber, how his own body had nearly shut down from exposure to the simulated death. And now his son? Now they were luring his son in there to do the same thing? No! David pressed his forehead, trying to physically clear his mind, to stop it from spinning. No! It had happened once, they had taken his first child; they would not get his second!

Impatiently, he looked at his watch. It had been twenty minutes since they'd decided to rescue Luke—just Preacher Man, himself . . . and Lawrence.

"It will serve no purpose for me to sit here," Lawrence had complained at the shelter's computer. "Luis obviously has his own agenda. There is nothing I can do to assist him." Turning to David he had added, "And your girlfriend, she's safe and out of the picture. So there's no one left to help but you."

David had nodded. Gita would be long gone from there by now. But long gone to where? Even with Luke and Emily heavy on his heart, there was still room to worry about Gita.

"How can you help us?" Preacher Man had asked Lawrence.

"There just might be a security issue or two, have you ever stopped to consider that? And if there is, I just might be able to offer some insight, did you ever think about that?"

Admittedly, Preacher Man hadn't. Reluctantly, he complied.

And, miraculously, they had caught a bus going the direction they wanted it to go at the time they wanted to go (a real miracle in Los Angeles). Now, as the sun began setting, street action around Echo Park had started to pick up.

"Give it another try," Preacher Man called.

David turned the key. Again there was nothing.

Preacher Man wiped his hands on a cloth and shut the hood. The metal creaked and groaned in protest. "I can't figure it out. Thought it was a clogged fuel line, but—"

Suddenly, the car behind them roared to life. David glanced in the rearview mirror and saw Lawrence emerge from the driver's side of an ugly, baby-blue Cadillac.

"What'd you do, son?" Preacher Man shouted. "Hot-wire that thing?"

"Didn't I say there would be security issues? Now are we going or what?"

David looked at Preacher Man, then quickly scrambled out of the car. They headed to the rusting Cadillac and climbed in—Preacher Man taking the front passenger seat, David the back.

"Is everybody set?" Lawrence asked as they slammed their doors.

"Let's go," David ordered. "Let's go!"

"All right, all right!" Lawrence dropped the car in gear and swerved into the traffic, causing more than one car to slam on its brakes and blast its horn.

W here is David?"
Gita had used what little money she had left to grab
a taxi from the hospital and head back to the shelter. Amidst
all the hospital confusion it had been easy to slip away. She'd
caught a glimpse of Luis heading back for the video van, but
thought better of following him. Instead, she chose to return
to David, repair whatever damage Luis had done, and decide
upon the next move. But when she arrived there was no
David, no Lawrence, no preacher—only Adrianna and Starr,
who were busy changing sheets on the cots.

"We tried to stop him," Adrianna replied.

"Where is he?"

Starr answered, a cigarette dangling from her mouth,
"Went to see your boss."

"He what?"

"Yeah, over in Malibu."

"That is—that is not possible!"

"Possible or not, that's where he is."

Adrianna explained, "They tricked his son into going
there—to try and rescue his dead sister. Your man took off as
soon as he found out."

Gita stared in disbelief. But only for a second. She spun
around and started for the hall. She'd have to go to the complex. Who knew what Griffin was pulling. What trap David
was stepping into. But she'd barely reached the dormitory
door before she stopped and turned. "Does anybody have a
car? Is there a car I may borrow?"

Adrianna shook her head. "Sorry."

"A car?" Starr quipped, taking a drag from her cigarette.
"No problem."

Adrianna looked at her. "What are you talking about? You
don't have a car."

Starr gave a smile then swaggered toward Gita. "It's Friday
night, why would we need a car?"

Gita frowned. "I do not understand. I must go to the Santa
Monica Mountains near Malibu."

Starr broke into a mischievous grin. "A couple hot babes like us on a Friday night." Flipping her stringy hair aside, she wrapped an arm around Gita's waist and headed for the door. "We'll go there, girlfriend. We'll go wherever we want."

Thick evening fog crept over the mountains as Griffin's BMW Z8 slid around the hairpin curves of Decker Canyon. He was on his way to the 101 Freeway and he was not happy. The last thing he wanted was to drive all the way into town to hold the congressman's hand. But the phone call had made it clear the situation had to be taken care of immediately.

"What have you done?" Hagen had shouted into the receiver.

"Pardon me?"

"Have I got some pervert's heart in me?"

Griffin had gone cold. "What?"

"Answer me!"

"What—what are you talking about? I don't understand what—"

"Did you give me some pervert's heart? Is that what you put inside me?"

"Sir, is this line secure?"

"Answer me!"

"How . . . where did you hear such a thing?"

"I swear to God, Griffin." He heard the man breathing heavily. "You know I hate their filth. They're disgusting. And you had the gall to—"

"Congressman—"

"And a greaseball to boot? Some slimy wetback?"

"Sir, if you'll—"

"Hector? His name was *Hector!*" Hagen coughed out the words, "A gay *and* Hispanic!" He paused, catching his breath. "A taco-eating queer? What have you done to me, Griffin? What have you done?"

"Congressman Hagen—"

The man resumed coughing.

"Are you all right?"

"You get down here and you get down here now!"

"Yes, sir. I'll—"

*Click.*

"Hello? Hello?" That's when Griffin knew it was time for an immediate visit. It had taken him longer than anticipated to wrap up and get going. But when he finally left he put his assistant, Wendell Nordstrom, in charge, giving clear instructions what to do with Kauffman's son when he arrived and what to do with Kauffman himself. Now he was racing down Decker Canyon through the thickening fog. He had not called 3316, he had not called anyone. With luck, Hagen would have the sense to do likewise. How did he know? How had he made the connection? He even had the name. No one knew the name. No one but—

Headlights glared, jarring him from his thoughts. He swerved hard to his right, but caught the left side of a car, hearing and feeling the sick shriek of metal against metal. Instinctively, he slammed on his brakes and slid to a stop. The car, an old Cadillac, did the same.

Griffin sat a moment, catching his breath. Then he stomped on the accelerator and took off—tires spitting mud and gravel. Hit and run, that's what he'd tell the insurance company. It was hit and run.

Ten minutes after their near collision on Decker Canyon, David sat in the stolen Cadillac, his head pounding and swimming. They'd parked a hundred yards from the Orbolitz gate, out of view of the security cameras. Now they were wasting valuable time shooting down each other's plans on how to get inside.

"All I'm saying," Lawrence insisted, "is that once we cut the lines to the cameras I can rewire the security box and open the gate within thirty seconds."

"I understand," Preacher Man argued. "But how likely is it that some guard's gonna sit still once he loses the picture?"

Lawrence sighed heavily.

"He's right." David rolled his head, stretching his neck. "Let's just circle the fence by foot and see if there's some other way to get over it—"

"Or through it," Preacher Man added.

Lawrence sulked, "Talk about unlikely."

"You're the computer whiz," David snapped. "Why didn't you hack into their system before we left?"

"Because you didn't give me time to think."

"Help us with security?" David muttered. "What did you expect to find, a mat with a key under it?"

"David," Preacher Man cautioned.

David closed his eyes, fighting for control.

"All right," Lawrence replied. "I will go, but you have to know that I do not appreciate—"

The rapping on the passenger's window caused all three to jump. David turned to see a thin young man with a stringy goatee. He was accompanied by a security guard.

"Mr. Kauffman?" The man smiled at him through the glass. He looked vaguely familiar as he motioned for the window to be lowered.

"Yes?" David fumbled for the power button, but it would not cooperate. He reached for the door handle.

"What are you doing?" Lawrence reached past him for the door.

David pushed him aside and opened it. The door creaked loudly.

"Mr. Kauffman? I'm Wendell Nordstrom. Dr. Griffin's associate. We met the other day at the VR lab."

"Yes, yes, of course," David heard himself say, as he opened the door further and rose from the car. "I've uh . . . that is, we . . ." He looked around, hard pressed to find an excuse for where they'd parked.

"Come on." Nordstrom motioned toward the gate. "We've been waiting for you."

N obody knows?" Hagen bellowed. "What do you mean, nobody knows?"

Griffin tried to reason. "All I'm saying is that if we stay calm, we can keep this contained—"

The congressman struggled to rise on one elbow. "Contained?"

"Congressman . . ." The aide laid his hand on Hagen's shoulder, trying to ease him back down, but the man would have none of it. His face was red, and his forehead wet with perspiration.

Griffin tried again. "I agree, there seems to be a minor leak of information, but it's really nothing we can't—"

"I have a pervert's heart beating inside of me! Do you understand that? Some degenerate, wetback's heart, and you have the gall—" He gasped for a breath. "And you have the gall to tell me it's—"

"Sir." Again the aide tried to ease him back—this time successfully as Hagen took a moment to breathe.

Griffin watched, hoping the situation would cool. His cell phone chirped. He did not answer it, but reached into his pocket and switched it to vibrate. Then, speaking as calmly as possible, he explained, "We can find these people, I assure you. We can insist upon their discretion, or their—"

"Or their what?" Hagen demanded.

"Their . . . removal."

"You know them, then?" the aide asked.

"Yes," Griffin lied, though he had a good idea. "And believe me, if it comes down to their word or ours—who is the public going to believe? Some Latino greaser, or—"

"Hey, Dr. Griffin. How's it goin', man?"

Griffin spun to the door. No one was there.

"Up here. I'm up here, man."

Griffin turned to the TV and spotted the street kid on the screen, the one whose finger he'd broken.

"So how you doin'?" The kid grinned his dead-tooth grin.

"Where—where are you?" Griffin demanded.

"You know us cockroaches, man. We're everywhere."

Griffin quickly scanned the room until he spotted the security camera in the corner. He threw a glance to Hagen. The man's eyes were wide with surprise and rage.

The aide stepped toward the TV. "What do you want? What are you hoping to get out of this little game?"

"Oh, it's no game, man. Just ask Dr. Griffin there."

Feeling the eyes turn to him, Griffin took a half step forward. "Listen, uh . . ."

"Luis."

"Listen, Luis. I don't know what you know—or what you think you know—but whatever you've dreamed up won't survive under the light of cold, hard facts."

"It won't." The kid cocked his head. "Tell me, el Doctor, what exactly do I know?"

Griffin hesitated, unsure how to respond. The aide saved him the trouble.

"Luis, listen, son. This is no way to carry on a conversation. If you have something to share, then we need to get together, discuss it face-to-face."

"Yeah." The kid nodded. "I get you. I mean, who knows who could be listening, right?"

"Exactly."

"Yeah." Suddenly an idea came to him. "Hey, Mr. Congressman. Remember I was talkin' 'bout my uncle's porn video shop in Sunset?"

Griffin threw a look at the congressman. His face was redder and covered in perspiration.

"Well, I got something you'll like even better." The kid reached in front of him. "Check it out, man."

Suddenly his image was replaced by a high-angle shot of a hospital room. *Their* hospital room. Only Griffin wasn't there. Just the congressman and the aide.

"*One wonders which is worse, pushy Jews or pushy queers,*" Hagen was saying.

"*I hear you,*" the aide chuckled.

Griffin spun to the aide who stood, staring up at the screen in disbelief. Then to Hagen, whose color continued to darken.

"*Just to have them touch me makes my skin crawl.*"

Griffin looked back to the TV as the congressman continued:

"*If there was one mistake we made in history, it was stopping Hitler too soon—after he was done removing the Jews, next on his list would have been the homosexuals.*"

Luis's face popped back onto the screen. "Now that's what I call entertainment!"

The aide was the first to find his voice. "What ... what do you want?"

"What you got?"

The congressman growled, "Listen, you little—"

"But wait," the kid interrupted, suddenly sounding like an infomercial. "There's more. If you're the first thirty to forty million national TV viewers to see that, then you won't want to miss ..."

Again the picture changed to the hospital room. This time Hagen was on the phone shouting: "*Did you give me some pervert's heart? Is that what you put inside me?*"

A jump cut in the video showed the congressman coughing and shouting: "*A gay and Hispanic! A taco-eating queer? What have you done to me, Griffin? What have you done?*"

Griffin felt his cell phone vibrate in his pocket. He turned to Hagen, who was breathing even harder. Luis reappeared on the screen, pretending to listen to a newscaster's earpiece as he spoke, "We interrupt this program with an even juicer quote."

Again the picture changed. Now Griffin saw himself standing beside Hagen's bed as the man gasped and shouted, "*I have a pervert's heart beating inside of me! Do you understand that? Some degenerate, wetback's heart, and you have the gall—*"

Griffin's TV image interrupted, "We can find these people, I assure you. We can insist upon their discretion, or their — "

"Or their what?"

"Their . . . removal. Believe me, if it comes down to their word or ours — who is the public going to believe? Some Latino greaser, or — "

Luis popped back on the screen, grinning. "I just love home videos, don't you?"

But Griffin was too distracted by Hagen's gasps to respond. The congressman's eyes were bulging; his face had turned burgundy. A quick glance to the wall monitors confirmed Griffin's suspicion. The man was going into cardiac arrest. Fortunately, the monitors had also alerted the nurses' station. The doors flew open with a nurse and a crash cart.

"Clear the room!" the big woman ordered.

There was confusion and some protesting by the aide.

"Clear the room! The man is in V-fib!"

The security agent moved to herd Griffin and the aide out.

As he was pushed through the door, Griffin felt his phone vibrate again. He took several steps into the hall before pulling it out and with shaking hands opening it.

It was a text message. Two words:

Kauffman's here.

All Dr. Griffin said was to keep an eye out for you."

"That's it?" David demanded. "He didn't say anything about my son?"

"Who?"

"Luke, my son. He didn't say anything?"

Wendell Nordstrom shook his head. "No. Not a word."

David paused, searching the technician. He wasn't sure if he believed him or not. "But he knew *I* was coming."

Nordstrom nodded. "He suspected you might, yes. He said, 'If you see Kauffman, bring him to the VR lab and wait for me.' That's all he said."

David began to pace. They were below the VR console directly in front of the chambers. "And no boy has been admitted. Twelve, tall, skinny?"

"By himself? Without an adult?" Nordstrom shook his head. "It's against policy. All minors have to be accompanied by an adult."

David closed his eyes, trying to think through the pounding headache, the rage, the exhaustion. He was on empty now, flying on fumes.

"He might have gotten lost," Preacher Man offered. "These mountain roads can be tricky. And if he's only twelve—"

David turned back to Nordstrom. "Griffin knows I'm here?"

"You saw me text-message him."

David nodded, his mind chasing itself, trying to figure the game.

"Listen," Nordstrom asked, "can I get you guys something while we wait?"

Preacher Man shook his head. David didn't bother.

"What about you?" Nordstrom turned to the control console above them—the console that Lawrence had been studying ever since they arrived in the lab.

"I'm fine," Lawrence said. "Listen, if all we're doing is waiting around, would you, you know—" He motioned to the controls in front of him.

"Explain some of it to you?" Nordstrom asked.

"Well, yes, I mean, if it's not classified or anything."

The technician chuckled and stepped up onto the platform. "No, there's nothing classified here. State of the art, maybe, but nothing you haven't heard or read about. Actually, it's not all that complicated. Over here is . . ."

As the two talked, drifting from earshot, David continued to pace, rubbing his neck, trying to clear his mind.

"What you thinking, brother?"

He glanced up to see Preacher Man beside him. "I don't know. The pieces are there, but—"

Preacher Man nodded. "We know somebody talked to your son over the computer; they pretended to be your daughter."

"Maybe."

"Maybe?"

"Maybe they weren't pretending."

Preacher Man's voice grew gentle. "Friend, your daughter's dead."

"I understand that, but—"

"I saw her, brother. Last night I was standing in her grave; I was looking down at her body."

"Right, but . . . maybe her spirit was trying to contact us." He glanced up to see the man shaking his head. He felt his anger returning. "How can you be so sure?"

The old man quoted softly, "'Absent from the body, present with the Lord.' Accordin' to the Bible there ain't no stoppin' off at séances or hidin' out in fancy machines. You're either dead or you're alive. You're either in your body or you're goin' to face God's glory and judgment."

David nodded, glancing to the chambers, remembering all too well the light he'd seen inside them. "But . . . there's got to be some exceptions."

Preacher Man shook his head. "Only two things contact us beyond the grave. And both are imposters. You've got your evil spirits, pretending to be loved ones—"

"Demons," David impatiently said, remembering his past conversations.

Preacher Man nodded. "Or you got con artists bilking folks outta their hard-earned money with fancy parlor tricks."

"You sound like Gita."

"We read the same Book."

David rubbed his head, scowling. "You're both positive that the Emily I contacted in there"—he motioned to the VR chambers—"was something programmed into the computer."

Preacher Man nodded.

"Which means the Emily who contacted Luke—"

"Was also man-made."

David nodded as the pieces arranged and rearranged themselves. "So we're back to someone pretending to be Emily to lure Luke here. But why?"

"Maybe it's not Luke they're after. Maybe he's just the bait."

David looked at him. "For me."

Preacher Man nodded.

"*If*," David emphasized, "what you and Gita say is correct."

The man held his gaze.

David looked back at the chambers. Everything seemed so real in there. But according to them it was all smoke and mirrors, carefully crafted illusions. Like the séance at Alcatraz. Like Emily's contact over the radio, his cell phone, the computer. Real or make-believe, true or false. On the surface they appeared identical—impossible for a person to tell the players without a program. A program . . . Gita and Preacher Man certainly felt they had one. And it certainly helped them see the difference . . . *if* it was right.

He recalled the pressure suit, the goggles, all of the paraphernalia necessary to—suddenly, he came to a stop. On the wall, near the third chamber, the small glass enclosure was open, its 3-D goggles missing.

He turned to the platform behind him. "Excuse me. Where are the goggles to that chamber?"

Nordstrom looked at him. "Pardon me?"

"The goggles. To that chamber. They're gone."

The technician blinked but did not speak.

"Is the chamber in use?"

Nordstrom continued to hesitate.

David moved around to the platform and stepped onto it, his mind already racing. "There's somebody in there, isn't there?"

Before Nordstrom could lie, David spotted one of the monitors. It was displaying an image he'd seen when he was inside. The image of the garden. "Who is it?" he demanded.

"That's, uh, proprietary information."

But it was information David suddenly pieced together. "How long?" he cried.

Again, Nordstrom hesitated.

"How long has he been in there?"

"Uh ..." Nordstrom glanced at the digital readout on the console. "Nineteen minutes. He entered just before you arrived."

David exploded. He stormed the technician and grabbed him by the collar, pulling him into his face.

"David!" Preacher Man called.

"What are you doing?" Lawrence cried.

"Tell them!" David roared.

Nordstrom sputtered. David spun him around and shoved him hard against a bank of instruments. The entire platform shook. "Tell them who's inside that chamber!"

Eyes wide in fear, Nordstrom repeated, "I–I can't! Proprietary information. Dr. Griffin will be here shortly. He can—"

Incensed, David flung him against the opposite console. "Nineteen minutes! He'll be dead by then!"

He heard Preacher Man approach. "Brother ..."

But he did not respond. He pulled the technician back into his face, shouting, spittle flying. "You know it and I know it!"

"Dav—"

"He's got my kid in there!" He shouted into Nordstrom's face. "Don't you!"

"No, no—"

"*Liar!*" Unable to contain his anger, David threw him across the platform. The technician stumbled and fell. "Shut it down! Shut it down now!"

"I can't!"

David started for him. "You will, or I swear—"

The technician scrambled backwards. "It will kill him! Don't you remember? The shock to the system is too great! It will kill the participant!"

David hesitated. He did remember. And he remembered how Griffin had to intervene to save him, how it had been the only thing that had saved his life. Instantly, a thought took shape. "Then suit me up."

"What?"

"Suit me up, now!"

"I can't!" Nordstrom rose unsteadily to his feet. "Not without authorization!"

Once again, David lunged at him. Only this time he grabbed him by the throat and began squeezing, squeezing with all his might.

Nordstrom coughed and gagged.

"David!" Preacher Man grabbed his shoulders, but he shook him off.

Nordstrom's eyes bulged.

"You will get me in there and you will get me in there now!"

Nordstrom continued gasping.

David tightened his grip. "Now!"

"David!"

Eyes ready to explode, Nordstrom nodded.

David released his hold but gave him no time to recover. As Nordstrom coughed and gagged, gasping for breath, he pulled the technician off the platform and toward the VR lockers. He caught worried glimpses from Preacher Man and Lawrence, heard their cautions, but he paid no attention. He paid attention to nothing but saving his son.

# thirteen

The door sealed shut with a hiss. David had wanted chamber two, to be closer to his son, but Nordstrom had said it was unavailable, that he was busy downloading and filtering raw data into it. Besides, it made no difference; once the program began, the experience would be identical. Of course, he'd insisted over and over again that it wasn't Luke inside the chamber, and over and over again David knew he was lying.

Now David stood alone in chamber one, nervously adjusting his goggles. He nervously glanced down to their left-hand corner and saw the digital readout:

*00:12:00*

It was double the time of his last foray, but his past exposure to the program had allowed him to build up some resistance. True, twelve minutes was pushing it, but he figured he needed all the time he could get. Earlier, as he had suited up and entered the chamber, there were the expected protests from the other three urging him to at least wait for Griffin to return. But David had made up his mind. He'd gone against his instincts in the past, and it had killed his daughter. He would not do it again with his son.

"All right," he ordered as he positioned his feet on the roller pad, "let's get started."

"Brother," Preacher Man spoke through the headset, still working him, still trying to change his mind. "A few more minutes won't make that much difference. And if this Griffin fellow knows—"

David reached to the intercom button on his collar and pressed it off. He was frightened enough; he didn't need more excuses to back out.

A moment later the walls of the chamber went black. The sound of rushing wind filled the speakers. Dark, indistinguishable figures once again blurred past, forming a tunnel. He adjusted his breathing, staying as close to the center as possible. The last thing he wanted was another encounter with one of the creatures. Up ahead, in the distance, he saw the light—awesome in its beauty and brilliance.

Luke had been in the program nearly twenty-four minutes and according to the monitors he was still alive. David wasn't sure how he'd survived this long without his system being fooled into shutting down ... and Nordstrom was giving no clues. He remembered Griffin saying something about younger, more elastic brains lasting longer. It really didn't matter. What mattered was that David would track him down. Wherever he was, David would find him and get him out before it was too late.

He rose toward the top of the tunnel—an indication that he was still breathing too hard. He forced himself to exhale and remain calm, working to keep his breathing even and constant. Looking back to the light, he began hearing the music. As before, it was awesome—majestic melodies, intricate rhythms, and harmonies that wanted to seep into his pores.

But he would not let it. Whatever solace the light provided, he would not accept it. He had another agenda. With determination, he forced himself to look from the center of the light to its rainbow edges. Still breathtaking, but the effects weren't quite as overpowering. He continued forward, approaching the end of the tunnel. At last the garden came into view with its glowing trees, its shimmering flowers, its shrubs and grass. And, of course, the people. So many people.

He glanced at his digital display for the remaining time:

    00:11:05

He exited the tunnel and slowed. As Griffin had taught him, he blew the air from his lungs and floated toward the ground and the people—all smiling, all waiting in eager anticipation. He began searching their faces. Luke was here somewhere. But where? With so many people, how could he possibly find him?

He'd not even landed before he saw heads tilting back up, looking past him. He followed their gaze, turning just in time to see someone reenter the tunnel. He caught only a fleeting glimpse of the form—gangly frame, skinny arms, long legs—

"Luke!"

Without hesitation, he inhaled and rose back toward the tunnel's entrance to catch his son.

But why? Why was he running? Surely he'd seen David's arrival. Everyone had. Why was his boy running from him?

As he approached the tunnel he felt its current. It seemed to flow in whatever direction he looked—as if his will somehow determined its course. And by turning away from the crowd and the light, by looking directly into the tunnel, he was immediately sucked into it. The sensation was unnerving, but he did not resist. Because there, just fifty yards ahead, was his boy.

He picked up speed.

So did his son.

"Luke!" he shouted over the wind. "Luke!"

The boy did not respond.

Once again David started rising toward the ceiling and once again he exhaled, forcing himself to stay centered in the tunnel. "Luke!"

Suddenly he heard a voice. "Three-quarter speed!"

Immediately, the program slowed. And, just as quickly, the blurred walls and ceiling took shape and definition. There they were, the spiny, amphibian-like creatures, shiny from the blood of their open wounds, their fangs bared as they screamed.

Stifling a gasp, David fought to keep his breathing as even as possible. But not his son. To his horror, he saw the boy rising toward the roof of the tunnel!

"Luke, no!"

The creatures scurried toward him, lunging with snapping claws and gnashing teeth.

"Luke!"

Then suddenly, and quite remarkably, his son disappeared between them.

*"Luke!"*

Keeping his eyes fixed on the exact location, David continued forward until he saw the opening—a hole in the black quartz, four to five feet in diameter. What had Griffin called them ... wormholes? A labyrinth of holes leading to, to ... he didn't remember. But, wherever they led, his son had just entered one and disappeared.

He drifted closer. Most of the creatures around the hole were small, the size of average dogs, scrambling and slithering over each other. But each one gave wide berth to the largest—a glistening, reptilian-faced gargoyle, nearly the size of a man. Spotting David, the thing hissed and bared its fangs, slashing the air as it darted back and forth across the hole's entrance. It appeared outraged at Luke's passage and was not about to let another get by.

But David had no choice. His son was in there. Despite memories of his last encounter, he slowed to a stop, just beyond the gargoyle's flailing arms and talons. Carefully, he watched the creature, searching for any pattern in its movement—when it would snap and snarl, when it would dash and scurry. In some ways it reminded him of a crab, the way it darted back and forth across the entrance. But there was a rhythm, distinct times, fractions of seconds when the opening was clear. Clear enough to pass. It would be close, but as Luke had proven, it was possible.

David waited, watching and calculating. Then, at the exact moment, he inhaled sharply and flew toward the ceiling. The creature tried to counter, to adjust its movement, but it was too late. David entered the hole headfirst. He nearly made it past the gargoyle until it dove and caught his left calf with its claws, then sank its fangs deep into his heel. David screamed and slammed his foot against the jagged entrance, once, twice. But the creature hung on, shrieking in its own pain. The third slam loosened its grip, but not enough. Shoving his foot back outside the hole, David dragged it hard across the razor-sharp stones, shredding the animal's face, but cutting his own foot as well. The thing howled, opening its jaws and releasing him. David quickly tucked in and inhaled. He shot up through the tube. He could hear the thing screeching and roaring behind him, but it did not pursue.

The capillary quickly narrowed until it was the size of a large man's chest. He tried not to touch its sides, but brushing against them was inevitable. And when he did, he noticed they were not solid at all. Unlike the opening into the main tunnel with the scurrying creatures and sharp quartz rock, these walls felt like ... fog. Icy, black fog. So cold that wherever he touched them, he felt the heat of his body being sucked away.

He glanced at his remaining time:

00:09:48

Several yards above, at the far end of the tube, he saw a deep, red glow. It was punctuated by bright flashes and flickerings—as if a giant electrical storm was in progress. Accompanying the flashes were crackling snaps and pops, obvious sounds of energy being discharged. There was no music here. Only the fading screams of the gargoyle behind him, and the storm ahead.

Again David was amazed at the power of his own will to direct his course. He didn't know how that translated into the computer program; maybe it was unconscious movements of his head or body within the VR suit. Whatever the case, it made him think of his first meeting with Preacher Man. How he'd said it was his own will that had driven him out of heaven. David didn't know about that, but he did know it was his own will that had brought him to where he was now.

But where was that?

And where was Luke?

As he approached the end of the capillary more and more of the flashing sky came into view. He exhaled to slow and finally came to a stop. Then, ever so cautiously, he raised his head up and out of the opening.

It was some sort of . . . cavern. Huge. Immense. There were thousands of other tubes and openings, just like his, jutting up like giant stalagmites. And a hundred feet below them, surrounding the base of these tubes were . . . people. A vast sea of people. But, unlike the garden, none of these people were looking up at him. Instead, each was screaming and writhing, lost in pain. And for good reason. The red glow he had seen did not radiate from a central light source. Instead, the cavern was lit by the glow of their burning flesh. Arms, heads, torsos, portions of their bodies, igniting, flaring up, and burning before dripping and falling into a lake that rose to their waists. A lake, not of water, but of fire.

Panic seized David. "Luke!" He spun around, searching in all directions. *"Luke!"*

But he did not see him. Nor, did he figure, could he be heard over the continual shrieks and screams. Still his son was there, somewhere. He took a shallow breath and finished rising out of the capillary. Looking to the left, he willed himself beyond the tube. Once clear, he exhaled and dropped toward the burning lake.

H ow much farther?" Starr wheezed. They'd been running through the rain less than five minutes and she was already out of breath.

Gita nodded up the dirt path that she often frequented during her noon-hour jogs. "Just a few hundred yards."

"No sweat," Starr gasped.

Gita eased back on their pace. Starr had been right. It had taken little effort for the two of them to be picked up on the Boulevard. And little more to convince their "dates" that they had a particular romantic place in mind up on Mulholland Drive—more precisely near Decker Canyon and Mulholland.

Fortunately for Gita, her date had been driving. All she had to endure was the lingering stench of marijuana, spilled beer, and the leers of the balding thirtysomething. She'd been more concerned for Starr in the back. But the girl had held her own with an incessant stream of chatter. Nonetheless, the men, the smells, and the raw lewdness had stirred vivid, horrific memories deep within Gita.

God was at it again. It hadn't been enough for Him to make her watch others live out her past—now He'd dropped her into the very center of it, forcing her to actually experience what she'd denied for so long. And, strangely enough, she was beginning to understand the reason. What had Adrianna said?

*"They can't fully love others ... 'cause they don't know how fully loved they are."*

God was tenderly yet thoroughly stripping her, "scalping her naked soul." He was showing her what she'd really been like, the complete foulness of who she'd been ... to prove the complete depth of who He was.

*"Amazing, isn't it ... The Creator of the universe loves us more than His own life. Regardless of what we've done. And once we get ahold of that, I mean, once we really understand and accept that, then the love, it just starts gushing out, and there's nothing we can do to stop it."*

It was as if He forced her to see everything she'd been—clearly, without denial—so He could prove He loved her ...

*more than His own life.* For this it was necessary to revisit everything . . . except the actual sinning.

Thanks to Starr's pepper spray and Gita's knowledge of self-defense, the sinning wasn't necessary. Once they arrived at a secluded spot, the girls had suddenly changed their minds. The boys had insisted that was not an option and were in the midst of proving it when Starr had emptied the can of pepper spray on her date and Gita had exercised a little Tae Kwon Do on hers. Of course she felt terrible about the blatant dishonesty and manipulation, but figured she'd just add it to the rest of the day's list.

Now the two ran up a dirt path that led to the back of the Orbolitz compound. There would be no cars and their dates would not be looking for them here. Once the compound's fence came into view, they could circle to the gate and enter with her security code.

The electrical storm continued as David, remaining close to the towering capillary, lowered himself toward the lake of burning bodies. At one hundred feet from the surface he could feel the heat. By forty, it was nearly unbearable.

"My son!" he shouted to the burning corpses. "Have any of you seen my son?"

But no one heard. They were too immersed in their own pain.

He forced himself to drop lower, wincing against the heat, raising a hand to shield his eyes. The closer he approached the lake, the more he realized that the people were not only writhing and screaming . . . they were also involved in very specific activities. Independent and totally oblivious to those around them, each was enacting some sort of crazy pantomime.

He glanced at his time remaining:

*00:09:15*

He drifted closer to one of the burning bodies—a woman, as best he could tell by what remained of her flesh. He watched as she appeared to pour the contents of a nonexistent bottle into a nonexistent glass. She raised the glass to her burning skull and tried to drink. But of course there was nothing to drink; it was only an illusion. Realizing the fact, she glared at her hand and shrieked in unfulfilled desire . . . which ignited even more of her body.

Then, as if suddenly forgetting, she saw another imaginary bottle, grasped it with her burning hand, poured it into her imaginary glass, and raised the glass to her bare, gleaming teeth until the illusion again evaporated and she again screamed in rage. And so the cycle continued. Though there were minor variations, the basic action repeated itself again and again . . . each time igniting more and more of her flesh.

Another cry drew David's attention to his left. He guessed the corpse to be a man's, though so much of his flesh had burned away it was hard to tell. He seemed to be grabbing fistfuls of imaginary food and shoving them toward his open jaw. Each time his hand arrived, he would breathe in as if savoring the aroma, then cram the contents into his mouth. Only then would he realize that his hand was empty. He could see food, he could smell it—but when he tried eating it, it did not exist. And with the realization came his desperate scream and the flaring up of more flames . . . before the pantomime started over again.

David looked on, trying to remember, trying to understand if this also related to what Preacher Man had said. Was this more free will being enacted? Was this what he meant about life molding the clay until death's kiln hardened it? Were these people merely enacting what they had permanently decided?

And the fire, the flames that charred and burned and melted—they didn't originate from outside these creatures; they didn't even come from the lake. No, the flames were coming from within them—lapping and leaping from inside them—as if the insatiable hunger inside was so hot that it ignited them, consuming all of who they were—mentally and physically.

David heard another scream and spun around to see a younger cadaver. It seemed to be leering at an unseen partner. It raised its burning hands, moving them through the fiery air, as if undressing the person—caressing them, fondling what was in reality nothing but smoke and flame. And then, just as he was about to pantomime the very act of sex itself, everything dissolved before him and he realized he was holding nothing, caressing no one. Outraged, burning with unquenched desire, he screamed in torture . . . until he spotted another imaginary partner, reached out to caress her, and began the pattern all over again.

David glanced at his time. He was down to:

*00:08:32*

He looked out across the burning sea of people, each entrapped in his own private prison, each suffering his own self-induced hell. Off to his left, not a hundred yards away in the red flickering light, he saw someone else hovering over the lake. The thin, wiry body was leaning over, carefully studying a burning corpse fifty feet below it.

"Luke!" David willed himself forward, quickly closing the distance. "Luke!"

But the boy did not respond. And the closer David approached, the more he realized the reason. The arms and legs were as skinny as his boy's. He was just as gangly and nearly as tall. But this person was not his son. He was too stooped. And his hair. At this closeness David could see that it was gray and thinning. Was it possible? All of this time had he been pursuing the wrong person?

David slowed to a stop, less than twenty feet away. The man did not look up, but remained bent over, examining the burning cadaver.

"Who . . ." David cleared his voice and shouted over the screams, "Who are you?"

The man did not look at him.

David floated closer. "I said, who are you?"

At last he spoke, his voice thin and airy. "I s'pose in this particular place, that really ain't the question." He raised his head, looking out across the burning sea. "I'm bettin' the more appropriate question is . . . who are *you?*"

David swallowed, studying the old man's profile. "Where is my son? Do you know where my son is?"

"Your son?" The man shrugged.

David drifted closer, striving to stay in control. "Who are you? Are you one of Griffin's associates? One of his employees?"

"An employee?" The man chuckled. "Hardly."

A nd the boy never showed up?" Griffin demanded as he peeled off his jacket and joined Wendell Nordstrom behind the VR console.

Wendell shook his head. "Best we figured, he got lost in the mountains. Kid's not even old enough to drive."

Griffin nodded. Not that it made any difference, now that they had the father. "How long has he been in there?" He motioned toward the VR chambers. "What do they have left?"

Wendell looked to the digital readouts for chambers one and three. "Kauffman has just under eight minutes."

"And Mr. Orbolitz?"

"Close to thirty."

Griffin looked at the two video monitors before him, each displaying what the men saw through their goggles. The burning, suffering forms in the background made it clear they had passed through the wormholes and had entered the giant, infinite cave.

"You've tried communicating?" he asked.

"Mr. Orbolitz never opens his intercom."

"And Kauffman?"

"He shut it off before he started."

Griffin swore. It was a lousy break that Orbolitz was using PNEUMA when Kauffman arrived. Just as lousy that Wendell had allowed Kauffman to enter the first chamber—though all three could be run independently. But now that they were communicating, now that the two programs were linked, there was no way to shut down one without affecting the other. The shock would be too great to both men's systems. And, if Kauffman discovered the truth, there was no telling what he'd do to Orbolitz. The last thing Griffin wanted on his hands was another murder . . . or two. But it wouldn't be murder if he could lure his boss away and encourage Kauffman to stay over his allotted time. Isn't that what happened his first time inside? Regardless, it was important for Orbolitz's safety to get in there and separate them as quickly as possible.

"All right." He motioned to the other two visitors who had come with Kauffman—some gay kid and an old black man. "Let's clear the lab. Get them out of here."

"Where?" Wendell asked.

"I don't care!" Griffin snapped as he reached over to adjust chamber two's calibrations. "Take them to the cafeteria. Buy them a cup of coffee. Anyplace but here."

"But—"

"I don't want them in this room!"

"Why not?" the black man spoke up. "You planning on hurting him?"

Griffin answered without looking. "Whatever happens to him will be his choice, old man, not mine."

The gay kid spoke. "You're planning to kill him, aren't you?"

Griffin glanced to the boy and saw definite attitude. He could be trouble. Turning to Wendell, he ordered, "Call Security."

"I can handle it," Wendell said as he stepped off the platform and reached for the kid's arm. "Come on."

The boy shrugged him off. "Honestly. Do you really believe, in your wildest dreams, that you can just herd us away while you kill our friend?"

"Nobody's killing any—"

"I am staying right here!"

Once again, Wendell grabbed the boy's arm.

The youth resisted. "Let go of me." He tried pushing Wendell away and a scuffle began.

Griffin shouted impatiently. "Wendell!" But they continued to struggle. Irritated, he hit the intercom button. "Security—VR lab. Stat!" He glanced up to see the old man enter the fray, trying to separate them.

"Lawrence . . . son!"

The struggle was almost comical—a feeble old man, one queen, and one geek. It was not so comical when they tripped over themselves, tumbled to the floor, and Wendell slammed his head against the corner of the console. He went out like a light.

Griffin sighed at the annoyance and returned to the controls just as two security guards entered. "Get them out of here," he ordered.

The guards moved to action, one pulling the old man and the boy to their feet, the other kneeling to examine Wendell.

Distracted by the commotion, not to mention the pressure of time, Griffin decided the calibrations were close enough. He raced off the platform, side-stepped his unconscious assistant and the guard, and quickly headed to the VR locker.

"Is he gonna be okay?" the old man asked.

Griffin didn't reply. He had more important things on his mind. He spoke to the locker. "Dr. Richard Griffin. Suit."

The door slid aside and he removed his VR suit.

"You ain't goin' in there, are you?"

Griffin ignored him and glanced at Wendell as the guard helped him to his feet—dazed, barely coherent.

"Get them out of here. All of them."

The guards nodded and moved the three toward the hallway. The old man tried to resist and shouted, "He said chamber two was unusable. He said—"

But the old-timer was no match for the security guards as the men hustled him along. Nor was Griffin listening. He was too occupied with how to confront Mr. Orbolitz and separate him from Kauffman. And after that? After that, it looked like he would have no alternative but to make sure David Kauffman never left PNEUMA alive.

"—said somethin 'bout downloadin' some—"

"Get them out of here!" Griffin shouted at the annoyance as he suited up. "Now!"

W ho are you?" David repeated. "What do you have to do with the Orbolitz Group?"

The floating figure adjusted his goggles as he continued looking out over the sea of bodies. "Like I said, I don't reckon our names are too important. Not in this place. Neither, I figure, is our position." He glanced back down at the burning cadaver he'd been studying and continued more quietly, "Only our passion."

David followed his gaze to the tortured figure. It seemed to be in the midst of a workout—frantically doing jumping jacks, then side bends, then skipping an imaginary rope—each jerk of movement causing intense pain as more of its flesh ignited and fell away. Finally, after curling imaginary weights, it sucked in what was left of its gut and posed before what must have been a mirror. But instead of a muscular, sculptured body, it saw the reality of its burning, melting flesh. It screamed in horror—which caused more flames to rise up, setting even more of its flesh on fire.

Turning from the grotesqueness David again asked, "Do you know where my son is?"

"One question at a time, ol' buddy, one question at a time." His calmness infuriated David. Looking across the sea, he said, "So tell me, what do you think this here place is all about?"

"I think they're people," David impatiently answered. "Dead people ... who somehow got caught up and trapped in their own passions."

"Nope." The man shook his head. "'Course that's what I used to think too—during my first visits. But it's more than that. These people here, they ain't imprisoned by their passions. They've *become* their passions."

The creature below screamed. David looked back to see it turning from its imaginary mirror and beginning the work-out cycle all over again.

"And you think they've been pretty foolish, don't you," the old man said, "puttin' their passion into such uselessness?"

"Please, just tell me if you know where my—"

"Don't you?"

"Yes, yes. They are foolish and they are to be pitied. Now if you'll just—"

"But exactly what type of foolishness is it, David Kauffman?"

The use of his name caught him off guard. "What do you mean?"

"Come with me." The old man drifted several yards away until he hovered over a burning woman. Only a patch or two of hair remained and large portions of her chest were missing. But there were still features of her face. At the moment she was bent over and seemed to be talking, even smiling, to what must have been an imaginary child or children.

Despite the searing heat, David willed himself closer.

She continued listening and talking, often breaking into gentle laughter. The imaginary companions seemed to bring her great joy . . . until she finally reached out to embrace them and discovered there was no one there. She looked about desperately, searching for them in all directions, but no one could be found. And, realizing her abandonment, an agonizing wail rose from within her breast and ignited more of her body.

Watching, the old man calmly observed, "We become whatever our passion is."

David nodded, watching with sadness. "A mother's love for her children."

"Not just a mother's love, Mr. Kauffman." The old man turned to him. "It could just as well be a father's."

"What?"

"That could just as easily be you down there."

David felt his anger rising. "It's not wrong to love our children."

The man gave a shrug. "We become our passion. That could be you . . . just as the fella consumed with his body could be me, or for that matter, any of these folks who lust after power, or wealth, or empires."

"You're . . ." Griffin swallowed, then stated his growing suspicion. "You're Norman Orbolitz."

The man nodded.

Filled with a dozen emotions, David spat out, "You had my daughter killed."

"Of course."

The feelings focused. "Why?" He seethed. He felt himself beginning to tremble. "What did she ever do to you? Why would you have an innocent child killed?"

Orbolitz did not respond.

Rage filled David's body. "Why? You're supposed to be this great, respected humanitarian!"

"That's what I hear." He looked out over the burning corpses. "But, as you see, things ain't always as they appear. Which is why I'm doin' everything I can to avoid this place— postponing my fate for as long as possible."

"Why her? Why my daughter?"

"Your daughter and me, we had identical tissue matches. The odds of that are pretty rare. Fact, our program has only found two other people in the whole region with that match. Sadly enough, I've already had to use them."

"Use them?"

"My first was a heart transplant, nearly three years ago. A college athlete. Quite satisfactory. Should keep me goin' for years."

David recoiled at the thought, but the man was not done.

"Then, thanks to some irritating diabetes, I had kidney and pancreas problems."

"Had?"

"She was a mother of three. Again the tissue match was perfect, which meant minimal complications and virtually no antirejection drugs. Nasty side effects, those drugs."

"But . . . my daughter—"

"Let's face it, son, she was a mental. Already tried to kill herself. The chances of that happening again were high—so high that she might not be around when I needed her. So . . . not liking to be wasteful, I simply sped up the process."

"Sped up?"

"Her suicide overdose."

David went limp, his rage suddenly draining. It took all of his effort just to croak, "So . . . it was *you*. Why?"

"They call it 'diabetic retinopathy'—when the whole retina falls apart."

"What are you talking about?"

"I'm talkin' about goin' blind, son. No cure. 'Cept for this newfangled operation they're experimentin' with where *everything* is replaced."

"What?"

Once again Orbolitz turned to face David. Only now as he turned, he removed his goggles. And, for the first time in months, David Kauffman looked directly into the beautiful violet blue eyes of his daughter.

# fourteen

To Griffin's surprise, the VR program did not begin with the dark tunnel and bright light. Instead, he seemed to be floating in some sort of star field. It surrounded him on all sides—up, down, around. He glanced at his digital readout.

00:27:45

That was his correct allotment. But where was he? He looked at the stars and tried to recognize them. Not a single constellation appeared familiar.

What was going on? Granted, he hadn't done as thorough a check on the system as he'd have liked, had been somewhat distracted, but this? He strained a moment to listen. There was no sound. No rushing wind. Only stillness.

Except for the whisperings. Like a soft breeze. So faint that at first he wasn't even sure he heard them.

He continued staring at the star field. It was unfamiliar, and yet there was something about it he had seen. And not so long ago.

The whisperings increased. To his left, he noticed three or four of the stars growing larger. No, they weren't growing larger; they were coming closer. And the closer they approached, the more he realized that they weren't stars at all. They were . . . eyes. Two pairs of eyes. He watched as they continued their advance, until he was finally able to discern the outline of their bodies. Reptilian, with long hooded necks and pointed snouts. They approached him at a strange, ninety-degree tilt. As they came closer he could see their leathery skin and glistening white teeth. In many ways they looked like the creatures attached to the tunnel. But these were free, able to move wherever they wished.

Their whisperings had grown loud enough to hear, but their language was foreign, impossible to understand. They were now close enough for Griffin to judge their size. Standing on their hind legs, they were between eighteen and twenty-four inches tall.

He heard more whisperings and turned to see three additional creatures approach from his right—same ninety-degree tilt, but looking a bit more amphibian.

He tried to remember what the old man had said in the lab about this chamber, about chamber two. Something about downloading. He turned to the first group and was astonished when one creature suddenly hopped onto his left leg and started walking up it. It was not heavy, weighing no more than a large cat. Immediately Griffin tried to shake it off. It was only then he realized that his leg was restrained. But with what? He tried his right leg. It was also tied.

The second creature jumped onto his right leg and started up it. Griffin tried to swat them both away but discovered his arms were also restrained. He twisted, turning first to his left, then to his right, feeling the pressure of something hard and rigid against his back. He seemed to be tied to a board, an upright table. The two creatures continued up his legs, chatting, as they effortlessly defied gravity. On second thought, maybe the table wasn't upright after all. Maybe it was horizontal—maybe he was lying down and the creatures were walking on top of him.

What about this seemed so familiar?

Other eyes approached. Coming at him from other directions. Griffin lifted his head to watch, breathing harder, faster. What had the old man said? Chamber two was what? Downloading what?

The first creature walked across his abdomen and arrived at his chest. Griffin stared wide-eyed as the thing curled its lips at him with what may or may not have been a grin. Because of the weight, it was harder to catch his breath. Because of the weight . . . and the terror.

Other creatures arrived behind the first, some standing on his chest, others his stomach, his lower abdomen. They formed a line, forking at his waist and continuing down each leg.

Suddenly a pair of razor-sharp talons dug into his jaw. He screamed and looked up to see one of the creatures standing above his head, grinning at him upside down, pulling open his mouth with its claws. Griffin shook his head, fighting, but the claws were too powerful. Inch by inch, they pried open his jaw.

He gasped at a sudden pressure against his chest and looked down to see the first creature had pushed off, leaping into the air. It sailed directly over his face, hovering a moment, and then dissolved into a thick, black mist. A black mist that immediately shot into his mouth and the back of his throat. He gagged and coughed, but it did no good. He felt its freezing cold seeping into the base of his skull, then burrowing higher into his head, his brain, until it had lodged itself into a small portion of his mind, of his thinking. He could actually feel it there, beside his own thoughts. And this is where it remained, its cold presence attaching to his own.

Another leaped off his chest. It also turned to vapor and rushed into his open mouth and up to his brain. And another, and another. He tried fighting, coughing, gagging, but they could not be stopped. They continued pouring in, faster and faster, an icy stream filling him with their presence, replacing his thoughts and existence . . . with their own.

Gita and Starr hurried down the hall with Wendell toward the VR lab. He'd regained most of his strength and quickly filled them in on all that he knew ... until the alarm sounded.

"What's that?" Starr asked.

Gita and Wendell exchanged looks then picked up their pace, breaking into a run.

"What's going on?" Starr called.

"It is somebody's vital signs!" Gita shouted over her shoulder.

"What?"

"We are losing somebody!"

They raced into the lab and up onto the platform, quickly scanning the displays. Gita found David's. His clock indicated he still had four minutes.

"It's Griffin!" Wendell shouted.

Her eyes darted to chamber two's monitor. On the screen were strange, reptilelike creatures standing on top of Griffin's chest. She leaned closer, not believing what she saw. Those that weren't standing were leaping into the air, floating over his face, and shooting into his mouth!

"I was downloading data into chamber two!" Wendell turned to the console behind them and hit a series of switches. "Some druggie's hallucination! I was running it through PNEUMA, filtering and cross-matching his experiences!"

Gita stared at the images as Griffin writhed and screamed under the creatures' attack until, suddenly, they disappeared. His cries and convulsing continued, but the creatures were gone. She spun around to see Wendell at the back console. He'd just removed the volunteer's data disc from the system.

But the alarm continued.

He crossed back to chamber two's controls and punched a half dozen buttons.

Down below, the chamber gave a loud hiss and the door slid open. Wendell hurried off the platform and raced to it. Gita followed. She still hated the machine, feared the chambers and what happened in them, but surely she could help. She arrived and saw Dr. Griffin splayed out on the black rollers. Wendell had already dropped to his knees and was rip-ping off the goggles and VR suit.

"Get the medical team down here!" he shouted as he checked the man's pupils. "Dr. Griffin! Dr. Griffin, can you hear me?"

Gita turned and ran to the control platform. Fumbling with the phone, she entered the emergency code . . . as the alarm continued to sound.

S uddenly David heard laughter. And, just as suddenly, Orbolitz had disappeared.

Still breathing hard, head reeling from the shock of see-ing his daughter's eyes, he tried to focus. Below him was the endless sea of burning bodies. Orbolitz was gone. But his son? He still hadn't found Luke. Or had it been Orbolitz all along? He tried clearing his mind, thinking it through, but he was too overwhelmed, far past exhaustion.

"Luke!" He scanned the lake, willing himself forward, searching. Someone would know. If his boy was here, some-one had to know. "Luke!"

W hat about David?" Gita stood at the entrance of chamber two. "His time is nearly up."

Wendell continued stripping Griffin of his suit. "The alarms will warn him."

"Not if he thinks his son is in there."

He gave her a look.

"I know him. I know he will stay there until he finds his son. We must warn him."

"He shut off his intercom."

Gita's heart missed a beat. "Then we must go in. We must retreive him!"

"Both chambers are in use."

"Not this one."

"No!"

"Why?"

"There's no telling what that program did to this chamber's system." Wendell paused to wipe his face on his sleeve, then continued working over Griffin. "Look at him! No way am I going in here without someone monitoring me every second."

"I can monitor you! I can—"

"You barely know the sytem."

"Wendell . . ."

"Absolutely not!"

Gita stared at Griffin's body, her thoughts frantically searching for a solution. One came to mind but she immediately pushed it aside, looking for another. But there was no other. Before giving herself time to think, she cried, "Then send me!"

"What?"

"Send me!"

D avid drifted toward a young man. He seemed to be performing. Like some rock star, he screamed into an imaginary microphone, pouring out his heart and soul to an imaginary crowd.

Despite the seering heat, David forced himself to drop lower—so close he feared his skin would blister. As he looked through the buckling air and flames he saw much of the young man's flesh had already fallen away. Around the bare vertebrae of the neck he noticed a gold chain. Attached to it was a pendant, a pointed tiger's tooth made of swirling gold with a large green emerald in the center. At this level he could also hear some of the words the youth screamed. They were faint but sounded like accusations. Accusations of friends, of family. He seemed to be blaming everyone for his fate. At last he reached the end of the song—screaming, wailing, belting out the last notes in a grand finale, before collapsing into an exhausted heap in front of the cheering throngs.

But, of course, there were no throngs. There were no cheers. Only silence.

He rose, looking about, shocked, outraged.

"Excuse me!" David shouted.

But the man did not hear. Desperately, he searched the nonexistent crowd looking for someone, for anyone, to praise his work, to acknowledge his labor. But there was no one. Not a soul. And the silence, the absolute lack of response, forced an agonizing scream from his chest that rose until it ignited the little remaining flesh of his face.

The sight was too grotesque. David could watch no more. He inhaled and rose above the heat. Again he tried to think through the mental exhaustion. If Luke was still alive within the system, he would not be looking for Emily here. He'd know she was in the garden. He'd be searching for her there. And if he had not survived—David shuddered—if his son had died, he wouldn't be here either. Not with these people. What had Preacher Man said? Life was pliable clay, a time for making eternal choices? There was no way Luke's clay had time to set. Not yet. He was just a boy. He'd not had time to choose his passion.

No, he wouldn't be here. Alive or dead, Luke would be back in the garden.

David spun around and looked up to the thousands of towering columns, the vaporous passageways from the tunnel to this cavern. But which one was his? Which had he passed through?

A low throbbing filled his ears. He glanced to the digital display in his goggles as it clicked to:

00:01:59

D r. Patekar, can you hear me? Dr. Patekar?"
Gita nodded, chest heaving, heart pounding so hard she could barely hear Wendell through the intercom. She was

inside the chamber now, preparing to enter PNEUMA—the last place she ever wanted to be. But David was there and he needed help.

"You've got to relax," Wendell ordered. "You've got to slow your breathing."

She nodded.

"If you don't, you won't make it through the tunnel."

"Yes," she gasped, trying through sheer will to calm herself.

The medical team was just outside her chamber finishing up with Griffin. They'd managed to stabilize his heart and other vitals. But his mind . . . By his wild looks and erratic behavior, it was clear the monsters were still there—and they had no intention of leaving.

"All right," Wendell continued. "He's on the other side of the wormholes."

"Which one?" she asked, still breathing hard, still trying to slow herself. "There are thousands of—"

"I'm replaying his video now. I'll track and isolate the one he entered."

Gita tried to swallow but her mouth was bone dry.

"Are you okay?"

She nodded.

"You sure? Because we can't continue until you're—"

"He has no time."

"I understand that, but—"

Closing her eyes, she fought to remain calm. "Now, Wendell! If I go, I must go now!"

"All right." There was a brief pause as he made last-minute adjustments. "Here we go, then. Hang on."


Choosing the most familiar-looking column, David willed himself toward it. The low pulsing alarm continued in his ears. Once he arrived at the base, he inhaled and rose, following the black, vaporous pillar to its top. He drifted to the opening and, being careful not to touch its sides, peered down into it.

The blackness was absolute.

He looked back out over the lake. So many columns and so many appeared the same. How could he tell? How could he—

A shrill *beep-beep-beep-beep* startled him. He glanced down to his readout. It had just clicked to:

00:01:00

The images in his goggles began to pulse, overexposing at each beep. With little time remaining, he stuck his head back into the hole, kicked his feet up over him, and exhaled.

He quickly dropped. But he'd traveled only a few yards before the sides closed in around him. It was too narrow. The wrong passage. Cold mist brushed against his shoulders, touching his arms, his chest, sucking the heat from his body. But it was more than heat. He could actually feel his thoughts, his emotions, everything that made him who he was, being sucked into the icy vapor.

Fighting to clear his mind, he inhaled and slowly, carefully, backed out of the passage, trying to avoid the sides, but bumping against them once, twice, three more times—each touch drawing away more and more life.

The beeping increased. The images in the goggles now pulsed red. He glanced to the digital readout. It was just as he feared. He was down to:

00:00:29

Struggling to hold his panic in check, he continued easing out until he was clear of the opening, once again floating in the cavern.

W endell's voice broke through the roar of the wind. "I'm slowing you to three-quarter speed."

Gita nodded and watched as the sides of the tunnel shifted from a blur to distinct images—images of grotesque creatures. She'd seen them thousands of times before in paintings, statues, sketches by people with occult experiences, and of course she'd studied them from their own images recorded right here inside PNEUMA. But, even though she'd seen them before, the effect of the 3-D goggles and the sounds of their growling and screeching were so realistic that she instinctively sucked in her breath and rose.

"Exhale, Doctor!" Wendell shouted. "You've got to keep your distance from them!"

She blew out the air until her position inside the tunnel stabilized. "Sorry."

"Don't worry, it happens to everyone. Now, the entrance is just ahead, fifteen meters. Look up and a little to your right. Remember, I can only see what you see."

She nodded and searched the ceiling of the tunnel some six or seven feet above her. She struggled to keep her breathing constant as the slithering creatures lunged at her, snapping and snarling, their eyes bulging with rage, fangs dripping in one another's blood.

"The larger, dominant ones rule the wormholes. Look for a big one with a froglike face—should be five meters ahead now."

As Gita searched, a larger gargoyle emerged from the swarming mass. It hissed and flayed its long spindly arms.

"I see it! That is him, yes?"

"Hang on ... Yep, that's our boy. And that's the opening directly behind him."

Gita squinted and saw the dark hole above the creature. It was no more than five feet in diameter. "What now?" she asked.

"Checking David's video, hold on."

"Hurry. He does not have much time."

"Neither do you, Dr. Patekar, neither do you."

She glanced down to her digital readout. As a rookie she'd only been given six minutes. She was now at:

*00:05:06*

"Okay. Do you see the way it's scurrying back and forth across the opening? Left and right, then left and hesitating, then left again, then right?"

Gita watched. "Yes."

"It repeats that same pattern over and over. There's some variation, but it's basically the same. That's how David got through. He found the pattern. Just watch until you see the pattern."

Gita nodded, studying the movements. The interval it gave her wasn't much, barely a second, but the entrance was left unguarded each and every time.

"When you think you're ready, go for it."

She continued to watch as it repeated the pattern once . . . twice . . . She nearly went the third time, but hesitated too long.

Four times . . .

"Dr. Patekar."

She did not respond but continued to concentrate. And then, on the fifth pass, she quickly inhaled and shot toward the opening.

For a moment she thought she'd made it. But the creature had anticipated her move and lunged toward her. Her head, neck, and chest made it through, but the thing managed to latch onto her left hip, digging its talons deep into her flesh.

She screamed.

"Doctor!" Her intercom crackled. "Doctor, are you all right?"

She tried to squirm away, but the claws dug deeper—the pain intense and unbelievable. She screamed again.

"Gita, can you hear me? Gita!"

The scream was so close David heard it over his alarm. It did not come from the lake below, but from one of the columns beside him. He turned, searching.

There it was again. To his left. The column to his immediate left.

He glanced at his display:

00:00:06

He willed himself over to the column. Once there he positioned himself to see inside. But, even as he looked into it, the flashing of his goggles came to a stop. So did the alarm. Again, he looked at the display. It read:

00:00:00

He watched as the numbers began to fade. In fact, all of the images in his goggles began to fade—as did the sounds from the speakers. Only then did he realize . . . they weren't fading, he was. He was starting to lose consciousness.

"David!"

Immediately, he recognized her voice. He squinted, looking farther into the hole, trying to clear his vision.

"David! It is me. It is Gita!"

He saw her floating inside the passage, not ten feet below him, her face twisted in pain. She struggled to move forward, to reach him. But something held her back. A vague form was attached to her side. "David! My hand! Take my hand!"

He squinted harder, trying to see. But the image of her face, the pleas of her voice were all fading—giving way to other images, other sounds. Fleeting snippets of his past . . .

There was Luke, his beloved Luke, standing with the soccer team that David had helped coach. They were laughing, fighting over who would raise the trophy over their head for the photo. The trophy that had once meant everything to them. But now . . . now, even as he watched the scene unfold, David felt a growing sadness. Not because of the winning, not because of the moment . . . but because the moment would not last. It had not lasted. It had existed only for a short time and then it disappeared . . . forever. It had been so important to them then, but now it was only a memory. Brief. Vague. How was it possible? How could something they'd worked so long and hard for disappear so quickly? Like steam from his coffee. A wisp, then forever gone.

"David!"

He blinked away the image, fighting to focus until he saw Gita again. She'd been dragged farther away, but she was still reaching, still calling. Her face flickered into another memory. This time, Emily.

Dear, sweet Emily. Clinging to his side, squealing in delight as they swung higher and higher in the hammock. What a moment that had been. Laughing so hard they cried. He was crying now. He could feel the burn in his eyes, the knot in his throat. Not because of the moment, but because the moment no longer existed. It had been beautiful, perfect ... but it no longer was. Simply a vapor, then gone.

*"David!"*

Again, he forced his vision to clear. His eyes had grown so heavy. It took such effort to keep them open. There was Gita still fighting, still reaching. But ... he saw it now ... now he understood. There was no need for her to bother. Even if she succeeded in reaching him, in helping him, it would only be for a moment. Just another moment that would fade and disappear. Didn't she understand? It didn't matter. None of it mattered. Everything was pointless. His whole life had been—

"David ..."

Gita—thoughtful, gentle, honest Gita. He loved her, there was no doubt about it. But it didn't matter. It was only a moment. And now ... now it was time to close his eyes. Time to—

"David ..."

Now he must give in to the pointlessness.

"David ..."

He must allow it to swallow him, immerse and envelop him.

D octor!" Wendell's voice blasted through the intercom. "He's gone."

"No, he's not!" Gita shouted through her pain. "He's—"

"His time is up! His system is shutting down!"

"Not yet, I still see him!" She stretched out to him for all she was worth. "David!"

The creature at her hip shrieked, struggling to pull her back, digging in its talons. White-hot pain shot through her body. She looked back to catch a glimpse of the thing, its hind feet gripping the outside of the tunnel, pulling with astonishing strength. But she would not give in. David floated so close. If she could reach his hand. If she could just—

"Doctor, look at your time!"

She glanced at the readout:

    00:01:42

"Leave him! He's gone! Leave him and get out of there!"

"David!"

She saw his mouth moving, "Gita ...," his voice a faint whisper.

"David, hang on!"

"It doesn't matter ..."

"What?"

The creature shrieked behind her, yanking and pulling.

"Nothing matters ..."

"What are you talking about?" She continued to fight, but the creature was winning, pulling her back. Inch by inch.

"... nothing matters ..."

"No ... No, that's not true!"

A nother memory flickered. Jacqueline. Their first date, the butterflies in his stomach, the thumping of his heart. It was love at first sight, that's what everyone said. So powerful, so overwhelming, he had not been able to sleep for thinking of her. But even that hadn't lasted. Even that ...

"David!"

Gita's voice was nearly gone ... as he and Jacqueline toasted cheap champagne in their cheap apartment. Celebrating his first book—something he'd been so passionate about, had sacrificed so much for. But now, like everything else, so ... useless.

"David ... something does matter ..."

He was receiving his college diploma. First in his family to graduate—another passion, another empty pursuit. Who cared? Who would remember?

"David ..." He barely heard.

There was Molly, his childhood dog. So loved he would have died for her. And she for him. But now, now she was dead, another pointless memory. That's all they were, memories. Passions that had disappeared. After all these years, he finally understood. The people in the burning lake were not foolish after all. They understood. They understood that nothing mattered, nothing lasted. Only those brief moments of joy, those fleeting moments of fulfillment. And now he would choose. Now he would decide which passion was his greatest. Which passion to live in, to be lost in. It was the only thing that mattered in a vain and pointless universe. And it was the only thing that he would live in, dwell in, be consumed by ... for eternity.

"David ..."

"Good-bye, Gita." His lips moved, but there was no sound. "Good-bye ..."

# fifteen

D avid!"
But David no longer answered. With eyes closed, body unmoving, he floated just yards from her reach.

"Gita." Wendell's voice broke through the intercom. "Gita, he's gone."

"No, he can't be. He's right—"

"You've got to come back! You're out of time!"

"But he's—"

"He's dead. His vitals are right here in front of me. Everything's flat."

Although the pain in her hip was unbearable, it was nothing compared to the ache in her chest. *"DAVID!"* The grief was so intense that she barely noticed the flashing in her goggles or the alarm beeping in her ears.

"Look at your time, Gita! Your time is up! Look at it!"

She glanced at the readout:

00:00:57

"I'm taking him off line," Wendell declared.

"What?"

"He's gone. I can take him off line now without affecting you."

She looked at David's form flashing in her goggles—so close, so agonizingly close. "We cannot leave him here! We have to retrieve his body!"

"He's not there! He's in chamber one!"

Gita closed her eyes. Of course, what was she thinking, it was all virtual reality.

"Now get out of there! You're down to forty-five seconds!"

She watched David as Wendell shut down his chamber. His image flickered once, twice, then disappeared. Suddenly she was all alone in the tube—just her and the creature digging into her side.

"Doctor!" Wendell called. "Gita!"

"Can you revive him?"

There was a pause.

"Wendell, is the medical team there? Can they revive him?"

"He's been in too long. He was way over his allotment. And you will be too. Look at your clock!"

She glanced down.

00:00:24

The images in her goggles were no longer flashing white, but red.

"You've got to get out of there, now!"

But an idea was forming.

"Doctor!"

"Wendell . . ." She cringed as the gargoyle continued to pull, digging in deeper. "How long has he been gone?"

"You don't have time to—"

"How long has he been—"

"Three minutes, almost four."

She nodded. "It takes twelve minutes for the brain to completely shut down."

"What? Yes, that's the maximum. What are you—"

"So if I can retrieve him, if I can convince him to return—"

"He's dead, Gita. And you will be too, look at your time!"

She did.

00:00:15

"But, if I can reach him—"

"You can't reach him! You're here! You're still in virtual reality and he's—"

"I understand, but if I could—"

"There's no way! He's dead, Doctor, you're alive! There's no way you can reach him, unless you—" Suddenly he stopped. "No. You can't, there's no way you would—"

"If I die, we'll be in the same reality."

"Gita—"

"I'll have six to twelve minutes to go after him."

"You'll both be dead!"

"But only for a few minutes. If I can get him, if I can bring him back before my time is up—"

"No. I won't allow it."

"—then you can revive us both."

"Doctor . . ."

She looked down at her display. It clicked to:

00:00:03

"I won't allow it. There's no assurance I can—"

She reached up to her intercom switch. "I trust you, Wendell. If anybody can do it, I am sure you can."

"But it's suicide. It's—"

The readout tripped to:

00:00:01

as she snapped off the intercom.

It wasn't suicide, she knew that. It was just the opposite. It was something she'd been afraid of her whole life. But something she finally understood. No logic now. No intellect. Yet she knew it, felt it to the very center of her being.

She watched and waited as her readout clicked to:

00:00:00

The alarm stopped. The images, the sounds, even the pain in her hip began to fade. No. This was not suicide. She knew what this was. Something so wonderful, so awesome. Something she'd begged God for her entire life. And now, through David, through his daughter, even through the shelter, God had finally stripped her naked enough to experience it.

The tunnel was more vivid than anything David had seen. By comparison, the VR program was a misty shadow. It was as if all of his senses had come alive for the very first time. And accompanying that life was a reality far more intense than anything he had ever experienced. Although he was moving too fast to see the creatures lining the tunnel, he could sense them, feel them. But it was more than feeling. It was like having a different vision. Deeper. And, were it not for the astonishing splendor of the light at the far end, he would have been overcome with terror.

The light ... so brilliant ... so powerful. As with the tunnel, his VR experience of it had been hopelessly inadequate—like holding a faint ember before the blinding sun—before a thousand blinding suns. But it was more than light. It was a presence. A presence that filled all of his senses. Through his ears he heard it as music, amazingly intricate, beautiful in its simplicity. With his nose he smelled it as a fragrance, subtle yet dizzying in power. His skin felt it as warmth, soaking through his pores, saturating his muscles, his bones, everything that he was.

When he reached the end of the tunnel, the light wrapped itself about him and gently lowered him to the lush green pelt of the garden floor. The same garden he'd seen before but, like everything else, so many times more real. Even the colors (some he never knew existed) were so rich and vivid that they almost seemed alive. Alive with light. Alive with *the* Light. Not so much illuminated by it, as actually containing a portion of it, a trace of its presence. Just as the illumination of hell came from the burning flames within the creatures, much of the illumination of the garden came from the Light shimmering within each of its objects ... Light that was an extension of the Light blazing in the distance.

"Daddy!"

David spun around and gasped. There was Emily. His Emily. Running toward him in a white, glowing gown. This was no facsimile as before. No VR image. Like everything else, his daughter was more real and alive than he'd ever seen. But it wasn't just physical beauty. Now with his deeper vision, he could see every detail, every nuance of her personality and character. All radiating and sparkling from the Light within her.

He barely had time to reach out his arms before she fell into them. And there, in the garden, he held his daughter. His wonderful child. He held her so tightly, so closely, that for a moment it felt as if she was a part of him—her breath, her life. Because she was his life. So much of it.

How long he held her, he didn't know. When they finally separated, he looked into her eyes, those beautiful, beautiful eyes. "I missed you," he whispered fiercely. "I missed you so much."

She smiled, giggling in delight. It was music that swelled his heart to bursting. She reached out and took his hand. He looked down to see her slender glowing fingers intertwined around his thick, solid ones. "How is Grams?" she asked. "And Luke?"

For the first time since he'd entered the tunnel, he felt concern. "Isn't he here? I thought he was here."

She continued to smile and shook her head, light sparkling and falling from her shiny dark hair.

David looked back up to the tunnel. "He should be here. I thought he'd be here."

"It's okay, Daddy." She gave his hand a squeeze and he turned back to her. "Everything is okay."

"But—"

"Everything is fine." She spoke with such peace and assurance that he found himself believing her. She pulled on his hand. "But you need to come with me. We haven't much time."

"Time?" he asked. "Before what?"

"Before you go."

"Go where?"

"Wherever you've chosen." She gave another tug. "Come."

They started forward. Of course he wanted to ask her a thousand questions, to know every detail of the past weeks, of where they were, of where they were going, of what happened to Luke. But for the moment that could wait. For the moment he was content simply to be with her. To be with his daughter and surrounded by the Light.

They'd only taken a few steps before they passed a rosebush that slowed him to a stop. It had no thorns and was covered in buds and flowers. At the center of each flower the petals glowed a rich burgundy that gently turned to lighter shades of pink until the outside shown a dazzling white. A white that, like everything else in the garden, shimmered with the Light's presence.

As a writer, he had spent minutes, sometimes hours, struggling for the right word, the right sentence, to capture the "honesty" of an object. There were dozens of phrases to describe something, and most folks would settle for any one of them. But the writer in David had always felt there was a perfect word, a perfect phrase, to capture its "truth." And now, in these petals he was able to see that truth. It was as if each petal was the original petal, the first petal ever created . . . and every other petal he had seen on Earth was only a crude copy of this original.

But it wasn't just the petals. He saw the same honesty in the leaves, in the entire bush. It was as if everything transcended the petal or leaves or bush to become their very truth, their very . . . *essence*.

"It's like poetry, isn't it, Daddy?" He looked up to see Emily smiling. "It's not what you see on the surface—it's not the words or the rhyme or the rhythm. Everything here holds the truest meaning of itself."

"Yes," he said softly. "Yes."

"But it's more. Not only is each object the perfect poem that captures itself, but each object, each poem, is a single word in a much larger poem. *The* poem."

David frowned, struggling to understand.

"Come." She gave another giggle and pulled his hand. "You'll see."

They continued walking until they came upon a river. But like everything else in the garden, it was more than a river. It was the original river, the quintessential river, its water sparkling so brightly that it appeared to be liquid crystal. At its bank a gazelle and her fawn had lowered their heads to drink. Just a few yards away a jaguar yawned, sunning itself on a glowing rock. Despite their close proximity, neither seemed concerned with the other's presence.

As David watched, a thought came to mind. Other than his daughter, he had not seen another soul. Although he enjoyed the privacy, he wondered why it was so different from his VR experience. Turning to her he asked, "Where are all the people?"

"People?"

"Yes, the friends and relatives to greet me. There were always friends and relatives before."

She smiled. "You'll see them. I promise. But not now."

He didn't understand and apparently she saw no need to explain. Instead, she pointed to a tree on the river's bank. It soared nearly a hundred feet into the air before its branches swooped back to the ground or out over the river. The glowing jade leaves were as big as a man's hand. And each branch was heavy with fruit.

He approached in quiet awe. "What type of tree is it?"

"I don't know its name, but we all eat from it."

They arrived at one of the branches and he stopped to look at the fruit. But it wasn't just one fruit. There were different varieties. And none that he recognized. Some were long and cylindrical, like bananas but purple. Others were round like oranges but blue. Another dangled from the branch long and thin like a pencil; another was cone-shaped. And, like the leaves, like everything in the garden, each glowed and shimmered with the Light.

"It's safe to eat?" he asked.

"Yes."

"Any of it?"

"All of it."

He reached to the nearest branch.

"Daddy, I don't—"

"It's beautiful." He pulled off a silver, pear-shaped fruit.

"Yes, but it's not for you."

"Why not?" He gave it a quick wipe with his sleeve.

"You chose not to eat it."

He shot her a grin, then raised it to his lips. "Looks like I've changed my mind."

"Daddy, I—"

He bit into it. The skin was thin, the meat sweet and juicy like a grape but with the slight tang of lime. He'd never tasted anything like it. Delicious, until it sliced and shredded the inside of his mouth.

"Ah!" He dropped his head, spitting, feeling as if he'd bitten into a razor. "What was that?"

His daughter reached to the branch and quickly plucked off a leaf. David's mouth was on fire. He spat again—the final remains of the fruit now mixed with blood.

"Emily!"

"Here." She raised the leaf to his mouth. "This will—"

He backed away. "What are you doing? What is—"

"It will take away the pain."

"Are you sure?" He could barely talk, his mouth burning and bleeding.

"Yes," she assured him, "it heals everyone." Again she reached to him. With some reluctance, he let her place the leaf against his lips, then his cheek.

Instantly, the pain vanished.

He looked at her in surprise, then bent down and spit again. There was no blood. Not a drop.

"What was that?" He reached to his mouth, though it no longer hurt.

"Its reality is too great for you."

"What?"

"I'll explain later. Please, we have to hurry." Again she took his hand and led him forward.

They crossed around the tree and followed the river. It took a sharp bend to the left, and suddenly a series of brilliant, glowing structures came into view. They were so bright that David could not make out specific shapes or forms—just the glowing presence of the Light.

"Is that where we're going?" he asked.

"Yes."

"Why, for what?"

"For your judgment, Daddy."

"My *what?*"

"For what you've decided. Come."

T he Light's power threw Gita to the ground. She covered her face, screaming, but she could not hear herself over the roar:

### "HOLY! HOLY! HOLY!"

Like the Light, the words had substance, a reality more real than anything she'd ever experienced.

### "HOLY IS THE LORD GOD ALMIGHTY!"

Clenching her eyes, she rolled onto her stomach, keeping her face to the floor, covering her head from the awful Light, the terrible booming voices:

### "WHO WAS AND IS AND IS TO COME!"

She didn't know how she got there or how long she could survive. One minute she was in the tunnel, the next she was before this terrifying Light. But it was more than light. And it was more than reality. Every fact, every figure, every certainty she had ever known was only a shadow of this crushing, overpowering . . . Truth.

## "HOLY! HOLY! HOLY!"

Power roared from the Light—smashing against her body, sucking air from her lungs. And yet, as terrified as she was . . . she felt an attraction. Though it would destroy her, she was drawn to it. Like thirst, like hunger, like having to breathe. The compulsion spread through her mind, her body, all that she was. This is what she had pursued her entire life. This Perfection. This Absolute.

## "HOLY IS THE LORD GOD ALMIGHTY!"

It had been her passion, her purpose. And if being destroyed by Its power meant her death, then she would be destroyed.

## "WHO WAS AND IS AND IS TO COME!"

Slowly, she pulled her hands from the top of her head. The Light assaulted her with hurricane force. But it was not wind. It was Truth. Truth she had to see. Experience.

Shaking, eyes closed, barely able to breathe, she used all of her strength to lift her face from the ground.

The Light pummeled her. But she would not look away. She would open her eyes. She would be overwhelmed, she knew that. But overwhelmed by the only thing she had ever desired. Mustering her will, crying out in terror and exertion, she forced them open.

But the Light was too intense. She could not look into it. She could only look to its outside edges—around it, below it, above it.

High overhead, through the blinding glare, she caught glimpses of giant, multiwinged creatures. A lion, an ox. Another was an eagle, another a man. But instead of skin or hair or feathers, each was covered in eyes. Every part of their bodies, eyes. Always watching, always seeing. These were the creatures who continued shouting:

### "HOLY! HOLY! HOLY!"

She'd read of them in the Bible—how they surrounded the throne, how they cried out the same phrase over and over again. Secretly, she had always thought their existence to be boring—flying around shouting the same phrases again and again. But as she watched, she realized how wrong she'd been. These were the most privileged of all creation. Not only did they fly closest to the Light and its Truth, but the words they shouted were anything but mindless repetition. Instead, each shout, each cry of holiness seemed to come from their amazement, from their utter astonishment. For every time they cried, they saw yet another aspect of the Light, another aspect of Its infinite Truth.

### "HOLY IS THE LORD GOD ALMIGHTY!"

Then, as she continued to stare, a most amazing thing happened. Through the brightness, the form of a man appeared. Before her eyes, a human being condensed out of the Light and walked toward her.

She watched in astonishment.

He continued forward, His eyes blazing with the Light, His feet glowing with Its power. But He was human, definitely human. And it was from that humanness that she felt understanding. More than that, she felt ... compassion. Truth and power were still very present, but they had reshaped themselves into the form of this man. And in that reshaping, she no longer felt the terror. Now she felt ... Love. His Love.

It wrapped around her, delighted in her. But it was more than that. It *adored* her. *He* adored her, He *treasured* her . . .

*". . . more than His own life."*

Gita's head reeled. Though the Light blazed and thundered around her, she was safe. As long as she focused on this Love, on this Man, nothing would harm her.

At last He arrived. But His Love, like the Light, was more than she could endure. Suddenly she was weeping. Deep, gut-wrenching sobs. She didn't know why—maybe the release of so many emotions, maybe the understanding that she no longer had to try, that she was loved regardless—whatever the reason, she could not stop crying.

She caught a glimpse of movement. Through her tears she saw the Man kneeling. Kneeling to her! Lowering to her! The action brought even more tears . . . until she felt His hand brush against her hair and touch her cheek.

She stopped breathing.

He moved his hand to her chin and gently raised her head until their eyes met. To her fear and amazement she saw that His eyes burned with flames of the Light. Of the Light's Passion. Of Its intense fervor . . . *for her.* She could not look away from the flames. They bore into her—penetrating into her thoughts, her emotions—until they reached the very center of who she was, the very soul of Gita Patekar.

Once inside, they began to expose all of her darkness— illuminating every hidden deed, every careless word, every disgusting habit, every act of dishonesty, selfishness, meanness—there seemed no end. And not just her deeds. Thoughts were exposed—secret hatreds, jealousies, lusts, envy, greed. And, though she was terrified at the revealings, though she cringed in embarrassment . . . she felt no condemnation. Not from the Man. Not from His Love. There was only the complete and total exposure by His all-seeing Light.

Finally He removed His hand from under her chin and stretched it out to her. She hesitated, still trembling in fear, still trying to catch her breath. But He waited. Patiently. For as long as it would take.

At last she placed her hand in His.

Gently, He helped her to her feet. Her knees were weak, her legs wobbly, but with His help she was able to stand. Then, ever so tenderly, He pulled her into an embrace. He wrapped His arms around her, and as He held her, she felt His Light soaking into her, from His heart into hers, filling her body, flooding her mind, returning to those same areas of weakness and failure and embarrassment. But this time, as the Light touched those areas, she felt It dissolving them . . . absorbing them.

Removing them . . .

Forever.

Suddenly her darkness was replaced with His Light. Where there had been shadow and failure, there was blinding glory. Where there had been shame and embarrassment, there was only His Presence.

At last they separated. Hot tears again streamed down Gita's face. And, as she looked up into those compassionate eyes of fire, she saw that they, too, were filled with moisture.

He placed an arm around her shoulder and they turned toward the exit. As they started forward, other creatures she had not noticed, some winged, some not, but all glowing with Light, dropped to their knees when they passed. She knew they were kneeling before Him. But because His arm was around her, she somehow suspected they were also kneeling before . . . *them.*

As they moved for the steps leading to an outside plaza, a question formed in her mind. But before she could even put it into words, she heard His gentle and powerful response:

*"We're going to warn David — to finish answering your prayer."*

D avid!"
He had entered the city with Emily. They were crossing a dazzling bright plaza when he looked up to see Gita

racing down a set of steps toward them. At least he thought it was Gita. It was hard to tell with the Light glaring from the structure behind her. She was with Someone. And, though he'd never seen Him before, David instantly knew who He was. Not because of the people dropping to their knees as He passed, but because the Light shining from Him was identical in every way to the Light pouring out of the building. And it was this same Light, only fainter, that he saw glowing within Gita as she approached, that he saw within Emily, within everything he'd witnessed since he'd arrived. Just as the rivers, trees, and roses that he'd tried to write about on Earth had their reality here . . . so everything here had its reality in this Man, in His Light.

The thought was so dizzying that David looked down, trying to grasp the implications. As everything he had ever beheld on Earth was a vague reflection of the reality surrounding him here, so the reality here was only a reflection of the Man. Wheels within wheels. Circles upon circles, all concentric, all finding their center, all having their origin . . . with Him.

*"Precisely."*

He looked up, startled. The Man was thirty yards away when He spoke, but David heard Him perfectly.

*"Just as your books reflect a portion of you, so My creation reflects a portion of Me."*

"It's true, then," David half whispered. "Everything I've ever pursued, the truth I've never been able to capture on paper—"

*"Is Me. Yes. I've always been with you, David Kauffman, always surrounding you, always hiding in plain sight."*

"David!" Gita was running to him. "David, you have to go back!"

"What?"

She arrived, and despite her urgency, despite their surroundings, she threw herself into his arms and he clung to her fiercely.

Finally, she looked up to him, exclaiming, "Luke's not here!"

"What?"

They separated and she continued breathlessly. "He never entered the chamber! He's still alive! You still have time to go back!"

Confused, David turned to the arriving Man. His eyes were like flames and their passion instantly captured him. They bore into him with an intensity that burned through his every defense. An intensity that revealed every dark and hidden area of his soul. But it did not condemn him. It simply exposed and revealed . . . and loved. For, despite the frightening purity of the flames, there was no missing their overwhelming compassion.

As he stared, David heard another voice. One he instantly recognized:

*"I don't know if You can hear me, God, but if You're there, I'm like really lost. All these roads up here, they all look the same. Please, if You could just help me find the right one . . ."*

Luke's voice faded as Gita explained, "He never arrived at the complex, David. He is still driving through the hills."

Staring into the eyes, David whispered, "Is that true?"

*"Yes."*

"But . . . what can I do? I'm here, I'm . . . dead."

*"Only if you choose to be."*

David frowned.

The Man replied, *"Your son still needs his father."*

"You . . . you would allow me to return?"

Suddenly, he heard another voice. Preacher Man's:

*"Please have mercy on my brother, here. He's been through a terrible lot — ain't had time to understand all the truth that's been pilin' up on him. I'd count it a personal favor if You'd just give him a bit more time and . . ."*

"He's praying?" David asked hoarsely. "For me?"

"He hasn't stopped since you entered the chamber." A playful smile danced across the Man's eyes. "And you and I both know how persistent he can be."

"But—but Emily," David said, turning to his daughter. "I won't be with you." Then to Gita, "Or you."

"You wouldn't be with us anyway, Daddy." Emily smiled sadly and pointed to his chest. "See."

He looked down. Like Emily and Gita he was also glowing, but not with the light of the Man. Instead, his was a rosy, reddish glow. Like what he'd seen in the cavern, in the burning lake of bodies. And for the first time since he'd entered this place, he felt uneasy, very uneasy. He turned back to the Man.

"You understand," the eyes spoke softly and David saw their pain. "You have understood since you first entered Gehenna."

David tried to play ignorant, but the burning eyes made it impossible to hide the truth that he'd already pieced together. He swallowed and quoted, "'We become our greatest passion.'"

"Yes."

"Just as Emily's greatest passion, Gita's greatest passion, is You ... they become part of You."

"Becoming one as the Father and I are one."

Emily turned to David. "He's what you see in us. He's the One burning inside us."

David nodded. "And my greatest passion ... My love for Luke, for Emily ... it becomes me."

"Yes."

"And since ... since that passion is about me, my love for my family ..."

The Man sadly finished, "Then it is you that your greatest passion will burn and consume."

Recalling what he'd seen in the cavern, David quietly added, "For eternity."

Instead of an answer, he heard Preacher Man's voice:

"Please bring him back, Lord. Come on now, You done it before, I know You can do it again."

"But . . ." David swallowed. "You're willing to answer him?"

There was that smile again. *"We both know how hard it is to say no to our children."*

David's mind raced. "What about Gita? What's going to happen to Gita?"

The Man turned to Gita and waited for her to answer.

She hesitated, then looked directly into His eyes as she spoke. "My greatest passion . . . my greatest desire is only for *part* of You."

"What do you mean?" David asked.

She turned to him. "I fell in love with His Truth, with His Words, but not . . ." Tears welled up in her eyes and she glanced down. ". . . but I did not love Him, I did not love the Author."

The Man gently wrapped His arm around her and corrected. *"That was true . . . until I answered your prayer."*

Surprised, she looked up to Him.

He quoted softly, *"'Whoever lives in love lives in God, and God in him.'"*

"But that is precisely the problem. I could never love. I tried. For years I tried, but I could never—"

*"'No greater love has a man than he gives up his life for his friends.'"*

She still looked puzzled.

*"Isn't that what you did for your friend here? When you finally understood the depth of My love for you, were you not able to express it to him?"*

She sniffed, blinking back the tears, her face beginning to brighten.

The Man waited.

"Yes." She started to nod. She wiped her eyes and grinned. "Yes, yes, I did love. I *do* love! I do know how to love! And . . ." She hesitated, then continued boldly, holding His gaze, "And I love *You!*"

Smiling at her excitement, the Man gently replied, *"Yes, you do."* He turned to David. *"And I want to thank you for your help."*

David stared, stunned. "You mean ... You mean You had all of this planned?"

The Man remained smiling.

*"All* of it?"

He gave no answer.

Finally, hoarsely, David asked, "Why?"

He motioned to Gita and Emily. *"For them."* Then turning to David, He added, *"And for you."*

"For *me?"*

The Man lifted his hands to David and slowly opened His palms. In the center of each was a large, oozing hole, wet with blood. *"I've paid a great deal for you, David Kauffman. And I will do whatever you allow Me to, so you do not slip through My hands."*

David stared at the wounds, dumbfounded—until the Man closed His palms and the Preacher's voice resumed:

*"We ain't got much time, Lord. Now I know You hear me. And I know You promised to answer my prayers, so I ain't gonna let up until You send him back here or ..."*

The Man interrupted. *"The choice must be yours. In this matter I limit Myself to your choice."*

David looked back into the eyes, still blazing with their purity, their compassion. And, though he knew he had the right to refuse, he knew the last thing he wanted was to disappoint those eyes.

Slowly he began to nod.

*"There is much for you to do, but I will always be with you."*

"Yes," David whispered, a tightness rising in his throat. "If it's what You want ... yes ... yes."

"Oh, David!" Gita threw her arms around him in another embrace. They held each other for a long moment. When they separated, she took his hands into hers and spoke quietly, "Thank you." There was no embarrassment in her look. No self-conscious timidity. Only the same love he had seen in the Man's eyes. "You have taught me so very much."

Feeling the ache tighten his throat, he could think of no other response but to gently raise her hands to his lips and kiss them. "Thank *you*," he thickly whispered. Then he pulled her into another embrace, holding her as tightly as possible. How deeply he loved this woman.

At last they separated. He wiped his face and smiled. Then he took a deep breath and prepared for the hardest good-bye of all.

He turned to Emily. Dearest Emily. It was their love that had started him on this search—his concern for her well-being that had ultimately brought him here. And now, at last, he'd found the answer. But it was an answer greater than anything he had expected. She moved into his arms and he held her, burying his face into her hair, swaying slightly as when she was a child, kissing the top of her head again . . . and again.

"I'll miss you so much," she murmured against his chest.

He clenched his eyes. "I'll miss you too, baby girl."

"But it won't be long."

"I know," he whispered, "I know."

It was time to separate. There could be no more delay. He took a half step back. Still holding her hands, he looked one last time at his daughter—the love of his life. Those beautiful eyes brimming in tears.

Holding out her hand she brought her five fingertips together, forming a set of lips. Their sign. He understood and did the same with his hand. Then they both reached out and "kissed," fingertip to fingertip.

"Good-bye, Daddy," she whispered.

"Good-bye, sweetheart."

He turned to the Man whose eyes were also moist . . . and beaming. Beaming over *him*. The look left David speechless. The Man gave the slightest nod, which he returned. And, instantly, David was falling back through the tunnel—back through the roaring wind and into the blackness that drowned out all Light, all sound, all sensation.

H e's back." A faint voice floated in the darkness. It grew louder. "We've got him, he's back!" As the volume increased so did the pounding in David's head. He winced in pain.

"He moved!" another voice called. "Did you see that, brother?"

"Mr. Kauffman." It was the first voice, the technician from the lab. "Mr. Kauffman, can you hear me?"

The pounding increased until his entire body throbbed.

"David?"

He tried opening his eyes but they were as heavy as lead.

"Praise God Almighty! Bring the boy in here. Bring him in."

"Dad . . . Dad . . ."

The sound thrilled his heart. He fought for all he was worth to open his lids until, finally, barely, he forced them apart. There was his boy, staring down at him.

"You okay, Dad?" Luke's voice cracked in emotion. "Are you all right?"

David tried to smile, unsure if he succeeded.

Dropping his head to his father's chest, Luke choked out the words, "I'm sorry . . ." He felt his boy's wet cheek against his neck. "I'm so sorry . . ."

"Give him air, son." David felt him being pulled away. "He needs air."

"Where . . ." David tried to speak but his mouth was dust-like.

"Take it easy," the technician said. "Take it easy."

"Gita . . ."

There was a moment's pause before Preacher Man answered, "She's gone, brother. She's not with us anymore."

"I'm sorry . . . ," a weary voice sighed.

With effort, David rolled his head toward it. There was Gita's body lying six feet from him. It did not move. A paramedic was snapping shut his case and sadly repeating, "I'm sorry ..."

David closed his eyes. Tears spilled from their corners.

"Dad ..."

"Let the boy back in here," Preacher Man insisted, "let him in."

Again David felt his son at his chest, trying to embrace him, trying to hold him. "It's okay, Dad, we'll be all right, it's okay."

Again, he was pulled away until Preacher Man barked, "Let him be! Let the boy be with his father!"

"You've still got me," Luke croaked. "You've still got me and it'll be all right. You'll see, Dad, we'll be okay, honest ..."

Using all of his strength, David raised an arm and clumsily dropped it across his son—an embrace. Tears ran down his face, tightness clawed his throat, but he knew Luke was right, it was going to be okay. Because he had his son. And in many ways he had his daughter. These were the greatest things of his life. And yet, as great as they were, he knew he now had something even greater.

# epilogue

O kay, okay," Luke laughed, "here's another one, let me read this one."

The friends and neighbors in David's backyard quieted as Luke, standing on the picnic bench, took the clipping from Grams and read yet another awful review: "'Although we've waited nearly four years for Mr. Kauffman's latest novel, his work makes one wish it had been another forty, or perhaps four hundred.'"

The guests whooped and laughed, slapping David on the back. He grimaced, sipping his ice tea as he moved through the crowd toward the back door.

"'This would ensure that none of our friends, loved ones, or vaguest acquaintances would be subjected to such boring detail and unending prose.'"

The group broke into applause, forcing David to resort to his very bad Elvis impression, "Thank you, thank you very much."

"'Although his work is graceful and poetic, often capturing life in the details—one wishes for far less detail and the tiniest trace of plot.'"

More applause, some glasses raised, as David gave a parting wave, slid open the screen door, and joined more guests in the kitchen—friends, relatives, and colleagues, all come to join in his book's celebration . . . or in this case, its wake.

Thirteen months had passed since the incident in the VR lab, since his death and return. And, though the experience had done much to unstick his creativity and break through his writer's block, in many ways it had also ruined him. Now everywhere he looked he saw the detailed wonders of creation—the truth within the gauzy wing of a fly, the wind whispering through pines, a baby's gurgling smile. So much life around him—from the microbes in a drop of pond water to a glorious bursting sunrise. How could he possibly write about something as mundane as car chases or shootouts when he was surrounded by so much greater drama?

His writing had finally come to life—after so many months and years of numbness. Unfortunately, his understanding of life had little in common with the public's view. Not that he blamed them. To the impatient eye, jet fighters and car bombs were far more exciting than the smell of orange blossoms or watching a ladybug herd aphids across a leaf. But these were the nuances that shouted to him of the Eternal. What had the Man said . . . *"I'm all around you, hiding in plain sight."* Well, he saw Him now—wherever and whenever he looked, he saw Him.

"David—"

He turned to Jonathan McClure, his agent. The guy stood at the kitchen counter. He was nervously thin, prematurely bald, and definitely a few margaritas to the wind. And why not? One of his favorite clients was sinking before his eyes.

"—we've got to talk."

"Right," David said, knowing full well that the agency was about to cut him loose. "But later, okay? Not when we're 'celebrating.'"

"No, you don't understand—"

David waved him off as he worked his way into the living room where ghetto rap pounded and assaulted the ears—and all other internal organs. Here, Starr and some of the kids from the shelter had segregated themselves from the adults. At the moment she was dancing and gyrating with Nubee,

Gita's younger brother, who rocked and swayed in his wheel-chair with the best of them.

On the street, Gita's death had become urban legend—how she'd given up her life for the man she loved, how she'd blown the whistle on the "Freak Shop," and helped bust Congressman Hagen. Kids like Starr had been impressed. And, though the girl couldn't visit Gita, she could hang with Gita's only living relative. At first it was only the novelty of the idea, but she soon began visiting him more often. Visits which Nubee always insisted meant reading the Bible. An exercise Starr seemed to grow more and more interested in—despite Nubee's new and annoying habit of proclaiming that God would be coming in the next few weeks.

David watched in quiet awe as the couple "danced." Was Starr yet another answered prayer? He shook his head in wonder. Wheels within wheels.

Spotting Rosa, Nubee's caretaker, he strolled to the couch and shouted over the stereo, "How you doing?"

Pointing to her ears, she yelled, "Do you see any blood yet?"

"Not yet!"

"Then I'm okay!"

He laughed. "Any word on Dr. Griffin?"

"The same, I'm afraid. No change."

David nodded. Griffin remained near catatonic, the circuits of his brain still very fried. When he did speak it was with strange and foreign-sounding voices. And, as irony would have it, both he and Nubee now shared the same nursing home. Not really so ironic, he supposed, since the Orbolitz Group was still picking up the tab for both. A thought that gave David more than a little pause.

"We brought over the rest of the books," Rosa shouted.

"Gita's?"

She nodded. "They're upstairs in your office."

Originally, Gita had left all of her possessions to her little brother. But Nubee felt David would be far more appreciative of the books than he. And so far he'd been right. They'd brought several dozen over to the house, most on death and dying, and those David had read, he'd found extremely fascinating.

"Hey, brother."

He glanced up to see Preacher Man and Adrianna approaching.

"You don't have any more of those little sausage thingies with the dough all around them, do you?"

David chuckled. "If we do, they're in the kitchen."

He nodded in appreciation as Adrianna leaned forward and shouted, "Did you read that Hagen is going for reelection?"

"You're kidding! You don't think he'll make it, do you?"

Adrianna shrugged. "He's got the money, he's got the power. Don't know what else he needs. Look at Orbolitz. If he can get off anybody can." Then with an ironic smile, she added, "Look at you."

David nodded. It was true, though the heat had been turned up on Hagen, he had managed to spin and damage control his way out of any type of recall. Fortune had shone equally as bright on David's fate. It seems a neighbor just happened to be walking her dog past Dr. Schroyer's home when she heard men yelling and the distinct firing of a gun. Minutes later on her return, she noticed David and Gita stepping from their cars and approaching the front door, which was already ajar. There was also the minor fact that the woman happened to be the mother of an Orbolitz Group employee. It certainly went beyond coincidence in David's book, but not to the authorities. Instead, they'd immediately dropped all charges ... which did little to ease David's suspicions. What purpose did Orbolitz have for him to be free? He didn't know. Wondered if he ever would.

And Orbolitz himself? Despite David's filing of reports (he felt no great indebtedness toward the man), nothing stuck. Granted, the Orbolitz Group had received some bad press, the VR lab had supposedly been shut down, employees like Wendell Nordstrom and Dr. Griffin had taken the fall, and the Freak Shop had been closed, or at least relocated. But somehow the personal integrity of Norman E. Orbolitz had remained untarnished.

Not that David hadn't tried. Besides the police reports, he'd talked to multiple lawyers about civil suits. But those he trusted assured him he could never win. When it came to the legal system, money talked. Orbolitz had enough money to bankrupt David a thousand times over in legal loopholes and counter lawsuits. And that was too bad. Because if there was one wound David had not recovered from, it was the raw, open hatred he had for the man who had killed his daughter . . . and who had inadvertently taken the life of the woman he'd fallen so deeply in love with.

Oh, he knew what Gita would say if she could talk to him now. He knew how she'd insist that he let it go and forgive Orbolitz—after all, that's what the Bible commanded: "Vengeance is mine, says the Lord" and "In the manner you forgive, you will be forgiven." He'd read such verses a dozen times. But reading them and being able to live them were two very different things. Maybe Gita with her big heart and ability to obey could forgive, but not David. It simply wasn't possible. And if he ever saw Orbolitz again, if he ever had the chance, he'd—

"Come on, Addy!"

He glanced up from his thoughts to see Preacher Man dragging Adrianna toward the kitchen. "Let's get in there 'fore them thingies are all gone."

Rolling her eyes, Adrianna threw a look back to David.

He smiled and shouted, "Don't worry, if we run out we can always go to the store."

"The Lord bless you," Preacher Man called. "'When I was hungry, you did feed me . . . and did so abundantly.'"

David continued smiling as the couple disappeared into the kitchen.

"David!" It was McClure again. The guy would not give up. "Please, we've got to talk!"

Resigning himself to the inevitable, David gave a weary sigh and motioned toward the stairs. His agent gratefully accepted the offer. They started up the steps, David feeling very much like a condemned prisoner heading for the gallows. When they arrived at the top, they turned down the hallway—the very hallway whose memories had once haunted him and caused so much dread. But the memories didn't bother him now, not like they used to. Nor did they bother him when they arrived at Emily's room and he stepped inside. Emily's room which he had recently converted into his office.

He wasn't sure why he'd made the switch. Part of it was to feel closer to her. But not like before, not in some clingy, unable-to-let-go sort of way. On the contrary, the separation seemed to be healthy and on track. He'd even managed to donate or give away most of her personal belongings—except of course, for her writings . . . and the poem from her diary that he'd framed on the wall beside his desk. No, instead of grieving and clutching to memories, he was celebrating them. And by working there, within these walls, he was not only reminded of the life they had enjoyed on earth, but of the life they would enjoy again.

He crossed to the window, opening the white shutters and allowing bright shafts of sunlight to spill onto the forest green carpet. He offered Jonathan his overstuffed sofa and turned to sit on the edge of his desk. "Okay," he sighed, "break it to me gently."

"I got a call yesterday afternoon, offering us an extraordinary amount of money."

David raised an eyebrow. "Was this before or after they read the reviews?"

His agent brought the margarita he'd been toting to his lips and took a sip. "It has nothing to do with a book. At the moment no one is returning my calls."

"Sorry."

"No matter. But . . ." He took a breath and began. "With this offer we might be able to swing you a deal—if we document all the facts and throw together a killer proposal—

which I'm betting could snag you mid to high six figures plus a—"

"Jonathan—"

"—movie option with one of the major studios or independents that could bring in an additional—"

"Jonathan."

He came to a stop. "Yes?"

"What offer?"

"Oh, right." He took another breath and another sip. "Does the name Ashton Hawkins ring any bells?"

The name sounded vaguely familiar, but David couldn't place it.

"Some top-of-the-charts rock 'n' roller up in Seattle?"

David waited for more. "And . . ."

"And his wife, Savannah something-or-other, some ex-supermodel, wants you to help find him."

David frowned. "Find him? Why me?"

"Because he keeps telling her that you're the only one who can."

"I don't understand. He's lost, but he can talk to her?"

"Yes." Jonathan took another swallow

"Where is he?"

No answer.

"Jonathan?"

The man looked at him.

"Where?"

"He's, uh . . ." He lowered his glass. "Well, actually, he's in hell."

David blinked. "Pardon me?"

"He died awhile back . . . murdered. And he keeps appearing to his wife in dreams, in séances. He keeps insisting that you are the only one who can help him."

David felt the slightest chill across his shoulders. "That's crazy."

His agent nodded. "Yes, I'd agree, except . . ."

"Except?"

"She's offering $25,000 for you to fly up there and try."

"Try?" David scoffed. "Try what? The man's dead. You said it yourself."

"I said he's in hell."

"And—"

"And he says you saw him there. You talked to him."

The chill deepened. He didn't like where this was leading. Only a few knew what had happened inside the VR chamber. Even fewer knew of his death experience. No, this was absurd. Things had finally returned to normal. He was finally able to settle into a somewhat average life with Grams and Luke . . . and now somebody was trying to . . . to, well, he didn't know what they were trying to do, but he was definitely not interested.

"It, uh . . ." Jonathan cleared his throat. "It gets worse."

"How so?"

Another sip.

"Jonathan?"

"He says God's coming to visit you in a few weeks. Wants you to put in a good word for him."

David burst out laughing. "I'm sorry, Jonathan—that's just plain nuts."

"Did I mention the potential book deal?"

"Jonathan—"

"And a movie, don't forget the package we could—"

"Jonathan, please. I'm not interested."

His agent let out a tired sigh. It was obvious he knew the argument was lost before it began—and no amount of booze would change it. David looked at the man's sagging, watery eyes. "I'm sorry," he repeated more softly.

His agent took another breath and nodded.

"But I promise you, I'll get us back into the game."

Jonathan nodded.

"Seriously. I've had my fling at being artsy. The next book will have more clichéd characters and hackneyed plots than you'll ever want to read."

"I hope so," Jonathan mumbled. "I dearly hope so."

"Fine, then." David rose to his feet. "Now that we've settled that, let's get back downstairs. We've got a party to attend."

Jonathan struggled to rise. But the sofa was a bit deep, and his alcohol level a bit high. David reached down and gave him a hand. "Whoever this woman is, this widow, you be sure to thank her for me, all right? Thank her, but make it clear I'm not the guy."

Jonathan nodded. "Did I mention the $25,000?"

"Yes, you did, my friend," David chuckled. "Yes, you did."

If possible his agent looked even more depressed.

"Relax. We'll get back on top. I promise I'll write something so commercial it'll make you throw up."

"Good." Jonathan started for the door. "Good."

David slapped him on the back, directing him into the hallway. "Now go back down there and enjoy yourself."

"Right," Jonathan muttered. "Oh, here." He reached into his pocket and pulled out a business envelope. "She asked me to give this to you."

"Who?"

"The widow."

"No, I—"

"It's not money—we should be so lucky. She just wanted you to have it." He continued holding the envelope until David took it.

"And, if you should change your—"

"I won't," David assured him, "Believe me. Now go back down there and have a good time."

"Right," the man mumbled as he turned and shuffled down the hallway. "A good time. Right, sure, why not . . ."

"Uh, Jonathan?"

He looked back over his shoulder.

David pointed the opposite direction. "The stairs."

"Oh, right." He turned toward the stairs. "I knew that."

David watched the man pass, smiling sadly after him. He glanced back at the envelope in his hands, feeling its weight.

Something other than paper was inside. Curiosity got the better of him and he tore open the top, dumping the contents into his hand. It was a pendant—a tiger's tooth made of swirling gold with a green emerald in its center. He'd seen it only once before and very briefly, but he immediately recognized it—the pendant worn by the singer in hell.

David leaned against the doorway to steady himself. It had to be a fraud. Somebody was playing a hoax. No one could communicate from beyond the grave. Isn't that what the Bible said? Isn't that what Gita and Preacher Man had both made crystal clear?

His eyes moved to the stack of books across the room, the ones Nubee had given him. The ones Gita had used in studying death and the afterlife. He'd only read a handful, but despite the various cultures and divergent beliefs, he'd already seen similarities—dark, malevolent forces, intent upon destroying life . . . powerful forces of good intent upon protecting it. And, above all, a magnificent Being that had created all of that life, a Being of overwhelming compassion carved out of the brightest, most intense Light.

David mused a moment. The Man of Light. The Man with the holes in His palms. He glanced over to Emily's poem, then approached it and read as he had a hundred times before:

*I see Love's scarred hands*
*outstretched from Calvary.*
*"Come, come, come."*

*"But my filth and failures —*
*can't you see*
*my shame, shame, shame!"*

*"I see not your dirt,*
*I count not your losses.*
*Come, come, come."*

*"But I am worthless,*
*with nothing to bring but*
*Shame, shame, shame!"*

*"You've not even that,*
*For I've taken it all, even*
*your blame, blame, blame."*

The Man with the holes in His hands.

Hands with so much truth and power ... and love. And, if those hands had such love for Emily, for Luke, for Gita ... would they not have a similar love for a desperate widow in the Pacific Northwest?

Over the months he'd thought many times of the Man's final words to him: *"There is much for you to do."* And of His promise. *"But I will always be with you."*

Could this be part of it? Yes, he knew the importance of being a good father, a good man, a positive influence in his community. But somehow he'd suspected there was more.

*"There is much for you to do."*

At one point he'd even hoped it meant finding and stopping Orbolitz. But now he had his doubts.

And this business of God coming in the next few weeks. He mused quietly. Maybe this woman and Nubee should start a club. He looked back at the pendant. He had told no one of it. And yet, here it was in his hand, the very object he'd seen in hell. Again, he felt the slightest shiver. If he agreed to help, would it mean returning? Was it even possible? And what of the danger? There certainly had been in the past—for him, for Gita. And yet it had all worked out, somehow it had all managed to fit into an intricate plan.

*"I will always be with you."*

Wheels within wheels. Concentric circles within concentric circles, all focusing upon the Light. The Light with Its Truth and Its Love. Truth and Love. How could he withhold either of those from anyone who needed them? From anyone who asked?

# The Bloodstone Chronicles

## A Journey of Faith

*Bill Myers*

Through the mysterious Bloodstone, which symbolizes God's great love for mankind, three children are whisked into strange and wondrous worlds. Soon they are visiting places like the Sea of Mirrors, where they are nearly crushed by the weight of their sins, or the Menagerie, where prisoners are doomed to live in pure selfishness, or Biiq, where one doubting child is allowed to experience the same deep and unfathomable love that Jesus Christ has for us.

With the help of intriguing characters like Aristophenix, the world's worst poet; Listro Q, a tall, purple dude with dyslexic speech; and Weaver, who weaves God's plans into each of our Life Tapestries, the children learn the powers and secrets of living as citizens in the kingdom of God.

Hardcover: 0-310-24684-9

Unabridged Audio Pages® CD: 0-310-25347-0

*Pick up a copy today at your favorite bookstore!*

**ZONDERVAN**™

GRAND RAPIDS, MICHIGAN 49530 USA

WWW.ZONDERVAN.COM

# The Face of God

*Bill Myers*

That is the quest of two men with opposite faiths ...

### THE PASTOR

His wife of twenty-three years has been murdered. His faith in God is crumbling before his very eyes. Now, with his estranged son, he sets out to find the supernatural stones spoken of in the Bible. Stones that will enable the two of them to hear the audible voice of God. Stones that may rekindle their dying faith and love.

### THE TERRORIST

He has also learned of the stones. He too must find them—but for much darker reasons. As the mastermind of a deadly plot that will soon kill millions, he has had a series of dreams that instruct him to first find the stones. Everything else is in place. The wrath of Allah is poised and ready to be unleashed. All that remains is for him to obtain the stones.

With the lives of millions hanging in the balance, the opposing faiths of these two men collide in an unforgettable showdown. The Face of God is another thrilling and thought-provoking novel by a master of the heart and suspense, Bill Myers.

Softcover: 0-310-22755-0
Adobe® Acrobat® eBook Reader: 0-310-25702-6
Microsoft® Reader: 0-310-25764-2
Palm™ Reader: 0-310-25705-0
Unabridged Audio Pages® CD: 0-310-24905-8
Unabridged Audio Pages® Cassette: 0-310-24904-X

# Blood of Heaven

*Bill Myers*

Mass Market: 0-310-25110-9
Softcover: 0-310-20119-5

# Threshold

*Bill Myers*

Mass Market: 0-310-25111-7
Softcover: 0-310-20120-9

# Fire of Heaven

*Bill Myers*

Mass Market: 0-310-25113-3
Softcover: 0-310-21738-5
Abridged Audio Pages® Cassette: 0-310-23002-0

# Eli

*Bill Myers*

Mass Market: 0-310-25114-1
Softcover: 0-310-21803-9
Abridged Audio Pages® Cassette: 0-310-23622-3
Palm Reader: 0-310-24754-3